SEASON TWO

SEASON TWO

AN ALL ABOUT THE DIAMOND ROMANCE

NAOMI SPRINGTHORP

Season 2. How did this happen? Enough books for a second season collection and more to come. Thank you to all of my readers. This one is for you

Season Two
An All About the Diamond Romance
Including: Star-Crossed in the Outfield (Book 4), The Closer (Book 5), Up the Bat (Book 6), Falling For Prince (Short Stop)

Published by Naomi Springthorp

Print Edition ISBN 978-1-949243-81-9

Cover Photographer: Tonya Clark All About the Covers Photography
Cover Model: Matthew Carothers
Graphic Designer: Irene Johnson johnsoni@mac.com
Editor: Katrina Fair

CONTENTS

STAR-CROSSED IN THE OUTFIELD

AN ALL ABOUT THE DIAMOND ROMANCE BOOK 4

PROLOGUE

Chase

I spend the off-season looking forward to spring training, then I get there. I'm happy to be there, but talk about a grind! Every year it's back to the basics. Practice catching. Practice throwing. Practice hitting. Dive, slide, bunt, steal. Drill after drill. Long days with early morning workouts and afternoon games in the warm Arizona sun. It's always the same. All the younger dudes play with us until they get assigned to a lower camp and some of them are pretty cool. I was one of them and I'm still one of the youngest players on the big league team. I enjoy getting lost in that crowd during spring training and having fun. This season I've taken it to a new level because my best bud, Rick Seno, got married in the off season and all he wants to do is campout in his new wife's ass—figuratively, not literally, I think. The last couple of years he's watched out for me and even took the heat for me once to keep me in the lineup when I needed to be there or risked losing my spot on the roster. He invited me to stay with him and Sherry, and I took the room on the opposite side of the house from them because I don't want to miss out on Sherry's baking. Plus, I know he'll keep me out of trouble. Just because I have a room doesn't mean I have to use it. Our place has become pool party central for the team. The couple disappears into their side of the house at some point every night. Nobody even notices until they're gone. The problem with this is that I get out of control. Sadly, I need someone to babysit me sometimes. I've done some stupid things. It's not an excuse, but I'm only 23, male and single. The facts are that I'm a professional baseball player, have more money than anybody my age should be allowed, and women find me adorable. Shit happens.

CHAPTER ONE

Chase

Shit happens. I know I'm in the right place when I freak and immediately have Rick and Sherry both standing in front of me, focused on me sitting on my bed and their jaws both drop. Their view of the situation is worse than mine. I'm sitting front and center on the edge of my bed with my feet flat on the floor, buck fucking nude with a sheet wrapped around my good bits, my head bowed and being held up by my hands. I'm hungover and it's the mother of all hangovers. I have red splotches all over my chest, abs, thighs, and that's just the places I can see. There are three different women's bikinis on my floor and the tail from the team mascot seal costume. They stare directly at each other and laugh, full on belly laughs. They're laughing at me, not with me. Sherry stops laughing to make it worse, "Have you looked in the mirror yet, sweetheart? Looks like something bit you."

Seno shakes his head, "How the fuck did you get the tail of the mascot costume?"

A question I'd really like answered. I shrug my shoulders, not having a clue.

"Just relax and I'll get you some breakfast, maybe I can piece together what happened here." Sherry will always take care of me.

Seno shuts the door behind her and starts in on me, "Do you remember anything from last night? Do you know who you had in your room or how many? Do you know if you had sex? I thought you weren't doing this shit anymore! Who was hanging out at the pool last night?"

"Dude, just stop!" Still holding my head because it feels like that's the only thing keeping it attached to my body. "I don't remember having anybody in my room. I feel like I had sex. Mason, Stray, Clay, Bravo, and a couple of the minor leaguers were here late last night. Martin left earlier, not much after you went off to be married." I should know if I had sex or not and probably who I had sex with. "Pretty obvious there was someone in my room." I survey my room and hope I didn't manage to get bit everywhere while I was at the pool, though that would be kind of cool to get attacked by a bunch of women while I was swimming. I can see it now, skinny-dipping with women biting and sucking at me under the water, maybe even giving me head. My own personal kinky shark attack. Saving that one for later, filing it in my personal film collection.

"Sherry already thinks ball players are players. I don't want her having any extra stress or getting worried about me doing this type of shit. She needs to stay happy and relaxed. She's already dealing with enough and we want her to have a healthy pregnancy, so she can travel with me as long as possible. We're going to get this figured out. I got your back, but you need to work with me here."

"You're having a kid?"

"God damn it!" Rick shook his head. "Sherry!" He calls her and she appears a minute later with breakfast and coffee for me that smells delicious.

I don't know how she makes everything better with food. Waffles with bacon? It's like baked goods, but breakfast.

Rick gazes at Sherry and speaks sweetly, "Baby, I know you've been wanting to tell somebody. Why don't you tell Cross?"

Seno smiles when her face lights up. "I'm pregnant!" Sherry declares happier than I've ever seen her and everything starts to make sense. She turns to Rick, "And you need to be nice to Chase. He's just a kid and I know you'd never do those things. But, you might have to remind me of that when I'm eight months pregnant, look like a house, and can't travel with you."

"There's nothing sexier than you pregnant, my queen." Seno kisses Sherry and I can see where this is going.

"Congratulations. I can't wait to meet baby Seno. Now, take that, whatever you have going on out of my room." They leave me with my waffles and no answers about the night before.

I decide to text the dudes I was partying with and ask if they know anything, but I can't find my phone. I go for a swim to clear my head and look around at the pool for anything that might jog my memory. I find my cell phone in the planter, dead. I'm sure there were empty containers left out, but I don't find any. I'm guessing Sherry already picked up. I plug my phone in to charge while I shower and get another cup of coffee. I find Seno at the coffee pot.

"Bravo says the minor league guys were fucking with you

and planted the bikinis in your room, but he doesn't know anything about the seal tail. Clay says he's hungover, but swears you were humping the seal. I thought the seal was a guy." Seno turns to me questioning, but gets distracted by Sherry walking through the kitchen singing a mushy song by that Ed Sheeran dude. It's got this line about fingers and thumbs that's kind of sexy, but I don't know what it's called.

I get in Seno's face trying to get his attention back, "Dude! I need help here and you're doing your woman in your head."

"I was not." He grins and continues, "We need to get the tail from the seal costume back to the stadium somehow without causing a problem."

Sherry chimes in, "When do you want it at the stadium?"

"Earlier is better. Less people are there." Rick smiles and doesn't ask questions.

"I'll handle that right now. I'll drop it off and let them know I was helping clean it. I'll see if I can find out who's been wearing it. I've been making friends with the volunteers at the training complex. I need to go to the grocery store anyway. Barbecue this weekend, for you and the seal humper. I'll get enough for the team to come over. Last weekend of spring training there should be a party." Sherry smiles as she grabs the seal tail and leaves.

"I need a woman like that. Keep me wanting her and out of trouble. Fixes problems."

"You need a keeper, not a woman. The team knows it, the minor league guys played you!"

"Where did the splotches come from?"

"They look like hickeys. So, I don't really know what's going on with that. Maybe the seal is a vampire. Did you see the ones on your neck? You really don't remember anything?"

"It's weird. Maybe I got roofied or something." We talk as

we walk to the stadium for our morning workout. The grounds are busy with fans because it's the last week of spring training and they all want to evaluate the product the team is going to put on the field. The fans are roaming the backfields, taking photographs, asking for autographs, and watching us run drills. There are women out here for completely different reasons. Yes, they're fans, but they want more. They're after a baseball player of their own and these women come in all ages, shapes, sizes, and colors. The gold diggers can be any age and usually appear to be perfectly put together with every single hair in place, typically they're under 30. The cougars are over 40, appear younger, and are only after sex. Baseball players are a conquest. For some of us younger players, we have pumas to deal with. They're in their 30s and still at least eight years older than us, but they're tricky. Some of them haven't given up on getting a player of their own, which makes them a gold digger. Others, are after the conquest and a small number of them are really potential girlfriends. Of course there are women of all ages that are truly fans, but most of them still spend some time gawking at the players or have a favorite player or something. The team front office passed information on to us about the fans now being more female than male. I hope they don't change the uniform to make it more appealing to the fans.

> Text from Sherry - Seal tail returned no problems. A bunch of different people have played the seal in the last month, boys, girls, even retired volunteers. Still investigating.

Well, at least I don't have to worry about getting in trouble with the team. One problem handled.

Mason walks out to the backfield with me to warm up

and throw the ball around, "What was with you and the seal last night?"

I focus on him, "I don't remember. What do you know? Help me out here. Do you know who it was or if the seal went in the house with me or anything?"

"You totally took the seal to your room with you. I assume it was a chick, but I never saw her face. She was wearing pink flip-flops, so you're cool because it was a girl." He nods coming to the female conclusion. "I still want to know how you got her in your room and did her without taking her mask off."

The power of a baseball player that's been hanging at the pool in swim trunks and no shirt, showing off his body unintentionally. Combine it with my non-existent will power and the need to get laid. I humped the seal. Seno's right. I need to be more responsible for my actions and stop acting like a kid. It's driving me crazy because I either had her out of the seal costume or there's another girl. There's no other way I would've gotten all these hickeys. Maybe the minor leaguers took a vacuum to me, but I don't think it's possible to be so drunk that I could have slept through that. I wonder if I left hickeys on the girl. Okay, so I'm watching for a girl wearing pink flip-flops that may or may not have hickeys.

Seal Girl

What was I thinking? I'm probably going to lose my internship over this. For what? A baseball player. Of course, they're always trouble. I can't keep a job as a volunteer! It's embarrassing enough that I dress up as the mascot and now I'm going to be known as the girl that was cut from the volunteer team for losing the tail piece of the costume. I can't go back in there and get it, can I? He's pretty wasted. He might not notice. No, I can't trust myself. I left because I want him too much. I can't even get a quick meaningless fuck right. It wasn't the alcohol. I couldn't help myself. I shed the seal costume and dry humped him for hours in my PJs. I wish I could be there to watch him try to explain the hickeys I left him with to the next girl. I kissed him all over his body, biting and sucking and leaving him spotted like a leopard. What kind of guy hits on a mascot anyway? Seriously? All he could see was my pink flip-flops and polished toe nails. Maybe he has a foot fetish. Worse, a seal fetish. Maybe he's into plush costumes and gets off on the anonymity of the whole thing.

I know three things.

One, he made me hotter than I've ever been. If I didn't get out of there when I did, I never would've left. His hands were warm and inviting. His body solid and sexy. His kiss owned me. His hard naked cock? I wanted it and had to rub on it. I still want it.

Two, I can't let him get in the way of my goals. This internship may sound silly, but it's the stepping stone I need to get into media at the major league stadium. I can't mess this up. This can't happen again. Chase Cross is not an option for me no matter what.

Lastly, baseball players suck.

CHAPTER TWO

Chase

I chill at the pool and relax as much as possible for the rest of the week, doing my best to stay out of trouble and not get released or reassigned to the minors. I'll party when everybody comes over for the barbecue after the last spring training game, and Sherry has invited everybody. I mean everybody, including the people who work and volunteer at the stadium, even some of the groupies. I think she wants to know who was in my room with me. You'd think it was the only chick I had in there, but it wasn't. Nobody noticed the others. I know I shouldn't, but I'm single and horny. I had two girls over together on two different nights, the same two girls and they apparently like to work as a team —I'm not complaining. One night I had three girls over, but I was sure I was going to get caught. They were so loud! It was fun to have them all in the pool together with me, but they were too giggly and I took them to my room and turned on some music to drown them out. "Train in Vain" by The

Clash was playing. It was like hiding them from my parents, though I knew I wouldn't get in trouble. I don't disrespect them. I try to give them what they want. I've been told they like my blonde hair that's almost shoulder length and tries to curl around my ears, and that I'm tall and skinny and "have shoulders that go on for days." I'm not exactly sure what that means, but the chicks think it's a good thing and I'm going with it. Some of them like the way I play, I do put it all out there. I'm not afraid of diving for the ball. I've heard that chicks dig scars. I'll lay it all out there for the game and my team. I want to win and I refuse to be the reason we lose. The chicks say I'm the same way when it comes to sex, but I've never really thought about it like that. Game rules are that she's getting some and so am I. But, it's always just sex. Well, not just sex. Sometimes we do other things. We might order a pizza, or sit in the hot tub. I guess my point is that I haven't found one that I like. They like me and sadly I'm using them, so I try to stick to the groupies because that's really all they want. Fucked by a player. That, I can do.

I've been thinking about women a lot during the off-season. I'd already started to think I wanted a real girlfriend before last season was over, but then my best bud got married and I was best man. I don't think they're the norm for a couple. I like what I see and want some of it for myself. It'd be great if she likes to bake. I need to find a chick I like, not just girls that want me. Seems like it's one of those things I don't have control over and it's hard to meet chicks that aren't trying to meet me. I need Sherry to help me with this, but she's so determined to figure out who the seal is. I guess it'll take some time and I need to work on keeping it in my pants.

I've been volunteered to help prep for the barbecue. I'm in charge of cleaning the grill, cleaning the pool, and I'm supposed to go to the store with Sherry to be her bitch boy a couple days before because Seno doesn't want her lifting anything, and he needs her out of the house to do something for her while she isn't there. The bitch boy duty includes making sure I keep her out of the house for two hours and text him when we're on our way home. It's a special day or something, so many months since their first date or some silly thing he wants to turn the romance up for. I'm sure Sherry will eat it up. Maybe I should be talking to Seno about finding a woman. You know, I found Sherry and gave her to him. I mean it was clear that she was interested and not a groupie type. Maybe he can help.

While I wander around at the baseball complex, I'm on the lookout for the pink flip-flops and hickeys. I feel bad that I don't know who it was. Not that it's the first time that's happened, but she works for the team and I probably see her everyday. I probably walk right by her and don't even acknowledge her existence. That's just shitty. Why did she have to wear the mascot costume anyway?

While I sleep, there's a movie playing in my head and I can see the whole thing unfold in front of me. Shit, I can feel the whole thing. There she was with long dark hair, olive skin that's been tanned by the Arizona sun, warm green eyes with little gold flecks sparkling in them, and perfect curves on her slender frame. I see the seal costume on the floor in the background and I'm laying spread out flat on my bed and naked. We're making out and it's hot, I mean I'm hard and ready. Alcohol has helped her lose all of her inhibitions, or I think I would've noticed a girl that wanted to suck on my tongue like that sooner. She's wearing boxer shorts with pink sunglasses printed on them and a matching tank top that's stretched perfectly across her boobs that says "I wear my sunglasses at night." She wears pajamas under the seal costume, interesting. I remember things being a little blurry and I had drunk a lot. She asked if we could just kiss and I went along with her because I never push, it's always what they want. I suggested that we could kiss all over and she kissed me all over from my ears down my neck, across my chest, over my abs and I thought I was going to get a blow job, but she skipped that and went for my thighs, kissing and sucking and biting all over my thighs. Then she reversed and traveled back up my body with her teeth, biting and sucking until she got back to my mouth. She straddled me then and our kiss heated to the point where I really wanted her, and I absent-mindedly rocked my hips. It felt like she would leave if I pushed her, but she rocked back at me. This isn't the way I do things, it's always what they want. But, this girl was driving me, pushing me, making me want more. She was making me crazy.

I told her I wanted her and she whispered all sexy in my ear "I want you, too. You have to want me for more. You don't want me enough."

"I want you plenty. I want you now." I moved and took initiative, kissing her neck and sucking just below her ear. A little strange, since I don't put out any extra effort—I never have to. I held her tight against me when she tried to pull away. "I won't hurt you, baby. I won't do anything that you don't want me to." I pressed my lips to hers and took control of our kiss, sliding my tongue into her mouth and gliding it against hers. She tasted like cookies and then all I could think about was her "cookie." Fuck me, I had totally lost it. I rubbed my hard cock against her.

"Give me one second." She got up and I thought she'd changed her mind. But she put the costume back on and left in a hurry, leaving the tail behind. I don't think she's my Cinderella or anything, but a glass slipper would be easier to fit than a one size fits most mascot costume.

I wish I could remember the part at the pool, before I

took her to my room. Fuck she was hot and she told me no. She got up and left. Now I want her more and I don't even know her name. I don't think I've ever seen her at the complex.

I wake up the next morning hoping Sherry invited her. I get up early and sit at the kitchen counter chatting with Sherry. "Good morning, sweetheart. It's early for you." Sherry's surprised to see me.

I pour some coffee, "I went to bed early. Umm, did you invite a girl with long straight dark brown hair and green eyes, slender but with curves, maybe wearing pink flip-flops?"

She stops what she's doing and looks at me, "What's her name?"

Fuck! "I don't know."

"That's not a pretty name." Sherry torments me on purpose.

"I was drunk. At least I remember what she looks like now."

"Is this the Seal Girl?"

"I'm pretty sure. I remember how I got all the spots. Oh, I didn't have sex with her."

"You were naked. You have spots from her mouth all over your body. But, you didn't have sex with her?"

"Yes."

"That makes no sense."

"She said she only wanted to kiss."

"I suggested kissing didn't have to be limited to mouths." Proud that I didn't push her and then I remember that she left because I kind of pushed her. Damn it.

"And?"

"She got up and left, after she made me spotted and we made out for awhile. I shouldn't have told her that I wanted her. Sherry, I need help. I need a chick that I like and isn't after a baseball player."

"You need to talk to Rick about that. I'm good for other stuff, but not the part that has to do with you being a player. You need to know their name before you stick your tongue in their mouth and get naked. That's the first step for you."

I listen to her. She's right. I need to know their name. I'll talk to Seno on our walk to the field this morning.

"You need to take girls on dates a few times and see if they're player crazy, not just fuck them as soon as you meet them."

"Didn't you have sex with Sherry the night you met her?" I know he did, he came to the stadium the next day wearing the same clothes he had on when he left and had a huge hickey.

"That doesn't matter. We're talking about you."

"What's the difference?"

"I'm older than you. I've got more experience than you. You just want to get laid. Look, Sherry broke all my rules. I can't explain why or how. She's different and I just knew. Fuck, you were there! You saw how fucked up I was over her. I still feel that way, but she's mine now."

"So, you're saying that rules can be broken?"

"Yea, I am. If you find yourself breaking personal rules, you need to pay attention to what you're doing and not be fucking around. You have no idea how many rules I broke with that woman. Fuck, she broke all my rules. I did some seriously stupid shit and I don't regret any of it."

"Got it. Don't follow my dick."

"I wasn't following my dick! But, for you, yea, that's a pretty good rule. Also, always use a condom and no sex until at least the third date, unless it's just one of your groupie fucks that you're never going to see again."

"Do the twins count as groupie fucks?"

"If you want a real girlfriend, you need to let that shit go." Seno shakes his head as he walks into the clubhouse to get ready for workouts.

I know he's right. I guess it all depends on me. Am I ready to give up the groupies? I would give them all up for the right girl. I'll keep them until I find her.

CHAPTER THREE

Chase

Spring training is finally over. I'm cleaning the pool with a beer in my hand while Sherry sets out bowls of salads and sides that she made. Seno is manning the grill until Sherry takes the tongs from him and tells him to go have fun. It's going to be a good night. I know because I carried all the beer and ice in. Sherry has a display of jello shots out, too. She made some non-alcoholic just for her, so she can show us how they're done and drive Seno crazy at the same time.

People are everywhere for the next few hours. My teammates, the ladies from the team store, the group who work in concessions, the retired volunteers, there's a representative from every part of the sports complex. The team had clicked together, it's great to hang out and have fun off the field. We're pounding beer and that turns into doing jello shots. We're challenging each other and, well, we're all very happy —even Seno's wasted, so I don't feel bad about my state of hazy desire. Somebody walks in wearing the seal costume and I head straight for it, I need her. I put my arms around the bulky seal and give it a squeeze, "I'm happy to see you. I've been thinking about you since you left the other night. Can we talk?" The seal stiffens and doesn't make a noise. "Please tell me I didn't just hit on another person in the seal costume." The team is watching me from across the yard and trying to hide their laughter. Sherry looks up and notices me with my arm around the seal.

Sherry walks up to us, "Welcome seal! How about I help you get changed into something more comfortable, so you can enjoy the party and have some fun?" I don't know if she's rescuing me or still trying to find out who the chick I had in my room was, but she drags the seal into the house with her and leaves me standing there. I didn't see the seal again and I still don't know who was in the costume.

There's music playing and when a slow song comes on, Seno grabs his wife and holds her close as they sway to the beat. Then our other teammates that have women do the same and I'm left standing there like a wallflower. It's different to witness all these big, tough guys be turned to mush for their women. Watching how they act differently with them and the expressions on their faces, the way they move together knowingly.

I want to dance, too. I want someone to look at me like that when I have my arms around them and want to dance with me, without me asking. Someone I belong with. I glance around and there's a chick making eyes at me from the other side of the pool. I smile at her and wave, then gesture to her hoping she'll meet me in the middle to dance with the crowd. I keep eye contact with her as we walk to each other and reach for her hand as soon as I'm close enough to reach it. She takes my hand willingly, glancing up into my eyes and blushing while she smiles timidly. She's shy and it seems like she hasn't been drinking. I pull her a little closer and kiss her on the forehead as we start to dance. I'm drunk, but trying to follow the rules. Don't push her. I need to know her name first. No sex unless I feel it's appropriate to break the rules. I wonder if she knows the girl from the seal costume with the pink flip-flops. I step back and look at her, wondering what shoes she's wearing and if she has any remnants of hickeys. Her skin is soft against mine and she has dark chocolate brown eyes. Her warm brown hair is tied up into a ponytail, revealing her long sexy neck. We dance until the slow songs stop and all of the guys are back to drinking, but the women are happier because of the personal time they had with their men. Interesting things I'm noticing while I spend time here with the Senos. I watch her as she goes back to talking with her friends and grabs a beer. She glances over at me and smiles a few times, but then she turns away to concentrate on the conversation she's having with her friends. I want to go over there and ask her out, but what if she's friends with the seal? I at least have to get her name. I'm not used to these rules, I'm really going to screw this up. I look up to catch Sherry pulling something out of the oven and go directly to the kitchen because she's baking. I walk up to her as she pulls chocolate chip cookie bars out of the oven and they smell delicious.

"Hey, Sherry. Are these for me?"

"Of course, sweetheart. I need to tell you something about the seal." Sherry focuses on me with a funny grin.

"Did you find out who she is?"

"It was a him tonight."

"Shit! I hit on a dude?"

"Maybe you just like the soft gray plush fur on the costume. He said he was flattered." Sherry laughs.

"Do you know who the girl I was dancing with is?"

"You danced with her and don't know her name? What did you talk about while you were dancing?" I feel like I'm being scolded.

"We didn't talk. We were just quiet and happy. At least, I was happy."

"Okay," I watch Sherry cut up the warm cookies and put a few on a plate. She hands me the plate, "Now, you go take these to her and offer her a cookie. Or, lead her away from her friends somewhere you can talk—Not your bedroom. Find out what her name is. Maybe find out how old she is, what does she do, does she work at the stadium, is she a student, where does she live," Sherry went on and on with things I should talk to the chick about. She stops and stares at me, "Never mind. You're drunk again, aren't you?"

I smile awkwardly, trying to remember what she said. "I'm going to walk over there with cookies and find out what her name is. Maybe get lucky and bring her back for more cookies and milk. Or, something more adult like sitting on the couch and talking. Maybe kiss her on the forehead again. Her skin is really soft." Sherry shakes her head at me like I've lost it as I walk out the door with a plate of cookies as an ice breaker to talk to the brown-haired girl.

I walk up to her, "Hi, would you like a cookie?" All of the sudden I'm reminded of wanting the girl from the seal costume and her "cookie". I'm torn and I don't want to lead anybody on. I don't even know who she is.

She takes a cookie, "Thank you."

I start talking to her and I don't know what I said, something about baked goods. I step a couple feet away and she follows, so I lead her off to a corner of the yard with swings and sit with her sharing my cookies. "I'm Chase, you probably know that."

She smiles, "Yeah, kind of. Everybody knows who you are. I'm Syl, it's short for Sylvia."

"Hi Syl." I smile at her and we talk while we eat cookies. I hear Sherry in my head and ask thoughtful things like she suggested. I learned that Syl was a college student and hoped to transfer to San Diego in the fall. She's not a groupie and I'm not going to be in Arizona long enough to date her the required three times, but she didn't seem like a player chaser. She works at the sports complex. I get her number, since I'd managed to talk to her without fucking her and consider kissing her. But, that would be it. A lesson in restraint. I need lessons and practice. She gives me her number and I send her a text.

Text to Syl - You have beautiful eyes.
Text to Syl - I'm leaving tomorrow because it's time for baseball season to start.
Text to Syl - If I wasn't leaving, I'd kiss you.

I gaze into her dark eyes and she smiles as my phone vibrates.

Text from Syl - Please kiss me.
Text from Syl - Let's get out of here.

I stand up immediately and take her hand, leading her to the empty family room via the kitchen where I pick up more cookies. I sit in the comfy chair and pull her down onto my lap with my arms around her. I hesitate, trying to be a good guy and not wanting to take advantage of someone a couple years younger than me. She giggles and puts her arms around my neck. Then shy, sweet Syl surprises me. She leans in and kisses me, licking my lips and sliding her tongue into my mouth to seductively caress mine. I let her take the lead, she can decide what direction we take and how far we take it. I'm pretty sure she's not the girl from the seal costume. Her eyes are the wrong color and they don't kiss the same. I may never figure out who the girl from the seal costume is, so I have Syl right now. At least I got her name before I kissed her. That's progress, right? A step in the right direction. Syl moves her lips to my neck and her hands to my chest, running her fingers across my chest and digging her fingers into my shoulders. I move my hand to her back and the other to her head, so I can hold her against me and run my fingers through her silky chestnut hair. I bring her lips back to mine, tasting her and feeling her full soft lips pressed to mine. Her kiss wants more, but I wait for her to show me what she wants. She moves her hands under my shirt to touch my abs, but really she's trying to get into my pants. I stop her and bring her hands up around my neck, but she goes right back for it and rubs against my now hard cock. I whisper in her ear, "What do you want from me, Syl? Are you just after a ball player? Thrill of the chase?"

She moves her mouth to my ear and whispers, "I like you. You're gorgeous. I want to fuck."

Alarms go off in my head, even in my drunk state I know this is a bad idea. Seno had managed to get something to sink in and I'm tired of being the dude who has sex with different chicks all the time. That's a lie, but I want a chick that likes me, doesn't care if I'm a baseball player and sticks around for repeat performances—and I don't think I can have both. "How about we just kiss?" I hear myself say and I don't know where it comes from.

Syl pulls back, and looks at me with big eyes, "We could kiss all over." I watch her eyes heat, "You know, naked."

I'm pretty sure I should be keeping my clothes on, but I

don't want to. Her breathy voice and hands all over me have my body ready and willing to do about anything. I've said almost the same thing to get chicks naked in my bed before and one step closer to sex, hoping to at least get head. That has to count as kissing all over. I love it when a chick sucks me off. Fuck! I need to get some distance. "Be right there!" and I get up carefully leaving Syl in the chair. She looks at me questioning, "I'll be back, Sherry needs help." I didn't hear her call for help, but in my head it was there and I needed to escape.

I walk into the kitchen to find Sherry leaning against the wall and sliding down slowly. "Sherry? You need help with something?"

"No, I'm just tired. I think I overdid it today."

I'm glad I came to the kitchen when I did, Sherry loves time in the kitchen and is apparently still learning her limits. She doesn't act like a pregnant woman, but maybe she should. "Let me help you get to bed." I walk toward her and she gestures for me to get her a chair. I slide a chair over to her and leave her sitting in the chair, with her head leaning against the wall. "I'll be right back." I run outside to find Seno before she can tell me not to. That woman is headstrong and wouldn't want to be a bother. Seno sees me walk out of the house and notices the look of urgency on my face. He's running to the kitchen before I can say any words. "I walked into the kitchen and she was leaning on the wall. She wouldn't let me help her get to bed, so I got her a chair and was going to get you," I fill him in as he goes to Sherry.

He looks at her and picks her up, carrying her off to bed, "It's okay, my queen, I've got you. I shouldn't have let you do so much today. You're fine. You just need some rest." I watch as they disappear into the bedroom, wondering which of them he's trying to comfort. "Thanks, Cross." I need to take over the party and I need to get to know Syl, not just fuck her.

I walk into the family room and Syl's gone. I should let it go and be done with it, but I can't.

Text to Syl - Hey... where'd you go?

Text from Syl - Getting a beer. Out by the pool.

I walk out and join her, but I'm done drinking for the night. I need to be the responsible one. We talk and I give her a goodnight kiss, not anywhere kinky.

CHAPTER FOUR

Chase

I wake up the next morning and wander out to take a swim before packing up my stuff for the drive back to San Diego. My head is clear, I'm not hungover, and I don't have any regrets about last night. I'm looking forward to getting home to my little bungalow by the beach and hitting the waves with my surfboard. It's early for me, so I do a double take when Seno's sister, Sam, is in the kitchen. "Hey, Sam, what's up?"

"Just here to help. Rick wanted me to come help them for a couple days, get them back home, keep Sherry from doing too much. Duties of the older sister," she smiles.

"Give me a few minutes and I'll help you get them packed up to go." I swim some laps, thinking about what I need to get done today and know I'll be on the waves tomorrow morning. I wish I could find out who the Seal Girl was, and I'll probably never know.

After my swim I find Sam texting and laughing, she left

me with instructions to pack up the food into the ice chest and left to take care of an errand. I'm left to my own thoughts and I'm not sure that's good. I think about the seal and when I think about the girl who wore the costume, I envision the seal and not her. Maybe I'm losing it. Maybe Sherry was right and I like the soft plush costume. I'm a sick puppy. I need to get home and everything will make more sense.

It's a five-hour drive to get home. I get my stuff loaded into my pick-up and stop at the stadium on my way out of town to clear out my locker. I have mail waiting for me, so I grab it and take it with me to deal with later. I hit the road and turn up my radio for the drive across the Arizona desert to San Diego. I listen to the new wave station on the satellite radio on my drive, I love that old British DJ dude and all the new wave music. I'm a bit eclectic, I like new wave and surfer music and a little punk, as well as current top forty and oldies. He was playing a set of Depeche Mode and talking about an upcoming tour as he played "Blasphemous Rumors," "People Are People," "Strangelove," and "Just Can't Get Enough." I needed something with more for driving, so I switch over to listen to The Wrecks on repeat for most of the drive home. Still, I find myself looking at the cars I pass and searching for the girl from the seal costume, hoping maybe she's going back to San Diego, too.

When I finally get to San Diego, I pick up my favorite pizza from Little Italy on my way home and sit on my patio eating the whole thing while I watch the waves roll into the shore. It's nice to be home. I'm tempted to hit the ocean and forget about unpacking, but the season is starting in a few days and I won't have any extra time. There's laundry to be done, or at least dropped off at the fluff and fold. Either that, or I really need to hire a maid that does that stuff for me. It would be nice to have fresh sheets more often and clean towels all the time. My patio is the reason I bought this tiny bungalow. It's a huge concrete slab that drops off into the sand and it's fenced with a worn out wood picket fence that's about three feet tall with huge gaps between the slats. It doesn't keep anything in, or anything out for that matter. You can step right over it and see right through it. But, it does have a gate that works and leads you to the white warm sand of Ocean Beach, and the Pacific Ocean just steps away. The bungalow itself is small. The realtor called it a two bedroom, but it's more like a master suite and a small office, den or maybe a large closet. It doesn't matter. It works for me. There's only one of me and I don't take much room. Yep, I have 800 square feet of living space with unlimited beach-front. It's a good thing the flat screen is mounted on the wall because there isn't even enough room for an entertainment center and a sofa in the living room. Then again, that's based on my standards and everybody doesn't require a sofa to be long enough for me to stretch out my 6'4" frame on for naps. My bedroom is a good size, I painted it myself and put in new bamboo flooring. It's exactly what I wanted with dark brown and teal throughout the room, on the bed, and covering the windows. It's my personal space and I've never brought a chick back to my place. It's rare I bring the guys over. Usually, I'm picking them up because they're on my way since I live farthest this direction from the stadium. Can't get any farther than the ocean. I get my things unloaded and put away. I end up sitting on the beach, letting the water come up to meet my toes.

Text to Sam - I'm home. Did you get the Senos home? Do you need help with anything?

Text from Sam - We just parked. Everything is fine. Thanks for the offer. Kris is already on his way.

Text to Sam - Cool. Let me know if you need me.

Interesting, I'm Seno's buddy. But, I guess this is Sam's show and she's always gotten along better with Martin. Sam thinks I'm a kid and, honestly, she's probably right.

When I finally go in for the night, I open the mail from my spring training locker. Mostly, it's fan mail, autograph requests, photos that fans have taken of me and letters from younger guys telling me how they want to be like me when they grow up, asking for advice and I think I'll always find that weird. I don't think of myself as a role model. Then I find the pink envelope that just has my name written on the outside and I open it to find a letter that's handwritten on matching pink paper.

Chase,

I didn't mean for it to end this way. I left because I didn't want to be just another baseball slut. I thought I was going to see you again, but I have to leave before spring training is over for a job opportunity. Probably better this way anyway. We didn't exchange numbers or anything. It would have just been sex and I'm being a dumb girl if I think anything different. Better that we didn't. No regrets.

Good luck this season.

The Seal

It even smells like her. I still don't know her name. I still don't have her number. I look to see if there's anything giving me a way to respond to her or contact her, but there isn't and I'm sure that was intentional. I need to get over it. Maybe I need a seal costume for my own personal use. What am I supposed to say? It's either her or the costume and I can't have her.

I enjoy the few days before the season starts and relax on the beach, spending hours floating on my board waiting for my wave to come. Can't beat surfing in early spring, only in San Diego is the weather always right for surfing.

I only leave the house to pick up food and I get fresh baked cookies while I'm out, dropping them off for Sherry so she doesn't bake. I want to do my part and she has always taken care of me.

CHAPTER FIVE

Chase

It's opening day and we're playing LA, which is the same most years. The stadium is clean, fresh, and shiny. The field is manicured to perfection. All of the opening day decorations are out, the paint on the field, the banners, the bunting—it looks like there's going to be a party. All of our lockers are full of uniforms, caps, gear, deliveries from sponsors and endorsement contracts, everything new for the new season. We've been briefed on opening day festivities. We know we'll each be introduced as we run out to the first base line in front of our home dugout and there will be fireworks shot off with each introduction, which is better than last year and the attempt at the smoke screen we were supposed to be magically appearing out of.

The stadium is buzzing. The gates open early and season ticket holders are able to come in and watch our early batting practice. It's an attempt to make getting into the stadium easier for the sell out crowd and reward the regulars at the same time by making them feel special. Make no mistake, they are special. Without them, the seats are empty and nobody cares. We need the fans and we feed on their energy. I watch them swarm around the dugouts and behind home plate to get a good look at batting practice, they're happy to be here. I remember when I was a kid, going to my first big league game of the year always made me happy. It's something about walking into the stadium, seeing the field, getting the ballpark food I'd missed in the offseason and anticipating the win. I can only guess that's how all these people feel and they're the extremists being season ticket holders. Losing is not an option. They're in it heart and soul, committed to the team like they're in a marriage. Yea, that's exactly what its like.

I wander off into the underbelly of the stadium to get some quiet time and I swear I see the seal out of the corner of my eye. It kind of jars my state of calm before the game. It's weird. The seal isn't the problem, it's the memory that it gives me. I'm going to have to make an effort to not let the seal get to me. Fucking mascot. That doesn't help. No fucking the mascot.

I turn around to go back to the clubhouse. I need my safe place. I need to be with the team. I need to stay focused. I see a girl walking away quickly, as if it's only a shadow and I think it's her. The Seal Girl. I try to catch up and get a better look, but she's gone. That's it! I'm going to the clubhouse. We're winning this game. I'm getting laid tonight. This is bullshit. I should've jerked off.

The clubhouse is amped up. The team is getting pumped up for the game and looks sharp in the new uniforms. Everybody showed up today with clean haircuts, trimmed beards, just looking good overall. Well, except me. I'm not cutting my hair and I couldn't grow a beard if I wanted to, I don't have the facial hair for it. Skip gives us a quick pep talk and we all walk the clubhouse high-fiving. It sounds funny, but its team bonding. We're all loose and ready to go. Most of the starting nine go out on the field pre-game and get warmed up. Stretching, doing sprints, throwing the ball. Seno and the starting pitcher, Rhett Clay, walk out to the bullpen early. It's Clay's first opening day with the team and to get called for the start, that's a big deal. I know he'll be great, Seno has his back. Seno was cutting up about it this morning because Sherry called it after Clay had only played with the team a couple times last season, she said he was going to be an ace.

I check behind home plate to see if Sherry's here and she's in the first row center, sitting with Sam. She won't miss a game unless she doesn't have a choice. She lives for baseball and she knows Seno wants her here, cheering for him every game. Hell, I love to hear her cheering for me, too. She has spunk and she isn't afraid to use it. I can't wait to hear what she calls the LA pitcher and what creative things she has to say about their hitters. She has had the whole offseason, so it should be good. The expression on her face tells me she's happy to be here. She's the definition of Seals Fan. I'm sure it made her happy to walk into the stadium today, even knowing its just the beginning of the season and having already been to spring training games.

I keep seeing the seal and the Seal Girl out of the corner of my eye, but then neither of them are there. Focus Chase. It's almost game time.

I'm lined up in the dugout for my name to get called out as part of the starting lineup, announcing me as I run out on to the field to fist bump all my teammates. I'm pumped, listening to the buzz of the crowd and cheering for the players announced before me. I'm in the lead off spot today, that makes me the first hitter of the season. The coaches and players that didn't make the starting lineup today have already been announced and are lined up waiting for me. The fireworks will start with me. I feel the pressure and hope I get a good reception from the fans.

Then I hear it over the loud speakers as it echoes through the stadium, "And now your Seals opening day starting nine as written in by the manager Butch Hopp. Leading off, in center field, number 17, Chaaaaaaasse Crooossssss!" I run up the steps of the dugout and the stadium explodes, calling out my name and screaming. I smile uncontrollably. I'm not an attention whore, but who wouldn't like this? It's a total ego trip. Fans hanging over the railings like they're reaching for me from the upper decks. Lots of girls wearing jerseys with my number, 17, on the back.

Sherry is out of her seat, yelling and I can hear her, "Go Chase" She's holding up a sign that says "Chase #17 Home!" and wearing a shirt that says "Future Seals Fan" with an arrow pointing to her belly. I can't help but chuckle and I can't take the smile off my face. The rest of the lineup gets announced:

Hitting second and playing Short Stop, #28, Jones Mason

Hitting third and playing first base, #2, Kris Martin

Hitting fourth, your catcher, #6, Rick Seno

Hitting fifth and playing third base, #13, Lucky Lucine

Hitting sixth and playing in right field, #10, Mark Rock

Hitting seventh and debuting at second base, #29 Andrew Brandt

Hitting eighth and playing in left field, newly acquired Seal, #15 Cain Simms

And, hitting ninth, your starting pitcher, #20, Rhett Clay

Nobody gets the cheers like Seno and it all comes from behind home plate. You can hear where Sherry's biases fall. The cheers for Kris were louder than mine, but that was Sam adding in. It's funny how you can still hear Sherry over the rest of the stadium, even on opening day, or maybe we're conditioned to listen for her because we know she's here for us. I find myself scanning the stadium, wishing the Seal Girl was here cheering for me. I know she's gone and I need to forget about her. If she wanted to be found, she would've given me a way to contact her.

We get to our positions and I hear "Make it a win, Seno!" yelled out and followed by a "Wooooo!" as he gets set behind the plate. Yep, it's time for baseball and the team is ready. I take the minute I have in the outfield before the first pitch and look around, enjoying the field and taking in the full stadium. I always forget to take time to enjoy where I am and have fun. I'm consciously trying to change that. I've seen what happens to players over the last couple of years and there are no guarantees I'll still be here next season, or even tomorrow. It's my reality. I think it's why I play with the groupies, it all kind of goes together—nothing is permanent. The thing is, I want more. I want permanent. I want to be better at baseball, I want to be a record breaker, and I want to show everybody that I'm an offensive and defensive force. While I'm wanting things, I want more time for surfing and sitting on the beach, and it would be great if I had a woman to sit on the beach with me. Just one.

Clay handled the top of the first inning perfectly, he's on

point and I may never get a ball in center this whole game with the way he's pitching. Bottom of the first, time for my lead off at bat and I've never wanted to make an impact so badly. I want to be noticed. I want to give Clay some run support. My job is to get on base. That's it, just get on base. My teammates will knock me in. I've got the speed. I can outrun the throw. I'm aware on the base paths and I can steal, it's why I lead off. Mason and I get on base, then Martin and Seno bring us home to score. It's the plan. It doesn't change. The team roots me on as I step into the on deck circle, I hear my walk up music "Turn It Up" by the Wrecks and Sherry yells, "You got this, Chase! Knock it!" The whole stadium is calling out to me. I get my footing in the batter's box and eye the pitcher, ready for whatever he has to send my direction. The first pitch is way outside, ball one. The second pitch is down the middle and low, ball two. The third pitch is a curve and the bottom drops right out of it, I swing and miss. 2 - 1 count. Keep your shoes on, Chase. Chill out. You got this. The fourth pitch is on the outside corner, my favorite pitch location, and I ground it up the middle. I'm safe on first and I did my job leading off the game. Mason strikes out. Martin looks better than normal and I can hear that he's still getting the extra support from behind the plate, he's actually smiling and he's all business on the field. The first pitch to him and he knocks it out of the park. I run the bases and he's right behind me when I get to home plate, just enough time to turn around and high-five.

Sam and Sherry, "Wooooot! Go Kris!" He turns to look at them, especially Sam, and I swear it's a look I've seen between Seno and Sherry.

"Nice work, kiddo!" Sherry gives me a thumbs-up.

Seno was up to bat and I don't know what he saw, but he

did a repeat performance of Martin's hit. Home run. The score is 3-0 Seals at the end of the first inning.

I walked once, and didn't get any more hits. The 5th inning was a merry-go-round of Seals scoring 4 more on seven consecutive singles. Clay pitched a complete shut out. Seals won 7-0 and everyone was happy, well except for LA and they don't count in my world.

I hung out around the dugout signing autographs for the fans while Clay did the on field interview with Hannah. I caught Seno before he disappeared into the clubhouse and told him I need him to find me a woman, while he signed some autographs with me. The team wants to celebrate together and our regular place, the Batter Up, won't work on opening day, too many fans. So, I invite the team over to hang on my patio and tell them to bring their beach blankets. I have to get food, get beer, and clean before they get there. I quickly get out of the clubhouse and run to my truck in the garage, where I find Sherry and Sam waiting for Seno.

"You ladies need to make Seno bring you to my place. Party on the beach."

Sherry stares at me in disbelief, "There's no way you're ready for that."

Of course she'd know, "I'm making it work. Just bring your beach blankets, bikinis, towels, whatever." I stop and look at her, "Any suggestions for easy food?"

Sherry smiles at me, "Order pizza, pick up fried chicken and salads from the deli. Everyone will be happy. You're going to need a huge ice chest for how much beer you're going to get, or a few small ones and you can divide up the options–like one with sodas, water and non-alcoholic options." Sam picks up her phone and orders a bunch of pizzas. "We'll pick up the pizzas and hit the deli for you on the way to your place, but you better have a comfy place for my pregnant ass to sit."

Sam chimes in, "So, is everybody going?"

"You should come, Sam. You'll like my backyard. I think the guys are all coming and you'll need to make sure Seno doesn't decide they're going home like old married people." She nods and I'm happy they're helping me. Though I'm worried that I might get beat for letting Sherry go to the deli for me. I take off to get things ready and I'm actually kind of excited to have everybody over.

When I get to my neighborhood, I stop at the liquor mart and get three ice chests filled with ice. I buy all the beer that looks good and a few sodas and a case of water, my pick-up is loaded and I drive the few blocks home. I pick up inside and make sure the bathroom is clean. I get the ice chests unloaded and fill them with drinks. I pull out my few beach chairs and flip on the patio lights, which are Christmas lights that I hung up all around the fence and under the patio cover.

Text to Sherry - Plates? Napkins? Chips? Dip?

Text from Sherry - Already picked it all up.

Text to Sherry - Thank you

Text to Sherry - Is Seno bringing me a chick?

Of course she did. What was I thinking? She's organized and knows how to do these things. I'm still learning. No response on the chick.

A few minutes later the team starts showing up and I lead them through to the back, so they can grab a drink and relax on the beach. I hear Seno coming through the door, "Cross! Don't give my woman jobs to do, it makes more work for me." He looks around and walks through the house to the patio, leaving his armload of stuff on the picnic table and going back for more. "You need to help me unload. Sherry's going to love this place."

I go to help unload and find Martin leaning on the roof of Seno's Challenger talking to the two ladies, and very gallantly escorting the two of them into my backyard while Seno and I unload. When I get back to my patio, Sherry and Sam are getting everything set out. Everything's perfect except Seno, he's ready to skin me. "Dude, you can take her for a walk out to the ocean. Let her get her feet wet. Whatever it is that helps her relax and will make you both happy. Then come back and make a nice spot on the sand with your beach blanket. It'll be fun. All of us kind of camping out at the beach." I walk back into the house and get some music playing, I set my music library on shuffle and "Rock & Roll Queen" by The Subways starts to play. I grab a beer and mingle with my teammates. It's interesting watching how everybody responds to my bungalow and how they embrace the beach. The women enjoying the opportunity to relax on the beach while the team drinks and talks about the game. Some of the dudes split off to hang with their women. It's kind of sexy seeing these players get close to their women. All different and like they're in their own space. Some walking off hand in hand on the beach. Others stretched out together on a beach blanket, or wrapped in each other's arms. The food, beer, and people are disappearing, but nobody is actually leaving. It's cool and I think they like it here. The problem here is that there are no extra women. I want you to understand what I'm saying here, I don't have a woman and there are no single women here for me to get to know. That's making it hard to get laid tonight. I need to get laid to get the Seal Girl out of my head. I need to be able to focus.

I find Seno leaning against the outside of my patio fence with Sherry sitting in his lap and his arms wrapped around her. "Dude, I need a chick. I keep thinking that I see the seal or the girl and neither are really there. I just need to fuck her out of my head."

"I'm not helping you get a chick when you're just trying to get laid. Call the twins or one of the baseball skanks." Seno was forceful with his words as he held Sherry tight.

"Twins?" Sherry questions.

"He's got this pair of twins that he's hooked up with a few times." I glare at Seno, thanking him for sharing.

Sherry looks at Seno, "I told you he wasn't ready. He's still just a kid. Give him a break." She turns to me, "Sweetie, you should call the twins. Twins sound like fun. Do you know their names? How can you tell them apart?"

I think I might die now. Then I realize that I can't remember their names. "The older one keeps her hair shorter and the younger one usually has her hair tied up in a ponytail."

"What if they change their hair?"

"They both have little tattoos. One has a baseball and the other has a heart. But, you'd never see those." I say and blush as I remember finding them hidden low on the inside of their hips. "I always call them Chip and Dale because they remind me of happy little chipmunks." I smile hoping that keeps me out of trouble and think that the twins might not be a bad idea. Except, I don't bring chicks to my place and I have the team over, so I can't leave. Why did I feel like I had to share all of that?

Text to Chip and Dale - Hi Ladies! Just wanted to let you know I'm back in town. ;)

But, there was no response from Chip or Dale. I move on to my other guests and enjoy the evening. I drink more than I should, but there are no girls so I figure it's safe. When I finally climb into bed, everybody's gone except for Mason who's passed out on my couch. It's a good thing tomorrow's game isn't an early one. I can't sleep. I'm horny and I'm tenting the sheets. I don't like being thought of as a kid. I know what I want. I just need to figure out how to get it. Maybe I can play that kinky shark attack in my head and handle business to get me through.

CHAPTER SIX

Chase

Over the next few weeks, I manage to stay out of trouble. The team is winning and my place has become the preferred post-game destination for early games. I'm cool with that, maybe a little flattered. I've got it down. I always have the drinks on hand and order pizza delivery from the place that does chicken, too. All I've done is play ball, work out, surf, hang with the team and spend time at home. No chicks. With the winning, and my hitting streak—it's going to stay this way. I know it's superstitious, but I never mess with a streak. I'm not going to wear dirty clothes or anything like that, but I'll keep my daily routine the same. Over the last eighteen games I've got a hit in fifteen of the games and the team has won thirteen of the games. We all know the games we won were the games with Seno behind the plate, Lucky on third, Mason at short and me in center, but none of us have said a word. That's not true, Sherry has pointed out that her lineup wins a couple of times. It happens to be the lineup that she shared with Seno while he was suspended last season. The other games had us moved around or gave one or more of us an off day. It all has to happen and every member of the team should get to play. If we can do it from first place in the division, even better.

It's a Saturday game and we've been playing at home for over a week. I've gotten control of seeing the mascot roaming the park. I'm out on the field stretching pre-game when I hear the public address announcer's voice fill the stadium. "Welcome to Seals Stadium. My name is Kristina. I'm the gofer this year, and I'm covering as PA Announcer for Kenny who's out ill today. So, let's get this rolling!" I recognize the female voice, but I don't know why. It's different, our announcer has always been a dude. I look up to the control booth, but can't see anything. I look at the Jumbotron, and there she is. My Seal Girl, or at least my vision of the Seal Girl from my dream. She's here. She's the stadium gofer. She's probably been here all season and I just haven't seen her, or maybe I have and I'm not losing my marbles like I thought I was. I run into the clubhouse to send a quick text.

Text to Sherry - The PA girl—I think it's her. My Seal Girl.
Text from Sherry - Really? Let me see what I can find out.
Text from Sherry - Go play hard and stay focused! She isn't going anywhere.

That's what I needed to hear.

Text to Sherry - Okay :)

Kristina

I've been on a high since I found out I was covering the PA Announcer today. It's my dream job. It's the perfect media position for me. I get to announce and I'm never on camera other than an occasional shot on the big screen. The fact that it's at the baseball stadium is interesting. I know baseball very well and I'm comfortable with all the ins and outs.

I went to every high school baseball game from my sophomore year on, home games and away games. I dated a utility player and when he got switched to pitcher he asked me to be his girl. I was loyal and I loved him, even when I heard rumors about him with other girls. They were simply jealous and wanted my guy. I helped him with his homework and he knew I'd always be there to support him. We did everything together for the first time. He got a full baseball scholarship and went away to college, while I went to a school specializing in communications, media, and journalism a couple hundred miles away. He dumped me after his first homecoming week and then posted all the pictures of him partying with other women—even a couple from high school. Baseball players suck.

The worst part is that I should've learned the first time. I didn't. I love the game and jumped at the opportunity to announce at a little league championship game. I didn't consider that the volunteer coach played on his own college team. I adored that he was coaching the team of eight year olds, it endeared him to me and I let my guard down. Of course, he wasn't what I thought he was unless we were in the same zip code. Yes, he believed that he could have a different girl in every zip code. He had someone waiting for him at every away game and me at every home game, not to mention all of the little league games he coached. Well, until I realized he was also fucking a couple of the little leaguers mothers. He was into MILFs. Jerk. I love the game, but the players suck.

Baseball players aren't an option for me. I've learned my lesson. I need to stay focused on my stadium internship and achieve my goal. I can't screw up my chance to show them what I can do. I need to stay away from Chase, he can't be a distraction. He'd be my downfall. I'd end up blacklisted in baseball media and labeled a player chaser, or simply thought of as a silly girl that can't handle her own emotions. I need to remember, he's nothing but cheating baseball player number 3.

It's my first time and I thought I'd be nervous, but I'm not. This is my opportunity to shine. Stadiums need more female announcers. The Seals need me. I keep repeating this to myself as I'm directed through the process by the control booth staff. Everything is timed and typed out. It's basically reading clearly on queue. It's obvious they're making it easy for me this time and I hope they take me seriously. I read through the required greeting and emergency information on queue and wait for my next mark while the control booth runs the disabled list on the big screen to the theme of an old hospital drama. It's time for the visitor's lineup and I read through the names plainly, perfectly on my mark. I want to put my own spin on it and show them what I have to offer, but I'm told to speak clearly and not go crazy. Then I get my queue for the home team, "And now for your starting lineup as written in by your manager Butch Hopp." I'm told to stop and wait for a beat. I'm told when to announce each player in the lineup. Time is going slowly in my head and I don't want to be plain, I want them to remember me. Never waste an opportunity. I can be plain for everything else. But the lineup? No way! And I get my queue. "Leading off and playing in Center Field, number 17, Chaaasse Crooosss!" I get a thumbs up from the booth director as I'm looking out over the field and see Chase smiling up at me. No distractions. The beat between each player gets quicker and quicker, but I know its really just in my head. It's timed perfectly. I'm just falling into sequence. "Hitting second and playing at Short Stop, number 28, Jooonesss Maaaaasson!" The wait gets shorter between announcements, almost non-existent. "In the third spot, your first baseman, number 2, Krrrrisssss Maartinnn! Hitting fourth, your catcher, number 6, Rrriickkk Seeeenooo! Hitting fifth and covering the hot corner, number 13, Luuuckyyyyyy Luuuciiiiine! In the sixth spot and playing in Left Field, number 15 Caaaaaaiinn Siimmm-mmms! Hitting seventh, your pitcher, number 8, Coooreeeyy Graaaaaaace! Hitting eighth, in Right Field, number 10, Maaaaark Roooock! And, hitting ninth, your second baseman, number 29, Aaandreeew Braaandt!" There's room to breathe now as I wait for my next mark and I glance around the stadium. They've got me on a small corner of the big screen and Chase Cross is focused on me, along with a portion of the crowd. He's just a guy. I don't like baseball players. I'm not interested. Clear your head! The stadium is full and buzzing, ready for the game to start. Ready for the Seals to get another win.

I follow along with the game and the scheduled announcements that are interspersed with introductions of the players coming up to bat. I have to be ready, but I get to watch the game and it's a great view of the field. I can see everything from the bases to the outfield wall and into the Seals dug out. It's going well and I haven't caught any flack for how I announced the home team. We should all be excited for the home team.

It was a great game! Seals won 8-5. I hope I get a chance as PA Announcer again.

Chase

The game went well, and we won. I admit I was slightly distracted, but it was good to listen to her voice over the loud speaker for the whole game. Sherry was right, she isn't going anywhere. And, now I know her name—Kristina. I need to figure out how to talk to her, get her to go out with me. Yes, I need her to go on dates with me. I'm not screwing this up. Martin was the player of the day again, it seems like it's his year. While he's doing the on field interview, I walk over to the net to find Sherry.

"How do I get her to talk to me? I want to take her on a date."

Sherry stares at me like I just grew three heads, "What about the twins?"

"I haven't been with any women since we got back to San Diego. I don't want the twins or the groupies. I want my own chick. I want her. I still haven't stopped thinking about her."

"Are you sure? The twins sound like a lot of fun."

"I want to date Kristina."

"Are you allowed in the control booth or up in the press boxes?"

"I can get up there, but they might not let me in everywhere."

"Okay. We need help from somebody in the office or maybe Carter. Or, are you up for something kind of public?"

This could be bad, "Like what?"

"Well, you could go get interviewed on the field now and use the opportunity to talk to her and ask her to meet you before she leaves the stadium. It's the quickest way to get to her."

It sounds crazy, but Sherry's right. I've been waiting for her and I don't want to wait any longer. I walk over to the dugout and nod at Hannah as she finishes the interview with Martin. Hannah waves me over, "Chase, that was a great catch you made at the wall this afternoon and your hitting has been off the charts. What do you attribute your hitting success to?"

I check the control booth to see if Kristina's still there and paying any attention to me at all, "I've been more focused on the game this season, trying to do everything right to make my game better. I want to be a Seal permanently and I'm trying to make that happen. I'd like to compliment Kristina on a great job as PA Announcer today, it was nice to hear a female voice coming out of the control booth for a change." I glance up to see her sitting there stone cold and move forward with my plan. "Kristina, you should come out and celebrate with the team tonight, you earned it."

"You both were awesome today. Thanks, Chase." The camera goes off and Hannah starts talking to me, "I didn't think you guys paid any attention to people like Kristina."

I smile, "We don't notice everything. Some people stand out."

"I'm going to be talking to the control booth, would you like me to pass along a message?"

"Can you do that for me? That would be great."

"I'm happy to."

"Give Kristina my number and ask her to call me or text me, please. Or, get her number for me?" I know I'm asking for too much, but she offered and I'm going with it. "Would it be easier to ask her to meet me somewhere in the stadium?"

Hannah looks at me like a horn is growing out of my head, "Let me call up and see what happens." Hannah turns away and makes the call. A couple minutes later, "She's not interested and she's getting ready to leave the control booth right now."

"How do I get up there? I need to talk to her." My eyes tell my story and Hannah's all in.

"Come with me." I follow her as she takes me to an elevator at the center of the stadium and uses her media card to get us to the control room door. She knocks and verifies that Kristina hasn't left yet. "This is the only door out, so unless she jumps to the field you'll see her come through that door. I'm leaving the rest to you." She winks at me as she turns and walks away, "Good luck, slugger."

I wish I had my phone, so I could text Sherry and find out what to do next. It feels like forever that I'm standing here, waiting for the door to open and see Kristina come walking out. I'm still in my dirty, game worn uniform and cleats. I probably smell like a stinky dude that's been working out in the sun all day. I know I've got dried mud on my pants and possibly a hole. My head is racing thinking about her and how it's been weeks since I've seen her. I try to ignore that she said she isn't interested. Maybe she's not interested in celebrating with the team. That doesn't mean she's not interested in me. I start to get a little bit crazy and I'm afraid I'm going to do something I shouldn't, but I can't leave. I need to see her. I want to talk to her. I'd love to touch her. There's something about this chick. I get in my head and start to wonder if it's really her or if I'm making it all up in my head, as the door opens and a dark haired gentleman walks out, with Kristina a few feet behind him.

"Hi, Kristina? Can we talk?"

"We don't have anything to talk about, Chase." I can feel her voice as it touches my ears.

"Kristina, will you go out with me tomorrow night? You're welcome to join the team tonight at my place, too. Please let me take you out on a date." She stares at me blankly. "I'm sure this sounds crazy, but I've been waiting for you."

Kristina glares at me, "Why?"

"I want to get to know you and spend time together."

She stares at me blankly and I don't find any of the fire I could hear in her voice when she's announcing. I reach for her, putting one hand on each of her upper arms gently and I'm happy she doesn't back away. I gaze into her eyes and lean in, pressing my lips to her soft, full lips that are exactly as I remember except she tastes like chocolate chip cookies. I think it's her lip balm. I don't push further, I simply hold my lips to hers until it runs through my head that I'm kissing her and I'm not supposed to do that and it's basically like kissing a co-worker while you're at work. I needed to make sure it's her. I needed to know it's really her and not a chick I made up in my dreams. I pull back and search her eyes, "What do you say? Will you let me take you out?"

She stares at me blankly and I can see the no coming.

"The team is going to my house to celebrate tonight and you should join us, bring a friend if you want." I give her my address and my phone number. "See what you think and then let me take you out tomorrow night."

She's still giving me the "I really don't want to talk to you" look.

"Kristina? I don't know why you don't want to talk to me. Give me a chance. Come by my place and see who I really am." I lean in to whisper in her ear and end up smelling her hair, "Please. I just want to talk. I promise all my clothes will stay on." I lean back and smile at her hoping for something positive.

"I'll think about it."

"At least text me, so I have your number."

"I'll think about it."

Better than a no. I give her a quick peck on the cheek and take off to the clubhouse. Hoping to see her at my place.

CHAPTER SEVEN

Kristina

I walk into my apartment and go directly to my room, tossing my bag into the corner and changing into my PJs before I plop down belly first on my bed for some alone time.

I turn the lights off and start to shut my bedroom door, but my roommate, Michelle, blocks my actions. "How was it, PA Announcer?" She asks all smiley.

"It was fantastic. It couldn't have gone better!"

"Then what's with the mood?"

"I'm not in a mood. I want to soak it all in and relax."

"I call bullshit."

I glare at her and force a breath out.

"Who is he?"

"Why does it have to be a guy?"

"Do we have to do this every time? It's always a guy."

"I don't know what you're talking about."

"Overly obstinate, nice. He must be a baseball player."

I screech at the top of my lungs and bury my face in my pillow.

"Why don't we skip to the chase?"

"How did you know?"

"Know what?"

"Chase."

"Chase Cross? Are you kidding me? The guy you jumped in the mascot costume? He's here?"

She laughs at me and the story I'm now wondering why I told her.

"Let's talk it out now, so we can drink tonight and get it out of your system."

"I don't want to talk about him."

"Oh, you like him. Like, really like him."

"Shut up!"

"You want to kiss him all over and jump his bones."

I swear I'm going to strangle her in her sleep.

"Oh, wait! You already did!"

"Stop! None of it matters! I'm not going!"

"Going where?"

Shit! "He invited me over to his place to celebrate with the team. I'm not interested and I'm not going."

"This is the hot blonde ballplayer that you humped for hours? I'd say you're interested."

"You know how I feel about baseball players. They're bad news. I don't want anything to do with any of them."

"They can't all be bad. It's mathematically improbable. So, you talked to him?"

"Yea, he was waiting for me outside the control booth."

"So, he went looking for you? Put effort into finding you? Waited for you to finish working? And asked you to come over?"

"Yea, and he asked me out on a date." I remember the kiss that accompanied the conversation.

"You kissed him!"

"I did not." I stop and look around my room smugly. "He kissed me."

"I knew it! This would be so much easier if you just told me what happened. Why do you always make me figure out the details?" She does this little dance she does when she's right. "Tell me about the kiss."

"It was just a kiss. Forget it."

"I saw your eyes glaze over when you remembered him kissing you. Your eyes don't glaze over for nothing."

"Look, it doesn't matter. I don't date or do anything else with players."

"Stop holding out and tell me about the kiss. What did he do with his hands? How did his lips feel? Was it hot?"

"You really need to get a dude."

"Whatever. Give me the deets."

"Fine, but only because I think it's the only male interaction you've had this year."

Michelle scoffs at me and waves me on for more details.

"He took me in his arms with passion and dipped me leaving me completely in his control while he kissed me senseless until I begged him to carry me off to my cubicle and have his way with me."

She glares at me and shakes her head, "Start with where his hands were."

I thought about his hands and how they felt on me. I'm reliving the warmth of his touch and the feel of his body.

"Hey!" Michelle snaps her fingers, "Out loud please."

"His hands are large and warm, slightly rough to touch yet tender in their actions." Michelle drops to my bed and makes herself comfy while she melts into my words, "He placed one hand on each of my upper arms and held me gently, making sure I was paying attention to him. His eyes," I stop as I remember the look in his eyes and gather myself.

"What about his eyes? Keep going. Tell me about the kiss!"

"His eyes were focused on me. I was the only thing that mattered and it was more than desire. Then he kissed me."

"He just kissed you, like a peck on the cheek?" she rolls her eyes at me in irritation.

"He leaned in slowly with need, completely focused on my lips. Softly placed his lips to mine and pressed against them gently, holding his lips on mine and not asking for more."

"And?"

"That's it. He asked me out again, reiterated the invitation to his house and told me I could bring a friend."

She raises her hand, "Friend!"

"I already told you I'm not going."

"Then tell me about the rest of the kiss."

"That's it. There's nothing else to tell."

"No tongue?" She looks confused. "Was it a good kiss? Did you like it?"

"No tongue." I consider the rest of her questions and realize there's no reason to keep it to myself. She already knows. She saw my eyes glaze over. I take a deep breath, "It was amazing. Electric with only his lips."

"Why aren't we going to his party?"

"I'm not interested in a baseball player. I don't need the drama. He thinks I'm that crazy seal girl. Forget it."

"Not interested doesn't mean you don't want him."

"Shut up."

"Don't you wonder what that kiss could turn into?" Michelle stops and waits for me to respond, but I hold my ground. "Get ready we're going. I'll be your DD. We need to find out more. Consider it a research mission. Hurry up!"

I stand up ready to go off on her and hold my ground, but why fight it. She's right, I want him. "Do you promise not to leave me alone with him unless I approve?"

"Of course."

"Fine. Get ready. I'm sure there will be other single guys there and you need a man."

"Whatever." She gets up like a shot, changing to go to the party.

Chase

A couple hours later the whole team is hanging out on the beach around my place, when Kristina shows up with a friend. "Hi, I'm happy you decided to come by." I smile at her and give her a quick hug. "This is my place. Food and drinks are out on the patio. We've got a bonfire going out on the sand tonight and some video games in the living room. Mostly the single dudes are playing video games and the couples are out on the patio or the beach somewhere." I walk them out back to show them where everything is and notice the couples have gotten closer to each other, all snuggling in their blankets on the sand and watching the waves while they're warmed by the fire. "I have some extra beach blankets if you would like to use them. Please make yourselves at home." I stop, focusing on Kristina, "I'd really like a chance to talk with you. I'm here when you're ready to talk or if you want someone to keep you warm out by the fire." I turn to her friend, "Hi, I'm Chase," and I reach my hand out to shake hers.

This warm girl with a sweet, innocent face takes my hand and shakes, "I'm Michelle. Nice to meet you." She smiles, "Thanks for inviting us over. So, can we play video games with the guys?"

Kristina shoots her a quick stare and I respond, "You're welcome to do whatever you like. Let me introduce you to the gamers." I lead them into the living room and point to each of my teammates as I introduce them, "This is Nathan Stray, Jones Mason, Rhett Clay, Cain Simms, Andrew Brandt, and Corey Grace. Dudes, this is my friend Kristina and her friend Michelle." Look at me getting names and making sure that everybody knows who everybody is. I realize Kristina hasn't said a word and I don't know if that's good or bad. "I can take you around and introduce you to everybody outside, too, if you'd like."

Michelle is still the only one talking, "No, this is cool. I'm comfortable with the video game crowd." She smiles awkwardly like maybe she shouldn't admit that. "Hey guys, do you mind if I join in and play?" She asks as she settles into a spot in the living room, making herself at home.

"What can I get you two ladies to drink?"

Michelle responds quickly, "An energy drink or a soda would be great, thanks."

Kristina wanders out to the patio to get food and pick a drink from the ice chests. Getting Michelle something to snack on, too. She settles in next to Michelle, quietly eating and watching everybody play games. When she finishes eating, she throws away her trash and walks off, checking things out around my bungalow and finally making her way out to the beach. I go after her when she gets to the beach, "Hey, did you want to go for a walk? May I escort you, so you aren't out here alone tonight?"

She glances up at me and we walk down the beach

together, "I don't understand why you're paying so much attention to me. I told you I'm not interested. I'm only in San Diego to work for the Seals and I'm trying to get a permanent gig."

"We have that in common. I'm trying to show the Seals they want to keep me. It's an everyday thing, making myself better and proving myself," I say sincerely.

"Yea, but you're a player and I'm an intern that gets coffee for the media and fills in whenever I possibly can."

"You really did sound great as PA Announcer today."

"Thanks." Her accompanying smile makes my heart skip a beat.

I know I shouldn't ask, "Kristina, what happened between giving me hickeys all over my body and now? What made you not interested in me? I know I was drunk and that means I'm a jerk. I'm not doing that any more."

She glares at me disgusted, like I should know. "I'm just not interested. Girls can change their mind, you know."

"Maybe you're not interested in that guy who wanted you in the mascot costume. But, how about me now?" She turns away from me and starts to walk away down the beach, but I go with her because I'm not giving up that easy and it's getting late for her to be out here by herself.

She sighs derisively, "You know I was trying to walk away from you, right? I don't need you to walk on the beach."

"Yes." I touch her cheek and make her look into my eyes, "Give me a chance here, get to know the real me. We can start from the beginning and pretend we just met. I haven't had another chick in bed with me since you left me. I've only wanted you and I thought you were gone." I feel my emotions in my throat as I say the words. I did think she was gone and now that I know where she is, I'm not letting her go. I need to be clear with her, she needs to know how I feel. "I'm not just looking for sex. I can get that whenever I want it. It's more than that." I'm really not good at this shit. No wonder she left in the middle of the night. I suddenly remember her words from that night. "I remember what you whispered in my ear before you left me that night. You said 'I want you, too. You have to want me for more. You don't want me enough.' and you were probably right. But, you wanted me then. I want you for more. I want you more than anybody else. Please let me show you." My hand still touching her face, I can feel her warm breath and her pulse quicken. I want to kiss her, but I don't want to do the wrong thing. I don't want her to run off on the beach. The wind off the ocean is getting stronger and cold. I brush her hair out of her face and I can't help myself, I lean in to kiss her. She surprises me by meeting me halfway and kissing me back. Relieved, this tightness that has been growing in my chest releases. The touch of her soft full lips to mine are an adrenaline rush to my system. I try not to push the kiss forward and instead wrap my arms around her, holding her close to me. I want to keep her warm. I want to take care of her. I don't want her to leave. I have no fucking clue what I'm doing. I can't believe I'm even thinking these things. The ocean roars and the lights on my patio twinkle off in the distance. I feel her lean into my body and she pulls back quickly, as if she's burned herself. "I like it when you're close to me." My voice comes out low.

"I should go back and check on Michelle. I shouldn't have left her with a bunch of guys she doesn't know." Kristina pulls away from me and I grab her hand, intertwining my fingers with hers as we walk back to my bungalow.

The crowd has gotten smaller and the bonfire is dying down. We catch Seno wrapping a blanket around Sherry as they're getting ready to leave. "Kristina, this is Rick Seno and his wife, Sherry."

Sherry immediately reaches for Kristina and gives her hug, "It's nice to finally meet you. Chase is one of the good ones." Sherry stops and stares at me, "Give her my number." It's more of an order than a request. Seno smiles and leads his wife away to take her home.

I start to go inside and check on the other dudes, but Kristina stops me. "How does she know who I am?"

"Uh, Sherry's my buddy. She bakes for me. Seno is my best bud, so I spend some time with them." That's good enough, right? She hasn't pulled her hand away from me yet, so it must be okay so far.

We walk into my living room to find Stray and Simms sitting on the floor playing a game with headphones on, and Mason sleeping on my couch with his arms possessively around Michelle. I didn't think we were gone that long. I glance at the clock and it's been longer than I thought, but not that long. The rest of the gamer dudes are gone. I look at Mason and Michelle. They're comfortable together and kind of match. I think that maybe we could double date, that would be fun. But, my thoughts are interrupted by Kristina. I feel her start to shake and she takes her hand from mine.

"Michelle!" Obviously upset at her friend. "What are you doing? Get up. Let's go."

Hold on. What happened? It was good and now she's freaking out.

Michelle opens her eyes and looks at Kristina drowsily, "What? I don't want to go yet." Mason's arms tighten around her and she smiles. "I like it right where I am."

"You don't even know this guy. He's a player. He won't even know your name tomorrow." Kristina throws the words at Michelle.

Michelle rolls her eyes, "You need to get over it. He's been nothing but nice to me. His hands feel amazing holding me and I like him. So, again, get over it. All of them aren't bad. Remember? Mathematically improbable?" She talks to Kristina like nobody else is in the room or she doesn't care if there is.

"Michelle, get up and let's go!"

"No, I'm staying right here. If I'm wrong, then it's my problem." Mason whispers in her ear and her face lights up, it doesn't look like she's wrong.

Mason looks to me for some help. I put my hand on Kristina's back, "Let me give you a ride home. I'm happy to do it." I want to tell her she's always welcome to stay here with me, but I don't want to push her and even if I promised that I'd just hold her—it would be pushing her. She looks at me questioning, "I didn't drink tonight. I wouldn't offer if I had." I wonder if that's what she's questioning, or if it's maybe something else. "You're always welcome to stay." I lean in to her ear and whisper, "That doesn't mean you have to stay in my bed. I have plenty of blankets and pillows, you can sleep wherever you want." I want her bad. I want her in my bed. I want her naked. I want to kiss her lips and feel her warm against my skin. What I would do to hold her like Mason is holding Michelle right now. That's what I want. What the hell is wrong with me? I just want to be with her.

Kristina goes back to Michelle, "When are you going to be ready to go home?"

Mason whispers in her ear again before she speaks, "I'm not going home tonight. Just crash here or let Chase take you home." Kristina's frustrated, but I can't help the smile on my face because both of those options work for me.

"I'm never taking you anywhere again." Kristina turns to me, "Please take me home."

I smile, "I'd be honored," I realize this means I get to know where she lives and I still don't know her phone number. I gesture to the door and follow her outside. I open the truck door for her and make sure she's in before I close the door. I'm going to drive her home. I'm going to walk her to her door. I may get to give her a kiss goodnight. I'm not going in her place. "So, where am I taking you?" She punches her address into my navigation system and doesn't say a word. "Is this going to be a silent trip? Are you mad at me or Michelle?"

I know she rolled her eyes and I didn't have to look, "Both. She ditched me to stay with a guy that she just met. You won't leave me alone."

"And, I'm not going to leave you alone. Isn't it kind of nice to be wanted?"

"Find another girl. It'll be better that way."

"First, I don't have to find chicks. Chicks find me and it requires no effort from me at all. Second, I don't want some chick. I've been turning away all the chicks. I want more and I only want you. I'm not going away."

"Whatever." She looks out the window while I drive her home.

This girl is driving me crazy. I know she kissed me back. "Will you go out to dinner and a movie or something with me tomorrow night? Or, I guess that's later tonight now."

"No."

"Can I have your phone number? How do I find you on social media, so I can message you while I'm on away trips?" Either one will work. Just give me something. Please don't leave me with nothing.

She does something on her phone and I hear mine beep. "I just followed you. I'm @Kristeeeeeena."

"And your phone number?"

"No. One thing at a time."

"How about breakfast in the morning before the game?"

"I have to be at the stadium at 9am. I'm not getting up early enough to go to breakfast."

At least that wasn't a no directed at me. "If you want to come by my place after the game, I'll be there. If we win, the team will be there and you can bring a friend with you or whatever you want. Doesn't have to be Michelle."

"I can't believe my roommate did that! She said she'd be my designated driver. That bitch!" Kristina is laughing now and I love the sound.

"Mason is a cool dude. Very chill. I haven't seen him with a single woman since he joined the team. Not that it matters. Michelle is the only one I've seen him even get close to. That probably makes him better than me, but I know what I want now and I'm not doing that shit anymore."

I pull up in front of her building and she goes to jump out, but I grab her hand, "Hold on, let me park." I find a spot quickly and hop out to go open her door.

She smiles at me, "Thanks for the ride," and turns to run into the building like she's trying to get away from me.

"Why are you running away?" I walk to her, "Let me walk you to your door." She slows down and I take her hand as we walk through the door and up the three flights of stairs to her floor. We get to her door and she unlocks it, reaching in to flip the light switch on. I want to touch her and kiss her, I haven't released her hand and she hasn't pulled it away from me. I whisper, "Kristina," sweetly in her ear as I pull her into me for a hug. She reaches her arms up around my neck and runs her fingers through my hair. I'm trying to be on good behavior and her mixed signals are confusing. I want to ask for permission to kiss her, but a kiss with permission isn't the same. She's gazing up at me and I can't help myself when I see those eyes looking at me. I lean down to her and press my lips to hers repeatedly, sweetly giving her lower lip a suck and holding her head with both hands. I want to inhale her into me. I want to be closer to her. I want to taste her. I lick her lips and she separates them for me like an invitation. I touch the tip of my tongue to hers and wait for her reaction before going further. She opens further and sucks on my tongue. I move my hands to her back and splay them across her, while I hold her to me. I don't want the kiss to end and my tongue dances with hers while I soak it all in. She's not pulling away from me and shows no signs of running. I hear her little whimper as I feel her lean into me and I feel like I can die now. She tries to pull me with her into her apartment, but I stop myself at the door, "I'm not having sex with you until after we've been on at least a few dates. It needs to be more with you and I want you to know that I want you enough. I want you to know you're special to me." I close my eyes because it's one of the hardest things I've done. I want to go in her apartment and fuck her senseless. I want her legs wrapped around me. I know she'd be tight and slick around my hard dick. My voice goes deep and raspy, "And, trust me, I want to. Very few things I want more than that right now." My head is spinning and I want to go in her apartment and see what happens.

"Tell me what you want more." Now she decides to talk.

I don't even think, I just spill, "I want your phone number. I want you to go out with me. I want you to be my chick. I want to know why you don't want me anymore. I want to hold you and maybe kiss you more." She puts her finger to my lips, so I'll quit talking.

"I never said I don't want you." She goes up on her tiptoes and gives me a quick kiss. "Goodnight, Chase." She slides into her apartment and closes the door, turning the lock behind her.

My phone beeps as I'm walking down the stairs.

From @Kristeeeeeena - Thank you for the ride home :)
To @Kristeeeeeena - You're welcome. Maybe you'll have a thank you kiss for me next time I see you?
From @Kristeeeeeena - It's waiting for you now, if you want to come back and get it ;)

I'm a fool, but I turn around and go back to her apartment. I find her changed into her tank top and boxers with the sunglasses on them, hanging out at her door. She smiles as soon as she sees me, like she wasn't sure I'd come back. The sight of her in the tank top and boxers brings back memories of our night in Arizona. I see visions of her all over my body, kissing, licking, sucking, and I can almost feel it. When I'm in her reach, she grabs me and pulls me into her apartment, locking the door behind me. She takes me to her bedroom, climbs into bed and holds the blanket up, inviting me to join her. I have will power, but I don't know if I have enough strength for this. Those short boxers with the easy access and her tits bouncing around all over.

"I came back for the kiss." I say as I take in the view of her lying in her bed and inviting me in.

"The kiss is here, you should come and get it."

"You make me want more." I walk over to the other side of the bed and lean over her, planting a kiss on her with passion and claiming her as mine. I'm crazy hot and my dick is hard, yelling at me to just fuck her. I suck on her lips and push my tongue into her mouth over and over as if it was my dick in her sex. I keep kissing her and dial it back to show her how much I want her. I kiss her tenderly with desire. I stand up. "Goodnight." I turn around and leave. Ignoring the noises my phone is making until I get all the way to my truck.

From @Kristeeeeeena - I can't believe you left.

From @Kristeeeeeena - I don't get it.

From @Kristeeeeeena - Just fuck me and get me out of your system.

From @Kristeeeeeena - Then you can leave me alone.

To @Kristeeeeeena - Not going to fuck you out of my system.

To @Kristeeeeeena - That's not possible.

To @Kristeeeeeena - I want you and I want more.

To @Kristeeeeeena - Goodnight, beautiful.

I get home to find Mason and Michelle still sleeping on my couch, but everyone else is gone, the party has been cleaned up and the house is locked up. I go to bed and fall asleep happy.

CHAPTER EIGHT

Kristina

I'm not a morning person and my phone is going off like crazy much too early. I've gotten at least three text messages, that I have chosen to at least attempt to sleep through and now my phone is ringing. I have to open my eyes and answer it, it might be work. I reach for my phone while I struggle to open my eyes and expose my relaxed sleep state to daylight. It wasn't a good night for sleep. I don't sleep well as a general rule, but it's worse when I'm home alone. It's only 7:00am and I'm ready to scream at whoever is calling me this early, but it's the stadium.

"Good morning!" I answer bright and cheery and not at all like I'm ready to strangle the person on the other end of the phone.

"Hi, we'd like you to fill the PA Announcer position again today," the human resources representative for the stadium states politely.

"Absolutely, I'd love to!" It's confirmation that I did a good job.

"Can you come in early enough to get your regular tasks done before the game?"

I pinch my eyes closed as tight as I can and suck it up, because I want to be the announcer, "I'm happy to do it. I'll be there in time to get everything set for the broadcasters before the game starts. Thanks for giving me another shot in the booth."

"You deserve it. Keep showing us what you've got. Thank you," he hangs up.

I check my texts and Michelle has been texting me for the last hour.

Text from GamerGirlM - Are you up yet?

Text from GamerGirlM - Of course not. Too early for you.

Text from GamerGirlM - Wake up!

Text from GamerGirlM - Are you still mad at me?

Text to GamerGirlM - What? You need me to pick you up?

Text to GamerGirlM - Jerk ballplayer ditch you after he got his?

Text from GamerGirlM - Get over yourself

Text from GamerGirlM - We're going to breakfast. Want to go?

I stop and think to myself, I'm up anyway and I have to go to work early.

Text to GamerGirlM - I'm PA Announcer again today.
Text to GamerGirlM - I'll be by if I have enough time
Text from GamerGirlM - Can you hear my eyes rolling?
Text from GamerGirlM - I'll see you at breakfast. Jones is asking Chase to go, too.
Text to GamerGirlM - Whatever
Text from GamerGirlM - You know you want him

Another text pops through with a string of emojis including a bunch of hearts and an eggplant. I respond with an eyeroll emoji and toss my phone to the side as I get ready for my day.

I find myself paying more attention to my appearance than normal. Why? I don't even know if Chase will be at breakfast. It must be for work. Dress to impress, though I don't think the control booth crew will appreciate my perfect fitting jeans as much as the outfielder. I don't want to date or do anything else with a baseball player. I guess there's an exception to every rule. Michelle's logic isn't wrong, they can't all be bad.

Driving to breakfast the radio plays his walk-up song and I can't help but think about him. Damn it! I want to see him.

Chase

Mason wakes me up early, "Cross, we're going to get breakfast before stadium time. You want to go with us?"

"No, I'm cool. Thanks."

"Kristina might be meeting us."

"No, dude, she said she had to be at the stadium early when I asked her last night."

"Schedule changed. She's PA Announcer again today."

I'm torn because I don't want to be the third wheel when she doesn't show up and I want to take her on a real date, not just hang out. I'm hungry. "Okay, I'm hungry now that I'm awake." I get ready quickly and we stop at the Yolk on the way to the stadium. We walk in to find Seno and Sherry, already sitting there eating their breakfast. This place is always good to us and makes sure to get us tables quick on early game days like today. Michelle is cool, doesn't seem crazy at all and definitely not a player chaser. Mason with a chick is different, he's always respectful and his midwest upbringing shows. But, with a girl, I don't know, it's like she deserves and gets all of his attention, almost like she's on a pedestal for him to look up at and desire. I can see it's working for him with Michelle. I wonder if Kristina will show up for breakfast and I go with the flow, ordering and talking with Mason. I really want to talk to Sherry and Seno for advice, but it's not the place. This girl has me confused.

I walk over to Seno's table, "Dude, want a ride today? I'll pick you up after breakfast. I need to talk."

"Sure. Come by and get me."

But, Sherry wants to run with it, "What's up?"

"I don't know. This chick has me confused. She won't give me her phone number. She won't go on a date with me. But, when I kiss her she meets my kiss and kisses me back. When I drove her home last night she called me back to her apartment and dragged me into her bedroom, wanting me to get in bed with her. I left and she messaged me asking why I didn't fuck her so I could get her out of my system. I told her I want her for more and it's not possible to fuck her out of my system. I don't get it."

Sherry looks at me and smiles, "And, she's here." She waves at her from across the restaurant. Kristina scowls at Michelle and walks right by her table without stopping, sliding in next to me at the Seno's table. "Hey, Kristina. Did Chase give you my number?"

"No." Kristina trades numbers with Sherry.

"So, Sherry can have your number and I can't?" I protest.

"That's right." Kristina smiles, looks at Sherry and laughs, "I don't give my number to boys. I don't travel with the team and I'm happy to help you while the team is away."

"I appreciate that. We're not looking forward to that. I always travel with Rick and we never spend a night apart." Sherry confesses her dread.

"I know, I see you at the stadium early and for every game. It'll be an adjustment, but well worth it." Kristina states supportively.

The waitress brings the food over to me and we leave Mason some private time with his chick. I like that Kristina and Sherry get along. That should help me.

Sherry looks directly at Kristina, "So, what do you think about our boy here?" Gesturing to me as I pound my head into the tabletop.

"Sherry, we don't need to talk about this." I look to her pleading.

Kristina starts in, "He's a great baseball player. He's a good kisser. He doesn't listen well and I think he has a seal fetish."

Sherry continues on, "I don't know about the kissing, but the seal fetish is interesting. I think he associates the seal with you, so technically he can't stop thinking about you. I haven't experienced the not listening."

They keep talking like I'm not right there listening to

everything they say. Seno is taking it all in and enjoying that it's not him they're talking about.

"I keep telling him to leave me alone and he blatantly refuses. I ask him to spend the night with me and he leaves. I decline a date and tell him I'm not giving him my phone number, but he keeps asking for both. Do you think he's mentally impaired?"

"Well, he's male." They both laugh like this is simply a fact. "I think he hears you and he's just persistent. Maybe you should try telling him yes to a date and see what happens."

"Maybe, but I don't want to lead him on and it's weird after Arizona. I know he's thinking of me as that drunk girl in the mascot costume that left him covered in hickeys. I don't want to be thought of like that. That's the only time I've ever done anything like that. I never get drunk. I'm not that girl and I know that's what he expects."

I look straight at her ready to tell her she's wrong, but Sherry stops me. "I don't think that's true. He didn't even remember the night, he was so hungover the next morning. You should've seen his face when he found the tail piece of the seal costume!" Kristina cocked her head to the side, like she was listening. "You should give him a chance. Don't worry about leading him on. He's a big boy and he can handle himself. I'll tell you, spending time with a professional baseball player isn't what you think and you won't want it to be any different once you've done it."

Kristina turns toward me and examines me. She turns back to Sherry, "I'll think about it."

The whole time they're talking, Kristina is eating my breakfast like it's her own. She gets up to leave and I walk her out to her car. My body humming just being near her. "I heard you're PA Announcer again today."

"Yes! I love it. I wish they'd hire me to the position

permanently." Kristina gets a daydreaming look at the thought.

"Good luck. I know you'll do great today. I'll be listening to your voice while I'm playing. Can I see you after the game?"

"I might come by if you win today." I have my hands in my pockets, to keep my hands to myself. But, she doesn't. She reaches her arms up around my neck and goes up on tiptoes to kiss me. She presses her lips to mine softly and holds them there for what feels like a long time, but I know it's only a couple of minutes at the most. She pulls back and I see her drag her teeth over her lower lip as she looks at my mouth.

She turns to leave and I can't help myself. I grab her and hold her against me. I bend down and kiss her neck at her ear, breathing in her scent. "I know you want me, too. Stop fighting it. Give us a chance, Kristina." I kiss her on the lips with the intent of things that I can't even understand myself and turn away as I walk back into the restaurant. I look out to the parking lot when I sit down at the table and see that she's still standing there.

To @Kristeeeeeena - Are you okay? I see you standing there in the parking lot.
From @Kristeeeeeena - No. I need another kiss.

I smile uncontrollably and get up, running back out to the parking lot. She's watching me run toward her with a huge grin. I take her in my arms and swing her around, holding her up to my lips. I kiss her, letting her know how much I want her, it's almost a need. Fuck, I need her. I need to have her. Her lips are so soft and giving, she tastes like my waffles. Out of breath, I set her back on the ground, "We can kiss for hours after the game."

She gets in her car, “I’m still not giving you my number,” and she drives away.

I sit back down with the Senos and eat the remains of my breakfast while Seno chuckles and Sherry provides commentary.

“Well folks, she came and ate most of his breakfast. Then she kissed him. Then she called him to the parking lot wanting another kiss. But, she’s not giving up the digits and won’t go out with him. The only hope he has is if the team wins today, she might visit. I’d say it’s a pretty good bet, what do you think Mr. Seno?”

Seno nods, “We need to make it a win for Cross today, so he can make out later. You should send her flowers or a note or something, so she thinks about you.”

“I was thinking about changing my walk up song, like a message for her.”

“I like that, too. You could do both. Maybe tie them together.” Seno continues.

“Okay, take me home so you two can have some guy talk. I can’t handle this right now.” Sherry has had enough.

CHAPTER NINE

Kristina

Am I truly considering Chase Cross as a potential boyfriend? He's everything that I avoid. I can't be in the same room or the same parking lot with him and maintain control. And his kiss! It's like potato chips, I can't have just one. Or, maybe M&M's, except I melt in his hands when he kisses me. I need to stay away from him, but, what if I don't want to? His fucking lips! One touch and I'm willing to give him anything. Distance is the answer. How am I going to do that when we work at the same place?

Can I be with a baseball player? My body wants to. I can't let my head give in.

I'm sitting in my car in the stadium employee parking lot and don't remember how I got here. All I can remember is how his lips feel pressed to mine, soft and warm. The happy grin he had when I wanted another kiss and how fast he ran to me, like he was stealing second. When he kisses me, I'm the only thing in his world, and his job is to please me and protect me. He takes my breath away with his touch. I wish I had his confidence. He believes we belong together. He must be crazy.

Chase

Mason catches me and Seno walking into the clubhouse, "Michelle knows absolutely nothing about baseball. I'm fine with it, but she wants to learn about the game. I need help with this. What do I do?"

Seno and I reply at the same time, "Sherry."

"Get her the seat next to Sherry for a few games and she'll know more about baseball than you do." Seno smiles, "Make sure both of them know what you're doing and tell Michelle to check with Sherry for what is acceptable food to eat around her that day. Garlic fries have been making her nauseated the last few days."

"She wants to come to the game today and I need to get her a ticket."

The three of us invade Carter's office. "I need a ticket to the game today for my girl and I want her to sit next to Sherry," Mason starts.

"It's a day game, so she's going to need a cap. Get her the game day cap and have Mason and his number put on it for her. While you're at it, have a game day cap made up with Cross and his number on it, too, and have it delivered to Kristina in the control booth. Oh, and take Sherry some chocolate soft serve ice cream in one of those little helmets and a bottle of water around the fifth inning please." Seno takes control of the situation.

"And, can you take Kristina some flowers with the cap

please? I want to write a note to put with it, if you can. I want to change my walk up song, too."

"Hold on... Two caps, a ticket for the game, ice cream, water, flowers and change a walk up song. Is that everything?" Carter inspects the trio curiously.

Mason adds, "Can you get my girl a shirt with my name and number, too? And, do you think she can get in early to watch BP with Sherry?"

"No BP today, but I'll get her added to the early entry list. What's the new walk up song?"

"'I Want to Hold Your Hand' by the Beatles." I find a piece of paper and a pen, to write a quick note.

Kristina,

Hope you like the flowers. Listen for my walk up song, changing it for you. Please come by later, I have kisses waiting for you.

Chase

I get it folded up and sealed in an envelope, leaving it for Carter to deliver with the flowers and cap.

"Alright, I'll get it handled. Now, get out of here so I can get working on it all." Carter evicts us back to the clubhouse and we all walk away satisfied with ourselves.

I walk out of the dugout to warm up before the game, earlier than usual because there's no batting practice today. Some of the team have been in the batting cages down in the stadium, but I need to get outside. I need to get some extra stretch time in and run some sprints, plus I want to see what everything looks like on the social side of things. Sherry and Michelle are sitting behind home plate all chummy and talking. Sherry looks excited, so they're probably talking baseball. Michelle is proudly sporting a new baseball cap and a Seals shirt. I can't see the back, but I know she's marked with Mason. I look to the control booth wondering what Carter managed to get done for me and there's a bright colored bouquet of flowers laying on the desktop near the microphone, but no cap and no Kristina. The Jumbotron is on an automatic slide rotation and there's music playing, but no announcements yet. I check the time and scan the stadium, hoping for a glimpse of Kristina. I want her to be wearing her cap with my name on it as proudly as Michelle's wearing Mason's, but I never know how she's going to respond to things. She might hate it or not wear hats.

I hear a female yelling, "Jack ass!"

I hear Sherry calling me, "Chase!"

I turn to run over to Sherry and she's pointing to Kristina, so I change course for her. I'm happy that she's looking for me, but then...

Kristina

"Jack ass!" I can't believe he had flowers and a cap with his number on it left in the control booth for me. In the control booth! I've worked so hard for this and he's going to ruin it for me! Why can't he leave me alone? Damn it! The flowers are gorgeous and I want to wear his cap!

"What the hell are you doing? You know I'm trying to land a permanent gig here and you go sending me things to the control booth! Don't embarrass me! Don't make me look like a fool or a player chaser!" How many times do I need to tell him no? Why can't he fuck me out of his system and be done with me? Or just leave me alone!

He stands there in all his baseball player hotness, staring at me without a response. I'm entranced by his shining light green eyes and watch them darken as I grab his jersey and pull him to me. I yell at myself internally as I kiss him and feel him smile against my lips. What the hell am I doing? I can't help myself. I hate baseball players! I press my lips against his harder, needing more and needing to have him. My heart beats faster and I feel his energy run through me, pushing me to give him more. I slide my tongue into his mouth, needing a taste of him. Damn it! What am I doing! Baseball players suck! I break the connection and try to hide that I'm breathing hard. I whisper in his ear, "Thank you." And as I'm running through the stands so I can get to the control booth on time, I yell back at him, "Now go win, jerk!"

Chase

Her lips were on me like never before, she sent a new electricity running through my body and I feel like I can do anything. I've never been so happy to be a jack ass and a jerk and get shoved away.

I turn back to the field and walk to Sherry and Michelle. They're laughing and Sherry points at me, so I question my decision to go talk to them. "Hello, ladies."

Sherry can't maintain herself, "It looked like she just went off on you, then took a kiss and shoved you away, but I couldn't hear anything other than the jack ass part in the beginning."

"She did say thank you and told me to win, too." I smile at

the whole interaction. "She doesn't want me to have things delivered to her in the control booth." If she's going to kiss me like that when she gets mad at me, I'm going to keep pissing her off. I look to the control booth and see Kristina sitting there now, reading the note with her flowers while she wears the cap with my number on it backwards with the headphones over the top. It's perfect, even if all she wants to do is kiss me.

The rest of the team comes out for warm up. Mason goes directly to Michelle and I hear giggling. Everything else is the way it's supposed to be, other than my distraction of Kristina as PA Announcer and that really isn't a distraction—I like to hear her voice. She announces the lineup and I love the way she says my name. I know she does all of them the same, but mine feels different to me. She reads through all of the pregame and we take the field.

I'm first at bat for the Seals and as I stand in the on deck circle swinging my bat I hear "I Want to Hold Your Hand" start to play, my new walk up song. The other team is still throwing the ball around the field and I take the opportunity to glance up at Kristina and see if she gets it. It's pretty straight forward. It's one of the first things you do when you meet someone or start dating someone—hold their hand. I've managed it a couple of times with Kristina and I love the way her hand feels in mine with our fingers locked together. Her skin is soft and while she's not delicate, her hands and fingers are feminine and slender. More so in my large man hands that have been beaten up by the sun and the game. When I hold her hand, she doesn't pull it away from me. It's like when we kiss, she meets me halfway. Kristina's smiling up in the control booth, but I don't know if that's my walk up music or her happy to be the PA Announcer again today.

"Chase," Sherry gets my attention, "Did you change your walk up song on purpose?"

"Yea," I think to myself that at least Sherry noticed, "What do you think?"

"I like it and it's very sweet." She gives me a happy nod of approval.

"I hope Kristina feels the same way." I look at Michelle for feedback since she's Kristina's friend and roommate, but all I get is a shoulder shrug.

I step up to the plate, digging my cleats into the clay and I hear her announce my name. Her voice wasn't as stable as it had been and I want to think that I could detect some emotion there, but it could be wishful thinking. The first pitch comes in low, then the second is outside, the third was high and inside causing me to lean back quickly to avoid getting hit by the wild 96 mile per hour fastball. That's when it happened. I heard the audible gasp come over the loud speakers throughout the park. I knew it was her. I knew I was in trouble because she would think that she'd messed up her opportunity for a permanent gig and it's my fault. I don't want to make things hard for her, but her gasp is proof that she cares. It means the ball getting that close to me scared her or worried her. While I don't want to scare her or worry her, I'm warm all over knowing how she feels about me. I knew she wanted me. I step out of the batters box to get my head straight and swing the bat a couple times, then get right back in there ready to get on base. I hear Sherry cheering for me and Michelle is yelling, too. The next pitch is low and I walk to first base without even swinging my bat.

Mason is up to bat next and just slams the ball on the very first pitch, hitting a home run to the left field upper deck. I think it's his first homer of the season. It's gotta be Michelle and she's out of her seat, yelling at the top of her lungs, "Go JJ!" and clapping. I cross home plate and wait for Mason to catch up with me, celebrating with him as he jumps on home plate. 2-0 Seals. Mason is focused on Michelle, I can see them smiling at each other and flirting as we walk back to the dugout.

Mason got a hit at each of his at bats, scoring three times and bringing three of his teammates home. Final score 10-3 Seals. The other two runs were home runs from Martin and Seno with Mason on base. I wasn't much help at the plate today, but I was all over the outfield like a dog playing fetch and had to climb the outfield wall to keep a ball from getting out of the park.

The way Mason hit today, you'd think he's a new man. They slept on my couch last night, there's no way he got laid. Then again, maybe he's being smart. I should probably take a lesson. Hannah grabbed him for the on field interview and I check to see if Kristina is still in the control booth while Seno walks over to the net checking on his woman. Michelle's eyes are locked on Mason doing the interview, I guess it would be different if you'd never been to a game before. Playing the game and giving interviews are part of the day for us, typically nothing special. Kristina's still sitting at the microphone, watching the interview. She must not be done announcing yet. I wave at her and smile, but she doesn't acknowledge me. I know she wants to kiss me. Even if she's mad, she wants to kiss me. I go to the clubhouse to get cleaned up and change. It's early and the team is coming over. I want to talk to Kristina and make sure she's coming over, but I don't want to appear needy. I guess it's my turn though, she did come find me to yell at me and kiss me before the game. Is it a problem that thinking of her yelling at me makes me happy? I must be a sick puppy.

To @Kristeeeeeena - Will you go out with me?
From @Kristeeeeeena - Give it up
To @Kristeeeeeena - Can I have your phone number?
From @Kristeeeeeena - Why would I give you my phone number?
From @Kristeeeeeena - You sent me gifts to the control booth! Jerk!
From @Kristeeeeeena - I totally screwed up today and it's your fault!

I wonder if her complaints that no other chick would complain about are some type of foreplay. I can't help myself.

To @Kristeeeeeena - You should give me your number, so you can kiss me sooner.
To @Kristeeeeeena - Phone number = quicker access
To @Kristeeeeeena - How did I screw you up?

I know, the gasp at the high and inside wild fastball. I want her to say it. I wait and get no response.

To @Kristeeeeeena - When you kiss me, I feel like I've won.
To @Kristeeeeeena - Your lips are soft and you taste sweet.
To @Kristeeeeeena - I want to hold your hand.
To @Kristeeeeeena - I want to hold you with a blanket by the bonfire.
To @Kristeeeeeena - Your hand just feels right when our fingers are locked together.
To @Kristeeeeeena - Please come over. You can stay over if you want to.
To @Kristeeeeeena - We can go surfing in the morning.
To @Kristeeeeeena - Whatever you want.

I'm ready to apologize for whatever I did to screw her up and I don't think I did anything. Why won't she respond? Twelve messages in a row. Shit, I look like a stalker. What am I thinking? I can't think straight with this chick. I shove my phone in my pocket and go home to get ready for the team. I don't want to play games with her. I want her. I hope she comes to find me.

CHAPTER TEN

Kristina

I refuse to lose what I've worked so hard for when I'm this close. I've replayed my reaction to Chase almost getting hit by the ball over and over in my head. Every time the shock and concern gets me. Every time I gasp louder than I did live in the game. I've watched the video replay and it looked worse from my vantage point, like it almost hit his chin. In reality, it was almost straight across the top of the Seals lettering on the chest of his jersey. Not much difference, but the difference of a potentially life altering injury and it didn't stop him. I don't want to be known as the announcer that can't control her emotions or isn't professional. This is my first big break and I can't screw it up. I can't afford the wrong reputation. I don't have any other professional experience to prove who I really am.

I really am this girl that can't help but be affected by the man she wants getting hit by the ball or injured in the game.

It's expected when you care about someone. I don't have the luxury to show it and get where I want to be professionally.

Baseball players are out for me. I need to stay away from him. If I'm outside of his atmospheric pull, I'm able to maintain my composure. That's it. No going to his house. I need to keep my distance.

I get home and change into my PJs, plopping down on my bed. I have the apartment to myself and leave the lights off to watch the replay of the game on my laptop, fast forwarding through and listening to my announcements. I get distracted and watch Chase's plays, replaying them and admiring his skill in the game. He doesn't get shook by anything. He knows exactly what he needs to do and he does it dependably. He doesn't let his team down. I also notice the way he stands with a masculine authority and flexes his muscles while he's at bat. The way his legs stretch his pants as he runs to catch the ball. How his helmet flies off his head as he's running the bases because of his sheer speed and dedication to winning the game. I need to stay away from him. I still want him.

Text from GamerGirlM - Why aren't you here yet?
Text from GamerGirlM - Chase has been watching for you.
Text to GamerGirlM - Not going.
Text from GamerGirlM - What? Why not?
Text to GamerGirlM - It's better this way.
Text from GamerGirlM - He's a good guy. Not a jerk player.

I know she's right and that's why I need to stay away. I can't get involved with someone real. I knew he was real. I should've fucked him in Arizona and forgot about it. Damn it! I want him.

Text to GamerGirlM - It's a work thing. I need to focus.

Text from GamerGirlM - Don't wait too long.

Text from GamerGirlM - He may be the one.

Text to GamerGirlM - That's stupid. That's not real.

Text from GamerGirlM - I was there when you got home that night in Arizona.

Text from GamerGirlM - You told me why you didn't have sex with him then.

Text from GamerGirlM - I know the truth.

Text from GamerGirlM - Were you lying to me then or are you lying to me now?

I love Michelle, but sometimes it would be nice to have a best friend that hadn't been my roommate since we got out of high school and that couldn't read me like a book because we've known each other for so long. I need to walk away from Chase.

Chase

The team is relaxing on the sand and the waves are raging. Kristina hasn't shown up and I haven't gotten any messages from her. I need to surf and get it out of my system. I grab my board and head toward the water, stopping just short to watch the waves. I'm familiar with the surf break. I've spent hundreds of hours floating on my board here waiting for my wave and weeks sitting on the sand observing. I swim out, diving into the waves with my surfboard. I feel alive. The ocean always makes things better, even if it's only a temporary distraction. I swim out at least a hundred yards and lay flat on my board watching the surf as it rolls in, waiting patiently. Floating calm on the raging ocean and letting the waves break, while they allow me to ride them. The waves are coming in sets of six and about every other set has my wave. I catch a few rides in, making it up to my feet each time and needing the rush of adrenaline. It's addictive, I immediately turn around and swim back out for more.

I walk up to my bungalow, dripping wet and cold. I observe the couples snuggling at the bonfire, wondering why it can't be like that for me. Why can't Kristina be here? Or, maybe she could message me. Anything would be nice. I watch Mason with his arms around Michelle as I approach, "Anything from your roommate?"

"Sorry, she's not coming."

"Did she say why?"

"She said she can't be with you and get the job she wants, that it's better this way." Michelle leans her head to the side with kind eyes, "I'm sorry. I tried to get her here. I'll keep trying. I think she's just upset today and I'm hoping she'll come around for you. I believe you're a good guy."

"This morning she was kissing me and wanting to kiss me more. I don't get it." I shake my head as I walk off to shower.

Chase

After everyone has gone home, I climb in bed and lie there thinking about Kristina. Not that different from the rest of the evening when I was hoping she'd show up. I'm not crazy. I know she wanted to kiss me this morning. She called me to the parking lot because she wanted another kiss and I'll never forget that feeling. I was happy in a new way, comfortable with her as I swung her around and kissed her. I know she was happy, too. I heard her need for me in her voice, and her joy when I had her in my arms. Shit, I've never felt so good as when she planted that kiss on me at the stadium today—even if I was a jerk and an asshole. I need to make her think about me.

To @Kristeeeeeena - Sorry you couldn't make it tonight.
To @Kristeeeeeena - Goodnight

I didn't think I'd get a response, but a reply popped through immediately.

From @Kristeeeeeena - Goodnight

I don't understand this chick.

To @Kristeeeeeena - I was thinking about you.
To @Kristeeeeeena - Wish you would've come over.
From @Kristeeeeeena - It's better if I don't.
To @Kristeeeeeena - How's it better not seeing each other and not kissing each other?

I'm frustrated and turn the sound on my phone off before she can reply. I wish she were here with me and remember her kiss as I fall asleep.

Kristina

I want to be kissing him right now, but I can't let myself get lost in his world. He's not good for me. I have a goal and I'm going for it. I need to stay away from him. He just makes things harder. Chase is a distraction I don't need. I need to focus on the gig I want, not the baseball player I want nothing to do with.

To @RookCross - You're bad for me.

I expect a quick response, but there's not one. He's not trying to change my mind. He's not saying anything. He's gone. "He's already off with another woman!" I yell out and throw my journal against the wall. "Damn it!" I kick the blankets off my bed and pace around talking to myself. "I knew it! Baseball players suck!"

"Excuse me, I'm a baseball player," I hear through the wall.

Shit! I didn't know they were here. "Michelle! Do you have a guy in your room?"

"We're playing in my room."

"What?" She's never had a guy over before.

"Not like that. Perv." Michelle calls back through the wall.

"Baseball players don't suck." Mason adds to the conversation and I hear giggling. I can only imagine the conversation about what else he would do to make up for not sucking.

I shake my head, "I can't believe you have a guy over in bed with you."

"I'm an adult and I can do whatever I want, mother."

"You could've at least given me a heads up before you brought your boy toy over for a romp. Why didn't you go to his place? I'm sure he's got a nice ball player bachelor pad." I joke, continuing the conversation through the wall. I hope she gets laid.

Mason complains, "Hey, you're messing with our mojo here."

Michelle responds to him, "Just put it on pause." I hear her bedroom door open and her walking toward my bedroom. "Are you decent? I'm coming in there either way." My door opens and there stands Michelle with the coolest wireless gaming headphones I've ever seen wrapped around her neck, fully dressed in leggings and a Seals T-shirt.

"What the?" I look at her confused.

She rolls her eyes at me, "Where do you think we were? We were at his place earlier."

"Then why are you here now? I'm sure his place is better."

"He doesn't have my gaming machine. I want to play my games, not his." She turns to leave, but changes her mind. "Why were you throwing shit? What did you do? It's about him. It's always a guy. Why didn't you just go to the party?"

"I told him he's bad for me and he didn't respond. He's probably busy with another girl. No time for me."

"You're a nut job! What do you expect? You keep telling him to leave you alone. He does what you want and you freak out. We all saw you kissing him. You were happy and wanted more. Why wouldn't you want more? Chase is fuckin' hot."

Mason interrupts, "Hello. Current guy you're dating is right here in the other room. Also a baseball player."

"I know, Mase. You're hot, too. And, you smell good." Michelle closes her eyes and continues, "You can't have it both ways. He wants you." She turns to the wall, "Mase, any chance Cross is with another girl tonight?"

He groans, "I'm sure there's one available and trying to get his attention."

"Not helping," she yells back at him.

"He's not into that anymore. I haven't seen him so much as call another woman."

I add on, "So, you're a guy, right?"

He groans, "Yes."

"Why wouldn't he respond to me?"

"Maybe he hasn't seen your message. Maybe you should call him or actually go to his house when he invites you if you want to talk to him instead of staying home. Fuck, maybe he's sleeping."

Michelle looks at me, "He could be sleeping. You need to figure this shit out. Mase is right and Chase won't wait forever." She stops, but gets the last word as she walks out of my room, "Love you to the moon, Kristina, but he's a good guy and he shouldn't have to wait. Figure it out."

"Thank you, Michelle," Mason calls out proudly.

She whispers to me, "I was referring to Chase." Then louder while shaking her head, "I know, I'll be right there."

"Hey, wait! What's up with you and Mason?" I whisper, "Did you get laid?"

"No! We just met. Perv!" She slams my door behind her and goes back to her room.

I grab my phone to look for a response from Chase, but there's still nothing. Maybe Mason is right. I should sleep, too.

To @GamerGirlM - Did he kiss you yet? Or anything?

From @GamerGirlM - He's sweet and respectful.

From @GamerGirlM - Not an intrusive perv like you.

From @GamerGirlM - Details later… when there are some.

I laugh out loud and Michelle yells through the wall, "Shut up! You could be getting laid if you wanted."

I'm not sure she's right. Chase wants to date me and kiss me. He's turned me down for sex. It doesn't matter. He's bad for my focus and I need to focus on my goal. If he doesn't wait, then he isn't the right one. Listen to me! He's not the right one. Baseball players are never the right one.

CHAPTER ELEVEN

Chase

I wake up to a missed call and texts from Mason.

Text from Mason - Dude! Where are you? Going to breakfast.

Text from Mason - Kristina is with us.

Text from Mason - She was freaking out about you not responding to her message last night.

I check my twitter.

From @ Kristeeeeena - You're bad for me.

Text to Mason - Thanks for the heads up.
Text to Mason - Fuck! How am I bad for her?
Text from Mason - I don't get that girl. She was watching for you at breakfast and waiting for your response last night.
Text to Mason - I don't get her either.

To @Kristeeeeena - Good morning. :)
To @Kristeeeeena - Sorry I missed our breakfast date.
To @Kristeeeeena - I was sleeping and my sound was off.
To @Kristeeeeena - Let me make it up to you over late night dessert at the diner after the game tonight?
From @Kristeeeeena - I don't think it's a good idea.
To @Kristeeeeena - Okay

Text to Carter - Hey Carter! Is Kristina PA Announcer again today?
Text from Carter - Yes.
Text to Carter - Perfect. Can you deliver the game day color cap with my number on it to her in the control booth please? I want her to match the team and feel special.
Text from Carter - No problem.
Text to Carter: Can you take her one of those plush seals with the jersey on it, too? Please. The larger one?
Text from Carter - I'll take care of it.

If I have to piss her off to get her to come find me and kiss me. I can be the jerk. Now I simply wait for her to get mad.

Kristina

What doesn't he understand about not sending me things to the control booth? I thought I was very clear. Maybe he really is mentally impaired! I have a goal here and he's getting in the way. He makes me look like a girl instead of an announcer. His truck is in the player's garage. I know he's here. He's not on the field or anywhere I have access to. I'm going to rip him a new one! Jerk!

Chase

When I get to the stadium, she's already been looking for me and she's pissed off. I take batting practice in the cage and do an extra work out on the weights, staying in the clubhouse until its time to go out and do my pregame warm-up.

Sherry and Michelle are behind home plate again and wave me over. "Kristina's been looking for you again and she didn't look happy." Sherry warns me, but I smile.

"That's part of my plan. She finds me when she's pissed and I'm betting I get another kiss."

"Sneaky. I like it," Michelle chimes in. "That girl doesn't think she can get the announcer gig and the guy. She acts like it's one or the other."

"I don't know what else to do. I'm open to suggestions." I see Kristina out of the corner of my eye, "I've gotta go." I turn and walk toward the outfield to warm up just in time for...

"Don't go running away from me, you jerk!"

I keep walking and pretend I don't here her yelling.

"Chase Cross! What the hell are you thinking? Idiot!"

I turn like I'm just noticing when she says my name, and

run toward her with a grin plastered on my face. "Hey! What's up?"

"What's up?" She stares at me like she's trying to bore a hole through my body. "You sent me another gift to the control booth! I specifically told you not to send me things to the control booth! Is the plush seal supposed to remind me of your furry fetish or my stupid decision to make out with you in your room? Jerk!"

I watch her go off on me and take the opportunity to gaze into her gorgeous green eyes. Her anger has the gold flecks dancing around the edge of her irises and her cheeks flushed. I'm prepared to respond, but I don't think I'll have to. I wait her out and let her finish yelling at me.

"I swear you either don't listen or you're just plain stupid!"

Sure enough, she reaches for me and pulls me to her by the front of my jersey. This time I'm ready and when she plants that amazing kiss on me, I wrap my arms around her and I take control. I lift her up and hold her against me. Kissing her with every bit of passion I have and not letting her go. She tries to push me away, but gives in to my kiss and melts into me. She's kissing me back and her heartbeat skips, beating hard against my chest. I press my lips to hers repeatedly, tasting her and drawing her into me. I push my luck, licking her lips and slipping my tongue into her mouth to stroke hers. I want more. I want all of her and it's not the place to go further. It's not the time. I need to prove I want her enough, but I have to get her near me to do that. I hold her tightly against me, so she can't get away and I whisper in her ear, "Feel us together. I want us. I know you want us. I can feel it in your touch and taste it on your lips. Let me show you that I want you enough. Please, stop fighting it. Give me a chance, Kristina. You're beautiful. You're everything I want." I don't know where it came from. It's not what I planned to say. I should release her and put her down, but I kiss her sweet lips and pull her head to rest on my chest.

She pulls away from me and gets to the ground. Glaring at me, she stretches up on her tiptoes and gives me a quick kiss on the lips. Then as she runs off to the control booth, "You're hot, but you're still a jerk and a ball player."

I turn away smiling uncontrollably and get ready for the game.

Kristina

His hands are warm and protective. His lips tell me his story and make me want more. His body against mine is solid and gives me his heart. His words and breath at my ear promise me the world—but I can't believe him. I want to. I want to go to him and be with him. It's not an option. My world revolves around me, not a baseball player who will ditch me as soon as he gets what he wants. Maybe I want the same thing. It doesn't matter. I can't have it.

Yet, I allow myself the indulgence of kissing him and I allow him to distract me when I need to get to work. He's bad for me and the first thing I do when I sit down in the PA Announcer's chair is put on the cap he sent me backwards and kiss the plush seal on the nose. I look out over the field as I put my headphones on and he's looking up at me, grinning from ear to ear and blowing me a kiss.

The field clears while I run through the scheduled announcements and lineups. Then as the National Anthem starts I notice a tweet.

From @RookCross - I hope you caught the kiss I blew to you.
From @RookCross - I know you always want a second kiss.
From @RookCross - Would you like me to come over after the game?
To @RookCross - I'm working here.
From @RookCross - You look hot wearing my cap.
From @RookCross - Have I told you how much I like hearing your voice during the game? Nobody announces my name the way you do.
To @RookCross - Can you leave me to work? Go win, jerk!

I turn my phone to silent and flip it over, so I'm not interrupted during the game. It doesn't help. All I can do is think about him. Do I want him to come over after the game? The crowd starts to yell and Cross is running for the wall. He jumps and reaches over the wall to snag it, getting the third out of the first inning and leaving two runners on base for the other team. I want to cheer for him and holler out his name, but I stop myself and have some decorum in the control booth. Bad enough they probably saw me making out with him on the field. I'm sucked into the game and Chase is leading off for the Seals. I hear "I Want to Hold Your Hand" play as he walks up to bat. I catch myself smiling and my voice sounds different when I announce his name. I hear Sherry cheering for him and wish I could. I watch each pitch get thrown, aware of the microphone in front of me and not wanting to make any noise.

First pitch: Low strike on the inside corner.

Second pitch: Swinging strike, low below the strike zone.

Third pitch: Ball inside.

Fourth pitch: He hits the ball foul.

Fifth pitch: Ball high and inside.

I watch his lean back like the 90 mile per hour fast ball didn't just miss his chest by an inch. I could see his jersey move from the force of the ball and I'm sitting up in the booth. Chase doesn't even step out of the batter's box, he simply waits for the next pitch. He has a calmness about him when he's at bat that I can't understand. How can you be calm when somebody is lobbing fastballs at you? The count is 2 and 2.

Sixth pitch: The ball is low on the outside corner and he smacks it, grounding it up the center. Base hit.

He's safe on first base, I don't have to worry about him getting hit by the ball anymore. I realize I haven't been breathing when I announce the next hitter, Jones Mason, and I sound like an out of breath frog. Chase has a large lead off first and he's leaning toward second when I see him communicating with Mason at bat. I hear Michelle chanting, "Mason, Mason, Mason, Mason." Mason turns his foot in the clay, digging in, and Chase takes off for second on the pitch. Mason chopper's the ball through the center of the diamond and over the second baseman's head. Mason's safe on first and Chase is running to third, diving in to reach the base before the throw from right center field. He's safe. He stands up and dusts off, shaking his pants to get the dirt out or rearrange his jockstrap. I've always wondered what they're actually doing and I've never asked. I assume they get dirt in their pants and that can't be comfortable. That could lead to dirty peen. Why am I thinking about his peen? Focus! I announce Kris Martin as he walks up to the plate and I hear "Lights Out" by Royal Blood rock the stadium. He's swinging the bat as he steps into the batter's box and the first pitch is wild, slamming against the wall behind home plate and caroming toward the dug out.

Chase steals home, scoring the first run of the game and gets high fives from his teammates as he walks through the dugout. He turns and looks up at me, grinning. I don't know why he's looking at me. I wish he wouldn't. I'm trying to work. I simply smile, annoyed, and he blows me another kiss. Damn it, if I don't want to catch it! My mind wanders. Maybe he's right. Maybe if I was with him, it would be better. He wouldn't be a distraction, he'd be my—my what? Boyfriend? Fuck buddy? Booty call? Baseball player. He's always going to be a baseball player and I'm not interested in baseball players! Unless, maybe I am. No. No, I'm not interested in baseball players. I wonder if he has a brother who does advertising or sales or something other than being a baseball player. That's stupid, he wouldn't be hot then. I might as well give in, so I can get to the part where he breaks my heart and I can move on.

I get my mind back on my job and hitting my marks for the announcements. I'm doing a great job until the end of the second inning when I announce Cross is at bat again. The pitcher, Rhett Clay, is on first and Lucky Lucine is on third, with two out. Chase is first pitch hunting and not his normal ground ball to get on base. I could hear it off the bat. It was clean with a ring to it and I watched it land in the visitors bullpen, easily 415 feet on his home run hit. I want to jump out of my chair and scream out his name, but I maintain myself. He looks up at me when he steps on home plate and gives me a thumbs up. I smile and give him a thumbs up back. I don't know why. I shouldn't be encouraging him like that.

The rest of the game goes quick. Easy plays and nobody getting on base. Chase came up to bat in the fifth inning, but struck out. When he was at bat in the eighth he walked, but nobody brought him home to score. Then in the top of the ninth inning when the Seals were ahead 5-4 with two outs and ready to win this game, the pinch hitter for the opposing team hits one far into the outfield. Chase runs for it and flies through the air, doing everything he can to reach that ball and keep it from touching the ground. He catches it in mid-air, bounces as he lands on the ground, and slides across the grass in the outfield holding the ball up in his glove like a snow cone. Game over. Seals win.

I watch as the team walks off the field and Hannah grabs Chase for her on-field interview. She puts her arm around him, bringing him in closer for the interview and batting her eyes at him. What the hell? She never does that! She's all business. "Chase, that was an amazing catch out there to end the game tonight. You must be superman, flying through the air like that to get the ball."

He chuckles, "I'm no superman, just an outfielder. That's my job and I never want to let my team down."

"Well, you didn't let your team down tonight. Not only did you make that spectacular catch to end the game, but you smacked a ball into the bullpen for a 3-run home run. Not to mention stealing home on that wild pitch early in the game. You brought in 4 of the 5 runs tonight. This game was truly all you!"

"Thanks, but this is a team sport. I rarely get the opportunity to push my teammates home being lead off, so it felt good to hit the homer. But, the guys had to get on base for me to bring them in. Honestly, the wild pitch was an error I took advantage of. Part of this game is knowing when to take advantage of errors."

"It's nice to be reminded of what you're capable of. Great job tonight. We'll be watching for more tomorrow."

"Thanks." He gave her a hug and she lingered, saying something in his ear before he walked off.

What the hell? Is Hannah hitting on him? And he

smiled. He liked it! Jerk! I gaze down onto the field and he's standing there looking up at me. I'm supposed to be announcing the final numbers for the game and I'm off my mark. Shit! I quickly get the announcements done and he's gone.

Chase

Mason gets my attention as I walk into the clubhouse, "Nice grab. What was that with Hannah?"

"She noticed Kristina had been watching me and thought it might be helpful if she saw that I was in demand."

I check my messages and there's no response from Kristina. It's a late night, so the team won't be coming over. But, I'm not ready to go home. I turn back to Mason, "What are you doing to tonight?"

"Hanging out and playing video games."

Fun, that'll do. "Are the guys going to your place or what? I want to go."

He smiles at me deviously, "They aren't coming over, but you're welcome to join us. Bring your headphones."

"What?"

"I have a date with Michelle. We're playing video games at her place. She has better gaming equipment."

"Did you just invite me over to Kristina's apartment?"

"Yup." He smiles, knowing exactly what he did.

"Dude, is that going to get you in trouble with Michelle? I don't want to cramp your style."

"Nope. We're still in the getting to know you phase. I'm taking it slow. She'll think it's funny that you're playing video games with us and that it drives Kristina crazy will be a bonus."

"Drives Kristina crazy?"

"Yea man, seriously. That girl wants you, she just won't admit it."

It's nice to know I'm not the only one who thinks so. "I'm in. Should I bring anything?"

"Pick up snacks and you'll be golden with Michelle."

"Done." I'm not sending her another message. I'll show up at her place and I won't be looking for her.

Kristina

I check my phone as I'm leaving the stadium, expecting my twitter to be blown up by Chase, but all I have is texts from Michelle.

> Text from GamerGirlM - This is me giving you notice that Mase will be over tonight.
> Text from GamerGirlM - We have a video game date.
> Text from GamerGirlM - No "romp" in the plan. Perv.
> Text from GamerGirlM - Hope that's acceptable, mother.

I shake my head at myself, unconcerned with Michelle's antics and wondering if he has already forgotten about me. Should I message him? He better not be off somewhere with Hannah! The way she was pulling him close and hugging him, that's not her style. I bet she was propositioning him on the field when she was whispering in his ear! What does she think she's doing? He's mine! Except for one minor thing. He's not mine. I keep telling him to go away. Mason and

Michelle both told me he wouldn't wait forever. I should message him. I don't want him with anyone else. I guess I can't have it both ways. No. I need to let him go. It's better this way. No distractions.

The only problem is that I want him and I don't want to let him go. Maybe I want more than I'm willing to admit even to myself.

Tears stream down my face on my drive home. I keep imagining him with Hannah or some other girl. Giving up on me and agreeing to spend time with another girl who's after him because all I did was push him away. I kept telling him no and wanting him to get me out of his system. He shouldn't be with them. He should be with me. He should be kissing me and wrapping his arms around me. He should be spending the night with me. He should be naked with me. I want him. Why does he have to be a player? There's no way.

I sit in my car until I can get myself together enough to hide my tear-stained face. Times like these I'm glad to find an old bottle of water in my car, so I can wash my face and freshen up without anyone knowing the truth. I'm a grown woman and I can control my emotions, I just can't figure out how to have the job I want and the man I want at the same time.

CHAPTER TWELVE

Chase

I walk up to Kristina's door with a pizza, a pack of energy drinks, and a bag of snacks. I knock on the door and Michelle answers, "Hey, Mase said you might come by. Come on in."

"Thanks." I hand her the pizza and snacks.

She turns to Mason, "I like this guy. He can stay."

"I hope I'm not interrupting anything between you and your boyfriend."

"Who said I have a boyfriend?"

"I shouldn't have to, but me," Mason affirms.

"Interesting." She turns back to me, "Are you here to play with us or are you looking for my roommate, because she's not home yet."

"I'm here for the video games, but if your roommate wants to take my attention I won't fight it." The grin on my face tells her everything she needs to know.

"Works for me."

I play video games with the couple and they're serious gamers. It's work to keep up with them.

Kristina walks through the door, talking to Michelle as she walks through the room to her bedroom and doesn't acknowledge my existence. Just as she's about to step into her room, "I brought pizza. It's in the kitchen if you want some."

She hears my voice and stops in her tracks, turning to look at me. "Why are you here?"

"It's nice to see you, too. I'm here to play video games."

Michelle adds in, "He's not very good at it, but what he lacks in skills he makes up for with enthusiasm. You want to join us? We could team up girls against the boys and beat them worse than they've ever been beat."

"Maybe. Can we play the old school Mortal Combat? I want to see how many times I can chop his head off."

"Sounds good, but I'm committed to Wii bowling sometime tonight. Mase thinks it's more of a date game or something," she says making air quotes.

Kristina disappears into her room and comes back in my favorite PJs with the sunglasses on them. She sits down on the floor between Michelle and I, and leans against me comfortably while we play round after round of Mortal Combat. Each round ending with her brutally chopping off my head and sending it rolling across the floor. Kristina is relaxed and happy. Giggling and actually touching me willingly without being mad at me. I put my arm around her to support her better while she sits leaning against me and she accepts it, snuggling into my body. I kiss her cheek and she turns to me smiling, responding with a peck on my lips before she goes back to chopping my head off and watching the blood splatter everywhere.

She puts her hand on my leg and leans in to kiss me, blinking with her big eyes as she presses her lips to mine sweetly and then pulls back away. We communicate silently and I take her in my arms, pulling her across my body and lean down to kiss her. She meets me halfway with her willing lips and wraps her arms around my neck. Where did this come from? This is what I want. I want her and I want her to want me. She tastes so sweet. I'm beginning to wonder if she really tastes like cookies and it's not lip balm. I press my lips to hers open-mouthed, repeatedly. Wanting more of her and trying not to push or be inappropriate in front of her roommate and Mason. She nibbles on my lower lip and sucks on it, releasing a quiet whimper. She pushes me with her fingers exploring my back and shoulders, and her tongue sliding into my mouth for more. She twirls her tongue around mine until I meet her need with mine and she sucks on my tongue. Oh, fuck. This chick. I hold her close to me, not wanting to let her go and she moves her hands to my hair, holding my lips to hers.

Mason comments, "Uh, we're going to change over to play bowling. Maybe you two want to take what you're doing into the other room?"

"We could do what they're doing instead of bowling. It looks like fun." Michelle suggests to him.

Mason continues, "Please go in the other room."

I pull back and search her eyes for direction, she giggles and leans her head on my chest. "My bedroom?"

I stand up with her in my arms and carry her with me to her bedroom. It's not the first time I've been here and I hope it's not the last. I sit on the small loveseat she has in the corner, not wanting to push this faster. I want her, but I'm not ready to go there yet. I need her to know I want her enough. I want to spend the night with her and I need her to know it's for her. I want to hold her and kiss her. I want to feel her against me. Mostly, I just want to be with her. This is new territory for me. It's not hit it and quit it.

I wait to see what she does next and she climbs off my lap to close her bedroom door. She folds the bedding back on her bed and climbs in, holding it open for me, "Do you want to join me?"

I'm not telling her no this time. I smile at her and pull my shirt off. I can't sleep in my jeans. I fight with myself about the level of will power I have and if I can stay with her in my boxer briefs without getting in her. I don't know what will happen tomorrow or where this change in what she wants came from, but I'm not taking a chance on losing it. I can do this, I sit on the edge of her bed and take my jeans off. She reaches for me, touching my bare skin. "Don't get the wrong idea. I'm not pushing you. There's no getting you out of my system." I climb in bed with her and pull her to me. She moves to climb on top of me and I should stop her, but I don't. I run my hands up and down the length of her arms and pull her mouth down to mine. I want to kiss her. I take her hand in mine and lock our fingers, while our mouths meet. There's nothing like her sweet soft lips. I roll her off of me and pull her back against me, so I can wrap my arms around her and hold her against my body. As I pull her back to me, she's silky and smooth and sexy. A little curvy with her ass pushed into my dick. "Sorry, it's not intentional. I can't control how much he wants you." I change to a whisper and my voice gets raspy, "I want you, too. I want to hold you next to me and protect you, so you'll know you're mine. I can do that. I want to do that. It's more important to me than anything else because I want you enough."

She's silent, but I know she's awake. I hold her and kiss

the back of her neck. I explore her curves tenderly, my hands lightly gliding along the surface of her skin. "Goodnight, Sweetness." Falling asleep, happily holding her in my arms.

Kristina

His arms around me, holding me. His warm breath at my ear, traveling down my neck. His fresh manly scent. I'm not ready to sleep. I roll toward him, my body pushed to his, front to front. I run my fingers through his hair at his temple and down around his ear, he releases a soft groan. I do it again and pull my fingers all the way through, exploring the muscles in his neck and shoulders. His hands on me flex and his fingers spread. I place my hands on his face and pull his mouth to mine, kissing him sweetly. I draw a line of kisses down his neck and he gets hard against me. I move against him.

I want him, but it can only be sex. I don't know what I'm doing. Ball players are bad for me. Why am I so attracted to him? Why does it feel so good to have his arms around me? Why did I kiss him and bring him to my bedroom? He's not an option. I can't be with him. Can I?

I kiss my way back to his mouth and stop myself. I push against his hard length and his hands move to my hips, stopping my movement. I kiss him again, playfully I lick his lips and touch my tongue to his. I pull back, sucking on his lower lip. I want more. I roll my hips against him again and his hold on my hips tightens. I press my lips to his and he responds, taking control of the kiss and pushing his tongue into my mouth with need. His kiss is claiming and I feel it travel my body, flooding me with warmth. I meet his urgency, stroking and sucking on his tongue. Suddenly, he stops. He pulls back and gazes into my eyes, his more grey than hazel as they shine back at me. He wraps his arms around me tight with his cheek to my forehead and I can feel him relax. His whole body at ease with me in his arms. His strong heartbeat fading to rest and taking me with it.

CHAPTER THIRTEEN

Kristina

I wake up early the next morning in bed alone. I knew it. Stupid ball players! There's no way he stayed all night with me. I roll over and hide the tears that are forming on my pillow, I can't believe I thought he might really want me enough. A minute later there's a body in bed next to me and arms wrapped around me.

I smile internally and roll over, so I can use him as my pillow. My hands exploring his bare chest and abs while he cradles me in the crook of his arm. I gaze into his eyes, leaning forward to kiss his cheek before I burrow into his embrace. I fall back to sleep, not wanting it to end.

We're both startled by someone knocking on my bedroom door and I call out, "Yea? What?"

Mason talks through the door, "Uhhh, is Cross in there?"

"Yes. I'm sleeping," he responds on a grumble and pulls me closer to him.

"About that, we have to be at the stadium in less than an hour and I don't have my truck with me."

"Dude, we have time. Report time is three hours from now," Chase corrects him.

"I have to be there early. So, let's go," there's a nervous tone to Jones' voice. Makes me wonder if he's lying.

"I'm not ready to leave. Get an Uber." Chase focuses on me, tracing my lips with his finger.

His soft, warm touch melting me. I sigh unintentionally.

His eyes light up and he grins as he presses his lips to mine. "How do you taste so sweet?" He says softly and continues to kiss me. He swipes his tongue across my lower lip, then tugs on it and my belly flutters.

"Cross, come on! You owe me one," his tone is almost desperate.

Chase takes a deep breath, "Fine. Grab my keys and I'll meet you at my truck in a few minutes. I'll drop you off on my way home."

"Thanks, man." I hear Jones walking around and keys clanking as the door to my apartment closes.

"I wonder what that's about."

"I don't care what he's got going on. I've got you," Chase kisses me sweetly and brushes my hair out of my face.

I hear myself giggle like a schoolgirl, and it's new to me.

"I like that sound. Mason can wait," he trails off as he claims my lips gently with his.

Oh yes, Mason can wait. Chase can kiss me like this all day and anywhere he wants.

Chase

I finally have Kristina in my arms and wanting me. Fucking, Mason! He's full of shit. He doesn't have to be at the stadium early. He can wait in my truck until I'm ready. Her sweet laugh has me hard again and I already jerked off earlier when I woke up painfully in need. I need to have control. I don't want her thinking this is about getting laid. But, her skin is so smooth and she smells sweet, exactly like how she tastes. The way she's responding, she's giving herself to me. I can do this, I mean not do her. My will power won't let me down. It's okay, hold her and make-out with her. This chick, she fits in my arms perfectly like it's where she belongs. I want more of her. I'm in my head while I'm kissing her and my hands are on their own mission exploring her body. I catch myself with the tips of my fingers slid between her and the elastic waistband of her shorts, and my other hand up her shirt on her bare back. She wants more and I know my limit, any more and I won't be able to stop. I pull my hands back quickly and wrap my arms around her, not giving up her lips.

She whimpers a complaint at me and pulls away, staring into my eyes, "What happened? You don't want to touch me?"

"I'm sorry, I lost control. I want to touch you and so much more."

"What if I want you to lose control?"

I chuckle nervously, "I'm not ready."

"How many girls have you been with! You're not ready?"

"None of them mattered. None of them were you." What am I saying? She's a runner! I'll scare her away.

She looks at me funny, cocking her head to the side like she does when she's thinking, "Okay. I like how you were touching me. You made me relax last night and I never really sleep. Thank you."

I hold her tight against me and she snuggles into my chest, taking my hands and moving them where she wants them. One up her tank top on her bare back and the other at her waist. I move my hand slowly across her back, appreciating her, and I feel her breath hitch at my touch. "You're beautiful."

She gazes into my eyes and smiles. I'm drawn to kiss her. I can't help myself. I'm like a moth to a flame when it comes to seeing her happy, her gorgeous smile. I stop before I kiss her and move my hands to her head, threading my fingers into her hair and holding her where I want her. I kiss the tip of her nose and she giggles. I kiss each of her eyelids. I kiss her temple and drag a line of kisses to her jawline, appreciating every piece of her and tipping her head back ready to taste her neck. It's not time for that yet, so I press my lips to hers. Sucking and nibbling on her sweet lips, our tongues tied together in a seductive dance that's testing the limits on my will power. It's obvious she wants this to go further and she wants it now. I want it now, too.

Michelle's bedroom door slams and she shouts, "He really left!" Followed by an impressive string of creative cuss words, "Son of a mother humping burnt hairy twat waffle! Damn it!" Doors continue to get slammed in the kitchen and she's stomping around loud on purpose. I look to Kristina, "I'm guessing I should go now."

She nods in agreement, "Roommates can suck. But, I need to check on her." She stops and then starts again, gazing at me, "I don't want you to go. We both need to get to work anyway. I'll see you later."

My cheeks warm and I grab her, kissing her silly. I pull my jeans and shirt on, and she follows me to the door,

"Thanks for coming over. I had a good time." I grab her again and lift her off the ground to plant a kiss on her. I need her to keep thinking about me.

"You're still here? Gah!" Michelle walks into the room.

"I'm leaving, and good morning to you, too." I turn to my girl and give her a quick peck on the cheek, "See you later, Sweetness."

I didn't get laid and that's a good thing, though I don't think I've ever imagined myself saying those words together. I have more energy than usual as I run down the stairs to my truck and find Mason sleeping.

From @Kristeeeeena - I want another kiss, but don't come back up. Bad idea right now.

From @Kristeeeeena - Just want you to know I still want another kiss ;)

To @Kristeeeeena - Good

To @Kristeeeeena - I'll have some ready for you when I see you.

Kristina

"Why are you smiling like a fool?" Michelle walks into the room irritated, as I'm messaging Chase.

"I'm not." She glares at me. "Whatever, you've been with Mason every second since you met him."

"So, what's the deal? I thought there was a boycott on baseball players."

Huh, "The deal is that I was enjoying myself, but you and your boy kept blowing the mood with your interruptions and slamming doors. I'm allowed to enjoy myself, right? Boys are allowed in my room, mother?" My words spitting from my mouth before I filter them and not what I intended. "Besides, I think the issue we should be discussing is you? What's got you in a tizzy?" I'm not discussing Chase. "I'm waiting." I stare at her tapping my foot with my arms crossed. "Is he a bad kisser or something? Tiny peen?" In my head, refuses to give it up and get laid? "Spill it! What's the deal?"

"I don't know if he's a bad kisser. His peen is fine. His arms are strong and muscular, awesome wrapped around me."

"I know you've kissed other guys. He's just okay or what?"

Michelle hems and haws around, not wanting to answer my question. "He hasn't kissed me, other than a kiss on the cheek and forehead."

"What? Yet, you know his peen is fine."

"Oh yeah! I felt it against me when he was holding me. I give it an A+ and I haven't seen or touched it."

"You could kiss him."

"Nope. I leaned in to kiss him, made sure he knew I wanted him to kiss me. He hugged me so I couldn't kiss him and did his whisper thing."

"Whisper thing?"

"It doesn't matter. I think it's his own version of mind control. He uses his words. It's so sexy when a guy uses his words." Michelle turns visibly red and I feel like I should spray her down with a hose or something. Well, Mason should use his hose. "I need a distraction. Tell me about Cross."

"He likes me. He's hot. He's a great kisser."

"And?"

"And, what?"

"The sex."

"We didn't do that, but I think I could've got some if my roommate wasn't being obnoxious."

"He stayed all night."

"Yes."

"He slept in your bed with you? He kept his clothes on?"

"Yes and no, he slept in his underwear and they never came off."

"You turned him down because he's a player?"

"No. He didn't even attempt. He kissed me and held me all night. I wanted him to do more."

"This is crazy. Cross stopped at first base and I can't get Mason out of the batter's box! Aren't big league baseball players supposed to be *players?*"

The irony isn't lost on me. But, privately in my head I keep hearing him tell me, "I'm not ready. None of them mattered. None of them were you." There's no way I'm special to him. Is there?

Chase

I knock on my truck window loudly, waking Mason. He unlocks the door and I yell at him as I open it, "Dude! What the fuck? Are you trying to cock block me? Your girl put you up to that shit?"

Mason sits up and swings his head to the right, then the left, popping his neck. He lowers the passenger window and stretches out with his elbow hanging out the window in his now reclined seat. He's trying to ignore me and reaches to change the station on my radio, but I smack his hand away and point to the decal on my dash that says, "Driver picks the music, shotgun shuts his cakehole."

"What happened in the girls' apartment?" I ask.

"You won't understand. I had to get out of there."

"Why? I thought you dig Michelle. She seems like a cool chick."

"I think Michelle's great. I want to spend time with her and get to know her. I don't want to be led by my dick."

"Okay, what's the problem?"

"It's your fault. She's been fine with me being sweet to her, holding her hand, whispering in her ear, spending time with her. Then you go having a make-out session in front of us and carry Kristina off to her bedroom, shutting the door behind you."

"We were kissing."

"Kissing leads to other stuff."

"You haven't kissed her yet?"

He turns away and doesn't even look at me.

"Dude, you need to kiss her. You need to find out what it feels like to kiss her."

"No, I don't. It won't change how I feel about her. She's perfect for me in every way."

I lean over my steering wheel and turn toward him, "You spent the night with her on my couch and never kissed her?"

"Oh, I've kissed her, but only a peck here and there." Mason continues talking to the window, "I can't be one of those guys that fucks everything with two legs, that's not me. No offense."

"None taken, and for the record I only fucked the ones that were looking to fuck. I don't lead chicks on and I don't break hearts."

"Good to know. Michelle has been worried about that."

"I don't understand how it's okay to spend the night in her bed, but not kiss her."

"I slept on the couch. I know we were on your couch

together. I couldn't help myself. You weren't there to see it. I was grinning at her and we were making eye contact, she giggled and kept sitting next to me while we were playing games. She even brushed against me when we were goofing around. She had slipped her shoes off and was sitting cross-legged, and it was her turn to play. Man, she was beating me at my game and I was loving it. I reached over and broke her concentration, tickling the bottom of her foot. She squealed and hopped up real quick, dancing around like she thought a bug was crawling on her. I was interested before, but something about her reaction sealed the deal for me. It also got the attention of Stray, who suddenly had a Southern accent and was calling her darlin'. Cain stood up and took her hand, asking her if she was okay and offering to get her anything she wanted. And, Clay flashed his toothy smile at her and offered to let her sit in his lap, so he could defend her from creepy crawlies. Corey just sat there laughing at the whole thing and I had to do something. I grabbed her and took her down on the couch with me, kicked Stray off the couch and started whispering in her ear. I think she liked it because she rolled toward me in my arms and burrowed into my chest. It felt right, but I shouldn't have done that."

"Get over yourself and kiss her already."

"She wants me to. I want to date her and I've never been good at knowing when to stop. I'm kind of an all or nothing guy."

"You can kiss her and hold her without fucking her. That's what I did last night."

"It'll be better if I wait."

"Dude, she's going to think she's friend zoned."

"She wanted to make-out like you were doing last night, and got mad when I wouldn't. So far, my whisper has kept her attention."

"What kind of magic are you saying to her?"

"I tell her nice things. Nothing magic, just the truth."

"She was pissed that you were gone this morning. Interrupted me for the second time this morning. Cock blocker number two." The thought strikes me and I'm thankful for the interruption, my will power was losing this morning.

"Michelle will be fine," Mason nods his head and grins with confidence.

Since I'm already at the stadium dropping off Mason, I decide to stay and get a good workout in.

Kristina

As I wander into the stadium, all I can think about is last night. He actually stayed the whole night with me. He didn't expect anything. I don't think I've ever slept that well. His kiss, his hands, his body, he makes me want more. I pushed against his hard cock and he stopped me. He's not ready. It was the stupidest thing I've ever heard. He's basically been fucking every woman who wants him for years. But, he's not ready for me? I remember his words. "None of them mattered. None of them were you." My body tingled at his words. His honest and sincere tone leaving no room to doubt him. He wants me enough.

I want to find him and spend some quality time together in a private corner of the stadium. I know the stadium inside and out. There are plenty of places for some private time. I wouldn't get naked here, but I'm up for a serious make-out session. Maybe he could finally get to second base. I daydream about Chase holding me up against a wall in a dark room, covering me in warm open-mouthed kisses from my lips, down my neck. My legs wrapped around him and my heat rubbing against his hard length. His warm breath on my neck as he whispers in my ear, telling me what he wants to do to me and telling me how I make him lose control. Thanking me for giving us a chance because he knows we're right together.

Unfortunately, I'm the only intern that's not out sick today and I get to do everyone's job. It's going to be a long one. No time for fun. It's a challenge I'm up to and a reminder to stay focused on my goal.

CHAPTER FOURTEEN

Chase

It's almost game time. I haven't seen Kristina at the stadium yet today and there's a dude announcing.

To @Kristeeeeena - I had a great time with you last night. Can I see you tonight?

To @Kristeeeeena - I was hoping to hear you announcing today.

From @Kristeeeeena - Sorry. Crazy busy.

From @Kristeeeeena - Probably working late.

From @Kristeeeeena - See you soon! :) Go win!

I'll take it. At least she's not telling me to go away.

I walk up the steps from the clubhouse to the dug out and Mason grabs me to warm-up. I survey the scene as we walk out to the field. Seno warming up our pitcher. Sherry getting settled behind home plate. Mason starts in, "I got Michelle a ticket and she didn't come to the game."

"Dude, she has a life and it's not going to stop because she met you. She was pissed at you this morning."

"She'll be fine." He turns away from me and runs to the field doing sprints. He doesn't have my speed and I run after him, challenging him to keep up. He meets me back at the foul line and our teammates egg us on to race, Cain and Brandt joining the contest.

My speed is what I'm known for. I beat them all easily and hear yelling from the stands, "Woooowooo! Go Cross!"

I turn to find Kristina standing at the first base wall, clapping with a huge smile on her face. It's much better than yelling at me and cussing me out. She tilts her head to the side and waves me over. I can't control my smile, "Hey, Sweetness."

She goes up on her tiptoes and whispers in my ear, "I only have a quick break, but I chose to spend it on you." She kisses my cheek and turns around to run back to work, "I'll be too late for anything tonight. Go win!" And she's gone out of sight, but it makes me happy. She came looking for me and didn't have to be pissed to do it.

Chase

It's the fourth inning and I'm sitting in the dugout, Seno pulls my cap off and gets in my face, "Are you in there?"

"Dude. What?"

"You tell me. What're you doing because it's not playing baseball."

I have no clue what he's talking about and don't respond.

"You've missed two opportunities to steal. You were in the wrong place to catch a pop fly. You could've had a double and stopped on first. Where's your brain?" He shakes his head, "Did you fuck that chick yet?"

"No. I spent the night at her place last night. Nothing kinky, she wanted it though."

"Stop thinking about your dick and play the game."

Mason chuckles and Seno turns to him, "You, too. What's with missing that ball up the middle? You could've out run that throw to first." Seno shakes his head, "Grow up and play. We are winning this season. Rookies." He walks away leaving me and Mason nodding at each other.

Top of the 5th inning, we are down by two. Running out onto the field and Seno yells at us, "Focus!"

Kranston is on fire with 7 strike outs and he deserves better support. I smack Mason on my way by him, "Let's do this!" I focus on the game. We want to win.

Kranston strikes out the first two at bat. The third hitter pops it up short to Left Center Field. I run for it and Mason is backing up to get it. I call him off and make the catch. I throw the ball into the stands on my way to the dug out and get a high-five from Mason. I hear Seno yell, "That's it, more of that."

Bottom of the 5th inning, Kranston is leading off and gets a base hit. Mason and I keep each other focused as he steps into the on deck circle and I walk toward the batter's box to "I Want to Hold Your Hand." I can't help but think of her and then I hear the cheers. It's not just Sherry and the stadium crowd. I turn to look and Kristina's there with Sherry, cheering at the top of her lungs, "Let's go, Chase! Woooooowooo!" It means everything to me. She's here for me. I love it when Sherry cheers for me, but now I get it. Nothing's the same as your girl there supporting you and wearing your number. I blow her a kiss and her bright smile empowers me. "Knock it, Chase!"

I need to get on base and I know better than to crush it trying for a homer. The first pitch is the one I always watch for, my favorite location and I smack it clean and hard. My bat stays intact and I swing through. It feels good and before I can look up to see it sail twenty feet over the Center Field wall, the stadium is going crazy. I run the bases, pushing Kranston around to home and all I can hear is Kristina, "Woooowooo! Yeah, baby!" I step on home plate and point at her mouthing "all you" to her. Game is tied at two.

Mason gets a single. Martin hits into a fielder's choice, safe on first and Mason's out at second. Martin steals second and Seno hits a double driving him in. Cain walks. Lucky hits into a double play and the score is 3-2 Seals as we go to the 6th inning.

In the seventh inning I hit a double and Martin knocks me in. Our pitching held the opposing team to two and the final score was 5-2 Seals.

I went to the net behind home plate after the game looking for Kristina, but she was gone. Sherry grins at me knowingly, "She could only stay for her lunch break." I'll take it.

Kristina

My job as the intern, gofer, do everything that nobody wants to do and cover everyone that's out sick has been everything I hoped. Until the bottom of the eighth inning when, Hannah, the scheduled on-field reporter blew chunks all over the press box. I know how to do the task, it's just—well, it involves a camera and I don't like to be on camera. I prefer to be behind a microphone somewhere nobody can see me. My specialty is radio broadcasting and announcing. I'm not an on-camera personality. They didn't give me a choice and I need to do whatever I can to make this a permanent gig. I'm not dressed for this and I have hat hair from wearing my Seals cap with Chase's number on it. Apparently, I'm the same size as Hannah and somehow she managed not to get puke on her wardrobe for today. I change into the short, curve hugging, hot pink dress and look at the shoes I'm supposed to wear with it. Luckily, we don't wear the same size shoes and they allow me to wear the 3" espadrilles I'd left in my car when I opted for flip flops. I'd kill myself in those 4" spiked platform heels on the field. I'm bombarded by the hair and make-up people, they need to learn the term "personal space" and get out of mine. I understand that they have to be close to apply make up and fix my hair, but I didn't give anyone permission to adjust my breasts—which is apparently a thing and I was wearing the wrong bra, so now I've been taped up into place and I'm popping out the top of the dress. At least I know I can get Chase to do an interview with me and he'll make someone else interview with me, too. Fuck! Chase is going to see me like this. This isn't me. I look in the mirror and they've magically made me camera-ready without hat hair. In fact, I look fabulous. Not my style at all and completely uncomfortable in the dress, but fabulous nonetheless. I bet he doesn't even recognize me.

To @GamerGirlM - They're making me go on camera.

To @GamerGirlM - Don't tell anybody.

To @GamerGirlM - Maybe they won't recognize me.

To @GamerGirlM - Yes, it's that bad.

From @GamerGirlM - Don't worry. You got this.

From @GamerGirlM - It's not what you want, but you've been trained for it!

From @GamerGirlM - What position?

To @GamerGirlM - On-Field Reporter

From @GamerGirlM - Oh Shit! With our guys?

From @GamerGirlM - Forget that.

From @GamerGirlM - Show them you're better than Hannah.

To @GamerGirlM - I don't want this job!

From @GamerGirlM - Just do it! Try it! You might like it!

To @GamerGirlM - I'm wearing hot pink and its short and snug.

From @GamerGirlM - LOL If you're good, they'll get you appropriate wardrobe.

She's got to be kidding me with this. She's never steered me wrong when it came to the professional or education world before. I don't have time to question it. Michelle said it, "Just do it!" They shove the earplug in my ear and the booth starts talking to me. It's already the top of the 9th and it doesn't look like there will be a bottom of the 9th. Unless something crazy happens, they want me to interview Cross and Kranston or Martin. Seno as a final option. They've got the stats for the game ready and will feed me the details I need for each interview.

I walk out to the field and watch the last out of the game, a pop fly caught by Chase at the wall in Center Field. The crew leads me to the area in front of the dug out and I'm supposed to grab the players as they come in from the field. I focus on Chase and watch as he runs in and goes straight to the net behind home plate. What's he doing? I need him over here. I stand watching for him to walk toward me. Honestly, I want to see the expression on his face when he realizes it's me. Kranston is already gone to the club house. I grab Martin, "Can we do a quick interview?"

He looks me up and down, "What's your name, sweetheart?"

"My name is Kristina. I'm covering for Hannah. I seem to be covering for everyone this season."

"No problem."

"Thanks. Let's get it done. I need to get Cross before he goes in the locker room, too."

"Wait, you're the chick Chase has been talking about. I saw you kiss him at the wall."

"Yes, well, either way I need to do the interview. He doesn't know I'm doing the on-field interviews tonight. I didn't know until thirty minutes ago."

Martin laughs, "This is going to be fun. Let's do it."

I lead Kris Martin to the camera and I'm getting nothing from the control booth. I know my baseball. I can wing it. "Kris, you did some great hitting tonight and that golden glove of yours was flashing at first base. What do you do to maintain your superior skills on the diamond?"

Kris blushes, "Thanks, Kristina. I try to stay focused on the game and sacrifice most of my personal life during the season. I know I'll only get to play for a short time and I want to be the best I can be for as long as possible."

"It's been noted that you're hitting and fielding better this year than you have in years past. The sports writers have even written articles about how it's your year. Are you doing something different to achieve the higher stats across the board?"

He grins and I know he's not going to give me the real answer, "I've felt my strength and confidence grow consistently over the last few years. I think I'm finally hitting my stride and I'm not stopping here. Having said that, this team makes all the difference. Without a leader like Seno, we wouldn't be where we are now as a team and this season we are a family."

"Thank you so much for your time. Good luck on the road trip!"

Kris smiles and shakes his head as he walks off. Then he looks up at Cross, "Cross, on field reporter wants you." He chuckles, "And she's hot." He walks down the steps into the dug out and stands there watching.

Chase looks at me and does a double-take as his face lights up. He walks toward me quickly. "Hey, Sweetness." His eyes land on my breasts and he stops talking.

"Hey. Ummm, sorry to spring this on you like this. I didn't know I was doing this until last inning. This isn't even my dress." I lean closer to him, "I'd never wear this dress."

"You're gorgeous in it, but it's not you." He leans in and whispers in my ear, "You're beautiful no matter what. I especially like it when you're wearing my number or those PJs with the sunglasses on them."

I know I'm turning red. I'm not supposed to be interviewing players, especially not players that know what I look like in my PJs! "I need to get through this interview with you, okay?"

"Anything for you, Sweetness."

"I'm going to need you not to call me Sweetness during the interview."

"I can do that."

The cameraman nods and we're ready to go, "Chase Cross, you had some great plays today. But, it seemed to start out slow for you. What do you contribute the significant change to the second half of your game to today?"

He gazes directly into my eyes and I know it has something to do with me, "I feed off the crowd and they were cheering louder during the second half of the game. Also, our team captain gave the rookies a pep talk and that made a huge difference."

"You hit a home run that flew at least twenty feet over the Center Field wall. That's not something we normally see from you. Have you been concentrating on your hitting?"

"My job in the leadoff spot is to get on base, not get out hitting a pop fly that comes up short. I have the speed, so I usually keep the ball on the ground. Sometimes, like today, I get a pitch I can't pass up. Baseball is a team sport, you have to work together to generate runs."

"Good job today. Thank you for taking the time to do this interview." The camera is finally off.

Chase pulls me to him, "That home run was all you. You make me stronger and I want to impress you. The first half of the game I was somewhere with you, not on the field. And, that dress? It makes me want to take you out of it. I know it's late, come to my house tonight?"

"I can't. I'll be here at least another three hours. Too many people out ill today."

He whispers in my ear, "You wanted me this morning. I wanted you. I still want you. I'm not after sex, I just want you with me. It felt right to hold you all night. I want to hold you every night."

I smile at him unable to put the words I want together.

"You did a great job with the interview. Can you do one thing for me?"

"What?"

"Change out of that dress before I have competition." He starts off into the clubhouse.

"Yeah, I can do that. Chase?"

He turns back, "Yeah?"

"Nobody can compete with you."

He gets a big grin and blows me a kiss before he disappears into the club house.

I made it through the interviews, now to get the rest of my work done.

From @GamerGirlM - Great job!

From @GamerGirlM - I saved the interviews, so you have them for your portfolio.

From @GamerGirlM - Also, I'd like to dissect the interaction between you and Chase.

To @GamerGirlM - Thank you.

To @GamerGirlM - It wasn't as bad as I thought it'd be.

To @GamerGirlM - Let's not and say we did.

To @GamerGirlM - Late night. See you around 2am or later.

From @GamerGirlM - Are you going to Chase's?

To @GamerGirlM - I'm working.

To @GamerGirlM - Will Mason be there when I get home?

From @GamerGirlM - No. I put him on a time out. He doesn't know.

To @GamerGirlM - Why? Still mad he left?

From @GamerGirlM - I need time to decide if I want a boyfriend or not.

From @GamerGirlM - He said he's my boyfriend, but he never asked me if I wanted that and he still hasn't kissed me.

To @GamerGirlM - Makes sense. Why commit to the guy that won't even kiss you?

From @GamerGirlM - That is the question I'm trying to answer.

From @GamerGirlM - You should know I think Chase is a keeper.

From @GamerGirlM - Bye!

CHAPTER FIFTEEN

Chase

> To @Kristeeeeena - You can come over any time.
>
> To @Kristeeeeena - Doesn't matter how late it is.
>
> From @Kristeeeeena - It's 2am and I'm still at the stadium working.
>
> To @ Kristeeeeena - Can I help?
>
> From @Kristeeeeena - No. I just need to get done.

I want her here with me. I want to hold her. I want to kiss her. It's late and the team leaves early in the morning. I need sleep.

Chase

My alarm goes off early and I wish she were here with me. I don't have much extra time this morning. The team is leaving early and flying out to play three games against Washington.

> To @Kristeeeeena - Good morning, Sweetness.
>
> To @Kristeeeeena - I'm at the stadium. Are you here?

Nothing. I wander around a bit and check with Carter. She's not here. She's off today.

> To @Kristeeeeena - Wish you were here. See you in a few days.

Chase

I take my phone out of airplane mode when we land inWashington and it goes crazy.

From @Kristeeeeena - Wish I was there to see you this morning.
From @Kristeeeeena - Phone was dead at the end of my work day and I was tired.
From @Kristeeeeena - Happy to have a day off.
From @Kristeeeeena - Win for me!
To @Kristeeeeena - Wish I was there to spend the day with you.
To @Kristeeeeena - I'm saving up kisses for you.
From @Kristeeeeena - :) :) :)
To @Kristeeeeena - Will you go out with me when I get back?
To @Kristeeeeena - Can I have your phone number?
From @Kristeeeeena - I told you I don't give boys my number.
To @Kristeeeeena - I'm a man, not a boy.
From @Kristeeeeena - That is very true. I don't give men my number either.

Chase

The team has batting practice on the field and I find myself leaning on the backstop between Mason and Seno.

"You rooks got your shit together today?" Seno asks as he stares at Brandt taking swings.

"The chick won't give me her number and ignores me when I ask her out," I say trying to focus on the game.

"Michelle is 'busy' and her responses are all one or two words. She'll be fine," Mason adds his current standing.

Seno releases a sigh and scratches the back of his head. He looks at me, "You need to keep her thinking about you and don't message her too much. You don't want to look needy." He looks down and shakes his head, then turns to Mason, "What did you do to piss her off?"

I laugh, "I think it's what he didn't do."

"Shut up," Mason snarls at me.

"I don't know what the fuck you did or didn't do. I do know you pissed her off and I don't care if it's your fault or not. Send her flowers. You can make it right when you get home." Seno gives each of us a questioning look, "Anything else?" He waits, but neither of us respond. "Good. Remember, women like winners not losers. My queen likes to see her team win, let's show these women what we've got."

We each take our turn at bat. Seno's on point and he has been all season, he's on a mission. I hit a couple grounders because I know that's what I'm supposed to do and then I let it rip knocking a few in a row out of the park. It feels good to smash the ball, freeing. Mason swings and misses the first two pitches, then hits a couple to the outfield and a grounder. He needs to get his head straight

"Dude, call her and use your magic whisper."

Mason blushes, "Naw, she'll be fine."

CHAPTER SIXTEEN

Kristina

"Are you watching the game today?" Michelle asks.

"I have the day off. No baseball."

"Really? We could watch the guys."

"I thought Mason's on a timeout?"

"He is, but that doesn't mean I have to be. I can watch him and he'll never know."

"Fine, I'm in."

We need a girls' night. It's almost game time. Michelle orders a pizza. I turn the television on and they're announcing the team.

"Look at all of them in the dug out, it's hottie heaven!" The camera pans, "Our guys are sitting together. Woah! Did you see Cross look into the camera and smile? He's so hot!" Michelle exclaims and I wonder if she's been drinking.

"You have your own player to drool over."

"Whatever. I don't know why you don't claim Chase and keep him."

I've been wondering the same thing myself. I know baseball players are bad for me, but when we were together he made me want him. "His eyes change color and give him away, gorgeous light green hazel to a shiny grey." I remember him in my bed, gazing at me with those eyes and holding me all night. "I don't know how Mason can spend so much time with you and stay the night holding you without kissing you."

"He only held me all night on Chase's couch."

"He stayed over night before last."

"On the couch."

"And the other night you two were in your room."

"He slept on the floor." The doorbell buzzes and Michelle gets up to get the pizza, "I don't get it. I don't know why he had to leave early." She opens the door to a large mixed bouquet of pink and yellow flowers.

"I'm looking for Michelle?"

"That's me."

"These are for you. Beautiful flowers for a beautiful girl. Have a good evening," and he walks off down the hallway. She turns around, her face glowing as she admires her flowers. She takes the card and walks toward me.

"Those are beautiful, who are they from?"

Michelle glares at me, then her expression changes and she opens the card quickly, "I think we know who they're from." She points at Mason on the TV and he hits a home run, bringing in Cross in the top of the first inning. I totally missed Chase getting on base.

"What's the card say?"

"The card says, 'Please be patient with me, JJ,' and it has a heart on it." She immediately picks up her phone and I know she's sending Mason a message.

I sit back and watch the game while my roommate is in La-La Land.

The doorbell buzzes again and Michelle gets up to get the pizza, she opens the door to another delivery guy, "I'm looking for Kristina?"

She calls out to me, "Um, it's for you."

I run over to the door, "I'm Kristina." He hands me a crystal vase filled with two-dozen long stemmed delicate pale pink roses. "Thank you." Warmth hits my cheeks and I realize I'm as bad as my roommate. I breathe in the fragrant scent of the roses and open the little card, it says "Sweetness: You are more beautiful than any flower. I'm thinking about you—Chase," and the card has a stuffed bear holding a heart on it.

To @RookCross - Thank you for the flowers.

To @RookCross - They are gorgeous (and better than Michelle's).

To @RookCross - Message me later :)

The pizza finally gets delivered and we sit happily watching our players on the field.

Chase

The game started out pretty well. I did my job and got on base. Mason hit a dinger and brought me home. Nobody has scored since. I'm standing in the outfield in the bottom of the eighth inning and the roof is open. It's a clear night and I look at the dark speckled sky wondering what she's doing. I hear the pop of a bat and a ball is heading my way. I run for it and make a diving grab. I wouldn't have needed to dive if I was paying attention. Focus, Chase. She'll be there after the game. Seno is up out of his crouch watching me, he shakes his head and gives me a thumbs up. He knows I'm distracted.

Bottom of the ninth, still 2-0 Seals. Seattle has runners at the corners with one out. They hit a sac fly that comes directly to me and the runner on third scores. I throw the ball to the infield quickly and catch the runner from first trying to advance. Mason gets the ball and tags him out as he slides into second base. Final score 2-1 Seals.

Chase

I'm finally checked into my room for the night and have time to relax. I haven't eaten and all I can think about is her. I check my phone and see that she messaged me when she got the flowers I sent. I have a reason to respond.

To @Kristeeeeena - Hey Sweetness.

From @Kristeeeeena - Hi :)

To @Kristeeeeena - Do you want to talk?

From @Kristeeeeena - I'm not giving you my number.

To @Kristeeeeena - I know. I meant chat.

From @Kristeeeeena - Oh. Sure.

From @Kristeeeeena - Nice win.

To @Kristeeeeena - Thanks. The game felt long.

To @Kristeeeeena - I've been thinking about you.

From @Kristeeeeena - What were you thinking?

To @Kristeeeeena - I like the way you sit with me playing Mortal Combat while you're chopping my head off.

To @Kristeeeeena - I like holding you all night.

To @Kristeeeeena - I like tasting your lips. You taste like cookies.

From @Kristeeeeena - *blush*

To @Kristeeeeena - Will you have kisses for me when I get back?

My phone rings and it's a blocked number, "Hello?"

I hear the sweetest voice ever, "I've got kisses waiting for you."

I want to melt, but it's interrupted by Michelle in the background, "Seriously?"

I hear a slight scuffle and Kristina tells her, "Go call your boyfriend, if you can call him that. Don't you have to get to first base before he can be your boyfriend? Goodnight!" A door slams and she's back to me, "Sorry, peanut gallery."

"No worries, so are we alone in your bedroom again?"

"Yea," she giggles. "I liked having you in my bed."

"Maybe we can do that again?"

"Maybe somewhere without my roommate, somewhere with no interruptions."

"You're always welcome at my place. I hoped you would show up at my place last night."

"One thing at a time."

I chuckle, "I'm pretty sure you wanted my thing when I stayed at your place. Seems like dating comes first in the timeline."

Her voice gets low, "I know better. You're a baseball player. You fuck. You don't date."

I can't deny my past, she was there, "You're right, that's what I did in the past. That's not me anymore. You make me want more."

"How long until you go back to fucking?"

"I'm not going back to that. I want one special chick." I take a deep breath and feel my words in my stomach, "I want you."

"You're crazy."

"Tell me what you want. Do you want me?" I immediately wish I didn't ask. I don't want the answer and I don't want to be pushing her.

"I want to kiss you again. I want to know why you're not ready with me."

"I don't know what I'm doing with you. I want to make sure I'm doing it right. The only chicks I've been with since high school wanted one thing and got it. None of them wanted me, they wanted a player."

"What if I want the one thing?"

I chuckle, "I know you want the one thing, but your kiss and touch tell me you want more. I have to want you enough."

Her tone changes and she starts talking faster, "I have work in the morning. Goodnight."

She hangs up before I can respond.

To @Kristeeeeena - Did I say something wrong?

To @Kristeeeeena - I'm sorry if I did. I have to learn how to do this.

To @Kristeeeeena - Can we message tomorrow?

From @Kristeeeeena - Yes

To @Kristeeeeena - I wish I could hold you and kiss you goodnight.

From @Kristeeeeena - That sounds nice. Goodnight :)

I didn't lose her completely. I'm surprised she called me.

CHAPTER SEVENTEEN

Kristina

I should've worked yesterday. It would've been easier than making up for it today. Nobody prepped today's broadcast and I have a list of things that I need to do before I do live stats research during tonight's game.

> From @RookCross - Good Morning, Sweetness :)
> To @RookCross - You got the morning part right.
> To @RookCross - Busy.
> From @RookCross - Remember you're beautiful. I'll be home tomorrow night.

Chase

It's raining today. The roof is closed. My girl is busy and I won't be distracted by the night sky. The rain seems to have set the tone, dreary, gray, and cold. I take advantage of the closed roof and run the warning track with Seno. It requires no talking, we just run. We don't stay at the same pace, he doesn't have my speed, and I need to open up the throttle. I run a couple laps with Seno to get warmed up and then I stretch out my pace, finally increasing my speed.

My brain closes down when I'm running, clears everything out. Today I'm daydreaming. I'm holding Kristina on the beach when a storm hits. Water falling like buckets dumping from the sky. We're instantly soaked and cold. Her long dark hair dripping. Raindrops on her face and hanging onto her eyelashes. Her warm eyes looking up at me, searching mine with no concern for the rain. My wet hair falls into my face and she reaches for it, grazing my face and softly tucking it behind my ear. I grab her wrist and kiss it tenderly. She goes up on her tiptoes to kiss me and wraps her arms around my neck, running her fingers through the ends of my wet hair. Her sweet full lips worshiping mine until she drags her teeth across my lower lip, tugging on it. I lift her to me and she wraps herself around me instinctually. Our clothes sticking together and wet hair in our eyes. Thunder crashes loudly and I can see flashes from the lightning through my closed eyelids. Her body shakes and I tell her it's only thunder, but she's shaking for me. She wants me. I slide her down my body and take her hand, quickly leading her across the beach to my bungalow. We step inside and I pull my wet shirt off, tossing it to the floor. I gaze into her eyes and feel how hooded mine are. I reach for the bottom hem of her shirt and pull it off over her head, dropping it to the floor. She's gorgeous standing in front of me, wearing only shorts and a bra. Fresh from the rain and cool to the touch. I pull her against me and press my lips to hers, my hands splayed across her back. She reaches around my waist and slides her hands into my shorts, gently squeezing my ass. I move my hands up her sides and cup her tits. She kisses me open-mouthed as she drags her hands up to my hair and holds my mouth to hers. I move my hands to her neck, holding her and kissing her. She unbuttons her shorts and drops them to the floor, puddling at her feet. She unties my shorts and slides her fingers between me and the waistband. I push them off and take her hand in mine, wrapping her fingers around my dick that's hard for her. Her breath catches audibly and I pick her up, feeling her skin against mine. I kiss her with need, lifting her higher so I can bite and suck at her collarbone. She releases a moan and I take her to my bed. I'm hot, and heavy with desire. Everything is hazy. I've wanted her, needed her for so long and I finally have her. I want to love her and make her cry out my name. The haze takes over and everything is just happening. We're one, and it's how it's meant to be.

"Cross! Time for BP." I'm startled and I still don't know what it's like to have her. I'm dripping sweat. I'm also hard, I'll have to handle that.

To @Kristeeeeena - Been thinking about you. Hope your day got better.

Chase

Nobody had said the word streak out loud, but when we saw the lineup for today we knew it was over. Stray catching instead of Seno. Mason is day to day, apparently he got cut on the cleats when he was tagging the player out at second at the end of the game yesterday. New guy George Hart is in the lineup covering shortstop for Mason. And, Mark Rock is covering me in Center Field with Bubbles in Right. We haven't won a game with Bubbles in the starting lineup all season. Seno told us that Skip was right, we all needed a day off and not to push. He'll put us in to play if he needs to. We're confident we'll be back to winning tomorrow.

Watching the game from the dug out is interesting. One, it reminds you what you're doing and refreshes your perspective. Two, veteran players do some crazy shit in the dug out. You'd think it would be the rookies, but it's not. The veterans have spent so many hours in the dug out that they have games to play. Everything from an old school hot foot to throwing seeds and shells at their teammates.

We lost 3-1.

I go out to eat with Mason and go back to my room. No messages from Kristina. I turn up the volume on my phone in case she calls and turn in early.

CHAPTER EIGHTEEN

Chase

> To @Kristeeeeena - Good Morning, Sweetness...early game today, see you tonight!

The lineup is back to normal and we're ready to play. They taped up Mason's hand, he's even good to go. The team is amped up, ready to go home and face Florida. We needed the day off. Time to beat Washington.

I get a four pitch leadoff walk to start the game and take my base. Mason hits a ground ruled double on the first pitch, he's becoming a double making machine. He could be a middle of the lineup hitter. Martin hits a double bringing us home, score 2-0 Seals and Washington has pitchers up warming in their bullpen. Seno works the pitch count up and draws a walk. Lucky Lucine is feisty today. He's communicating with Skip and the runners, and he's all smiles—a play is on. He's crowding the plate and almost dancing in the batter's box while he waits for the pitch. I look at Seno and Martin, both trying to keep their game face on. The pitcher buries a slider in the dirt and it gets away from the catcher, both runners advance on the passed ball and Lucky keeps dancing. Lucine gets hit by the pitch and the bases are loaded with Seals. Brandt comes up to bat and skies one to right field on the first pitch. His first grand slam in the Bigs. 6-0 Seals with no outs. Washington changes pitchers, and strikes out the next three Seals.

I'm leading off again in the second inning, which doesn't happen often, and work the pitch count full. I hit a grounder up the third base line and leg out the throw, safe at first. Mason pops up on the fourth pitch and I make it a sac fly, getting to second base safely. Martin strikes out on five pitches. Seno crushes a homer to the parking lot. Lucky choppers one up the center and gets tagged out at second. 8-0 Seals.

Washington responds in the bottom of the second by making me cover every inch of Center Field. Every hit is in my zone and I don't let the ball touch the ground. We get on base, but nobody scores in the third, fourth, and fifth innings. I'm jumping at the wall, sliding across the field and diving to get the outs. I make it a rule not to show injuries or pain. I don't want to be pulled from the game.

Skip makes me part of the double switch in the middle of the sixth inning and I make my case, "I've got Center covered. Leave me in. I'm a dog playing fetch today."

He looks me up and down, "You're scraped up, bloody, dirty, and have more holes in your uni than I've ever seen in all my years as coach here. See first aid and get cleaned up. You're done for the day."

"Yes, sir." I storm off to the club house and indulge myself with a long hot shower before the rest of the team gets there.

The medic is waiting for me when I come out of the shower, ready to disinfect and bandage up my battle damage. I played hard today and it feels good.

Kristina

I feed the lineup change to the broadcasters and ask for more info when I see the double switch taking Chase out of a game that he's been the star in. There's no details, just a double switch at this point.

To @RookCross - Pulled you out on a double-switch?

To @RookCross - Are you okay?

I go back and scan through highlights from the last few innings. He's made some unbelievable plays and has some serious hustle, but his uniform is getting more blood soaked as the game goes on.

To @RookCross - Chase?

Chase

I'm putting my phone in airplane mode when I see I've missed a call from a blocked number. There's no voicemail. I check my twitter and see the messages from Kristina with no time to respond.

To @Kristeeeeena - Planes taking off. I'm fine.

Kristina

Why isn't he responding? He was playing his position better than anyone else in the league. He must be hurt or they wouldn't have pulled him. I go back to the feed searching for details. Why haven't they said anything? How hard would it be to give a quick update? The game is finally over and I get a break from assisting the broadcasters. I resort to a bathroom stall and social media. I need to know what happened. He always tweets, nothing. Nothing anywhere. I can't do this. I go to my cubicle and replay the game on fast forward searching for something, anything that will tell me what happened. He's got holes in his uniform at the knees and along his thigh near his hip. His pants are bloodstained at the knees and he's bled enough for it to drip down his leg. His forearm is raw. No matter his condition or injury, his expression is determined.

I notice the team is on their way home and watch the coach's post-game presser hoping one of the reporters asked about Chase. Finally, something! Nothing about any injury, only praise for how hard he plays and a joke about the coach not liking the holes in his uniform, but he did give confirmation that we will be seeing Cross in the lineup for the next game.

My whole body relaxes and tears stream down my face uncontrollably. I can breathe again. I stop and gather myself. I can't be this person. Fucking baseball players! Why did he do this to me?

Chase

The plane lands and I turn off airplane mode to find my message to Kristina didn't go through. It sends and I message her again.

To @Kristeeeeena - Sent that message before we took off and it didn't go through.

To @Kristeeeeena - Just landed in San Diego.

To @Kristeeeeena - I'll be at the stadium soon. Are you there?

I'm suddenly excited, I know she's working today. I'll get to see her soon.

I drop my stuff off in my locker and wander around a bit, hoping to run into Kristina.

Carter pulls me into his office, "I saw you looking all lost puppy dog and checked to see where she is today. She went home early. She left an hour ago."

"I don't get this chick. Thanks."

To @Kristeeeeena - Are you okay?

To @Kristeeeeena - Did I do something wrong?

From @Kristeeeeena - Please leave me alone.

I hear Seno in my head, "Keep her thinking about you and don't message her too much." I go home and attempt to get my laundry done.

Text from Mason - Video games at your place?

Text to Mason - Sure. Bring pizza.

The pizza is gone and Mason's phone has been blowing up. I've only got two messages, and they're both unexpected.

Text from Chip - We miss you.

Text from Dale - Want to play?

Mason stretches and stands up, "Well, time for me to go. See you tomorrow."

"Dude, we're in the middle of a game."

"I'm tired," he fake yawns and laughs.

"Michelle?"

"Yeah."

"At least one of us can have some fun."

"Don't worry. I won't. Sticking to the good boy plan."

"Dude, you gotta do something. At least tell her what you're waiting for."

"I'm thinking about it. Maybe I can sleep in her bed, but on top of the blankets. Bye." He trots out the door to see his woman and all I've got is an invitation for sex with the twins. I never thought that would be a bad thing.

I'm going to bed before I make a bad choice.

To @Kristeeeeena - Goodnight

CHAPTER NINETEEN

Chase

I get to the stadium early, hoping to run into Kristina since she hasn't responded to my messages. I walk into Carter's office and he never even looks up, "She's PA Announcer again today. It's retro day and I already have a cap made for her."

"Perfect. Is there anything new and obnoxious in the team store to deliver with the cap?"

"Are you trying to piss her off?" He asks sarcastically.

"Yes."

"Whatever you want, man. How about a ragdoll Cross?"

"Are you fucking kidding me right now? They have those?"

"Oh yeah, they made ragdolls of you, Mason, and Martin."

"Take her that, too. The bigger the better." I grin, happy with myself and knowing I'll be kissing her at the first base wall before the game. "Thanks."

Chase

Michelle is back behind home plate with Sherry. It looks like Mason has hooked her up with retro gear. I wonder what he did to get back in good graces. No sign of Kristina. There's only a few minutes left before the announcements start. Where is she?

Kristina

What doesn't he understand? I told him to leave me alone. I've told him not to send things to the control booth, but he still does that too! I should throw the doll into the stands! Right out the control booth window! Or, maybe, hang it by a noose and let it dangle there for the whole game. Maybe that would get my point across. The ragdoll really does look like him, it even has muscles in the same places, the same hair. Damn it! I put the cap on backwards and get to announcing.

I see him look up to the booth and smile as I announce him and "I Want to Hold Your Hand" plays. He's irritating. I turn to the sound operator, "Would it be possible to change his walk-up for his next at bat?"

"Yes, but I need a written request."

I write a note and hand it to her, "Will that work?"

"No problem. This should be fun."

Chase is walking to first and I keep up with my announcing on queue. I hear Michelle yelling for Mason as he walks up to bat and decide, why not? I write a note requesting to change Mason's song, too. I know I shouldn't, but I'm done with the players. Mason hits a double and I try to focus on my task at hand.

Bottom of the third inning, I announce Cross and "I Don't Like You" by the Wrecks plays as his walk-up song. I watch as he stops halfway to the plate and swings his bat wildly. He hits a home run on the first pitch, knocking in today's starting pitcher, Corey Grace. I obviously don't affect his game.

Chase

Did she really change my walk-up song? She won't message me. She won't give me her phone number. She didn't find me at the wall and kiss me. "I Don't Like You," she's full of shit! I step on home plate and Mason shakes his head at me. She announces him and "Kiss Me" by Sixpence None the Richer plays.

He turns to me and mouths, "What the fuck?" I see him look at Michelle and she shrugs, but likes the idea. She makes kissy lips at him and laughs.

I yell into the clubhouse, "Carter!"

He pops his head into the dug out, "What do you need?"

"Change my walk-up song to," I stop and think for a minute and write it down. I hand him the note.

"No problem."

"Wait. Change Mason's, too. Make his," I add to the note.

"He's okay with that?"

"Um, yeah." What the fuck? Why not?

Carter nods and disappears.

Seno glares at me, "Are you causing trouble?"

"Just having some fun, I figure it can't hurt. It's making

her think about me." I'm surprised to hear the happy tone in my voice and realize it's because of her. I'm happy simply thinking about her or playing with her.

Seno shakes his head and I enjoy the game, waiting for the next move.

Kristina

Bottom of the 6th, I announce Chase again and his walk-up song changed to "My Favorite Liar" by The Wrecks. Are you kidding me! He doesn't believe me. Cocky bastard! Of course, all the women like him. He's not giving up on me and I'm trying to push him away. I almost miss my mark to announce Mason because I'm in my head. I look up and see that Chase got a double while I hear "The Last of the Real Ones" by Fall Out Boy play. I wonder which of them changed the song. I do like the sentiment, they are real. I immediately write a note and hand it to the sound operator.

She laughs, "You all are keeping me busy tonight."

Chase

Sitting with Mason in the dug out, "Did she change it again? How'd it get to Fall Out Boy?"

"I did it that time. Why not, right?"

"Good choice." He shakes his head in a way that tells me it's okay this time, but don't do it again. I'm cool with that.

It's a low scoring game and we aren't getting many at

bats. Mason and I will both get an at bat in the 9th if the other team scores, possibly the eighth if we score.

The score is 3-0 Seals in the bottom of the eighth and we're up at bat. I'm anxious to see if my walk-up song changes again. Swinging the bat in the on deck circle and she announces me, her voice sounding clear and almost chuckling. "Sunglasses at Night" blares through the sound system and I can't help but smile at the imagery it conjures in my head. All I can do is see her in those PJs. Fuck! I get hard walking to the plate. I bend over at the plate and rub dirt on my hands to buy me a minute and glance up at her, wondering if she knows what she's done. I do my best to concentrate on the ball, even asking for a time out and stepping out of the box to focus.

Seno yells from the dug out, "Get your head on straight!"

I see the ball in the pitcher's hand and try to slow everything down. It's straight up the pipe in the middle of the strike zone and doesn't look like it has any wiggle to it. Hoping for a walk, but I have to hit this. There's a crack off my bat and the ball is flying to Left Field. I drop my bat in pieces and run, hoping the ball won't get caught. The fielder couldn't get to it in time and on any other at bat I would've made this a double, tonight I'm happy to be safe at first and not sliding into the base.

Kristina announces Mason and "1950" by King Princess plays. She's on a roll! Mason looks irritated, but Michelle yells out that she loves that song and he's happy again. She'll get everything she wants from him. I can see it now. But, it's on his time schedule. I kind of respect that. I'd still be hitting it.

I hope for a walk or a home run, anything that keeps me from having to run fast. He choppers it up the diamond and I need full speed. Middle infielders miss the ball and the

Centerfielder is running in to back them up. I'm already on my way to third and need my speed. I don't want to slide. I have to slide. I make it to third base safely, even keeping all my good bits intact. Mason's safe at first. Martin hits a home run and I run across home straight to the dug out.

Seno's laughing at me, "Hard problem to have. I think she won that battle." She absolutely did, but I'll never admit it out loud.

Top of the ninth, Seals are ahead 6-1 and Skip pulls me for the double switch. Thank you for small favors because this hard-on won't go away. I head into the clubhouse, showering at attention and lean my forehead on my arm against the wall allowing the water to fall over me. I close my eyes and imagine us in the rain together naked, pushing into her heat with her lips at my neck. It's all it takes to relieve the pressure. I need this chick.

Kristina

Home games are better. I have access and verified he isn't hurt in seconds. Not that I care. Fuck. I care.

Chase

She still hasn't messaged me. I don't want to message her too much, but...

To @Kristeeeeena - I'm home for the night. You're always welcome to join me. Your terms.
From @Kristeeeeena - Okay
To @Kristeeeeena - Goodnight, Sweetness.

None of this changes the way I feel about her. I want her with me. I want her in my bed. I want my lips on hers. I know she wants me, too. I don't know why she keeps fighting it.

Kristina

I'm tossing and turning. In my bed. Alone. I don't have to be. I could be with Chase. I sleep when I'm with him. Maybe I should call him and have him over? I need sleep. Or, I could go to his place. He did invite me. He keeps inviting me. I love his arms around me. He gives me the protection I'm missing. It's more than comfort and feeling safe. It's not fair to use him like that. I can't keep him. I haven't cried and worried this much, well, ever. It's too much for me. I need to focus on my goal and get the gig I'm working for. No, there will be no baseball players for me.

What if I can have a baseball player? What if, hypothetically, I want one? What if I eliminate the whole ball player boycott? Is it a possibility? If not, I want a night with him. I want to know what it could've been like. If I regret it later, I want to know I did it and have the memory.

I pick up my phone, hoping there might be a new message from him. Of course there's not. It's 2am. I need to let it go.

CHAPTER TWENTY

Chase

Saturday's game was a total blow out. Seals lost 9-0. Skip instituted a new rule: No changing your walk-up song mid-game. I changed it to "Head Games" by Foreigner before the game started. I may not have won the game, but I made the final play.

Sunday's game is early and Monday is an off day. We all need it. We need a few off days, but that's not an option in the life of a professional baseball player. No BP and if we win, party at my place. I already restocked the party supplies. We always win on Sunday. Sunday is Run Day.

Fielding isn't looking good today, but the Sunday Run Day rule is holding true. Everyone on the starting lineup has a hit in the first two innings. I want the game over. I need a break and a couple days at my beach bungalow will be perfect.

Top of the 6th inning and the score is already 10-1 Seals. Skip pulls the key players and puts in the second stringers, they need playing time and we need a break. Final score 12-5 Seals.

> To @Kristeeeeena - Team will be celebrating at my house.
> To @Kristeeeeena - Hope you can join us.
> To @Kristeeeeena - I'm going surfing in the morning if you want to stay over.
> To @Kristeeeeena - No pressure. Whatever you want.
> To @Kristeeeeena - I wish you'd talk to me or at least respond.
> To @Kristeeeeena - Please, Sweetness.

I look and realize I've messaged her like a stalker again. I shove my phone in my pocket and go home.

Kristina

I've tried to stay away. He's my weakness. Sweetness. Every time he calls me that it goes straight to my heart and flutters down to my belly. He doesn't know that. Nobody does.

I've been hiding out a bit, trying to get my head straight and not do anything stupid. The problem is that quiet time can reveal the truth. It's not my head that's the problem, it's my heart. My head knows what I want to do and focuses on the goal, but it has nothing to do with what my heart wants. This time, my heart might be winning.

I worked as long as I could after the game, an intentional distraction. I leave the stadium on auto-pilot and go home. I can't get him out of my head, and maybe I don't want to. I walk into my empty apartment and texts pop through.

Text from GamerGirlM - I'm with Mase at Chase's.

Text from GamerGirlM - You should be here, too.

Text from GamerGirlM - No response required.

Text from GameGirlM - You know you want to.

Text from GamerGirlM - Do it already!

I toss my PJs, swimsuit, and clothes in my overnight bag. I'm going surfing with Chase in the morning.

I get to Chase's and walk in without being noticed. The team and guests are all outside on the beach, and who can blame them? It's the perfect day for it. Nerves hit me and I'm exhausted. I place my bag in the corner of his bedroom with intentions of going to find Michelle, but his bed is so inviting. It's a cloud of soft fluffy blankets. I run my fingers along his bed and imagine him sleeping there. His masculine scent overtakes my senses. I sit on the edge of his bed and lean back on his pillows. It's perfect. I sink in and it's so comfortable. I'm so tired. Maybe, just a quick nap...

Chase

The team is over to celebrate again, but my bungalow has turned more into a space that everyone can use. The permanent team bonfire. I'm okay with that, the team is family and I like having them around. It seems I'd be here alone without them.

The waves are coming in larger than normal and nobody here needs me, time to surf.

I go in my bedroom to change and hit the waves. I find an overnight bag in the corner of my room and look around. Someone's in my bed, sunk down into the mattress and buried under my comforter. I can only see their outline as they sleep in my bed and it's defined as the Stay Puft Marshmallow Man. I hear a sweet little noise and my body goes on high alert. Kristina's in my bed and she brought her overnight bag. I didn't even know she was here. I need to recap this. The woman I want is in my bed and brought what she needs to stay the night, but I can't have her because she won't date me. So, I can't have her phone number and she refuses to date me, but she's sleeping in my bed and seems to like to kiss me. At least she used to like to kiss me. And, she's planning on staying the night with me? How's this going to work? I guess I can sleep in the same bed with her and hold her again. It does sound nice to have her in my bed with me all night. Spending the night with her was, I don't know—special. She made it challenging to keep it in my pants. We both wanted more. Or, I could sleep on the couch, but it may be occupied again. Seems like one of the rookies is on my couch most nights. Feels like I'm set up for failure. I can't pick up where we left off. I need her to know that I still want her enough. Besides, I'm leaving for a road trip in two days. I can't be with her and then leave. I want to spend more time with her. What are the Las Vegas odds on me sleeping with her and not *sleeping* with her? Sounds like something I'd put money on and I know which way I'd bet. I don't think those odds are in my favor. I hope she's not still trying to get me to fuck her out of my system. I need Sherry.

I go to the bonfire to find Sherry cuddled up with Seno, and sit next to them. "What do you want?" Fairly rude reception from Seno, especially considering they're at my house. No idea what I interrupted.

Quietly, I share my situation and wait for advice.

"What do you want to do?" Sherry asks.

"That's not a fair question. I've wanted her for months.

It's the first time she's been in my bed and she's there alone, she chose to sleep in my bed and didn't even say anything. I'm supposed to take her to my bed, not find her there sleeping. She still won't give me her fucking phone number, but she'll walk into my place and make herself at home in my room? She brought her stuff, she's planning on staying over."

"Do you want her here?" Sherry questions.

"Yes."

"You need to find out what she wants."

"Fine. But, what if she wants me to fuck her out of my system? That's what she wanted when she tried to get me into her bed the first time. I don't want her to feel like that. I'm not using her. It could be awkward if she thinks I'm turning her down again. What she wants seems to change."

"Are you ready to have sex with her? Really?"

"Not until she goes out with me. I need her to know she's special and that I want her enough."

"So, tell her you really want her, but you aren't ready yet. She should respect that."

"Are we talking about the same confusing chick? She doesn't always make sense or do the logical thing."

Seno adds, "Sometimes rules are meant to be broken," as he holds Sherry tighter. "You have to do what's right for you. Everybody's different. Maybe she doesn't like to go out. Fuck, maybe she has a boyfriend."

"Do I leave her alone in my bed until later or let her know I know she's here or climb in bed with her? Never mind. I know what to do."

"Good luck," I get from both of them as I walk back in the house and into my room.

Chase

I carefully sit on the edge of my bed and roll over on top of the comforter, trying to find exactly where she's buried. I pull the blankets down to reveal her face and I'm driven to snuggle up against her. I put my arm around where I think she is and kiss her cheek sweetly. She's not fighting me, pushing me away, or trying to get me to fuck her. I want to climb in under the blankets with her and kiss her. I want to feel her warm body next to mine. I want to push my dick into her and feel her tight around me. I think the blanket barrier is a good idea for now and I probably shouldn't drink tonight. She looks so sweet and beautiful. Something about her being in my bed makes her feel like she's mine and gives me permission to kiss her. I press my lips to hers softly and feel a magnetic pull between us, pushing me to take more than one soft, innocent kiss. I want her badly, but I can't go there. Kissing her, well I have to—I need to. I press my lips to hers repeatedly with her between my arms and she kisses me back without opening her eyes. I nibble at her lower lip and she opens her mouth for me on a sweet moan. I slide my tongue across her lips and against her tongue, needing her kiss, needing to taste her and wanting more. She moves, pulling her arms out from under the blankets and pushes me away. She opens her eyes and looks at me differently. Without saying a word, she reaches her arms around me and pulls me back to her, kissing me senseless. Fuck me. I want to know why she's in my bed. I want to know what she wants. I want to know if she's really staying with me tonight. And damn Seno, now I want to know if she has a boyfriend and if she does, he has to go. Kristina's mine now. All I can do is feel her lips on mine and her arms holding me to her. She drags her teeth over my lower lip and sucks on it lightly while she pulls away from me.

She stops and gazes into my eyes, "Hi," is all she says and her voice is different. Sleepy maybe and sweet. Like she's let her guard down.

"Hi," I don't want to disturb the mood. I love that she's being so sweet.

She smiles, "I brought my overnight bag, so I can stay with you tonight and maybe go surfing in the morning."

That counts as a date. I'm not asking if she will go out with me anymore. I'm asking her to do specific things with me, like going surfing or maybe going out to eat. I love the sound of her voice saying, "stay with you." I'm feeling lucky and want to ask for her phone number, but I think better of it. I leave on a road trip Tuesday morning. I'm not having sex with her until I get back. I'm not starting something and then leaving her the next day, that can't happen. I'm suddenly slammed with the realization that I've never had a woman in my bed at my bungalow. It feels so right. Foreigner takes over ear worming me with their love songs and I must be going crazy. Does she feel it, too?

My body is humming happily, "I'm so happy that you did." I want in her so bad right now, the head on my shoulders is spinning and the one below my waist is throbbing. I need to stay in control. I bite and suck at her soft lips, and I feel her body moving underneath me. This blanket barrier needs to go, I need to touch her. Stop! I gather the calmest voice that I can, "Kristina, do you have another guy, a boyfriend?" It sounds so childish, but Seno said it and now I have to know.

She looks at me with big eyes, "I wouldn't be here if I did. I've never cheated and I never will."

I smile, "So, I'm your only guy right now."

"I'm not dating anybody right now."

"What do you call what we're doing?"

Kristina smiles, "Kissing in your bed." She giggles knowing that isn't what I asked.

"There will be no other chicks in my bed and I won't kiss any other chicks, unless you tell me we're done." I look into her eyes, wanting her to know how much she means to me. "Just you, Kristina." I take a deep breath. "Please tell me you want me and only me." I'm in uncharted territory. I haven't had any type of exclusive relationship since junior high. I haven't wanted one. But, Kristina—she's different and I want to be with her even if it's only kissing.

"I can't. I don't want you. You drive me crazy and freak me out. The one thing I've wanted to do is be in the control booth at the stadium and I get the chance at the PA Announcer, the ultimate gig—I totally fucked up and I wouldn't have if it wasn't for you. I couldn't help it! Then the afterthought about how often you're at bat and at risk, left me shook. No, I can't want you because you screw me up. You and your sending me flowers with sweet notes, caps with your name and number on them, you looking up and smiling at me in the control booth, you blowing me kisses and, seriously, changing your walk up song? I keep telling you no and I haven't even given you my phone number! Yet, you don't stop. No, I don't want you. I can't want you."

My heart sinks, but it doesn't make any sense, "Then why are you here? Why do you keep kissing me? Why are you fucking with me?" I stare at her and wait for an answer.

Kristina lets out a deep sigh, "That whole rant I just spat out at you doesn't matter. I can't stop thinking about you. I can't pass up a chance to kiss you. I don't want you. I have to have you, be near you, and it doesn't matter how much more sense it makes to walk away because I'll give everything else up before you."

All of a sudden the barrier and my dick, neither one of them matter. She's as messed up as I am. I get up and lock my bedroom door. I pull my T-shirt off and climb into my bed under the blankets wearing only my board shorts, reaching for her and holding her to me. I nuzzle my face into her hair, "I know. It's scary for me, too." It's amazing to have her in my arms. I can feel her breathing and her heart beating. I hold her curled into my chest and her warm breath caresses my skin. She entangles her bare legs with mine and I realize I don't even know what she's wearing. It feels like a silky little top and short shorts, probably pajamas again. It doesn't matter. All that matters is that I have her in my arms and I'm going to keep it this way for as long as I can. The team will pick up and lock up on their way out, they'll get it. I don't know if I should talk to her or just hold her. It's not about sex. Kristina touches my chest, delicately exploring from my collarbone to my pecs to my abs. Slowly moving lower and closer to things I'm not sure we're ready for. I grab her hand before she can get to my shorts. "Kristina, I," I groan at the words I'm going to say, "I leave Tuesday morning for a road trip. I don't want to have sex with you and then be gone for days. I want to be here with you and know we can be together for days, spend our nights together and spoil you." My voice goes raspy, "I want to push into you while you're kissing me and I know I shouldn't say that because it sounds like I want sex, but I want you. I don't want us to just be sex. I want you to know how much I want you and believe that I want you enough."

"Chase, show me how much you want me. Take me."

"Kristina, it's not a good idea. We need to spend time together. We need to get to know each other." She presses her lips to my neck and, "Anything you want. I'll give you anything you want." She climbs on top of me, her body laying on top of mine while she continues to kiss, lick and suck at my neck. Her breasts squish into my chest and her hands are in my hair. I can't control myself and I don't want to wait any longer. I know I should, but I tell myself this is one of those times that rules are meant to be broken. I slide her shorts down over her hips and touch her bare skin, I feel her breath hitch. I run my hands up her sides and pull her top off over her head. I have her naked, lying on me in my bed. She had no objections to me taking her clothes off. Her skin is soft and silky all over. I keep touching her, caressing her. I move my hands to her tits and take one of them in each hand, squeezing them gently and kissing them where they come together. I give each of them attention, licking, kissing and sucking at her nipples. Her reaction is crazy. I can feel her whole body needing me, wanting me. She said she doesn't want me, but it's a lie. She wants to protect herself and there's no protection from this. I move my hands down her body, simply touching her and getting to know her shape. I wrap my arms around her and pull her mouth up to mine, kissing her with no doubt of what's on my mind while I hold her tightly to me. I pull back, "Tell me to stop. Tell me to stop before I can't stop." My pulse is racing and I'm nervous. I'm never nervous. "Kristina."

"Chase, please, I want to feel you. I need you." She's breathless and her words make me want to please her. "Condom, okay?"

"I'll always protect you, I've got you." I kiss her neck and roll us over so she's naked underneath me. She reaches for my shorts and unties them, gesturing for me to get rid of them. I do as she asks, stripping bare and grabbing a condom from my nightstand. I hit the remote on the stereo, turning up the music in the house. Foreigner is playing "Feels like the First Time" and my nerves feel the same way. What if I'm not what she wants? What if I'm not any good? I lean on my arm and press my lips to hers tenderly, I want her and I don't want to just fuck her. I want to take care of her and please her. I move my free hand down between her legs, feeling how hot and wet she is. Fuck me, I need in. I need to feel her wrapped around me. I rip open the foil wrapper with one hand and my teeth, and roll the condom on. I rub my tip against her opening, she's tight and I can feel her nerves, "We can still stop. I don't want to push you."

"Please, Chase. I want this." She goes back to kissing my neck and it's my downfall. I slide my finger inside her, sliding it in and out of her wet heat. "Oh."

"Don't worry. I'll take care of you. That's my finger. I promise I won't hurt you." I want her to relax and she's too wound up. I understand, I could hammer nails with my dick right now. I slide in a second finger and she cries out. I can't do this. I'm too big for her. I'll hurt her. I kiss my way down to her sex and lick her clit while I stroke her with my fingers, flicking at it with my tongue and then sucking. I slide down further, pulling my fingers out and burying my face. Licking and sucking at her folds, she reaches for my head and runs her fingers through my hair while she feels me at her center. I feel her pulse quickening.

"Chase, please. I want all of you the first time."

I slide my finger back in and keep stroking her. "I want you to have me. God, I want in you. But, I'll hurt you."

"Please, all of you, now. I want you, okay. I want you!"

"I really do want you," I'm hard and needy. I press my lips to hers and she whimpers with need. Her sweet whimper. She rolls her hips and my hard dick feels her heat firsthand. I know it will hurt her, but she wants it anyway. I wrap my arms around her tightly, holding her against me while we kiss and push into her a little further with each stroke. I don't let her go and I keep it slow, giving her everything I can on each stroke. Feeling her so tight around me, "Oh, Kristina. We'll make it better, I promise."

"Chase, please don't hold back. I want all of you. Give me all of you." She says breathlessly.

I pull out and look at her lying there in my bed, asking me for more.

"Please, Chase, please." And I just want back inside her. I've waited for her for so long and she feels so good around me. I can't help myself and I slam all the way into her a couple times, "Chase! Oh! Chase!" She screams out my name and I push all the way in until our bodies are mashed together. I look at our connection and see how tight she is around me, knowing how hard I am and how much of me is buried inside her. How I slammed into that tight hole and made myself fit because she wants all of me. Fuck she feels amazing and she wants all of me.

"Kristina, tell me its good for you. Tell me you feel it, too." I stroke in and out of her slowly as I lean in and kiss her, claiming her mouth as my own, and in my heart claiming her as mine. She whimpers and cries out with every pass. "Tell me your mine. Tell me what you want. I'll make it happen. Anything and everything for you." Fuck! I'm losing it! The feel of our bodies together, my skin burns everywhere she touches me, like she leaves a trail of flames in her path. I want more of her. I whisper in her ear, "Does it feel okay? I need to know I'm not hurting you. I never want to hurt you."

She turns to face me smiling, "It's perfect, Chase. You're perfect." Her sweet soft voice cuts straight through me. Fuck me. "You don't have to be careful with me. Show me you want me."

She's killing me. I'm already thinking about baseball to keep from firing off. I kiss her, claiming her completely and taking control of everything, while I keep moving inside her, pulling out and then pushing back in repeatedly and slowly. I feel her arch in pleasure underneath me and I start to move faster. "Oh, Kristina." I need her to finish first. Finishing first is not an option for me. I sit back on my knees and lift her right leg in the air, kissing her ankle and leg, while I keep moving harder and faster. Her leg resting against my shoulder, I reach under her and grab her ass, pulling her closer to me. I hear her crying out my name and it's like magic. Her cry turns to a squeal when I feel her tighten up around me and she's pulling me with her, I couldn't stop if I wanted to and I don't want to. She feels amazing as I pound into her hard, pushing her orgasm and being overcome by mine. I feel like I'm going to explode like never before while her body continues to squeeze me.

"Oh, Chase! Chase! Oh! Fucking amazing, oh my..." She trails off and grabs me, pulling me down to her and making me stop moving. But, that's all it takes and I'm done. She kisses me, then stops and gazes up at me doe eyed. I'm not quite with her yet, I feel like I'm coming forever and keep moving as much as I can as I finish. I move to pull out and she stops me. "No, just stay here and kiss me. I want more of you, Chase." I smile and she continues, "Do you still want me or..."

I cut her off, "I told you it isn't possible to fuck you out of my system. It's not like that, Kristina. Of course I still want you. I want you more than I did before and I didn't think that was possible." Listen to me! Fuck! Can I really only have one chick? Fuck me. Yes. I press my lips to hers and I'm still hard, ready for more. Her lips are inviting and she's full of desire. I start to move inside her, but she stops me.

"I'm not ready yet."

"It's okay. I thought you wanted more. We don't need to do anything."

"I do. It's just, uh, you're big and I'm not prepared."

"I'm happy to hold you all night. I want you here with me." I smile at her. I pull out of her slowly and go handle some quick business in the bathroom. I return to find her dressed and putting her shoes on. I don't understand. "Where are you going?"

"Well, I thought I should go home."

"No." I walk over to her and put my arms around her, still naked. "You're staying with me tonight."

"We already..."

I cut her off, "No. I'm not playing this game with you any more. I know you want to be with me and you know I want to be with you. You have a choice: Get back in my bed with me right now or join the party with me and I'll hold you out by the bonfire. No more running scared."

She stares at me and doesn't speak.

"Are you just in this for sex? Did you just use me?" The words come out a little loud and more harshly than I'd intended. I guess it could be true. I did find her in my bed. She could've been waiting for me and hoping to get laid. Fuck! I gave her what she wanted and now she's out. This is why Seno said to date first, I need to know if they want me or a ball player. Now I'm angry. I've been waiting for her. I wanted her and no other chick. Fuck! "Kristina! You better say something quick." I'm pacing around my room while my head spins and I'm not letting her leave my room no matter what she says. I know the truth and this is bullshit.

She looks at me blankly and disturbed by my tone.

"You told me you wanted me to keep kissing you and now

you're up and dressed? Ready to leave? Tell me you didn't use me."

"I'm not using you. I'm embarrassed." She says quietly.

"You have no reason to be. You're staying with me."

"Okay."

"Good." I walk to her and make her decision for her. I unbutton her shorts and push them down until they fall to her feet. I pull her top off over her head and toss it on the floor. I take in the view of her in matching jade lace panties and bra. She's hot. Slender, but not skinny and curvy in all the right places. I pick her up, bringing her tits to my mouth, "Wrap your legs around me and hold on, I'm taking you back to bed." She wraps her legs around me and holds onto my head, playing with my hair. I lick and suck at her tits through her lace bra and she shudders. I sit on the edge of my bed and lay back with her in my arms. My dick is still hard and reaching for her.

She slides down my body wanting to find my mouth and bumps into my waiting hard-on. She reaches back and puts her hand around me, feeling me. Her touch sends more of that electricity through my body.

"Sorry, he can be rude." I laugh.

"Don't be sorry. Feels like he wants me."

"He definitely does. So do I, but I want more than him."

She giggles at me and slides down a little further, like she's going for my neck. She reaches behind her again and strokes my hard length, obviously liking the feel of it. In a second she's guided him in and slides onto me. She slides back and forth a few times.

"Kristina, you can't do..." But, I lose all ability to think and speak when she sits up and rides me like a cowgirl. Grinding against me while she's mounted on my hard dick. She's so hot and wet, and I can actually feel everything. Fuck me, fuck me, fuck me! I need to get her off of me, but she feels so good. "Kristina?"

"Yeah," She responds out of breath.

"No condom." I don't want to stop either, but we can't do this.

"Yeah, okay." What the fuck?

"Um, not okay."

"Feels good."

"I know, it's way better. But, we need a condom." Two months ago I didn't even know who I had in my bed and if I had sex, now I'm the voice of reason? This chick. I say things to her and I mean them. I told her I'd protect her.

"Just a little more, please." Her eyes are closed and her skin is turning red and blotchy.

"No, no more. You're going to make me come."

"No, I'll come and then I'll stop."

She doesn't seem to get it, "Kristina, are you trying to get knocked up by a ball player?"

"You feel good. I need you, Chase."

Fuck me. Baseball. Baseball. Baseball. What's worse, Basketball. Basketball. Men's stinky locker room. Dumpsters. Baseball. Baseball. Baseball. I need a plan here. That's it, get her off quick and get her off me before I blow. I press up into her and she cries out. She's close. I reach for our connection and it's crazy how solid I am right now. Don't get distracted from the mission. I reach for her clit and touch it lightly, circling around it softly and adding more pressure, then I press it and I feel her get wetter. "Kristina, listen to me." She nods. "You're fucking amazing. You make me so hard that I don't know how you and your tight little hole are doing this right now. I'm huge and up in you. I don't know if you looked, but I'm eight inches long or so and right now, you've got me at max. I couldn't be stretched any harder. I'm at least two inches thick and a while ago you could barely take my finger. Do you feel that?" I press up into her again and again and again.

"Yes," her voice shakes.

"Come for me. Feel how hard and hot our connection is. Come for me." I should pull out because I'm out of control, but I'm as bad as she is. "Kristina. Kristina. Kristina. Oh, fuck me! Fuck me!" I'm on the far edge and no better, but she starts to come and I can feel everything–Fuck, no condom. Baseball. Baseball. Baseball. Maybe I can bring it back in. I can have control. I can have control.

"Chase! I'm yours. I'm yours. Oh, God, I'm yours." She collapses on my chest and I pull out of her as quickly as possible. What was I thinking? Her wetness is all over me and I'm coming like a fucking hose in two strokes. This is crazy. I feel her heart beating against my chest and she's not moving.

"Sweetness, are you okay?"

"I'm better than okay. Sorry."

"Don't be sorry. Tell me your mine again." I'm such a fucking chick.

"I'm yours, Chase. I'm yours." Her voice is so sincere and sweet that my heart leaps in my chest.

I kiss her on the cheek, "No other dudes? Only me? And, you'll be my girl?"

She smiles giddily, "No other guys. Only you. Nobody compares to you. I'm already your girl." She laughs, "Does that mean you're my boyfriend?"

I hadn't thought about it but, "Yes. You're the only chick in my life." It makes me happy to say it. "Put some sweats on." She glares at me funny, "Work with me here." I pull on sweatpants and a zippered hoodie. I watch as she pulls leggings out of her bag and a T-shirt. "Hold on." I toss her a Seals pullover hoodie that will be huge on her and keep her warm. She pulls on her leggings and my hoodie, looking fucking sexy in my hoodie that fits her more like a dress. I grab my extra blanket and hand it to Kristina. I take her hand and lead her out of the bedroom to the bonfire. There's nobody left in the house and it's been cleaned up, no gamers left, and nobody passed out on my couch. I snag what's left of the food from the patio table and a couple bottles of water from the ice chest. We find the Senos, and Mason and Michelle both coupled up, wrapped together in blankets at the bonfire.

"Is everybody else gone?" I ask.

"Yea, everything is taken care of. Just us left enjoying the bonfire." Sherry offers the answer and smiles as she witnesses Kristina and I together.

I sit down on the sand and take the blanket from Kristina. I wrap the blanket around my back and pull her down to my lap. We snack on the leftovers and snuggle together with the blanket around us. I pull the blanket over our heads and find her lips with mine, simply brushing my lips against hers and I feel her smile. I whisper to her, "Will you stay with me until I leave Tuesday morning?"

"I'd love to. I might get called in to work tomorrow and I need to go home and get clothes before I have to work Tuesday morning. Okay?"

"I can work with that. Can I have your phone number now?" I still hesitate to ask, but I'm feeling confident.

"Yes. I'll put it in your phone when we go back in." I place my hands on her face and bring her lips to mine. I kiss her possessively, open mouthed and claiming. She's mine.

We sit together at the bonfire as it crackles and pops. It's starting to die down and we aren't adding to the fuel, it's getting late. The embers around the edge are glowing hot orange and the fire is still burning three or four feet high in the center. Sparks fly off into the night sky and the fire has a life of it's own. The flames are more yellow than orange, but it's still providing us with warmth on the beach and cutting the chilly breeze. I sit and stare into the flames while I hold Kristina. I've never noticed the depth of the flames and how they dance, a sexy seduction as the flames join each other and become one.

Mason and Michelle get up and leave with a wave. He has his arm around her and she's wearing his cap. Kristina's starting to get cold and the fire is fading. I pull the blanket around us tight to keep the air out and hold her, snuggling together. This is new for me and I like it. It's a new comfortable feeling that I've never experienced before and I'm happy. Seno gets up and puts his blanket around Sherry's shoulders. He holds his hand out to her and helps her up awkwardly. She's noticeably more pregnant every time I see her and that makes me happy that we've been winning because I know there's a very good chance that Seno will start to lose it when Sherry isn't traveling with him. Since he met her, he hasn't been the same when she isn't there with him. I'm hoping it will be different. I'm sure she wants to be with him. Seno smiles and gives me a high five, "Buy extra condoms and snacks. For you, probably cookies and don't ask Sherry, it's too much for her right now, unless you want to come over and do all the work. She needs to sit and relax, the kid is strong and keeps kicking, keeping her up at night. Remember to hydrate and be ready on game days." He walks away holding Sherry's hand and I realize his grumpiness lately is worry and I understand better than I did before.

"Sweetness, are you ready to go in for the night?" She nods and gets up, somehow managing to stay in the blanket. I wrap her in it and pick her up, carrying her into the house and kissing her. She holds on with her arms around my neck and doesn't complain. I take her to my bedroom and lay her down on my bed. "Can I get you anything? Snacks? Water? Me?" I chuckle and toss her my phone, so she'll add her number.

"I'd like all three, please." I laugh at her response and she makes sure I know she's serious, coming after me and going on tiptoes to kiss me. I put my hands on her waist and hold her there while we kiss, leaning toward never making it to get snacks.

I take her hand and drag her to my kitchen, "Make yourself at home. Take whatever you want." She slides her free hand into my sweats and grasps my dick in her hand. She makes eye contact with me and I can see her heat. She takes her hand from mine and reaches up to kiss me while she unties my sweats and pushes them down, releasing my dick and stroking it. She slides down my body and kneels on her knees in front of me, focused on my dick. She pushes me back against the kitchen counter and kisses my tip. I watch her soft full lips take me in her mouth and suck me in as far as she can, licking my length and dragging her soft lips along my dick. Her sweet lips and her hot, wet mouth on me, driving me crazy. I can't believe she's doing this. "Sweetness, I don't expect you to do that. I, uh, fuck me." She makes me unable to speak and it makes her giggle, adding a vibration to the sucking and licking. All I can think about is getting back inside her. I grab her hand and pull her up to standing, I slide her leggings and panties off at the same time, "Sweetness, you drive me crazy." I unzip my hoodie and pull hers off over her head, holding her bare skin to my bare skin. I lift her up and hold my arms around her tight, kissing her and she wraps her legs around me. I love that. I let her slide down a bit and bump my dick, "I need inside you, Sweetness."

"Yes, please." She gazes into my eyes, searching for something and biting her lower lip. I smile, happy we're in the same place and push my hard dick up into her roughly so I get all the way in. She screams out as I shove into her and holds onto me tight, biting at my collarbone.

"Okay, Kristina?"

"Uh, huh. More. Condom?"

"Don't worry. Under control."

"I trust you." I think is what she says next but she wasn't really talking, it was more trying to remember to breathe as I stroke up into her. I could set up camp when I'm inside her and stay there. She moves her hands to my shoulders and starts to move with me. The heat between us is growing and this is a bad idea.

"Taking you to bed, Sweetness." I carry her into my room and crawl onto my bed, still in her. I lay her down and stroke into her deep and fast a few times.

"Oh, Chase."

"I know, Sweetness. Me, too." She's so warm and soft, it feels right. I take both of her hands in mine and lock our fingers, while I gaze into her eyes and I don't know what I'm looking for. I push into her slowly and deliberately, over and over without taking my eyes off of her. She finally locks eyes with me and I feel it throughout my body, she can see straight into my heart and soul. I'm happy to be in her and I want to stay there as long as I can, but mostly I want to make her feel good. I want her to want me. I want her to need me. I want her to want more. Fuck me, I want more. I need to be thinking about a condom, not wanting more. I pull out quickly and put on a condom before I'm lost any further. I go back to where I was, holding both of her hands and moving slowly. I lean into her ear and kiss her all around it, sucking on her lobe with my warm breath at her ear. My body is on high alert. My heart is running the show and this has never happened to me before. "How did you get so far into my heart?" Please don't break me. She squeezes my hands and then releases them, reaching around my shoulders with her arms and holding me, burying her face in my neck while we move together.

It's never been like this before. I'm so lost and all I can think about is her. What can I do for her? How can I make her feel good? How long can I have her? How do I make her want me? What do I do to make her stay? Does she want me like I want her? Is it all in my head? Fuck! I'm all in my head! I knew I shouldn't have gone there. I knew I needed to wait until after the road trip, at the soonest. I shouldn't have broken the three dates rule, but she was never going to go on a date with me. I don't understand why, I have no clue. What do I know? I know she wouldn't date me. I know she wouldn't give me her phone number. I know she had to kiss me whenever we were in the same place, she couldn't help herself. I know she gets quiet when she's nervous or embarrassed. I know she yells and calls me names when she's mad, even if it doesn't make sense. I know she came into my house and slept in my bed like goldilocks, and didn't say anything, just waited to be found. I know she planned to stay the night and go surfing. I know her lips are soft and full, and she tastes sweet like cookies. I know she'll give everything else up before she gives me up, huh, and ain't that the kicker? She actually told me that. She tried to protect herself. She didn't want to want me or be with me at all—she doesn't have a choice, she has to have me, she needs me. I know one more thing, that's exactly how I feel. I just didn't try to deny that I wanted her. She already knew she was risking her heart and wanted to protect it. She's been in this place before. Shit, she's been hurt before. I don't want her to get hurt again. I won't be that guy. I said I would always protect her and that includes her heart. Right now I need to focus on making her feel good and we can talk later.

The friction and heat between us is building, but I can't wait. I push into her hard and fast. I'm out of control with need. I sit up and grasp my dick at the base, watching as I slide in and out of her, watching her face while she's taking me in. I let go of my dick and slam it all the way back into her, waiting to see her expression change. She cries out and starts to turn red. "Did you like that, Sweetness?"

"Yes."

"Do you want more?"

"Yes." Fuck me.

"Promise to tell me if I hurt you."

"Uh huh," she whimpers. "More, Chase. Please."

I lift her legs up and hook them both with my elbows. I push into her hard a few times and I can see that she likes it as she starts to writhe around underneath me and arches into me. "That's it, Sweetness. There's more coming. I'm going to hold you all night long and keep you safe. I'll always protect you." I keep pushing in and pulling out, over and over. I lean over her and take her legs with me, bending her knees back to her ears and push in as deep as I can get. "Kristina, oh you're so good. You're my good girl." I hear her whimper and pull out, watching her reaction. I slide back into her and pound into her hard, with her bent in half, getting as deep as I can on every pass and with every stroke sending myself closer to oblivion. Her breath is ragged and I don't want to be done yet. I lean in tighter and latch onto her tit, sucking on it and pulling it, not letting it go. I watch her expression change and feel her body tense. I slam into her more and keep at her tit. My orgasm sneaks up on me and I can't stop, my needs take over as I pound into her to completion uncontrollably and I cry out her name, "What are you doing to me? Oh, Sweetness!" She's right there with me as I fall over the edge and the intensity of her orgasm pulls mine further. Both of us crying out uncontrollably. "Kristina!"

"Chase! Please don't stop! Oh, Chase! Chase! Ohhh!"

"I'm not stopping. I've got you, Sweetness. I'm here." I release her legs and wrap my arms around her. I'm not sure if it's for her or for me, I just know I need to hold her.

Kristina

His arms are wrapped around me tight. He nuzzles into my hair with his lips at my ear and warm breath traveling down my neck. I can't remember a time when I've been so satisfied or desired. He bites my earlobe tenderly and kisses my neck. His body is hot and resting on me, his heartbeat slows and takes me with him. He whispers, "Stay with me, Sweetness." There's no place I'd rather be.

CHAPTER TWENTY-ONE

Chase

I wake up needing to pee and it's way too early. I'm not alone and I'm tired, sleepy, confused. I take stock of the situation. I'm entangled with a chick, mostly lying on top of her with my arms around her and my dick is still in her. The weird thing is that I like it and I'm not trying to figure out how to get away without gnawing my own arm off. Also, I'm in my own bed and I never have chicks here. I relax for a minute and remember the night before, finding Kristina in my bed and then doing my best to keep her there all night long. Oh yeah, fuck me. I must've fell asleep on top of her that last time. I hear her breathing, sweet and asleep. I don't want to wake her, but I kind of have to slide out of her and off of her. Not much chance that I don't wake her up. "Sweetness? I'm not leaving you. Have to take care of business and I'll be right back here to you. I promise, Kristina, I'll hold you all night long just like I said I would. You're my girl." I'm not getting any response, but I can't wait. I carefully slide out of her, making sure not to lose the condom and she whimpers. I get up and take care of business. I grab some water and go back to bed. I fix the blankets and cover us both up. I snuggle up next to her and kiss her cheek. I wrap my arms around her and since she's sleeping, I talk to her quietly, "You're so beautiful, my Sweetness. I promise to keep your heart safe. I won't break your heart. I need you. Please don't break mine." I look at her and watch her sleep until I drift off to sleep.

Kristina

I'm snuggling up to a warm, hard-bodied man and I'm naked. So is he and he's hard everywhere. I touch him gently, lightly tracing his features and exploring his toned muscles. I've had my night with him. No matter what happens, I will always have the memory of our night together. But, I can't imagine leaving him. He has control of me, maybe too much. I like it. I want more. My body hums and I want him. He's sleeping with his arms around me protectively. I think that's the sleep magic, he's protecting me and I trust him to make sure I'm safe. I don't always want to take care of myself. I can, but it's different with Chase. He needs to protect me and I want to let him. I snuggle in tighter and run my fingers through his thick blond hair, brushing it out of his face. I kiss his cheek and it leads me to his strong jaw, on my way to his neck and ear. His hands claim me appreciatively, but I don't think he's awake yet. I giggle at his ear, "Do you still want me here?" I ask, but I know the answer. He wants me here, even if it's just for sex. I kiss his neck open-mouthed and rub against him.

Chase

I wake up to warm soft lips on my neck and Kristina's arms around me. I love it. I've never had this before, but I could get used to it quick. I groan happily, "Good morning, Sweetness." I reach for her and pull her on top of me. She laughs and straddles my abs. I rub her bare thighs and gaze up into her eyes. "You make me happy. I'm glad you stayed with me. I was afraid you'd leave while I was sleeping."

Her eyes change as she stares at me, "I was worried you'd change your mind and I stayed too long."

"No, Sweetness. You're always welcome here and you can stay over with me any night you want. I like you here with me. That's not going to change." I don't have words for what I want her to know. I want her to understand what she means to me, but I don't understand it. I pull her down to me and press my lips to hers while I hold her between my arms and feel her body against mine. She opens her lips for me and I slide my tongue into her mouth, touching hers. I love the way she feels. She feels like mine.

She looks me straight in the eyes, "I won't break your heart, you'll be the one that breaks mine." My heart hurts hearing her words.

"I'll never hurt you. Who hurt you? What happened?" I shouldn't ask, but I kind of want to beat the guy.

"It doesn't matter. I'll always get hurt. I fall for the wrong guys."

"Not this time. I'm the right one for you, Sweetness."

She glares at me like I'm crazy. I understand because I feel the same way, I've lost it. "How can you say that? You can't mean it."

"I just know. You're the only one that makes me feel like this, the only one I want to be here when I wake up in the morning, and the only one I want to be wrapped around when I go to sleep."

"You're full of shit! You're just trying to make me stay and fuck you!"

I tighten my hold on her and run my fingers through her hair. Somebody has really fucked with her. My voice low, "I'll never lie to you. I want you with me, and we don't have to have sex." I hold her eyes with mine before I make my admission, "Kristina, I've never had another girl over to my house. Only you, Sweetness. I don't know what that means. I don't understand any of this. I know I want to be with you." I wait for some type of response, any reaction.

She continues unsure, "What if I want to have sex?"

"Condoms are in the nightstand. I won't complain." I smile and she rolls her eyes at my sarcasm. "How about breakfast and surfing?"

"Those things sound like we'd have to get out of bed."

"True."

"I don't think I'm ready to get out of bed yet."

"Let me hold you and we can go back to sleep."

She reaches for my nightstand to get a condom and turns around, giving me a beautifully curvy rear view while she touches my dick, kisses the tip and puts the condom on me. I've never had a chick put a condom on me and touch me like this. It's always more about fucking me. And fuck, her touch is life changing. She really wants me, needs me. She doesn't just want to fuck a ball player. I squeeze her ass cheeks and get a peek at her sex, she's already wet and I can't help but slide a finger into her to feel her heat. She pulls away from me and turns around, taking my view away. She leans in like she's going to kiss me, and goes straight for my neck. She already knows it's my weakness. She slides back and mounts my dick while she sucks at my neck, "Oh, fuck! Kristina!"

She moves on me, sliding her slick heat on and off of my dick. I don't know what she does to me, but I have no control. I move with her, trying to get more of her and she sits up straight, taking me completely. She watches my face while she rides me and I watch her. She moves constantly and starts to bounce on me like I'm her toy, and I happily accept the job —future title, "Kristina's Toy." The way she feels wrapped around me and in control is un-fucking-believable. I put my hands on her waist, guiding her hips and feeling her move on me. I don't understand what she does to me. I feel open and bare to her, like I belong to her and she has control of me—all of me. I'm overcome by emotion and I need to hold her. I pull her down to me and hold her tight in my embrace. I'm breathing heavy and it's not from the sex. She wraps her arms around my neck and cuddles into me, not questioning my actions.

"I'm with you, Chase." She whispers in my ear, "Am I your first? I mean, I know you've had a lot of sex, but like this?" I don't speak. "We're not just sex, baby. There's something. I can feel it and I know you do, too. I don't mean to freak out, it's self-defense. It makes it better when you hold me tight and take control." She stops and takes a deep breath, "I knew it was different for us when we were in Arizona, it scared me and I ran." Her voice is shaky and she keeps her face buried in my neck. "I don't want to get hurt again, but I couldn't stay away from you." I move my hand to her neck and caress her back, cherishing her because it's all I can do. I never want her to get hurt again.

I take control and roll over on top of her. I push into her slowly, feeling her and thinking about her. "Your eyes are beautiful. You feel so soft and silky under my hands. Your lips are full and sweet. I've never been with a chick that makes me feel like you do. You make me feel special, like I'm the only one that can make you feel like this. Like I'm the only man that has made you cry out his name. My dick is at your mercy, I lose control when I'm inside you." I'm lost in her, moving slowly and my heart is beating out of my chest.

"Chase, baby," she puts her hands over my heart, feeling it beat for her.

"Oh, Sweetness. You feel so good. Feel me hard in you, stroking you."

"Yea, Chase. I feel you. There's no way to not feel you. You're huge, baby. You make me feel so full. It's perfect and when you hit that deep spot, you own me."

Fuck me. I need to know when I find that deep spot and I need to find it now. I push all the way into her and she whimpers. I don't want to take her hard, I want... I really am losing it. She's just a chick. I'm leaving tomorrow morning and won't see her for days. Shit! She just gave me her phone number and I don't even know if she gave me her real number. Get out of your head! You know she's real. Take it slow. She's the runner, not you. I reach down between her legs while I move in and out, in and out, her tight heat pulling at me with every stroke. I spread her legs farther and work my way in deeper.

"Oh, Chase! More, baby! Oh!"

I touch her swollen nub and stroke it in time with my dick, moving faster and harder as I watch her climb to the peak.

"Chase! Chase! Oh Chase! Oh baby! Yes!" She cries out and screams out loud as she comes hard around me and pulls me with her unexpectedly. She has control of me and it's crazy. I hear myself call out her name in ecstasy as I grab onto her and hold her tight. Both of us reaching for the other, needing more contact.

I roll off of her and hold her to me. I need her. I want to

take care of her. "I'll be right back, Sweetness." I run to the bathroom, wash my hands and make my way to the kitchen. I look for something to eat, and a tray or something, but I'm not prepared. I pour milk into two mugs and find the last of the baked goods that Sherry left for me, to share with Kristina. Man, I really like this girl if I'm sharing my cookies. I walk back into my bedroom and find Kristina wearing my T-shirt, sitting in the middle of my bed. I smile because I love it. "I don't have breakfast or really anything to eat left in the house. I have milk and the rest of the cookies Sherry left for me. Want some?"

She looks at me wide-eyed and I think she's going to lecture me on breakfast, "Bring it over here! I love cookies and milk." Totally my girl. "Sherry made these?"

"Sherry bakes a ton, but not so much right now. She had some stuff frozen, so she could have it ready for me throughout the season. This is the end of it. It's too much for her right now."

"Why does she bake for you?"

"She likes to bake. Seno is my buddy. I was Best Man at their wedding and I kind of introduced them. She takes care of me like my baked goods dealer." I laugh. "Baking is relaxing for her and a hobby. Somebody has to eat it."

"These are delicious."

"She's a great baker. I love her chocolate chip cookie bars and her brownies. Those are the best. She makes all kinds of stuff. Everything is good."

There are so many things I want to talk to her about. I don't know where to start and I don't want to overwhelm her, but I don't want her to freak out. I hear my phone and grab it to see who's looking for me.

Text from Seno - Sherry can't travel. Want to share a room for this road trip?

Fuck. He's going to need me this road trip.

Text to Seno - Yes. Is she okay?
Text from Seno - She's fine. It's too hard for her and Dr told her to stay home. No more plane rides.
Text to Seno - Who is taking care of Sherry?
Text from Seno - She will be fine. Trying to get her to go to her Mom, but she insists she can take care of herself. Stubborn.
Text to Seno - What if I can arrange some company for her?
Text from Seno - I would love that, but she needs to relax.

"Kristina, do you bake?" It's not selfish if it helps Sherry, right?

"I wish. I can bake cookies from the pre-made cookie dough." I explain what's going on and Kristina texts Sherry, arranging for baking lessons while the team is away.

Text from Seno - Nice one! I'm not even in trouble for setting her up because I didn't! Thanks, Man.

"Do you work when the team is away?"

"Yes. Most game days and sometimes only half a day. I'm off today, like you." She smiles. "I know the team's schedule. I know you're in San Francisco tomorrow, then Houston, then Chicago, and then you're back home with an off day a week from Thursday. You should be home on Wednesday, I'm guessing."

I look at my phone and notice the text from Kristina, she sent me the kiss emoji. She also took a selfie while she was wearing my hoodie and added it to her contact info in my phone. She looks at me funny while I'm checking it out and takes my phone from me. I grab her and snap a selfie of me kissing her. I set it as my wallpaper and text the photo to her, finding that she changed her contact name to read: Kristina Girlfriend. I absolutely love it and decide to pick on her. "Is that your way of marking your territory?"

She laughs, "Trust me. I mark my territory."

We spend the morning together, lazy on the beach. We don't have enough energy left for surfing. I take her to her place to get clothes and I do some laundry for the road trip. At sunset I take her for a walk on the beach and hold her hand while we kick at the water that tries to reach us. I stand behind her with her in my arms, watching the last minutes of sunlight disappear.

"The sunset is beautiful with all the pinks."

"It's not as beautiful as you, my Sweetness." I turn her to me and kiss her, feeling it all the way to my toes. We're electric together. "You're gorgeous and mine." I smile as I say the words.

We walk back to my bungalow, "Can I take you out tonight?"

"I'm hungry, can we just order delivery? Maybe play video games?" Did my girl say that she'd rather stay in and play video games? She really is perfect.

"Whatever you want, as long as you're staying with me I'm happy." I call in an order of chicken parmesan for two and sit down on the couch with Kristina. I put my arm around her with intent of picking a game, but end up making out with her until the food gets delivered. The evening is comfortable as we eat together, enjoying each other's company on the patio with the lights twinkling around us, and the ocean roaring in the background. We talk about baseball, video games, music, goals, and home. The conversation simply flows and I always have something else I want to ask about her or tell her about. The chill finally chases us inside. We sit on the floor in my living room with our backs against my couch, leaning on each other while we play head to head video games and have a great time laughing, sometimes with each other and other times at each other.

After Kristina used her combo moves to chop my head off and laughed at it rolling around on the screen a handful of times, "Are you ready to go to bed? I have to be at the stadium early."

"You just don't like to lose," She retorts.

"I'm not losing. I'm winning because you're still here." I gaze into her eyes and feel my heart beating. I take her hand in mine, intertwining our fingers and smile. Kristina leans in to give me a sweet kiss on the lips and looks down, blushing and happy. We get up and go to my bedroom, changing clothes and getting ready for bed. "Will you get up early and go to breakfast with me?"

"Maybe," She says, teasing me.

"Maybe!" I repeat back at her as I reach over and pull her to me, tickling her until she's laughing to the point of tears and squealing. She feels so right.

I turn some music on low and The Damnwells start to play "I Will Keep the Bad Things From You." The melodic guitar and vocal tone suits my mood as I take Kristina in my arms, not wanting to let her go. I want to hold her and kiss her and... I'm going to be gone for ten days, I don't want her to forget me. I don't want her to remember me as the dude that kept fucking her. I want her to still want me when I get back. This is crazy. My head is my own worst enemy. It makes me vulnerable. "Kristina, Sweetness, promise me you won't forget me while I'm gone?" No, that's my fucking heart taking over my world. How did I get here? No, I'm not going to complain. I'm happy and feeling things I've never felt before. Scary things I don't understand and I don't know how to process. I want her. I need her. I need her to only want me.

Kristina smiles at me warmly, "Do you really think I could forget about you?"

I stare at her, unable to answer because my heart is in control and hasn't learned how to control my voice yet.

"There's no way I'll ever forget about you, Chase. You're not my first and you may not be my last, but one thing I know for sure is that I don't forget guys I fall for. And, Chase, I'm on the path to falling for you." The gold flecks in her warm green eyes sparkle while they look into mine.

I leave the music playing and turn the lights off. We climb in bed together and I want her near me. I want to hold her. I want to feel her against me. I want to feel her silky hair and smell her scent. I want her to know how I feel about her, without any question. I want to know that she's safe and with me.

I'm wishing that I had stuck to the three dates rule. I'm dreading leaving her in the morning, but it would've happened sooner or later.

Kristina

I wake up cold and lonely. It's dark, with only the shine of moonlight filtered by the draperies lighting the room. I have the blanket curled tightly in my fists and pulled up to my neck. My eyes adjust and I remember where I am. Chase sighs and I realize I'm hanging off the edge of his king sized bed, while he's still where he started the night and resting contentedly. I rarely sleep well, but the nights I've been with him are the best sleep I've ever had. Why am I so far from him? Clinging to the edge and blankets for comfort? He's so far away. I sit up and gaze at him, lying there comfortable and at rest. He's gorgeous and he wants me here with him. I release the blankets and move over to him. He's where I belong. I kiss his cheek sweetly and wrap my arm around his waist as I make his strong chest my pillow. Instinctively, he pulls me closer. I put my feet between his legs and accept him, snuggling against him and fall back asleep effortlessly.

Chase

I wake up in the middle of the night and she's using me as her pillow. She's sleeping and breathing deeply, curled into me with her head on my chest, her legs entangled with mine and her arm possessively across my body. My arm is around her back, holding her to me. She's beautiful. I push her hair out of her face and kiss her forehead, content and satisfied to have her in my arms. I close my eyes and start to drift back to sleep, when I feel her kiss my chest and her hand wrap around my dick. I splay my hand across her back receptively and only half awake. She makes sweet little noises and pulls herself on top of me, pressing her hands and lips to my chest. She's biting and sucking all over me. I'm hit with deja vu from that first night in Arizona and I know how I got the marks, I remember watching her then as she traveled my body just like she's doing right now. The thought of stopping her is not an option because she feels so good on my body, her hands touching me, her tongue licking me, her mouth sucking on me. The difference now is that I want in her and I know what it's like to be there. I reach for her hips and press her against my hard dick, so she can feel how hard I am and how much I want her. She slides her panties off, reaches for my hard length and guides me inside her without taking a breath. Oh fuck, she fits me better than my baseball glove. I move inside her mindlessly, unable to help myself. I can't stop myself from taking her selfishly. She keeps biting and sucking at my chest, pushing me forward and making me want more. I try to take control, I want her under me, but she stops me and sits up. She starts to ride me, grinding against me and touching herself. I'm watching her every move and it's driving me crazy—the way she takes control, the way she's touching herself. I look at her face, her eyes are closed and her body is relaxed. I push up into her and she cries out, leaning her head back and arching her body. Her eyes open, she finally looks at me and smiles. I don't think she's really awake and I wonder if she knows what she's doing. I know I'm only half awake and, man, this sleepy state I'm in is sexy, hazy, indulgent. I can't help but to keep watching her. She rides me harder and harder, pushing down onto me like she needs more, grinding against me and rubbing her clit. I'm just happy to be part of it and I keep watching her. She moves faster and rubs at her hard nub faster, harder, fiercely, until she suddenly falls apart, screaming out as she comes around me. I was in complete control, now suddenly I'm ready to explode and not prepared. Damn it! Fuck! I want to come right where I am. I just want to go with it, feeling her around me tighter and tighter. Fuck me! Fuck me! Fuck me! I groan, needy and on the edge.

"Just do it. It feels too good not to." Kristina says in a

sweet voice and I know I can't because I told her I'd always protect her. I'm still not sure she's awake.

"No, I have to protect you, Sweetness. You're my girl." I pull out and go for a condom, but I'm too far gone. Kristina watches me grasp my dick and start to stroke it. She leans down and takes me in her mouth, licking and sucking at my hard dick. It's the end of me. I come almost instantly in her hot wet mouth and she doesn't pull back or stop. She sucks and licks at me, like she wants more. Oh, fuck me I'm so done. I watch her and it's so hot to see her finishing me like this. Fuck! I can see her swallowing. She licks me clean before releasing me and all I can think about is her. I couldn't forget her if I tried. No woman has ever treated me the way she does, touched me the way she does.

Kristina lies down next to me and all I can do is look at her. I don't know what to do with myself, I just, she is, I mean, fuck me. I gaze into her eyes, baring everything to her and feeling things that I shouldn't. I pull her to me desperately, claiming her mouth with one kiss and pulling back to see her eyes. I want to know she's in the same place with me and I have no idea what I'm searching for. I roll her underneath me, burying her in my bed sheets and comforter like we're cocooned in our own private cloud. I touch my lips to hers softly and take a deep breath, inhaling her into me while our electricity shocks me through my limbs and stabs me in the heart. I put my hands in her hair, holding her head while I kiss her tenderly. I know I'm naked and on top of her, but I just want to kiss her. I love her lips. I want to cherish her sweet lips and taste her. I try to memorize her lips and the feel of her, her sweetness. I feel her heart beat with mine and I can't breathe. I can't do anything but kiss her like she's the air I need to breathe. I want her for more, and damn it, if I don't want her enough.

CHAPTER TWENTY-TWO

Chase

We wake up when the early alarm goes off, forehead to forehead with arms wrapped around each other and her feet between my legs. "Good morning, Sweetness," I say quietly and realize that even though the day is starting out better than almost every other day I've had in my life, I have to leave her to go on the road in a few hours and I'll be gone for ten days without her lips, her body, her. She rubs against me and snuggles in, not wanting to get up. "Sweetness, if we get up now we have time to get ready and go to breakfast before we go to the stadium."

"I don't want to."

"You don't want to what?"

"Get out of bed."

"I'll get up and get ready, you can stay in bed while I shower."

"No. I don't want you to get up."

"We can't stay in bed all day. I'd love to stay here with you, but it's not an option. You have work this morning, right?"

"Yes." She mumbles something to herself, almost like she's cursing herself out.

"You're going to the stadium with me this morning, right?"

"Yes."

"Sweetness, I don't like that I have to leave you. It's part of being a baseball player. We travel. But, I'll come home to you and I'll think about you while I'm gone. I told you, no other chicks. You're my girl." I brush my thumb across her cheek, "I mean it, Sweetness. It's only you for me." My voice is raspy and sincere.

Kristina smiles at me and her eyes light up, "Can we skip breakfast and stay in bed longer?"

"Whatever you want."

She focuses on me and I can see flames reflected back at me, "I know what I want."

"Yea? Tell me what you want." I want to hear her say it.

She looks around the room, before she finally focuses on me, "I want you to kiss me more, like you did early this morning when I fell back to sleep in your arms." She blinks a couple of times. "I want you on top of me and in control of me. I want the sex to match the kiss."

"You want me to fuck you while I kiss you?"

"I guess, not really. When you kissed me it was different. I don't know, like we were connected and I could feel it." She closes her eyes.

She felt it too.

"I'm sorry. I'm being stupid. Forget it."

I can't let her forget it. She needs to know I felt it, too. I have to know it's the same for her. I have to put it out there.

"You mean it felt like electricity was running through your body and we were somewhere alone where nothing else mattered? Just us and we needed each other to breathe?" I'm freaking out inside now that I've said it. What if I'm crazy? What if she has no idea what I'm talking about? What if it's only sex for her? I feel myself start to shake and I sit up, waiting for her response. This is the longest second of my life. Why did I tell her that?

She smiles at me, "I felt like you were sending sparks through my body. Like you were the only thing keeping my heart beating. Like you had whisked me off to a fantasyland that only we could go to." I gaze into her eyes and feel my cheeks get warm. "It didn't feel like something you could do while you were fucking."

I lean back against my headboard. I pull her to me, so she's straddling my legs while I start to kiss her tenderly. Honestly, the way I want to kiss her. The way I can show her how I feel about her. I can feel her melting in my arms. I remember last night and reach for a condom before we have a problem. I get it open and roll it on while I kiss her. I splay my hands on her bare back and hold her while my lips explore hers. I feel her breathing change and ask her, "Do you want more, Sweetness? Do you want me inside you?"

"Yes, baby," Slips from her lips on a sigh.

I lift her up and slide her down on me. She moves slowly, working me into her all the way. She feels crazy good around me. I simply hold her against me and continue kissing her lips gently, tenderly, telling her how I feel without words. I don't know how to show her how I feel with my dick and the rest of my body. Something I've never done. Something I never thought of. It was always chicks that wanted to fuck me. I guess I was a dick to conquer, a notch in their bedpost, a challenge maybe. Another ballplayer to fuck. I don't even understand how I feel. I don't know how to explain it. I feel her and place my hands on her hips, guiding her to slow movements with me. Feeling her body and desires with my hands, and making them happen. My body floods with warmth and the electricity is back, but more intense. "Kristina, do you feel the sparks, electricity, whatever it was like last night?"

"It's like the sparks have grown to fireworks shooting through my body." That's exactly what it's like and it drives me to give her more, unselfishly. More passionate kisses and more of my feelings, all of me, all in.

I lean my forehead against hers and smile uncontrollably, "I'm so fuckin' happy to be in the same place with you, Kristina. Fireworks. High voltage and combustible, my Sweetness." I hold her tight and need more. I roll her underneath me and stroke into her completely, in and out, in and out, feeling her like never before. I want more. She wraps her arms around my neck and pulls herself up to me, kissing me while we fit together in pleasure. I catch her legs and lean down to her to kiss her, taking her legs with me. I push in as deep as I can, wanting to get closer to her and needing to be as close as possible. I hold us together like two perfectly matched puzzle pieces and look at our connection, seeing my hard dick stroke in and out of her perfect little heaven. I see her nerve center, needy and staring back at me, so I touch her softly and she cries out my name.

"Chase! Oh Chase! More."

All I want to do is make her happy. She gets whatever she wants. I increase the pressure on her clit, circling it and teasing it. She arches into me and I feel her get wet at my touch. I stroke into her slowly, but hard and I can see her start to unravel. "You're amazing, Kristina. The things you do to me. Come for me. Come for me hard. Feel the fireworks. Maybe we can see them together." I push into her hard and fast, pounding into her while I have her bent in half and rub her clit harder.

"Tell me, Sweetness. Tell me everything." I whisper with my eyes closed, on the edge of the world and ready to jump off head-first.

"You cut through me. Straight to my heart, Chase." She starts to buck and I lose it completely.

"Fuck, Kristina. Come for me. Come for me now. Come with me." I call out to her even though she's right there with me. I need her to come. I can't finish before her and I'm out of control. "Please! Oh fuck! Oh fuck!" I can't help myself, it's intense and I press down on her hips, holding her in place while I stroke into my paradise found, losing it by the millisecond. I know she's with me, she's right there with me and I hear her scream out.

"Chase! I'm yours!" She squeezes me tight and I come hard as if on queue. She digs her fingers into my back and shoulders, as I push and pull us through knowing I have to leave her for ten days. Knowing we're in the same place. Knowing I'm falling, just like she is. Maybe I already fell.

Chase

We race to get ready and get to the stadium on time. We skipped breakfast and our morning activities still have us running late. I'm not complaining. No, I'm not complaining even a little. Kristina doesn't have to be at the stadium as early as I do, so she'll have time to get her day going. I'll have to settle for whatever is left in the clubhouse, if anything. That's fine. It was worth it. I'm hoping for a few minutes to say goodbye to my girl properly, but I don't know if that's going to happen either—I'd give up food for it. She picks up all of her stuff and tosses it in her bag, so she's ready to go. I toss my duffle bag over my shoulder and get her bag, ready to load up and get out. I see my hoodie that she's been wearing left on my bed and drop the bags. I get the hoodie and give it to Kristina, "Take it with you. You might need it to take care of you while I'm gone." She hugs me tight and I don't think it has anything to do with the hoodie. "I know, Sweetness." I hold her head to my chest and feel it in my heart. "I promise it will be okay and I'll be back looking for you as soon as I get off the plane next Wednesday. How about I pick you up when I get back next Wednesday? We can go out or order in or whatever you want." She half smiles at me. "We will text and talk while I'm gone. I'll call you everyday, Sweetness." I look at her and she's upset. "Trust me, I don't want to leave you. I'm going to miss you." I speak softly and lean my head against hers. I notice the clock and time issues keep getting worse. "We gotta go, Sweetness." She pulls the hoodie on and I grab the bags, ushering us both out to my truck.

We drive to the stadium in silence and she's staring out the passenger window. I get her talking, "Why don't we get to know each other better while I'm gone?"

She turns and glares at me like I'm crazy. "How's that going to work?"

"We text each other and ask questions. Not like Truth or Dare, or anything like that. Little things we want to know about each other. Say three or four each day. Could be fun."

"Okay."

"I was wondering, are you really interested in baking?"

"Yes, I've always wanted to."

"Do you have a mixer and baking stuff, tools, whatever to bake?"

"I have a bowl, a spoon and a little measuring cup."

"Well, Sherry has everything and you will be at her place. You should be good." I laugh, "Remember chocolate chip cookie bars and brownies are my favorite." At least I've got her smiling. We pull into the player's garage to park and I've got no time.

Text to Seno - Cover me… I'm here in the garage… need 5 minutes… please.

I get an immediate response of a thumbs up emoji.

I reach for Kristina's hand, pulling her closer so I can kiss her and she resists. "I only have a few minutes. I'm already late. I just want to give you a kiss, my Sweetness."

"It's better if I just go." She says grumpily.

"No. I'm getting my goodbye kiss. I need to have something to get me through to next week." She rolls her eyes at me and I realize it's part of her defense mechanism. I turn her face to look at me, "You don't need to protect yourself from me. Drop the self-defense. I'll always protect you." I get out of my truck and quickly walk around to the passenger side, opening the door and not giving her a choice. I claim her mouth with mine and wrap my arms around her, pulling her out of my truck in the process. "You're mine. Don't forget it."

"Chase..." I cut her off.

"Yes, my Sweetness. I'm yours, only yours," More than you know and more than I ever thought possible.

"Okay. I like being your girl." My heart sinks at her words and I kiss her again before running off into the stadium. Bad enough to be gone, I'm not going to be gone and scratched from the game.

Kristina

I'm left standing here watching while Chase runs off into stadium. I have a little time before I need to be at work and I don't want anyone to see me right now. I pull on the big hoodie and take off for a walk in the village. Hiding the tears running down my face more than anything else. He doesn't want to hurt me, but he is by simply leaving on the road trip. It's not his fault. It's work.

CHAPTER TWENTY-THREE

Chase

I walk through the stadium thinking to myself about how I can call her and text her. I might even send her dirty pictures and I mean pictures of me at the end of the game when I'm covered in mud and have holes in my uniform... and maybe some abs and happy trail. I want her to be happy while I'm gone and I want to buy her presents.

Text to Sherry - Hey lovey. Heard my girl is going to be hanging out with you to learn to bake. Thought you might order everything she needs to bake and have it delivered to her. You still have my credit card info. I mean everything. She only has a bowl, a spoon and a measuring cup. You can use my card for ingredients or whatever she needs. Make sure she learns how to make your brownies and your chocolate chip cookie bars. :) Don't overdo it, relax and make Kristina do everything. Don't worry about Seno, I've got him and we're rooming together this trip. Most important please take care of yourself and Baby Seno.
Text from Sherry - I'll order stuff later today. Love shopping therapy. What color does she like or what color is her kitchen?
Text from Sherry - And it's Baby Girl Seno :)
Text to Sherry - I bet she'll be just like you :) and drive Seno crazy!
Text from Sherry - I think she already has him wrapped around her little finger :)
Text to Sherry - I'll let you know about color later today.

Next on the list...

Text to Carter - Dude, can you get a jersey made up for the intern Kristina for me? My name and number. And an oversized hoodie the same way. Please.

Text to Carter - Can I have something left for her everyday of the road trip? Different jerseys, caps, shirts, hoodies, whatever I can get for her with my name and number on it.

Text from Carter - I can arrange that. Are you sure you want to do that? She was pissed about the things you've had delivered to the control booth.

Text to Carter - Does she have an employee locker or something you can leave it in for her to find?

Text from Carter - She has a small cubicle in the media offices. I can leave things for her there.

Text to Carter - She has a cubicle? Where pictures and stuff can get put on the walls?

Text from Carter - Yea, I guess.

Text to Carter - Leave stuff for her at her cubicle. Thanks.

I hope I don't get in trouble for having gifts left for her everyday, but I think it'll be okay. She's not going to be PA Announcer during that time because there are no home games. She'll get a gift and a reminder of me everyday that I'm gone. Perfect.

Text to Kristina - Waiting on the plane. Thinking about you, my Sweetness. <3

Text to Kristina - What's your favorite color?

Text to Kristina - What's your favorite candy?

Text from Kristina - You didn't forget me yet? :)

Text to Kristina - I'm not going to forget you, beautiful.

Text from Kristina - 10 days is a long time... you'll forget me

Text to Kristina - Stop. No, I won't forget you. I haven't forgotten you since Arizona.

Text from Kristina - Chocolate

Text from Kristina - Tiffany Blue

Text to Sherry - Tiffany Blue... Thank you

Text to Kristina - What kind of chocolate?

Text from Kristina - Milk chocolate... white chocolate is good, but not really chocolate.

Text from Kristina - Chocolate with caramel is good, but not chocolate with anything fruity...that just ruins it.

Text to Kristina - Will you be watching the game tonight?

Text from Kristina - Yes. Not sure if I'll be working or not yet. Michelle and I are planning to go to Sherry's.

Text to Kristina - Cool. Getting ready to take off. Talk to you soon, Sweetness.

My chest feels heavy. I miss her and I haven't even gotten to San Francisco yet.

Seno looks over at me, "Texting the girl?"

"Yea. Dude, I'm lost with her and I think she's right there with me. It's never been like this. I miss her already."

"It's just a new girl. Give it time."

I turn to Seno, irritated and quietly, "Then why does it feel like I have sparks and electricity running through my body when I'm with her? Why was I happy when she was still there in the morning? Why does her touch feel different than all the rest? Why can't I stop thinking about her?"

"Man, you're screwed." Seno chuckles. "Do you keep thinking things and not saying them? Have a hard time putting words together when she touches you? Can't keep your hands off of her? Want to tell her that you love her, but know it sounds crazy?"

"Fuck me! I really am screwed."

"No, you're fine. If it's real, you're lucky." Seno smiles and his eyes shine. "Thank you for telling me to ask Sherry out and getting me to go out." He takes a deep breath, obviously thinking about her. "When it's right, it's right and sometimes you just know. Do what makes you happy. Don't rush it. Get to know her. If that means you have her over every night, so be it. My Dad told me to do whatever I needed to do to make sure my happy didn't get away, that it doesn't matter what anyone else thinks."

"So, I'm not crazy and she didn't drug me or something?"

"I don't think so, but we can have you tested." Seno smiles at me and laughs. "Don't tell her you love her too soon. Might freak her out."

"I don't love her."

"Whatever you say. I'll be here when you need me."

"You think I love her?"

"Give it some time it could be lust." Seno stops and thinks, before continuing, "You miss her, what do you miss?"

"I just want to be close to her. I want to protect her."

"Yea, you're screwed." Seno pats me on the leg and smiles.

"So, is Sherry on the DL for the rest of the season?"

"Probably the rest of the regular season for away games. Everything should be good for the postseason. I expect she'll miss some home games, but not too many. And, yes, we're going to postseason and we're winning. I want a championship ring for the year my girl is born. My girls make me feel like I've already won."

He's so happy, it's crazy. "Does she have a name yet?"

"We're down to a couple, but Sherry can't decide. She's thinking something Hawaiian maybe, but then we found out she's further along than we thought and she already had a girl name picked out. She's due before the end of June."

"That's next month. Dude, that's insane."

Seno nods and sits happily as the plane lands and everybody gets their phones out, texting to check in. I turn on my phone to messages from Kristina.

Text from Kristina - Why me and not one of the other girls?
Text from Kristina - Why won't you forget me?
Text to Kristina - Landed in San Francisco

How am I supposed to answer those questions? This game might have been a bad idea. This isn't a conversation I want to have by text. I want to have it live and in person, not when I'm gone for the next ten days. I know I need to respond.

Text to Kristina - You're the only girl that has ever made me feel this way
Text to Kristina - I think our connection is special and I'm not referring to the sex, but the sex is our own fireworks show.
Text to Kristina - What duty do you have at the stadium today?
Text from Kristina - Just preparing pregame notes and the lineup for the broadcasters and getting it sent over to them in SF. I'll be off in time to go to Sherry's, but I'll be researching stat questions and feeding the information to the broadcasters for the post game.
Text from Kristina - Maybe you should see what it's like with another girl, now that you don't want to fuck every girl you see.

That's it. I call her and I shouldn't. I'm irritated and I'm with the team. The phone rings, but there's no answer. I know she has her phone, she's texting me.

Text to Kristina - Answer your phone.
Text from Kristina - Can't, I'm at work.
Text to Kristina - Answer your phone or I'll call into the stadium and get transferred to you. I'm not having this conversation by text.
Text from Kristina - I'll call you in a couple minutes.
Text to Kristina - Okay.

I'm frustrated. I don't know why she would suggest such a thing, unless she doesn't like me. She keeps trying to push me away, but when we're together she holds on to me.

The team is going directly to the stadium for practice. Everybody is pumped up and we're ready to keep the winning streak going. My phone isn't ringing and my head is all over the place.

Seno barks at me, "Stop looking at your phone. Shake it off. Everything isn't on your schedule."

He's right. I toss my phone into my locker and go work out, trying my best to leave Kristina in my locker with my phone. I put my earbuds in and escape everybody for a while with my work out playlist on shuffle, it starts with "Turn It Up" by The Wrecks. Working out always gets my head straight, puts me in the right frame of mind for the game. It brings everything into focus for me. Lying on my board out in the ocean is the only place that relaxes me more.

I take batting practice in the cages, enjoying my alone time and I'm driven to swing the bat viciously. I'm seeing the ball and feel like the bat is part of me. Connecting with no effort at all.

I go to my locker, prepared to hit the showers and get ready for the game. My phone is blowing up and I reach for it to turn the sound off, but I can't ignore the activity. Two missed calls and texts, all from Kristina.

Kristina

Why isn't he answering? He told me to call him. Damn it! I told him to be with another girl. He's probably doing it right now. There's always some slut ready for a player. Why did I say that! Answer the phone! My hands are shaking as I try calling him again. Straight to voicemail.

Text to Chase - I called, you didn't answer.
Text to Chase - Where are you?
Text to Chase - My break is almost over.
Text to Chase - Why aren't you answering me?
Text to Chase - I shouldn't have said that. I didn't mean it.
Text to Chase - I don't want you with another girl, not even just to see.
Text from Chase - Don't fuck with me. I don't play those games.
Text from Chase - Do you want me? You want to be with me? Be my girl? You wouldn't suggest another girl if you did.
Text from Chase - I'm all in with you, Sweetness. If you're not, don't fuck with me. Tell me.
Text to Chase - I want to be all in.
Text to Chase - I'm yours, Chase.
Text from Chase - I only want you, Sweetness. I miss you. I don't like being away from you.
Text from Chase - I'm not going to hurt you. Please don't play games with me.
Text to Chase - How do you know you won't hurt me?
Text from Chase - I just know. There's nobody like you. I'll always protect you.
Text to Chase - :)

He can't know he won't hurt me. I'll get hurt. But, pushing him toward another woman is hurting myself. Why do I do these stupid things when I want to be with him?

Chase

I hit the shower and let the hot water roll down over my body. The spray hits my face and I close my eyes. Everything from the world around me washes away and all I can see is her. I can feel her with me. My girl.

Going into the game today, it's going to be extreme. The question is will it be really good or suck. Too many things happening in the club house. First, Seno on the road without Sherry. Second, Mason hasn't stopped talking about Michelle since we got to the stadium. Third, Bravo is off the disabled list and getting texts from a hook up he has in San Francisco that he thought he was rid of.

And then there's me, and I miss Kristina. I'm not even sure that it's missing her, I won't see her tonight and I don't like it. I can't believe she told me to be with another chick. It makes me need to see her and show her she's mine. Since I'm on the road for eight more days, that's not an option. I'm not experienced with chicks. What I mean to say is I'm very experienced with sex, not experienced at all with having one chick all to myself. The part that gets me the most is that I never wanted a chick to be my girl. Fuck their brains out, yes. Protect them, no. I'm not concerned about being tempted or cheating, that's not me. But, Kristina makes me want her and I don't even notice anybody else. I know she'll be watching the game.

The answer is Seno was on point, hitting safely on all his at bats, scoring twice and bringing in three baserunners. Mason was on fire with two home runs. Bravo was brought in as designated hitter in the eighth, hitting a double. Everyone else did as they normally do. Me? I hit a triple and struck out my other two at bats. The real problem was my fielding. I pride myself on my fielding. I will dive for that shit. I will run for it like an Olympic sprinter. I will climb the wall and I will jump into the wall if that's what it takes. Today, well the best way I know how to describe it is from the movie Tin Cup when he got the shanks and his swing felt like an unfolding lawn chair. That was my catching. Awkward at best, if I was able to get to the ball, and I simply missed the ball more than once. I'm surprised Skip didn't pull me sooner than he did, and that was in the sixth. Somehow, we still won 9-7. Not our best showing, but a win is a win.

Kristina

I get to Sherry's to find her and Michelle already sitting in front of the TV watching the pregame. It's funny to see the teacher and student situation with Michelle as the student, she's always the one who knows everything. It must be killing her not knowing baseball, but she'll probably know it better than the rest of us soon. They're discussing the lineup and the impact of the order on the game. I hear them starting with Chase because he's leading off.

"Cross is perfect at lead off because he has the speed and we want him on the bases. Speed matters because he can outrun the ball when a grounder gets hit or he bunts. It's also a benefit for stealing bases, which he has proven with his record of stolen bases," Sherry goes on about my guy.

"His strong, long legs and coordination give him a significant speed advantage. Sometimes these long-legged guys don't have the control. Chase has excellent control," I chime in.

"Perv," Michelle interjects. "Though I do like the dirty uniform and he always seems to get a very dirty uniform."

"That's mostly the stealing and some of the sliding across the outfield to get the ball," Sherry says shaking her head at out interaction. "I'm a bit surprised Mason is hitting second. I suspect they will be moving him toward the clean up spot. He's been coming into his own with his hitting." She turns to Michelle, "That's a good thing. He's getting better and that's a sign of longevity in this game. There's always someone better waiting for the chance to take your spot in the lineup."

The game is starting and Chase is at bat. The first two pitches are balls outside and on the third pitch he smacks it fair up the first base line. The first baseman misses the ball and it bounces off the outfield wall before the right fielder can get to it. Chase is showing us a great example of his long legs and speed. He's turned up to full speed and running. I can see him watching the coaches and trusting their signs, not worrying about the ball or wasting time looking for it himself. He rounds first and second without concern and dives for third, sliding in hot and hooking the base with his foot to maintain contact. Sherry cheers for him and claps. I join her, getting to yell for my guy. I smile uncontrollably at the ability to yell for him freely and the sense of pride that runs through me knowing he's my man. Michelle and Sherry both look at me and smile, like I'm finally getting it. Maybe I am. Maybe I've known longer than any of them have had a clue and I'm good at hiding it.

Mason is up to bat and takes four balls in a row for a walk. "He's starting to get at bats like this because of his hitting. Teams don't want him to connect, but they don't want to give him the intentional walk because they know he won't swing for it out of the zone." Sherry gets this expression on her face that I've only ever seen when she's with Rick, "There's my Rick walking to the batter's box." She beams and yells, "Let's go Seno!" He swings his bat and stands ready for the pitch. The first pitch is low and inside, "See that? They are trying to back him up off the plate." The second pitch is placed the same and he doesn't move. "That's it, my king! Hold your ground!" The third pitch looks like a curve ball that lost its drop and his bat connects with a clean pop. "Yes! Run, baby!" Sherry cheers him on. "Home run! Woooo!" She puts her hand to her belly and smiles, baby must be cheering her daddy on, too. Seno scores, knocking in Mason.

CHAPTER TWENTY-FOUR

Chase

The team gets checked into the hotel and we all plan to meet in the bar. Seno and I get to our room, get our things unpacked and check our phones. He immediately calls Sherry and stretches out on his bed, settling in for what looks like a long call. I have messages and they're not all from Kristina.

Text from Sherry - Kristina and Michelle are here watching the game with me. It's fun.
Text from Sherry - Kristina says she's being stupid and she can't help it. I'm working on it.
Text from Kristina - Thank you for the jersey :) It was left hanging on my cubicle waiting for me before I left the stadium today.
Text to Kristina - :) I didn't want to get in trouble for sending you stuff to the control booth
Text from Kristina - You did good. You would've been in trouble if you called me at the stadium.
Text to Kristina - Don't tell me to be with other chicks and you won't have that problem.
Text to Kristina - Are you still at Sherry's? Want to talk on the phone? I want to hear your voice, Sweetness.
Text from Kristina - Michelle is driving us home right now. I'll call you when we get home, okay?
Text to Kristina - I'm looking forward to it. <3

Seno is obviously happy to stay right where he is and doesn't care if he goes to the bar or not. I'd rather be on the phone with my girl, too. I've never felt like that before. I've always picked on the guys that did it and dragged them out to the bar anyway. Besides, I got enough ribbing in the club house today about my hickeys. I order us dinner from room service and change into a T-shirt and sweatpants. It's kind of nice to relax and hang out in the room. Seno and I always used to room together, so it's like old times except now we both have chicks to talk to. Back then, neither one of us had a girl. I like having him as a roommate, and I finally understand why he spends so much time with Sherry. I get it, I want to be with Kristina, too. I thumb through the magazine in the room while I wait for Kristina to call and see an ad for an artisan chocolatier in San Francisco, so I go on their website and have a box of chocolate candies sent to her. I check out the options, choosing a box that is all milk chocolate, none of them have anything fruity and about half of the box has caramel. I have it gift wrapped and include a card that says "Sweets for my Sweetness." That's when my phone rings, "Hello?"

"Hi, baby." Her sweet voice coming to me through the phone is heaven to my ears. I love that she calls me baby.

"Hey, Sweetness. How was your day?"

"Good. I'm sorry about my text. My automatic defense mechanism kicks in. The thing is that every relationship I've had, ended. I'm afraid of getting hurt again. But, I really don't want you with anyone else. Only me, Chase." Her words cut right through me and my heart rolls over in my chest like a puppy that wants its tummy rubbed more.

"They were all idiots and didn't know what they had when they had you, Kristina. Besides, those relationships had to end otherwise you wouldn't have been available for me. I feel like a fool because I miss you so much and we only spent a couple days together."

"I guess that's true. I miss you, too. It was a great couple of days." I hear her happiness and daydreamy attitude at thoughts of our time together. "I love your little place on the beach, it's perfect. I think you're what makes it perfect." Fuck me, she kills me.

"I wish I was there with you, Sweetness. I'd show you how much you mean to me."

She giggles, "Tell me."

"I'm better with actions than I am with words."

"Then tell me what your actions would be."

Huh, "I want to hold you close to me and kiss you, until you can feel everything I feel for you." I remember the morning and take a deep breath. "I like waking up with you in my bed, with your arm around me and you using me as your pillow. I like holding you all night long, you between my arms, your hair silky against my skin and the sweet sounds you make while you sleep. No, Kristina, I'll never hurt you. I'll always protect you." I feel like I'm falling as I say the words, knowing that I mean them and realizing the truth.

We talk on the phone until room service delivers dinner and then call back to talk more after we eat. I can hear Seno questioning Sherry about how she feels, making sure she isn't overdoing it, and telling her how much he loves her and misses her. Kristina and I mostly giggle on the phone, still getting to know each other and not wanting to say the wrong thing. Making sure I don't tell her I love her too soon, and I don't know if that's what this feeling is or not, all I know is that I've never felt it before and I want to be with her all the time. The end of our phone call feels weird, like we both want to say more and neither of us do. It doesn't matter. We spent time together on the phone being together and that's good.

Kristina

I love the sound of his voice, it's deep and comforts me. Our phone call reminds me of being a teenager and spending hours on the phone with my boyfriend. Sweet and giggly. I'm never like that anymore. Except, Chase makes it okay. I block out the fact that the guy I was on the phone with back then dumped me and had probably been cheating on me the whole time we were together. That's been over for years. I was young and didn't know any better. Chase will always protect me. I pull the blankets up over my head and pretend I'm in his fluffy bed waiting for him to find me again, replaying his sweet words in my head until I fall asleep happy.

Chase

Road Trip Day 2: Wednesday - Game 2 in San Francisco

The game went well, mostly because I wasn't in the lineup. That's not a good thing. I need to figure out how to get this under control to keep my spot in the lineup. Seals won 6-1. I learned that Kristina really isn't a morning person and doesn't get out of bed any earlier than she has to. I also learned that I love to hear her voice when she wakes up in the morning, it gave me wood. As grumpy as she was, she was still hazy with sleep when my phone call woke her up and if I wasn't sharing a room with Seno, I'd probably have stroked myself. She sent me a couple of text messages throughout the day and we talked on the phone after the game.

Text to Kristina - What toppings do you like on your pizza?
Text to Kristina - What is your favorite restaurant?
Text to Kristina - What's your favorite song?
Text from Kristina - Bacon, sun-dried tomatoes, basil, and garlic
Text from Kristina - I'm not sure I have a favorite. I like to try new places all the time. Usually it's more about what's convenient. Coffee Shops are a creature comfort for me.
Text from Kristina - Like my all time favorite song or my favorite right now?
Text to Kristina - Both
Text from Kristina - My all time favorite is "Just Can't Get Enough" by Depeche Mode.
Text from Kristina - Right now I love "Dive" by Ed Sheeran, I think it's Sherry's fault.
Text from Kristina - Is there a song that makes you think of me?
Text from Kristina - What's your favorite thing to eat?
Text from Kristina - What's your favorite color?
Text to Kristina - There are a few songs that make me think of you.
Text from Kristina - What are they? All of them.
Text to Kristina - "Feels Like the First Time" by Foreigner.
Text to Kristina - "Just Like Heaven" by the Cure.
Text to Kristina - "Won't Stop" by OneRepublic.
Text to Kristina - "Turn It Up" by The Wrecks.
Text to Kristina - Pizza
Text to Kristina - I really like the blue color in my bedroom, but lately I find I'm fond of the warm green I see when I look into your eyes.

She had an oversized hoodie with Cross and the number

17 on the back of it left at her cubicle, she told me she loved it and felt like it was hugging her. She even sent me a picture of her wearing it and nothing else. I managed not to get in trouble today and she didn't tell me to be with another girl, so I think that's progress.

Kristina

I never thought I'd say this about a guy, but I miss him. I love how he leaves presents for me. He doesn't have to do that. I want to be with him and I'd be happy to have him in a small apartment alone even if he wasn't a baseball player. I don't care if he has money or any of the rest of it. He's all that matters.

The days while the team is away are standard, full of basic prep duties and nothing exciting. It's an early game and a short day for me. I see the lineup and there's no Cross. I guess everyone needs a day off. I wish we could spend our time off together. I wish his arms were around me right now.

Chase

Road Trip Day 3: Thursday - Game 3 in San Francisco

Luckily, I was back in the lineup. I hated being away from Kristina and not playing. What's the point? We swept the series, winning three out of three games. I hit two home runs, and brought in five of my teammates to score—that's 7 runs batted in. Every single one of us got at least one hit. I'm not usually a home run hitter, but the ball connected with my bat effortlessly. I didn't realize I was a triple away from a cycle until I reviewed my stats after the game. We won 14-2, a total massacre. It was awesome. The only thing that would've made it better is if she was here to celebrate with me. Woah! Who am I? Dude, be cool and give it time. She's yours.

I want to call Kristina in the morning again, but decide not to poke the tiger.

Text to Kristina - Good Morning, Sweetness. I don't to want to wake you up again. Let me know when you can talk.
Text from Kristina - You can always call me. :)

I call her and we talk about plans for the day. She's going to Sherry's after work to bake and I hope they save some for me. The game is earlier than normal because it's a getaway day and the team flies to Houston after the game today. One of the reasons I want to talk to her, in case it's too late later. But, that's been vetoed. She wants me to call her either way, no matter how late.

Text to Kristina - What are your favorite flowers?

Text to Kristina - What's the first thing you want to do when I get back?

Text to Kristina - Is there a song that makes you think of me?

Text from Kristina - Daisies

Text from Kristina - 2 songs... "I Want To Hold Your Hand" and "Dive"

Text from Kristina - Right now, I want you to hold me all night and let me spend the night with you. This could change though.

Text to Kristina - I've been hoping you would stay over with me again. I want to hold you every night.

Text from Kristina - Which side of the bed do you prefer to sleep on?

Text from Kristina - What's your favorite home cooked meal?

Text from Kristina - What's the first thing you want to do when you get back?

Text to Kristina - Left Side, closest to the bathroom and the bedroom door.

Text to Kristina - I love pasta and pot roast.

Text to Kristina - Hug you tight and smell your hair.

Text from Kristina - You might get tired of me staying over. I'd invite you to my place, but my roommate has already proven that your place is easier.

Text to Kristina - I'll never get tired of you. I want you with me every night.

Kristina

I never get two short days in a row. It's nice and the fact that I've been sleeping well the last couple of nights makes it better. I'm going to Sherry's right after work for baseball and baking.

> Text from Sherry - I used up some of my baking supplies. I needed cookies. Don't tell Rick I was baking. I only made a small batch for me and the baby.
> Text to Sherry - I'll pick up on my way. What do you need?
> Text from Sherry - Eggs, chocolate chips, peanut butter chips, unsalted butter.
> Text from Sherry - Tamales from the delicatessen would be great, too. :)

I laugh knowing it's a pregnant request.

> Text to Sherry - I'm sure I can manage all of that.
> Text to Sherry - I'll pick up on my way.

I walk into Sherry's with her requested supplies and tamales. The game is already on and she's focused on it with her hand resting on her belly. I put away the groceries and meet her in front of the TV with tamales. She nods at me in appreciation and we enjoy some baseball talk while we spend time with our guys. It's funny, I never thought of it as spending time together when I watch the game until Sherry said it. She's right. In the stadium with them or not, it's experiencing part of their life with them and making it our own. We cheer for them and I don't miss Chase so much when I watch him playing. I love the smile on his face when he looks up to see the ball he hit go out of the park.

I knew he was special, but it may be more than I expected. I want to be what he wants.

Sherry tells me about how she met Rick and how everything went so fast. She's happy and wouldn't change a thing. She never wanted to get married and never considered having a child, but Rick changed those things for her. There's nothing she wants more than the life she has now.

The game is over and it's time to bake. Sherry has a stool in her kitchen where she sits and gives me directions. She goes through everything step by step and I make chocolate chip cookies. I clean up after myself as I go and when I put the cookies in the oven, she instructs me on how to make brownies. It's not hard, but I need to follow instructions and Sherry does everything from memory. I make notes in my phone as we go, so I can try to replicate the process on my own later. The kitchen smells delicious and I made it that way. I can't wait to bake for Chase, I'm leaving these with Sherry.

Kristina

I get home for the night and I haven't heard from Chase. I call him, but he doesn't answer, "Hey baby, I'm home from Sherry's and going to bed. You were great tonight. Please call me. I miss you."

Chase

We land in Houston late. We had to wait on the plane and getting to the hotel took longer than it should've. By the time I call her, she's already asleep and I knew she would be because of the message she left me. I was hoping to hear about baking and get to talk sweet to her when I climbed into bed for the night. She did answer the phone in a quiet voice and I could tell she was sleeping, so I talked sweet to her, "Hey Sweetness. I wish I were there with you. I want to hold you and kiss you. I want to feel your body against mine, our hearts beating together." She made some sweet little noises. "Sleep and remember you're my girl. Goodnight, Sweetness." I made a kiss noise at her through the phone and hung up.

Kristina

I wake up early and feel spoiled as I put on my new Seals T-shirt that says "Cross" on the back. I take a couple selfies, front and back, and send them to Chase. His name on my shirt and cutoff short shorts only covering my ass. Nothing I've ever done before Chase. But this morning I'm happy and nothing can dim the light glowing in my heart. I'm proud to wear his name and waiting impatiently for tonight's game, so I can watch him play and spend some time with him. He's my guy and I'm his. I'm falling for him.

Chase

Road Trip Day 4: Friday - Game 1 in Houston

Friday morning we didn't have practice and didn't have to be at the stadium until noon. We slept in. I woke up to pictures of Kristina wearing the T-shirt with my name and number on the back, eating chocolates and texts. Fuck she's hot in my number.

Text from Kristina - Good morning, baby. :)
Text from Kristina - You don't need to keep giving me things.
Text from Kristina - The chocolates are delicious.
Text from Kristina - We'll talk about Houston and baking tonight.
Text from Kristina - Thank you for the shirt and candy... you really don't need to keep giving me things, but I do like it. :)
Text from Kristina - Which stadium do you like playing in the most?
Text from Kristina - Did you have pets when you were growing up?
Text from Kristina - Have you ever been in love?
Text to Kristina - What's your favorite thing to eat?
Text to Kristina - If you picked my walk up song, what would it be?
Text to Kristina - Did you pick media or is that just what the internship is for?
Text to Kristina - The stadium closest to you.
Text to Kristina - Yes. Two dogs, both Labs. My parents still have one of them.

I don't know how to answer her last question. This is not how I want her to find out I love her. If I say no, that means never and includes now. I don't want to tell her I don't love her, and honestly I think it would be a lie. At the same time, if I say yes, she'll ask me when or who or something. Can I blame it on the dog?

Text from Kristina - I picked Media. It's what I want to do.
Text from Kristina - Comfort food like waffles, pizza, stew, pasta.
Text from Kristina - Walk up song is serious business. It needs to have some intensity to it and some type of meaning. It needs to get you pumped up and send a message to the other team. I love the sentiment behind "I Want To Hold Your Hand," but I think it should be harder rock. Maybe even punk. I need to think about this one.
Text from Kristina - You never answered the third question.
Text to Kristina - Yes, I was in love with my dog when she ran away.
Text from Kristina - I meant with a human being.
Text to Kristina - I don't know.
Text from Kristina - If you don't know, then who does?
Text to Kristina - I meant that I don't know what that kind of love feels like. I just know how I feel.
Text from Kristina - Oh
Text to Kristina - What does love feel like? Is it the sparks and the fireworks? Is it always wanting to be together?
Text to Kristina - Are you asking me how I feel about you? That's not something I'm going to text you about, Sweetness. You know how I feel about you when we're together. You know I miss you and want to hold you.

Text from Kristina - Okay. Chase, you know love when you feel it. It could be the sparks and fireworks, or it could be something else.
Text to Kristina - When your heart rolls over in your chest helpless and bare because you need someone and want someone so much that it physically hurts?
Text from Kristina - I think it depends on what exactly you need and want.
Text to Kristina - Or, maybe it's just the person and you take whatever you can get just to be with them.
Text from Kristina - *jaw drop*

We go to the stadium and do our workouts. The team is in a good mood because we got the chance to sleep in and relax. The game is going to be a pitcher's duel between Houston's ace and Rhett Clay. I probably won't even see a ball in center field.

Text from Kristina - I'm watching the game with Sherry tonight… Make it a win! ;)
Text to Kristina - Anything for you, Sweetness.
Text to Kristina - Make sure Sherry is relaxing and not doing much, okay?
Text from Kristina - I'm on that… picking up dinner on my way.
Text to Kristina - You're the best. Beautiful inside and out, Sweetness. <3

Walking out onto the field at game time I point my gloved hand at Seno and wink, "Make it a win!" as I stretch and warm up. He smiles and nods. I can see him physically relax at the words and think that I need to say them before every game until Sherry's here.

The game was horrible. It was long, a test of endurance and patience. I caught myself staring at the stars while I was in the outfield, knowing she's closer than the stars and we'll be under them together soon. I need to stay focused and not let down time in the outfield get the best of me. All four of the balls that make it to the outfield land in my glove. Martin hit a double, knocking in me and Mason in the first inning, but Houston answers back in the second with a single and home run. We're tied at 2 in the second inning and it stays that way until the top of the ninth when I get to be the hero, hitting a home run and driving in Clay and Brandt. We win 5-2. Seno and Clay work the complete game together with precision, the relievers are thankful to get the night off.

Kristina

My day was crazy and all I could think about was Chase. I pick up Sherry's favorite tamales for dinner and get to her place in time for the second inning. I sit down in front of the TV with her and she starts in, obviously searching for something to distract her.

"So, how's things with Chase?"

Not sure how to answer, "Good. We haven't been able to talk much." I turn to her, "I bet you miss Rick."

"I do. I want to be there with him, but I know this is more important to both of us right now." She wraps her arms around her belly and offers a shaky smile.

I'm out of my zone here, but I want to be helpful, "I'm sure he misses you, too. He seems like a great guy."

"He is. He's perfect. I can't imagine being married to anyone else and I wouldn't want a family with anyone, but him." She rambles on, "Family is very important to him and I'm so happy to be giving him something he's wanted for so long. I still have to pinch myself to make sure this is my life. It's been such a roller coaster ride. I'm sure you are starting to see what the professional athlete world is like, being with Chase. You two are young, but when it's right it's right. I wish I'd met Rick sooner. I envy you meeting Chase so young. You two can do anything together and start your lives together."

I black out there for a minute listening to Sherry talk about my life with Chase. Suddenly all I can focus on is that she's pregnant, huge and uncomfortable. I flash back to mounting him bare and not caring about what might happen, simply needing him and having him was all that mattered. How could I be so stupid! I know he says he'll protect me, but he's still a guy. Damn it! I did it myself! It wasn't even him. He tried to stop it. I wanted more. I steer Sherry back to the game and try not to think about it. She needs calm company, I can be that for her tonight. We can cheer for our guys together.

CHAPTER TWENTY-FIVE

Chase

Seno and I have fallen into a routine, phone calls with our women and room service every night. We decide to stick with it since we're on a winning streak and you never fuck with a streak. I hesitate to even think the word streak because it could jinx it. It doesn't matter, we would be in our room and talking to our women even if we'd lost. We both change into sweatpants and dial our women at the same time.

"Hello?"

"Hey, Sweetness. I made it a win for you. Did you see my home run?"

"Yes, baby! It was a moon shot! We were both yelling at the TV!"

"Are you having fun baking and watching baseball with Sherry?"

"Yea, I'm staying with her tonight. Helping her get some things done that are hard for her and we're going to stay up and watch movies, because she's having a hard time sleeping." Her tone is different.

"Is something wrong? Are you okay?"

"Hold on a second."

Text from Kristina - She needs her Mom here or somebody. I don't know about this stuff. She's okay, but she's nervous and worried.

"Sorry, my friend was texting me."

"That was sly."

"I try."

I get Seno's attention across the room and signal for him to cover his phone, "Kristina's staying at your place tonight and thinks Sherry needs someone to stay with her that has more experience with pregnant stuff. Says she's okay, but looks nervous and worried." He nods at me and gives me a thumbs up.

"So, Sweetness, what did you bake? Did you have any surprises left for you at your desk today?"

"There was a baseball cap embroidered with your number on it in the regular team colors left for me today, thank you. I'm starting to feel like I'm getting a whole new wardrobe and everything has your name and number on it. Are you marking me?" She giggles.

"Yes. I want everyone to know you're mine. I'm proud to have you as mine and I don't want anyone else even thinking about having you." Fuck me, I'm starting to sound possessive like Seno. Maybe we shouldn't room together.

"Wow." Her breath hitched, "The way you said that gave me chills."

Fuck me, fuck me, fuck me, "It's simply the truth, Kristina. Good chills?"

"Very good chills." I can't help but smile. "I baked brownies and cookies. She said she'll show me more in the morning."

"Room service just got here. Let me call you back after we eat, okay? Or do you want to call me when you climb into bed, so I can tell you what I want?"

"I'll call you later, baby." I thought she was done. "Chase —I miss you, baby." She hangs up leaving me wishing that I could be with her right now. She misses me. It shouldn't make me feel good that she misses me, but it does. She fits, too. I mean, she belongs with me and fits the team dynamic. She's even helping Sherry, looking out for her and she doesn't have to do that. Shit, I was being selfish and killing to birds with one stone, thinking my girl would learn to bake and Sherry would have someone around—she took it to a whole different level. I love her heart.

Seno and I eat dinner while he calls Sam and she agrees to go stay with Sherry for a few days. I'm happy I ordered us a twelve pack of brews, we're going to need them this weekend. I turn on the TV and flip through channels, while the twelve pack disappears.

I'm stretched out on my bed, half asleep watching an action flick when my phone rings, "Hey, Sweetness."

"Hi, baby... What are you doing?"

"Seno and I are hanging in the room, tossing back some brews."

"Michelle says I have a big box from Amazon waiting for me at home. Do you know anything about that?"

"I guess that depends on what's in the box. Might be a delivery from somebody else."

"So, you did send me something? What is it?"

"You'll have to look for yourself, Sweetness." I don't know exactly what's in the box, Sherry did that part. I'd rather she be surprised anyway. I wouldn't tell her if I knew.

"You really don't need to keep sending me things."

"I want you to have things. I want you to have the appropriate team gear and things that you need. It makes me happy to give you things." I want to give you everything are the words going through my head and I realize my buzz may be getting the best of me. "So, are you curled up on the couch with a blanket?"

"Yes, and I'm lonely," playing with me in her sweet, soft girly voice.

"Oh, Sweetness, we can't have that. Close your eyes and let me make it better. I'm there with you right now. I lean over the back of the couch and kiss your cheek, your skin's so soft. You turn your head and look at me, I can only imagine the need in my eyes matches the need I find in yours. We claim each other's lips because we can't help it, we need the touch, the electrical contact. I wrap my arms around you and pick you up, bringing you close to my chest and holding you tight, never wanting to let you go. I carry you out to the balcony and you snag your blanket on the way. I sit down on the lounge chair under the night sky with you in my arms and get us both wrapped in the blanket. My hands hold you possessively because you're mine and I'm not going to share. I love the way your body fits perfectly against mine while I hold you and we look at the stars with the faint sound of the ocean in the background. The night sky is so dark that the stars shine and twinkle with more stars than you can imagine. The beauty of the night is breathtaking, but doesn't compare to my woman that I'm holding in my arms, my Kristina, my Sweetness. You make me warm all over. You make my heart beat faster. You make my pulse race. I want to hold you and protect you. You make me think things that I don't understand and want to say things that I know I shouldn't."

I'm interrupted by Seno throwing something at me and mouthing "Shut up! You're drunk!" at me.

I try to get my head straight. I don't even know what I was saying. "Sweetness, what would you do if you were here with me?" Seno gives me a thumbs up.

I hear a sweet sigh and I know she's falling asleep, "I want to be in your arms under the stars. Can't you be here with me under the stars?"

"Yes, my Sweetness. I'm with you under the stars. Tell me what you would do if I was there with you."

"My feet would be nestled between your legs. My arm stretched across your body and holding you at your waist. My head cuddled into your neck with my face resting on your chest. Relaxing to the sound and feel of your heartbeat. Absorbing your warmth and content being near you, I'd kiss your bare chest and move my hand up your torso to hold onto it. You'd kiss me on the forehead because it's the only place you could reach without disturbing our position. I feel tingles just being near you and I'm embarrassed by my attraction because I can't help myself as I lightly rub against your leg. I'm wet for you and I can't control it, when all I want is for you to keep holding me."

"I want to hold you, too, my Sweetness." I shouldn't, but... "Are you really wet for me right now, Sweetness?" No response. "If you're tired, I can let you go to sleep."

"I'm not ready yet. Um, maybe." That's a yes.

"Do you want to tell me about it?"

"Are you, uh, hard?"

"Trust me, as soon as you said wet I got hard."

She giggles and it makes it worse. Seno gets up and

stomps across the room, "Horndog," then locks himself in the bathroom and turns the shower on.

"How hard are you?"

"I thought you just wanted me to hold you."

"Mostly, but other things are good, too. Chase, baby, I want you bad."

"What do you want?"

"I want you to hold your cock and tell me how hard it is."

Oh fuck, "It's rock solid, thinking about you."

"I wish you were in me."

"Me, too... Sweetness, what are you wearing? I'm laying shirtless with my hand in my sweatpants."

"You should come out of those sweats and stroke yourself for me. I want to lick your cock and kiss it all over. You'd see my breasts bounce in the skimpy tank top I'm wearing and get a view straight down my shirt. You're so hard that I can only get half of you in my mouth and that's not good enough."

"No, my Sweetness deserves all of me. I pull you up to my lips and kiss you as you slide back onto my hard dick. Oh, Kristina, I can feel you on me and it's amazing."

"Stroke it like I'm on you, baby."

"Are you touching yourself, Sweetness? Please touch yourself. I would touch you and make you feel good if I was there. Do it for me, Sweetness. Reach your hand into your panties and feel how wet you are."

"Are you stroking your dick?"

"Yes, and imagining you on me. I want to make you come and I want to hear you. Find your spot, Sweetness, and rub it for me. Tell me how wet you are. Tell me how you feel."

"My panties are soaked, and I'm slick to the touch. So easy for you to slide in. I need you, Chase. Fuck, I'm falling for you."

"It's okay, Sweetness. I need you, too. Rub it and feel me

pushing into you. I'll always protect you, Kristina. Always you, Sweetness." I hear her whimper softly, sexy. I've heard it before and I know she's with me. "Feel how hard I am for you."

"I sit up straight and ride you hard because I can't help myself. Grinding against you at our connection. I touch our connection and feel how hard you are, filling me, stretching me. Oh!" Her tone changes.

"I'm here with you, Sweetness. You want to come?"

"Yes, oh yes, oh Chase."

"Rub it harder for me, faster, Sweetness. Don't stop, just don't stop. I want you on me. I want to push into you and feel you wet around me. I want you however I can get you." I'm getting close and start to lose my breath.

"Oh, Chase!"

"More, Sweetness. More. Don't stop. I won't stop, push it Sweetness. More."

"Chase!" I hear her cry out my name and whimper. I know the sound and it sets me off instantly.

I groan as I come, "Fuck, Sweetness. How do you do this to me? Oh, fuck... I'm still coming. Tell me you feel it. Tell me you want me in you. Tell me it's only you and me, Kristina."

There's only silence.

"Chase?"

"I'm here, Sweetness."

"I miss you, baby. It's only you and me."

I smile, "I miss you, too. I'm here to catch you if you're falling. I'll always protect you. I promise you're safe with me. I promise. I'm still holding you, Sweetness. All night long." We hang up and sleep, unable to keep our eyes open. My girl. All I can think about and I dream about her now, too.

Kristina

Five minutes ago I was listening to his voice and couldn't keep my eyes open. Now, I can't sleep. I can't believe I told him that I'm falling for him. Shit! This is how I end up pregnant and the size of a house! Plus, bonus! It will be my own fault! I'm the one that slides onto his cock without warning and doesn't want to get off of him. I can't be falling for him. This isn't part of my plan. I need to have a job and be self-sufficient. Being dependent on a man, any man, not an option. The tone in his voice tonight owned me. New, sincere and possessive, it shot right through me. I want him so bad that I had phone sex and fuck if I didn't start it! Yep. This is my end. The life I want goes out the window. I'm controlled by a man. This can't happen. Oh, and his possessive words. He wants us to be living together? He said he wants me in his bed every night. He said it's only me and him. He wants to be like them. He wants to move me in, get married and knock me up. I can't do this. I don't want to get hurt again. He said he'll protect me and I believe him. I believe every word he says.

I get home after no sleep and find the huge Amazon box waiting for me. It's full of everything for baking. Mixer with all the attachments, bowls, measuring cups, everything I could possibly need for baking and not the cheap stuff. I walk into my room to find all of my new Seals wardrobe hanging everywhere. Everything says Cross and has a big 17 on it. He can't buy me and mark me. He doesn't get to own me.

No, I can't do this. I want him. I think I love him, but this isn't me. It's too much.

CHAPTER TWENTY-SIX

Chase

Road Trip Day 5: Saturday - Game 2 in Houston

I wake up thinking about Kristina and I'm somehow satisfied from last night. I reach for my phone to call my girl and tell her good morning, but Seno yells at me from across the room, "Pervert! Keep that shit in your pants and under control. No more beer nights for you. Fuck, at least tell me to take a shower or something before you have phone sex and wack it."

"Sorry, it was her fault. I'll warn you if it happens again. Dude, she says the hottest things. Fuck me." I relax in bed thinking about our conversation, "Hey, she told me she's falling for me."

Seno stares at me, "Is that what you want? Just her? No more girls everywhere waiting for you to fuck them? No more nights with the twins? No more walking away the next day, without even knowing their name?"

"I want her. I know it sounds stupid. I need her. I want to protect her. I told her I'm here to catch her if she falls. I promised I wouldn't hurt her. I mean it. Dude, I understand why you want Sherry with you. The one special one that's yours, that you can share with and just be you, everything is better with them being in the same room or sitting in the stadium during a game."

Seno smiles, "You need to do whatever makes you happy and keeps you that way. Don't tell her you love her over the phone or text or anything stupid, do it in person with no alcohol in your system."

"I can do that."

I have pictures of a mixer and baking stuff from Kristina.

Text from Kristina - You need to stop.

Text from Kristina - I mean, good morning. Thank you for the baking tools and the outrageously expensive mixer with attachments that cost as much as my rent.

Text from Kristina - Sorry, please stop sending me things.

Text from Kristina - I don't think I can do this.

Woah! What the fuck happened? I call her, but she doesn't answer.

Text to Kristina - Good morning.

Text to Kristina - Please answer your phone or call me.

Text to Kristina - I thought you would like it because you wanted to learn how to bake.

Text to Kristina - You're still going to have things left for you at your cubicle everyday until I get back.

Text to Kristina - I'm sorry. Tell me what to do here.

Text to Kristina - You said you're falling for me. This doesn't make any sense.

Text to Kristina - I'll never hurt you. I mean it.

Text to Kristina - We won't end like the rest of them.

Text to Kristina - Don't run scared. Please. I need you.

I turn to Seno, "She froze me out and won't respond. Fuck!"

"Give her a chance to respond and see what happens. You can send her flowers or something if you want."

"No, she told me to stop sending her things."

"Concentrate on baseball. Only five more games until we go home. She'll come around."

We head over to the stadium early to work out and I need to run it off. I need to run her out of my system. Maybe I need to find a hook up tonight and forget about her. But, that's not what I want. Fuck. I want her. I keep checking my phone, but there's nothing new. I've run over ten miles and already spent too much time in the batting cage. I walk into the clubhouse and hang out with the guys, listening to music and playing cards. Trying to get through the day without my Sweetness.

Mason walks in, "What the fuck did you do? Michelle said Kristina freaked out and took off."

"Where'd she go? She's not at the stadium working?" I hear the worry in my voice.

Mason watches Seno drop his head and shake it, "Uh, I'm sure everything is fine."

Seno comments, "Mason, you're an idiot. See if you can find out where she went."

Text to Carter - Can you find out what time Kristina is working today? And if she's there?

Text from Carter - On it

Text from Carter - She called in sick.

Text to Sherry - Any idea where Kristina is?

Text to Kristina - At least tell me you're okay.

Text from Kristina - I'm okay. Please leave me alone.

Text to Kristina - I will do anything you want, except leave you alone.

Text from Sherry - Yes

Text to Sherry - Where is she?

Text from Sherry - She doesn't want you to know.

Text to Sherry - Can you help me? I don't know what to do. I need to know she's safe.

Text from Sherry - She's safe.

I'm completely lost and it's almost time for the game to start. I go through the motions, get ready and go out on the field to stretch and warm up. I don't know what to do, since she won't talk to me. I need to be in the same place with her and bring her back to me, tell her to stop running. I know that's all this is. She's running away because she's scared of getting hurt again. I guess from her view I'm not the best bet, but I'm not that guy. I was, but meeting her saved me. She saved me and made me realize what I was missing. She may be the only one that can save me. Why won't she let me save her?

I try to get the game started right. I walk through the

dugout clapping and say "Let's make it a win!" I'm first at bat and as I stand in the on deck circle swinging my bat, I wonder if she's somewhere watching me. The cameraman is watching me and I look directly into the camera as if I'm looking at Kristina, pat my heart and point at her. I step up to the plate and dig in with my cleats. The plan is the same as it always is, get on base and let the team bring me around to score. Keep it simple. Get a base hit. Take a walk. Whatever. Just get on base. It takes ten pitches, but I get the walk and making the pitcher throw ten pitches to the first batter is in our favor. Use the starter up and get into the bullpen early. Mason is at bat next and communicating with me. I steal second successfully and I'm in scoring position with no outs. Mason hits a double off the right field wall and I score. That's how we play baseball. We scored 3 in the first inning. One out in the bottom of the sixth inning and a fly ball is heading toward left center field. I run to make the catch and Simms is running toward me from left field. I call him off because I've got the ball, but he keeps coming at me. I catch the ball as he's grabbing for it and take his elbow to my face, knocking me backwards to the ground. I roll with it into a backwards somersault to help lessen the impact and somehow manage to hold onto the ball for the out. I sit up and Skip waves at me to see if I'm okay, I wave him off. I refuse to look like I'm hurt, even if I am. I'm staying in this game and we're winning. I'm not going on the disabled list and I'm not showing any signs of injury to anybody that might be watching me play. The last thing I need is another reason for Kristina to not want to be with me. Nobody is taking my spot on the team or getting anywhere near my girl, and she's still my girl. I just need to get to her and everything will be fine. Seno hit a homer in the 6th inning and a double in the 9th, driving in four runs. The streak continues, Seals win 7-1.

Kristina

It's stupid, but I find Sherry's is my safe place and I've taken up baking to keep busy. She suggested it, said it helps when she's nervous. She also said she wouldn't mind some cookies. Sam is visiting until the team gets back, so they turn the game on and cheer together. It makes sense, both of them are close to Rick. I'm trying the recipes she taught me on my own without her assistance and watching the game out of the corner of my eye, trying not to pay attention to Chase when he's at bat.

Sherry checks on me, "How are you doing?"

"I think I've got the cookies down. You'll be the test when you taste them."

She examines me, "Everything else okay, too?"

Sam yells out louder than expected when Kris Martin gets a hit and I let it distract me from Sherry's question.

She doesn't push me, "You're always welcome here. You know where to find me if you want to talk." She starts to walk away, but turns and speaks quietly over her shoulder, "Don't give up so easily, things have a way of working out. Cookies smell good."

I don't know how to make this work out. Sam yells again when Kris comes around to score. "What's with cheering for Martin?"

"It's been this way since I met Sam. I think he's her baseball fantasy," she laughs as she goes back to the game in time for Seno to bat.

Baking is my escape tonight. I don't want to think about my life.

Chase

Seno and I get back to our room and he directs me, "Get changed. We're going out with the team. Sam has Sherry and I've been told to go get wasted. You should, too. Hurry up!" He makes a quick check in call to his woman and he's ready in less than five minutes. "Why aren't you ready? Let's go."

"I'm going to stay here."

"I don't know what part of this you don't understand. You're going if I have to drag you with me. Not trying to get you hooked up or anything, I get it. But, we're going out and we're getting wasted. It's a bad decision with an early game tomorrow, and I'm not going to get away with those much longer. Work with me here and get your ass ready."

I start to argue, but realize that he needs this and no matter what, he's always had my back. Time to get wasted.

Seno leads me out of the hotel and we walk a couple blocks to the bar where the team is already drinking. The guys are doing shots and we need to catch up. We order a couple plates of appetizers, a round for the team and a couple extra shots each for us. It's a whiskey night. I know better. Whiskey nights always get me into trouble. I check my phone and it's still radio silence from Kristina. I want to talk to her and that means I need to get rid of my phone or I'll drunk dial her. It would also be a good idea to have a keeper. I know I'm an adult, but me and whiskey usually ends up me and at least one chick in my bed. I haven't tested this since I stopped fucking every chick that wanted me and the fact that Kristina is ignoring me isn't helping. Maybe I should text her before I give up my phone for the night or something. It doesn't matter, she's not going to call me tonight. Fuck it.

Text to Kristina - Seno dragged me out to the bar to get wasted. I'd rather be talking to you, but he insisted and you don't want to talk to me. Maybe wasted will be a good thing.

Three shots in and I'm feeling pretty good. Seno and I have been going shot for shot. We haven't drunk like this since before he met Sherry. It was always a challenge to keep up with him and I refuse to give up. I'm guessing that maybe he hasn't been drinking as much and this is my chance to out drink him. Mason has our backs to make sure we get back to our room safely with no women, he's even holding my phone to keep me from drunk dialing anyone. I think he's entertained by the drinking display and obvious intent to get wasted. It's a different side of Seno and very few of us have seen it. It's always been a few of us drinking when this happens, not the whole team. I mean, of course I'd drink regardless and go for luck, but I was being a kid that knew a chick would be waiting at his hotel room door to fuck him, too. The next two shots arrive together and they're doubles. We shoot them both quickly and hang out with the team.

Mason's looking at a phone and I'm hopeful that Kristina has made contact, but he sees me looking and shakes me off. Most of the team is in pretty good condition. Things are a little hazy for me around the edges. Seno stands up to go to the head and he's wavering, or maybe that's my eyesight. I'd say we both achieved wasted. He turns back to me and smiles, "My daughter's name is going to be Elle. Don't tell her it's because I like doing it in elevators, okay?"

"No problem, dude." He turns and walks away, and I know he's wasted. I smile at the information he provided. Who knew Seno was a kinky bastard! It makes me happy to know he isn't all business like he wants everybody to think.

Sherry got extra points with me, too. Lucky dude, got the right woman and she puts out in elevators. I'm happy for him.

It hits me like a brick that I may never talk to Kristina again. I don't really believe that will happen. She works at the stadium. But, the reality is she could be done with me. My chest hurts. I don't think she was using me. I don't think I was a notch on her bedpost or a player conquest to add to her collection. She's not that kind of chick. Yeah, she was at the party in Arizona, but she was working at the stadium there, too. And, she left me hard and wanting, she didn't fuck me. No, she's not that type of girl. Kristina's real. I'm worried about her. I promised I wouldn't hurt her and now I'm wondering if somehow I did without knowing it. I never want to hurt her. I wonder if she knows how much she's hurting me right now. This must be love. I've heard it's a blessing and a curse. Shit, I've seen it. If you love someone it gives them the ability to hurt you. The more love you have for them, the more they can hurt you. Yeah, I love her and I'm in deep. I hope there isn't another dude, that would kill me. I stand up to walk over to Mason and I'm drunk off my ass. I lean on him, "Does anybody know where Kristina is? Is she okay? Is there another dude?"

Mason gives me a painful grin, "I haven't heard anything about another dude. All I can get out of Michelle is that she's safe. I don't get it either."

"Ask for an update." I need more.

"I don't think it's that kind of a thing." He looks at me, not liking where this is going.

"Please." I look at the floor. "I need her to be okay. Do you think she'll talk to me again?"

"Man, you're drunk. Maybe we should get you back to the hotel."

"Just get her on the phone with me." I feel like I'm begging.

"No, that's why you gave me your phone. No drunk dialing." Mason stands his ground.

He's right. I go back to my seat at the table and nibble on the appetizers. Seno comes back and almost misses the chair when he sits down.

Mason comes to us, "She's just a chick. There's always another one. Maybe we should get you guys back to sleep it off."

Seno adds his two cents, "No, she's not just a chick. This fool's totally in love with her. He's not getting over it any time soon." He didn't tell Mason, he announced it loudly to the whole bar in his drunk tone. Fuck me. There were chicks hanging on me within seconds, all offering to help me get over her or show me that they were better for me anyway.

"I'm not interested." I get up and leave the bar. I don't know what direction I'm walking. I don't know which way to get to the hotel. I'm wasted and I hoped that would help numb me, if it's helping then I don't want to be sober because this still hurts. The lights all have a glow around them. The sky is dark and cloudy, not like when I have Kristina and the sky is clear with bright shining stars. I feel empty. I want to call her, but Mason still has my phone. I feel better getting outside and away from everybody. I wish she were with me. The other problem is that I don't have a clue where I am. I see a woman walking toward me and for a few seconds I think it's Kristina. I don't know how she found me. It makes sense because she saved me before, so why wouldn't she find me when I'm lost? Well, she's in San Diego and I'm in Houston, that's why not and I can see that it's not her as the figure walks right by me. I start walking back the direction I came from, thinking maybe I'll find the bar or one of the guys from the team. Maybe I can get another drink before I go back to my room. Nothing looks familiar. I keep walking because I didn't walk that far, or I didn't think I did. I see Mason walking toward me.

"Where did you take off to? You were gone quick and I couldn't find you. Let's get back to the hotel."

"Maybe we could get another drink first."

"You don't need it. Let's get you back. I already got Seno to bed."

"Can I have my phone?"

"No drunk dialing?"

"No drunk dialing." He hands me my phone and a text pops through. He looks at my face, ready to grab the phone back away from me.

"Maybe we should just turn it off for the night and you should go to bed." He tries to slide the phone away from me, but I don't let him.

> Text from Kristina - I wasn't looking for a ball player and I don't think I can be in a relationship with one. My heart has been broken too many times and I'm not strong enough for you. Goodbye, Chase.

Damn it! Damn it! Damn it! I want to throw my phone to the ground and watch it splatter into a thousand little pieces.

> Text to Kristina - No. This isn't goodbye. You are strong enough. You're everything.
> ***Error this number is not accepting your messages***

FUCK! She dumped me in a text and blocked me!

To @Kristeeeeeena - This isn't goodbye. You are strong enough. You're everything.

To @Kristeeeeeena - I'm not letting you go. I'm coming for you.

To @Kristeeeeeena - We're not over. You're still my Sweetness.

"Call Michelle and see if Kristina is there with her." I stare at Mason waiting.

"I can't do that. I'm not putting Michelle in that position with her roommate. I'll call her and let you know if I can find out anything. I know this is killing you."

"Then do it and get a picture of her if you can."

Mason shakes his head and dials. He starts talking to Michelle and finally gets to asking about Kristina. We get to my room and he directs me to go inside while he finishes his conversation, so I leave the door blocked for him to keep the door from locking. I hear him end his call and he comes into my room. "Michelle says that Kristina's a wreck. I was able to confirm that there isn't another guy. Something about a phone conversation you had with her last night, baseball, and Sherry. Honest, it didn't make any sense to me."

I get that we had a pretty deep conversation last night. I know because I felt our connection, too. Was I supposed to tell her I'm falling for her, too? Baseball is my job, I love it and it pays well, but it does have me on the road about ninety days a year, players get hurt and we get traded like commodities. Sherry? I don't get that part. Maybe Sherry was pushing me on her? I know Sherry thinks I'm a great guy. Maybe she was a mean baking coach? Maybe Sherry is in an overly emotional state, missing her man and Kristina decided it's too hard? I don't understand women.

I look at Mason, "Thanks for watching out for me tonight,

dude. I appreciate it. Please let me know if you get any more info on Kristina. If you can, please make sure she knows I'm still hers. I'm not giving up on her. I really do love her, Seno wasn't just being a dick. I'm going to tell her when we get home, even if she doesn't want me." Mason pats me on the back and takes off for his room.

Now, I'm sad and my chest still hurts. I admit that I love her and it makes me hurt more. I'm going to tell her when I get back to San Diego. It doesn't matter if she wants me or not, she needs to know. If it's my turn to have a broken heart, so be it. She deserves to know that I love her.

I call room service and order breakfast to be delivered, to make sure we wake up in time to get to the stadium and have coffee waiting for us. It's going to be a challenge and I won't be surprised if one or both of us get scratched from the lineup tomorrow. I'm feeling too much, so I raid the mini bar and throw back three bottles of whiskey. Seno is completely passed out. I open my laptop looking for a distraction and end up watching videos on youtube. Just when I feel like I might be able to sleep, a string of Foreigner videos starts to play and the whiskey has taken control.

Kristina

It's the middle of the night and my Twitter is blowing up. I've been tagged on a few posts and they just keep going. I check notifications knowing I don't have to respond and curious about what's going on. It's Chase. He's posting videos and directing them to me. I know I shouldn't, but I can't help myself and I go watch them as he posts them. No words in his posts, simply the link and video. A string of Foreignor,"Feels

Like the First Time," "I Want to Know What Love Is," "Waiting For a Girl Like You," "I Don't Want to Live Without You," and "Say You Will," followed by "Just Like Heaven," "Dive," and "Turn It Up." "I Want to Hold Your Hand" is last and the only one with a message, it says 'please, this is all I want.' His fans are commenting on the tweets, but he's not responding. I'm staying invisible, but that doesn't keep the tears from rolling silently down my cheeks as I watch every single video and realize he's hurting, too.

CHAPTER TWENTY-SEVEN

Chase

Road Trip Day 6: Sunday - Game 3 in Houston

I wake up, startled by room service banging on the door. I sit up and the room spins. Fuck me. Seno speaks, "I got it."

"I ordered last night to make sure we got up and had coffee. I knew it would be bad this morning."

"Good thinking. What were you thinking when you drank the mini bar?" With a chastising tone.

"Fuck me. Dude, the room is spinning." Room service wheels in a cart with breakfast and coffee. Seno tosses the waste basket on my bed and his timing is impeccable. I block rather than catch because everything is moving and blow chunks into the waste basket, as if it was on queue. Seno appears to be just fine and appreciating that I ordered breakfast.

"You need to get it together. We need to get to the stadium." He looks at me funny, "What were you doing with your laptop in bed last night? Surfing porn?" He walks toward me and clicks the touchpad to see what I was doing. "Fuck. What did you do?"

I look over and my laptop is open to twitter. I was tweeting videos to Kristina and apparently decided to drink more from the mini bar than I thought, since there are a pile of empty little bottles on the floor. I can't tell you more than that. It's all I can do to stop vomiting and I really just want the room to stop trying to spin.

"Man, you really can't be trusted to control yourself."

"Did she tweet me back?"

"Seriously? You can't get up, probably will be late to the stadium and end up scratched from the game. And you want to know if she tweeted you? Fuck, dude. You do have it bad." Seno tosses the other waste basket my direction and goes off to shower. I guess I have to look for myself and that's not an option right now. This has happened in the past. I blame the whiskey. I know that nobody made me drink it. But, all it takes is somebody to get me going and last night I didn't want to feel anything, so I had a few more and then the whiskey took over. I don't remember going back for more, but I know it was me. It reminds me of the nights when I would wake up with women in my bed and not know what I did or what their names were. Sometimes I didn't know where I was or how I got there. It reminds me of waking up in Arizona covered in hickeys and how the minor leaguers knew I was out of control. The night I was with Kristina and didn't know her name or who she was and almost lost her completely because I had no way to find her. The morning I woke up with the tail from the mascot costume on my floor and all I could remember was the seal.

This isn't me. No, this isn't what I want and it definitely isn't who I want to be.

I think about Kristina's words while I lay in my bed with my eyes closed. She doesn't think she's strong enough. I need to be strong enough for both of us. Whiskey nights are not the way to do that. Whiskey nights are me giving up and running away from the problem. I need to pull it together and get to the stadium. I need an update on my girl. I need strength to make it through three more days and then I'll find her. Yeah, I'll find her and I'll make everything right again. I know she still wants to be mine.

Seno drags me to the stadium and I get there on time, but Skip scratches me anyway. Fuck it. I sit by my locker in the clubhouse and mope, finally getting time to see what I did on social media last night. Videos. I tweeted videos at Kristina. Every Foreigner love song that's been in my head since she spent the night with me and every song we had ever talked about. I scan through what I did, hoping for a response, but all I got was comments from fans—nothing from the only person that matters. Still radio silence.

Seno walks through the clubhouse and glares at me. He sits in front of me and leans in so I'm the only one that can hear him, "You need to pull your shit together. You need to be in the game and not sitting here accepting that Skip scratched you. I don't care how fucked up you are or how shitty you feel. Your hangover is your own fault, suck it up. The girl will be there or she was never there to begin with. Don't waste your time, use it on productive things and get your ass on that field. If nothing else keep busy and get out of your head, the game is your distraction."

"But,..." Seno cuts me off.

"No fuckin' buts! I'm here. I'm playing. I'm not letting the rest of my life get in my head. No, I'm making this about being the best I can be. I want my girls to be proud of me. I know Sherry loves to watch me play, and that's what I'm doing. Don't you think that I'd rather be with my pregnant wife?" He stops and looks me in the eye. "Okay, now get off your ass and start harassing Skip. I want you on the field and I don't want to see you sitting around like an emotional teenage boy." He gets up and goes about his ritual of getting ready for the game.

He's right. Am I acting like an emotional teenage boy? Fuck that, that's totally unacceptable. I find water and start following Skip around, making it my goal to get into the game today. I've seen Seno do it and he may not start, but he usually manages to get into the game. I harass Skip and start working out, bugging Skip every step of the way and showing him I can do this, showing him that he wants me on that field and running the bases.

Skip finally puts me in as a pinch runner in the seventh inning and I end up part of a double switch, hitting in the pitcher's spot. I'm motivated and want to show Skip he's doing the right thing. Brandt is hitting and signs are getting thrown all over the diamond. Brandt and I are communicating with each pitch, I've got a huge lead off of first base and the pitcher throws to first. I dive for the base, making it back just in time. I stretch my lead off of first again and the pitch is wild, I steal second standing. The third base coach wants me to steal third, there's nobody covering second and I'm half way to third when the pitch is thrown. Brandt choppers the ball through the infield and I score on his base hit. The streak continues, we win 4-1.

The team is flying to Chicago tonight, so we're busy and that's good, helps me stay focused. That is until we get on the plane and everybody gets their phones out to call their women, and I can't because she blocked me. I want to call her and talk for a few minutes, like my teammates. Seno sits next to me and ends his call with Sherry. "Good work getting into the game," with an attaboy nod.

"Thanks."

With a deep sigh, "She was baking with Sherry this afternoon and they were watching the game together. So, she's safe and not hiding. Sherry said Kristina's been asking her questions about ball players and I don't think she'd do that if she was ready to be done with you. Give her the few days and when we get back I'll help you find her. But, I want to see you hustling in Chicago. No, whiny ass shit."

"I got it. Thanks for letting me know she's okay."

To @Kristeeeeeena - Flying to Chicago. Miss you.

Seno wakes me up when the plane is landing and I feel much better than I did earlier, I may have shook off the hangover. I'm hungry. We get checked into our room and settled. I take Seno and Mason out for a steak dinner, it's Chicago home of the steakhouse. I figure I owe them since I've been such a punk the last couple of days. We keep it an early night and I make up for my whiskey night by turning in early.

Kristina

"How could you jump in so quick with a baseball player? They're all players in every sense of the word."

Sherry grins, "You'd think that, but it's not true. Rick hadn't been with a woman in two years when I met him. That doesn't mean it wasn't a struggle. Their past isn't their present and they can't control the women that are after them."

"I guess. I don't know. They're gone so much and they could be doing anything," I should think before I speak. The last thing I want is a worried pregnant woman on my hands.

Sherry looks at me funny, "We don't like being apart, so I go on road trips. The rest doesn't matter. It's not a concern because we trust each other."

Do I trust Chase? I think I trusted him the first moment I met him. I hadn't considered him cheating until I told him to try another girl. So fucking stupid. Can it be cheating if I told him to do it? No, he wouldn't cheat. I don't have the luxury of being able to travel with him. I have to work.

"How do you deal with him getting hurt? Doesn't it freak you out when pitchers throw at him?"

"I never want him hurt, but when he got hurt last season it brought us closer together. It pisses me off when they throw at him and I yell at the pitchers when they do it. It's part of the game." She stops and turns to me, "We all have to live. Life has risks."

She doesn't ask me about Chase, she simply continues helping me learn how to bake and let's me do my own thing. She's content and happy sharing her life with a baseball player.

Wanting Chase could be a change to my whole life plan. I don't know if I can have what I want and him. What if he wants more than I'm willing to give?

CHAPTER TWENTY-EIGHT

Chase

The next three days I do my best to stay focused. Mason and Seno share info they get about Kristina —she's safe and still there. I can go find her when I get home and figure it out from there. Baseball is my world. No chicks. No booze. My team, work outs and games.

Monday's game was postponed due to rain. A day wasted. The team got together and went for deep dish Chicago Style pizza. Then I hung out with Mason, who I found out has been spending time alone in his room this whole trip. Well, maybe not quite alone, playing video games online with Michelle and talking to her through the game—basically whispering in her ear the whole time they've been apart. Luckily, she's busy with work today and the team takes over Mason's room with a video game competition. Yes, we played baseball.

I didn't realize Michelle works, but I guess she has to pay rent somehow. She's always available for games and it doesn't matter what time of day or day of the week. Mason has been spending all his free time with her, so I don't know when she's working. "Dude, what does your chick do?"

"She's a freelance contractor of some type. She doesn't go into it. She has some deadlines and mostly knows how much work she has to get done each day to stay on pace for her jobs," Mason shares vaguely.

"So, you don't know?"

"Pretty much. The only part I understand is that she's self-employed."

We all stay up too late for the doubleheader we have tomorrow.

Kristina

Between work and hanging out at Sherry's I haven't been home much. I get home and my apartment is silent, but I know Michelle should be here. "Hello?" I call out.

"SShhhhh... busy," comes through her closed bedroom door.

I've never got that response before. I knock on her door, "Coming in."

She groans and looks up at me as I stand in her doorway.

"Are you behind on work?" Michelle looks ragged, like she hasn't slept.

"No. Busy."

"Busy with what?" I walk over to look at her computer expecting to find she's on a video game binge. "What the..."

"Don't ask. I don't know where it's coming from. I can't help it and I can't sleep and I'm barely keeping up the minimums on my fantasy serials."

"Okay, but you need to get some sleep. What did you tell Jones you do?"

"I'm a self-employed freelance contractor. I got lucky and he didn't ask questions. I've learned to lean in for a kiss and he'll do anything to avoid it."

"I don't know why you put up with that. I can't believe he hasn't kissed you."

"I can't believe you don't claim Chase as your own and stop being stupid," she stares at me with disdain. "It's kind of sweet that Mase is taking it slow. At least that's what I keep telling myself and then I remind myself how amazing his hands feel when he holds me. I'm being patient."

"Whatever."

"Seriously, Kristina, he's a good guy and he's into you. Forget that he's a baseball player for five minutes and think about the man. The hot man with long legs and muscles and always in a dirty uniform. Maybe the uniform part doesn't help, but you get the idea."

"Michelle!"

"He gets my attention. Do you know how many other women are noticing him if I am? You need to get your shit together."

"I'm thinking about it."

"Like, really?"

"Yes."

"Don't think too long. I think you're good until the team gets back. Mase said Chase is going to find you when he gets home. You better know what you want by then."

"So, what's with the project you're working on?"

"It's extra-curricular and we are keeping it to ourselves."

"Um, what about your critique partner?"

"I don't want to have to explain him to Mason."

"That's not what I meant. Does he know about your project?"

"No. I haven't figured that part out yet. This may never get beyond my laptop."

"I doubt that, but whatever."

I walk away and leave her to her project. I have things to think about.

Chase

There's no time for anything other than baseball on Tuesday. We're playing a doubleheader to make up the rain out from yesterday. The lineups for both games are posted at the same time and game one starts at 11:00am. Doubleheaders are a mixed bag. Skip probably won't play the same guys both games and may make some last minute changes between games. Then again, if I'd look at the lineups I'd know.

```
Game 1
1 CF Cross
2 SS Mason
3 1B Martin
4 C Seno
5 3B Lucine
6 2B Brandt
7 RF Rock
8 LF Simms
9 P Grace

Game 2
1 2B Brandt
```

```
2 SS Hart
3 CF Cross
4 LF Mason
5 3B Simms
6 1B Saben
7 RF Bravo
8 C Stray
9 P Clay
```

It's going to be a long day for a few of us. I need to be in both games. The less down time the better.

Game one went like most games that have the lineup. We won 12-4 and Seno is pissed about the 4. I told him to take the win, but he doesn't listen. It's a good thing he's sitting game two out. Every single one of us got a hit, even Corey Grace and he hits for shit. Mason, Lucine and Brandt hit homers. I got on base four of my five at bats and my teammates brought me home three times. I stole second base twice, walked twice and caught six balls in the outfield. Center Field is my space.

Game two, I'm concerned it will be wonky. First of all, Bravo is in the lineup and we haven't won a game with Bravo in the lineup all season. Second, Seno and Lucine aren't in the lineup. Third, Mason isn't in the Sherry approved position. I spend the game leaning toward Right Field and covering half of Bravo's zone in addition to my own, pushing him farther right. I've been watching him and he doesn't have the speed or desire to cover all of Right Field. I've got this, and it's a good thing I do because I run for a pop fly in Right Center Field that he never would've caught. It's mostly rookies on the field for game two and they step up to show what they can do. I'm one of them, but I'm the rookie that's been a Seal the longest. Mason is fine in Left Field, but not as sharp as he is at Short Stop. I get the change though, Short Stop for two games would be too much. He hit two doubles and a homer, I won't be surprised to see him in the clean up spot more often. Stray brought his bat with him today, hitting safely at all of his at bats. A double and three singles. Brandt is new to the Seals, but not a rookie. He's good people, a little quiet maybe, and what the team has been looking for at Second Base. He walked twice, popped out and hit a single. Simms is still getting his feet under him, but the progress is there. He seems to be able to handle anything on the left side. He hit two singles, but got caught stealing both times he made it on base. It wasn't spectacular, but we managed to pull out a win. 2-1 Seals.

Wednesday I wake up anxious. I know we go home today and I've never been more ready to go home. It's an early game and we're going to win, keeping our streak intact. We fly home right after the game and I'm going to find my Sweetness. I know Mason has a date with Michelle tonight, Seno wants to go home to Sherry, and Martin is expecting a visit from a special friend. I'm not alone in my desire to get home and it shows in our playing. Shortest game all season at two hours and fifteen minutes, and that's fine—especially when Josh Kranston shuts out Chicago and pitches the complete game in only 80 pitches. Mason hit a homer in the 4th inning that knocked me in. And in the 7th, we strung together three singles and a walk to score a run. 3-0 Seals.

Kristina

It's hard to ignore baseball when you work in baseball media. More specifically, it's hard to forget Chase when he plays hard and he's the star of the game. I'm constantly writing copy and updating stats that surround him. His batting average and on base percentage keep going up, and his fielding percentage is one of the highest in the league. His UBR and UZR are both impressive, but what stands out most to me is his stolen base percentage. He's the best in the division and three of the top five are on the Seals. The problem is Michelle. Something about the dirty pants does it for her and Chase is always dirty. If she acted like this when Jones was around, he'd swear he has competition. And, that makes me think about him. It's hard not to when I know what he's capable of. It's not the sex. We are combustible together, but it's more than that. I'm relaxed around him and I'm never relaxed around anyone. I can't remember the last time I slept as well as I do when I'm with him. Everything melts away. I guess I believe he'll protect me, he takes away my worries. I like being close to him and that seems to turn into sex.

I wanted to get laid. Just once in my life I wanted to be the girl that gave it up to a baseball player that made it to the majors, a professional athlete. Baseball skank for the night. It's not me. But, the environment reminded me of my ex-boyfriend and he didn't make it to the varsity team in college. I'm sure he wouldn't have found out, but somehow it would vindicate me to know I was with a man that made it further than the jerk who cheated on me and therefore he had to be better. The fact that it was a one and done thing would be the icing on the cake. It's what I wanted and I went for it. I knew my target when I got to the party. Everyone knew Cross wanted to get naked and fuck. I didn't stop when he wanted me and I was wearing the mascot costume. I didn't care. But, when we kissed my heart immediately began to pound. I remember vividly how my heartbeat was so strong that I swear you should've been able to see it beating out of my chest. Like in the cartoons when the red cartoon heart flies out of the characters chest pulling the character off of it's feet and it shows it's warm glow out there for everyone to see the cupids and tweety birds flying around it. Completely exposed. He was drunk and I could read his eyes even if he wasn't coherent. He was with me. He wanted me. I wanted him. I still can't believe that I dry humped him in my PJs. He told me he wanted me enough that night and I believe that he did. I ran because I was afraid of the overwhelming emotions. There's no reason I couldn't have taken advantage of the easy ball player and went on my way. No, my fear won and my fear keeps getting in the way. It makes me say things I don't mean and hide from what I want. If I'm being honest with myself, it's not the fear that's the problem. It's how much I want to be with him. The only fear is that I'm not what he really wants or can't be what he really wants. Fear that I love him as much as I do and he doesn't know what love is or will choose not to love me back. I had to leave him. I can't get dumped by another baseball player. Baseball players suck.

CHAPTER TWENTY-NINE

Chase

The plane ride home was a bit rowdy, not uncommon when the next day is an off day. I bug Seno and Mason to see what they can find out about Kristina. I want as much info as I can get, so I can find her. It seems that she was watching the game with Michelle and disappeared as soon as it was over.

When the plane lands, I don't waste any time. I start my search for Kristina.

Always the last place you look, it's where you find what you're looking for. I've been all over town searching for her. I've been all over the stadium, to her apartment, to Seno's, I've even checked a couple places that Michelle suggested. No sign of her, so I go home to regroup. I need a new plan. If she's hiding from me or doesn't want me to find her, I'll never find her. I open up my bungalow to the beach and there she is, my Sweetness is sitting on the beach between the ocean and my patio. She's looking at the waves and the wind off the ocean is blowing her hair back. The sudden relief in my body almost knocks me over. I stay where I am and look at her. The sight of her alone has my blood flowing and my heart beating faster. I have hope. The fact that she's here on my beach, she must want me to find her. She must want to see me. I want to go to her and I realize that I've been waiting for this, I've been waiting for days to see her and hold her. I've been waiting to have her in my arms, so I can tell her that I love her. I don't want to push her or scare her, and I don't want her to think I'm saying it to get her back. It's not a trick. I'm stuck dead in my tracks, not knowing what to do and I hear Seno in my head telling me to do whatever I need to do to keep my happy. All that matters is that she knows I love her.

I kick my shoes off and run out to her on the sand, dropping down to sit in front of her and face her. "Hi." I watch for signs that she's going to get up and leave, or maybe I could somehow get lucky and she would reach for me to kiss me, or, shit, I'd be happy if she smacked me at this point. I get nothing. "I know you don't want to talk to me. I know you want me to leave you alone. I know you said you were falling for me. The only part I want to believe is that you're falling for me. I don't know what made you run from me, but I think you're afraid of us. I want to be with you. We should be together. I want to know what made you run and I will do anything in my power to fix those things. I care about you and I don't want to push you or pressure you. So, I'm going to say what I have to say and then I'm going in my house. You're always welcome and the door will be unlocked." I take a deep breath and gaze out at the ocean with the roaring waves, feeling a kind of peace fill me and I know I'm doing the right thing, "I didn't know how to react on the phone when you said you were falling for me. I'm not falling for you. I can't fall for you because," I gaze into her eyes and palm her head, running my fingers through her silky hair, "Kristina, I love you. I'm in deep. I couldn't say it over the phone, not the first time. You dumped me and it hurt in my chest, like I'd been cracked open and somebody took out everything that was good, leaving me to suffer with my pain alone. But, none of that matters. If you're done with me, I'll have to figure out a way to make you want me again. And, I'll do it. Right now, I want you to know that I love you. You and only you. In my heart, you're my girl and you always will be. I love you and I'll always protect you." She doesn't speak. She doesn't move a muscle. I lean in and kiss her forehead. I release her from my arms, as much as I don't want to and stand up. I walk back to my bungalow, doing my best to not look back and I know in my heart she'll come to me. I'm just not sure how long it will take and I want her now. I leave my sliding door open and walk to my kitchen, sitting at my counter drinking a bottle of water while I watch her sit there and hope she comes to me.

The sunset is taking over the sky and Kristina is still sitting on the beach, no action other than changing her position and stretching out her legs. The breeze off the ocean has kicked up. I run a blanket out to her and place it around her shoulders, returning quickly to my kitchen counter where I continue to watch her. I run in to my bedroom to change into sweats and use the bathroom, and when I return she isn't sitting on the beach anymore—she's gone. I yell out, "Fuck me! Damn it!" and storm around my living room as I search for her on the beach.

"Is something wrong? I can leave." I hear the sweet voice and turn around to find Kristina sitting on my couch.

"No, don't leave. Nothing is wrong. I ran in the other room real quick and then you weren't on the beach anymore, I thought you were gone."

"I'm right here."

"I see that now."

"Tell me again, Chase."

I smile and feel my body start to relax, "I love you, Kristina."

She smiles and it's the most beautiful thing I've ever seen.

I want to know what pushed her over the edge, but I'm afraid to bring it up. I need to know if I'm going to keep it from happening again. "Do you want to tell me what happened? I don't want you having any questions about me or how I feel about you or what I want from you. I want you to be mine and I want you to be happy."

"I don't want to talk about it right now. You're off tomorrow, right?"

"Yes."

"Me, too."

"Do you want to hang out with me tomorrow?"

"I was thinking I could stay here with you until we go to work on Friday."

"That's perfect." I walk to her across the room and press my lips to hers while I wrap my arms around her. She reaches her arms around my neck and holds on as she wraps her legs around my waist. My girl, my Sweetness, is here with me.

I'm in my head and I just want to hold her. I want to spend time with her. Her body wrapped around me and holding onto me like this makes me want more, but that can wait. I could be sliding into her in less than thirty seconds. I don't understand how she can go from wanting me to leave her alone to wrapped around me, and she probably still has me blocked. She confuses me. It doesn't matter. I need to hold her. I grab the blanket off of my couch and walk out to my patio, carrying her with me. I sit down on the lounge chair and she's basically sitting in my lap, facing me with her arms and legs wrapped around me. She takes over our kiss and is pushing me for more. I want her to know that we aren't just sex. "Lay next to me here, Sweetness." She looks at me a little funny and does as I ask. I lean back into the chair and kick my feet up, while she snuggles into my side using my chest as her pillow and burrowing her head in under my chin. She reaches her arm across me and holds my waist. I cradle her from behind and lean down to kiss her forehead, as we entangle our legs and I cover us with the blanket. I look up into the darkness to find the clear night sky, speckled with bright shining stars. "This is perfect, Sweetness. What can I do to make it perfect for you?"

"It's perfect, Chase. You're perfect. Am I still your girl?"

"You'll always be my girl. You're my everything. Please tell me why you think you aren't strong enough to be with me. What happened to make you dump me? What did I do wrong?" I say as sweetly as possible while I have her in my arms and she can't run away.

"I had time to think about being with you and the time we spent together. I've never been so reckless and I didn't even care. You make me lose all rational thought and all I can think about is you, us, together. And you weren't here. I was lost. I went to hang out with Sherry, learn to bake and watch the game. She tells me about meeting Rick, all I can see is that she's the size of a house and I mentally slap myself for being careless. I can't believe how stupid I was."

"I'm so sorry, Sweetness. I told you I would always protect you and I mean it. I should've made sure you were protected. Honestly, I was already lost in you and you do something to me that I don't understand. I couldn't help myself and I've never had another girl bare before. You felt so good around me, fuck, just thinking about it I want you again. Hot, wet and tight around me with nothing in between us." My stomach flips and my groin is doing somersaults. "It's the nothing in between us part that means the most, it's as close to you as I can get. I want to be as close to you as I can get," Comes out raspy and sexy, completely out of my control. "I promise you it won't happen again."

"I started it and I didn't give you any warning. It was all me."

"No. I wanted you just like that and I could've pulled out sooner. It was me, too. Don't blame yourself."

She swallows hard. "I don't want to be like them. I don't want to be living together, married and pregnant that quick. I don't think I can be what you really want."

"Hold on. That's not what I want." She stops and looks at me. "I mean, that's not what I want right now. I want a girlfriend who I love and I want her all to myself. I'm not sharing with any other dudes. I want to take her out. I want to buy her gifts. I want to spoil her. I want a girl who loves me and isn't a slut after a player. I want to spend time together and build a life that we both want. I'd love to have my girl in my bed every night, but that doesn't mean I expect her to move in with me. The other stuff, I don't know. I've never thought about getting married or having kids. How are we supposed to know what we'll want? I just want to have my girl with me and love her. Remember, I'm the guy who's never even had a girlfriend. I have a steep learning curve, but I'm trying."

Kristina smiles at me, "So, you really just want a girlfriend?"

"Well, not just a girlfriend. Someone special, I mean," This is going to go all wrong and I already know it, "I always want to be with you. I don't know what to call it, but I think girlfriend is where it starts. Fuck! I totally screwed that up, didn't I?"

"No, I understand. You want me and only me. You want

to keep me. You love me. You want to protect me. You want a future with me, but we don't know what we want yet."

I smile, "Yeah, does that work for you?" I can tell by the look on her face that I couldn't have done much better. I get the Sherry part of the problem now.

"Yes," She giggles happily. Someday, when I inevitably decide to propose it's exactly how I hope her answer sounds.

"Good. So, my Sweetness, what would you like to do until we go to work on Friday? Can I take you out to dinner? Keep holding you under the stars? Whatever you want, you get."

"Love me under the stars, Chase."

I pull the blanket up over us and maneuver her onto my lap, facing me. I claim her mouth passionately. I know she's mine. I hold her tightly against me and feel what it's like to have her in my arms knowing that I love her. It's different. I know I like her, care for her, that she's special, but feeling what it's like to love her and think I'd lost her. Feeling the pain in my chest. Now I understand because this feeling is so much more and I never want it to end. I run my hands along her body, feeling her and I know she wants more. Our electricity is shooting through me and I know she can feel it, too. I can feel her shaking.

"Chase, please."

Fuck me. I want more, too. I don't have a condom in reach when we are outside on the patio. Obviously, something I may need to resolve for the future. "I want you, too, Sweetness. Have to go inside for a condom."

"No, I need you now. Please." Her tone is needy and pleading. Fuck I want her bad. She reaches into my sweats and frees my dick, stroking it lightly and feeling how hard I am.

"You know I want you. Let's go inside," I plead with her,

fighting my own urge to slide her right down on me and come hard inside her. I've always wanted to do that and I know it's not an option.

"Now baby, please. Inside me."

Fuck, fuck, fuck. This is a disaster waiting to happen. I stand up and take her with me, she automatically wraps her legs around me and holds on. "I know you said under the stars, and we'll get there before the night's over. I need you to believe in your heart that I'll always protect you. You need to trust me and giving in to you for this will just make it worse. Sweetness, you need to know that I'd love to just slide into you and not worry about anything. No matter what, I'll always take care of you and it'll always be us. No blame, Sweetness." I get to my bed and sit down with her still in my lap, her legs wrapped around me. She pushes my sweats down and is sliding out of her shorts before I can even reach for a condom. I grab her around the waist and hold her to me tightly, trying to gain control of the situation. "Kristina. Please work with me here." I feel her rubbing against me and it's driving me crazy. I quickly rip open the condom and roll it on, and she's on me instantly. Her heat sliding down over me feels like I found my home and I never want to leave. Fuck me. She needs me, I can feel her need running through her body as she moves on me and I'm thankful that I'm what she needs. "Thank you, Kristina. Thank you for needing me. I love you, my Sweetness." I pull her down to me, slowing her actions and holding her tight. I touch my lips to hers and she opens for me, inviting my tongue to dance with hers. I may have missed kissing her more than anything else. Her soft, full lips and her sweet taste are things I can't get enough of. I run my fingers through her hair and hold her face to mine so I can keep kissing her and kissing her. I see things when I gaze into her eyes that I can feel in my heart. She moves her hips while we kiss and I'm overcome by emotion. I'm not used to this, I've never experienced this before. I, I just want to love her. I touch her face and I trace her features delicately.

"Chase, baby... oh, Chase." She keeps moving on me and buries her face in my neck, kissing and sucking me there. She finds the right places and I grasp her hips, guiding her and meeting her with my own motions. Causing her to shake and shiver with every stroke, whimpering and moaning my name like I'm what she needs to survive.

"Is it too much, Sweetness? Don't worry, I've got you. I'm right here with you. I didn't know how much I need you and how much control your body has over mine. Oh, fuck, how do you make me feel like this?"

"More, Chase... please. I need..." She sits up straight and bounces on my hard dick, grinding against me at every contact.

"Oh, Kristina... Don't stop, Sweetness, you're going to make me come like that, oh fuck me. I can't stop. Come with me."

"I want to make you go first, Chase. Feel me around you. Feel me tight, hot and wet, riding you while you're so hard up in me." I reach for her and feel how hot and wet our connection is and I feel her shiver at my touch. I push up into her, meeting her movements and I'm pounding up into her, I need to come so bad. I touch her clit and she tightens, fuck me. I rub it and feel her get wetter. "Chase, I need you... more... more... please." I want to roll her underneath me and take over, but we're past that.

"I've got you, Sweetness." I rub her clit faster with a light touch, getting harder as I go and she explodes around me.

"Oh, Chase..." I'm pounding in her and my dicks pulsating in pleasure inside her.

"Fuck you're amazing! Oh fuck!" I call out as I'm

completely drained. She collapses on me, hot and sweaty. I hold her tight as I try to catch my breath.

"Chase, do you still love me?"

I don't know where that comes from, "Yes. I'll always love you. Nothing is going to change that. You're my girl. I promise you that I won't break your heart, it's safe with me." Managing to get all the words out on the little breath I have. I squeeze her and kiss every piece of her that I can reach without letting her go.

She rolls out of my arms and I step away to handle business.

"How can you say that? You can't know that for sure. You might feel different when you wake up tomorrow or next week."

I wish I could make her understand. I wish I knew what her past had done to make her this way. "I don't think love is something that goes away."

She cocks her head to the side, considering my words.

"It's the spark, the fireworks, that zing I get when I'm with you. The emptiness when you wouldn't talk to me. The connection we have when we talk on the phone. The undeniable need between us, pulling us together. It's never been that way with anyone else. I don't want to be with anyone else." I don't know why I keep going on. I want her to agree with me. I want her to say she feels those things too. She doesn't need to tell me she loves me, though I'd love to hear the words. I've never had a woman tell me they love me.

She smiles at me, "Okay."

I get back in bed with intentions of showing her how I feel. I've got no clue what I'm doing.

Kristina

Chase is searching my eyes for something and not saying a word. His hazel eyes are darker and almost grey, yet bright against the teal sheets. He's a guy. I know what he wants. Love me or not, they all want the same thing. I can see it in his hooded eyes. He wants sex like all of the rest of them. That's what my ex-boyfriend wanted and as soon as I wasn't there for him, he found it somewhere else. That's not love. It's getting satisfaction.

He leans over me, kissing my lips delicately and pulling back away. The single touch of his lips increases my heart rate as it zings through me. He's focused on me and his smile widens, "I love you." His tone is full of devotion and I don't know why that makes me lust for him. He wraps his arms around me and holds me against him, his heart beating at a nervous pace. I nuzzle against his chest and lightly trace an outline of his muscles from his arm to shoulder, and then to his chest. Repeating the process back to where I started a few times while I lie silently in his strong protective arms. I trace up his neck to his lips and he releases a warm sigh. I kiss his neck and trace his lips again. He meets my finger with his tongue and kisses it. I want his lips. I pull my hand back and climb on top of him, needing my lips on him. I kiss him from his neck to his lips, dragging my tongue and retracing what I'd done with my finger. He meets my kiss willingly with desire. I'm already breathing hard and all I've done is kiss him. This is crazy! I want him so bad. No, I need him. His arms wrap around me and he takes control of our kiss, tugging on my lower lip. I can't help myself, I reach for his cock to guide him in.

"No, Sweetness. Me, not my dick." He takes control of the situation, "Please. Let me love you."

His hands warm and tender on my body, his lips attentively kissing me pull me into him. I want more and I feel his hand at his dick. It excites me. I want him inside me and I push back against him.

"If that's what you want, it's yours." Yet he didn't let me take him in. He sits up, "Hold on." He stands and wraps his king sized comforter around us like a cloak with a hood over our heads. I hold on tight and wrap my legs around him while I kiss his neck, enjoying the private darkness he's made for us. "I love your legs wrapped around me. Your lips on my neck may be my downfall." He turns all the lights off including the patio lights as he walks through his bungalow carrying me. He takes us outside to his patio naked and in the darkness, walking out to the sand so we can see the white caps on the ocean and hear it's roar. He claims my mouth as we stand there in our wide-open solitude. He turns to go back inside, but takes us to the back corner of his patio. He crawls onto a cushioned lounger on all fours as I cling to him. We lie there together, claiming each other with the blanket blocking out the world.

Chase mutters under his breath, "I have no idea what I'm doing. Sex won't prove anything to you." His kiss is aggressive and controlling, "I need you." He settles himself between my legs and keeps kissing me. His hands at my breasts, but then searching for my hands. He intertwines his fingers with mine and everything around us stops for a moment in time, it's just us. Nothing else exists as we gaze into each other's eyes and giggle happily.

"Please, Chase."

"I'm trying."

I don't understand what he means. Trying? I don't get it.

He lies on top of me and whispers in my ear, "You're special to me. You'll always be special to me. I'll never hurt you." He takes a deep breath, and pushes into me a little at a time. Tightening his fingers around mine, "Kristina..." He kisses me softly and open-mouthed. He's blocked everything else from my world, he's the only thing that exists.

He moves slowly, giving me more and more of him until our bodies mash together at our connection. He's buried deep inside me, yet focused on my mouth. He's somehow managing to continuously rub that spot that drives me crazy with little movement. But it's his hands that give everything away. The muscles flexing in his hands and the grip his fingers have on mine. He's not letting me go. He's holding on tight and I find I am, too. I open my eyes and he's looking at me. I try to pull my hands away and he won't let me. "I want to touch you. I'll give my hands back." He kisses me with more need than I've ever felt and loosens his grip. I run my fingers through his hair and wrap my arms around his neck, wishing I could reach around his muscular shoulders. He's hot to the touch and his warm breath is ragged at my ear. The friction between us growing as he moves faster. He pulls out and strokes back into me repeatedly, and completely. He's amazing, huge and hard.

"I need you," he declares on a whisper.

"You have me, Chase. I'm with you, baby."

I feel his grin against my cheek and his hands move to my hips. He caresses my thighs and lifts my legs, catching them with his arms and coming down on me while he strokes into me. "I need to be closer to you. I don't know how. I can only get deeper."

"Oh, Chase!"

He pounds into me wildly, "This isn't what I wanted to do. I can't help myself when I'm with you." He stops and rests his forehead against mine, "I love you. How can I show you I love you? How can I prove it to you?"

"You show me in your touch and in your kiss. You don't have to do anything special, just be you."

He consumes me. I hear the blood rushing through my body, our hearts beating, and our uneven breaths. The heat of his touch controlling me as he takes over my body. I'm hit with the sudden realization that I'm his. I feel my center tighten, spooling toward release. He takes me harder and faster, "You drive me crazy. Tell me what you want."

"More of you," slips from my tongue without a thought.

"I can do that. Tell me if I hurt you. I never want to hurt you."

"All of you, Chase. Harder, baby. Please. Send me to the stars." I don't know where my words come from, but he listens.

He takes my hands back in his, locking his fingers with mine and supporting himself on our hands pressed together into the cushion. He claims my lips and slides his tongue against mine in time to the stroke of his hard length inside me. Pushing into me harder and harder until he's slamming into me on every stroke and unable to get any deeper. I cry out to him with need and want to hold him, but he has my hands, "Chase!" It drives him further, faster. I'm suddenly ready to explode and see light flickering behind my closed eyelids. He feels so good, I'm calling out his name on every stroke. "I need you," escapes me and I'm out of control.

"I've got you." He releases my hands and wraps his arms around me, holding me tight to him. "You're amazing around me. Custom fit, Sweetness."

He keeps slamming into me, harder and harder. The flickering turns to a full-on fireworks display exploding just for me as I come harder than ever before. I tighten quickly around him and I'm reminded of his size as I scream out his name, "Chase, oh Chase! So big!" He slams into me again over and over, I come even harder.

He reaches between my legs, "I think that was two."

"Uh huh. Oh Chase."

He finds my clit and teases it, "I didn't give this any attention."

And I'm lost, coming a third time at his hand with him still buried in me. He's in complete control.

"I need to come. I'm so hard for you. I could stay this way all night. Do you want to come again first?"

"Come for me." All the words I can manage. He pounds into me with his fist around the base of his cock and then lets go and gives me all of him again. My orgasm rolls on and on. I'm out of control, flying through the stars.

"Kristina! Kristina! Oh fuck, Sweetness."

Suddenly he's there with me, holding my hand as I float through space looking at the stars. His arm around me, holding me against him in the starlit night.

CHAPTER THIRTY

Kristina

I wake up snuggled against him on his patio, lying side by side on the lounger. We're still covered, but we can see the sky through an opening in the blanket. I have no idea what time it is, but it's dark out. I move my hands to his chest.

"Are you back with me?" He asks.

"Yeah."

"Is this okay, or do you want me to take you back inside?"

"I want to stay right here."

"I lost you there for a while, are you okay?"

"There were fireworks and you held my hand while we floated through the stars."

"I was there, too. You were already in the stars when I got there. I'll try not to let you go there alone next time," He smiles at me content with himself.

We lie there together until I fall asleep in his arms.

Chase

When the sun comes up I take my woman to my bed and lock up the house. The sunrise is beautiful, but on the beach with the early morning surfers probably isn't the place to sleep naked. I don't know what she does to me, if it's how I feel about her or what, but I want to slide right back into her and claim her as mine again. I want to keep her. I hope she wants me to keep her. She already owns me. She was sleeping and didn't wake up when I brought her to bed. I hold her and go back to sleep.

Kristina

"Chase?" My eyes are closed and it's dark. He's holding me.

His arms tighten around me, "I'm right here."

I roll into him and kiss his chest, still half asleep. My hands wander his body, exploring his adonis belt. We're both naked. My hands travel farther south and I drag a finger along the hard long length of his cock. I wrap my hand around him and I can't reach all the way around. He's holding me close and I stroke him lightly, more of a caress. I kiss his neck and he leans in to meet my lips with his. Tracing my lips with the tip of his tongue, then kissing my upper lip, then my lower lip. Everything in slow motion. He rolls me underneath him and holds me with his arms around me. He kisses me, worshiping my lips and I'm lost in him. I'm falling for him. I knew it would be like this when I kissed him the first time. I love him and he makes me want to do crazy things. I rock my hips up at him while he's kissing me and I feel him hard at my entrance. "I trust you, Chase. I want to be closer to you."

He bends my knees and spreads my legs, his lips never leaving mine. He takes my hand and wraps it around his bare cock. "I want to be closer to you, too. I want to be bare with you, no condom separating us. I won't take you that way, you have to give yourself to me."

I feel him in my hand. I stroke him and his body shivers. I rub his tip against me and I'm wet for him. He groans under his breath at the feel of me. I push against his tip, taking him in. "I'm yours, Chase."

He takes control pushing all the way in quickly, "I love you, Kristina." He moves slowly and his kiss becomes more passionate. "Thank you, love. You mean everything to me," he whispers in my ear.

I should tell him that I love him, but I haven't said that to a man since my high school boyfriend. Honestly, nothing has ever felt like this and I'm not referring to his peen, though it is in it's own league. There's something about Chase. I've tried to fight it, but I find myself asking "why fight it if it's what I want?" He makes me want to take a chance. I believe him when he says he loves me. I believe every word he says. I trust him completely, more than I trust myself. "Chase, baby, tell me again."

He smiles against my lips, "I love you, Sweetness."

He doesn't expect a response or anything in return. He starts to move with long slow strokes, over and over. I squeeze him and cry out his name in pure pleasure.

Chase

The way she says my name, it's like she's saying she's mine. I can feel it in her body and hear the thoughts she has running through her head. I'm trying to clear them all away and be everything in her existence, like she is for me. "You feel amazing around me. I want you to come with me deep inside you. I want to feel you get wet for me and tighten around me. I want to feel that you're mine."

She nods, breathless as I kiss her neck.

"I want to be closer to you. Tell me if I hurt you. I never want to hurt you. I need to be deeper inside you. Do you feel my love?" I spread her legs further and push in as far as I can, holding myself deep against her. It's not enough. I lift her legs, bringing her knees to her chest and push in further. She squeals and I brush the hair out of her face, watching to make sure I don't hurt her.

"Yes, Chase. I know you love me. I feel it everywhere."

"Ready for more?"

"Please. More."

I pound into her hard. Watching my hard dick slam into her bare, over and over. Her tight little heaven, hot and wet around me. I'm not sure I deserve her this way. I'll ruin her for everyone else. It doesn't matter. She's not a fuck. I'm keeping her. There's nothing like this direct contact. Just us and nothing in the way. Nothing keeping us apart.

"Oh, Chase!" she cries out on every stroke into her. "You make me so full. You're so hard. Oh! Oh!" She starts to scream and I wrap my arm around her, muffling her cries with my kiss.

"Almost, Sweetness. You feel so good, just a little more. I've got you." I keep slamming her tight hole and I don't want to stop. She's coming hard around me. I feel her orgasm hit her. I'm not giving this up. I've wanted her for too long and to have her bare, fuck me. Fuck! I want to come inside. I want to come in deep with my tip pressing against her wall. Fuck. Fuck. Control! I want to stay inside her. I could go for hours, until she whimpers my name all sweet and sexy. It's my downfall and I try to make it last. I lean into her ear. "I want to see the stars with you, take me with you."

She arches into me, "You're the only one for me. It's okay, come inside. I want you. I know you want to."

I want to, but I can't, "We can't take that risk. I promised I'd protect you."

"Please, Chase, I want to feel you come inside me. I want to feel you hard and pulsating."

Fuck me. I want to so bad. Maybe it would be okay this once. Only once. She's so hot and tight, I want to stay inside her as long as I can. I'm pushing and pulling myself closer to the edge, while I listen to her sexy little cries.

"Nobody compares to you, baby." She starts to moan and I'm done.

I can't control myself any longer. I grab my dick and pull out quick, trying not to get any near her heaven. No stroking necessary. Fuck, I'm a fucking fire hose. I collapse on top of her and give it a quick last tug.

Kristina

Waking up in his arms, happy and content. I wonder why I ever questioned being with him. I love him. I want to make him as happy as he makes me. I'm all in. We can figure this out together.

I want to do something for him. I get up quietly, trying

not to disturb him in his deep sleep. I wander to his kitchen, hoping he has the ingredients to make cookies. No such luck, but I do find what I need to make French toast. I mix up soaking liquid the best I can with what I have to work with and search further for more flavor. I layer the French toast in a small baking dish with chocolate bits and bake it. When it's done, I plate up a few pieces. I add more chocolate bits and dust the plate with powdered sugar as I hear Chase call out my name.

CHAPTER THIRTY-ONE

Chase

I wake up the next day and I'm alone in my bed. I remember our early morning rendezvous and hope she didn't run. I did and said some stupid shit. I know better than to push the boundaries with her.

"Kristina?" I call out.

"Just a second. I'm almost ready."

That's when I notice the delicious smell. I stretch and sit up with the blanket pulled up to my waist, keeping my good bits covered. I straighten the sheets and put my hands on the back of my head as I lean back against my headboard. I don't remember ever feeling this content.

"Good morning," she smiles at me as she carries in a big plate with two forks and a glass of milk. "I hope you don't mind, I went through your kitchen. I didn't find everything I needed to make cookies, so I hope you like French toast. You don't have syrup so I added chocolate bits and extra powdered sugar."

"You cooked for me?"

"Yeah." She giggles, "Sherry taught me some things. I wanted to make chocolate chip cookie bars, but you don't have the ingredients."

I take the plate from her and set it on my nightstand. I grab her around the waist and pull her into bed with me. "We will get whatever you want for the kitchen today."

"Chase, umm. I need to talk to you about something."

Oh fuck. "Okay."

"I'm sorry about earlier. You make me lose my mind. Thank you for doing the right thing and protecting me."

"I'll always protect you. I'm sorry I got carried away last night. It won't happen again."

"It's okay as long as it's you. It will always be us." She kisses me sweetly and rests her hands on my shoulders, "I'll do anything for you, Chase. I'm yours. I love you."

I'm surprised by her words. My smile takes over all the way into my cheeks and I feel my eyes light up. "Tell me again."

"I love you, Chase."

"You love me? Are you sure?"

She laughs, "Yes! I'll always love you. Nobody compares to you."

"I love you, too." I take her in my arms, kissing her and loving her. She's the only one for me.

PLAYLIST

"Hearts Don't Break Around Here" by Ed Sheeran
"Train in Vain" by The Clash
"Tonight & Forever" by The Damnwells
"I Will Keep the Bad Things From You" by The Damnwells
"Graceless" by The Damnwells
"Favorite Liar" by The Wrecks
"I Don't Like You" by The Wrecks
"Turn It Up" by The Wrecks
"Automatic" by The Subways
"Rock & Roll Queen" by The Subways
"She Sun" by the Subways
"Blasphemous Rumors" by Depeche Mode
"Strangelove" by Depeche Mode
"Just Can't Get Enough" by Depeche Mode
"People Are People" by Depeche Mode
"Return of Mack" by Mark Morrison
"Cake By the Ocean" by DNCE
"I Want to Hold Your Hand" by The Beatles
"Kiss is on My List" by Hall and Oates

"Kristina" by Rick Springfield
"Waiting For a Girl Like You" by Foreigner
"Feels Like the First Time" by Foreigner
"Something So Strong" by Crowded House
"Won't Stop" by OneRepublic
"Dive" by Ed Sheeran
"I Want To Know What Love Is" by Foreigner
"Just Like Heaven" by The Cure
"Last of the Real Ones" by Fall Out Boy
"Sweetness" by Jimmy Eat World
"1950" by King Princess

THE CLOSER

AN ALL ABOUT THE DIAMOND ROMANCE BOOK 5

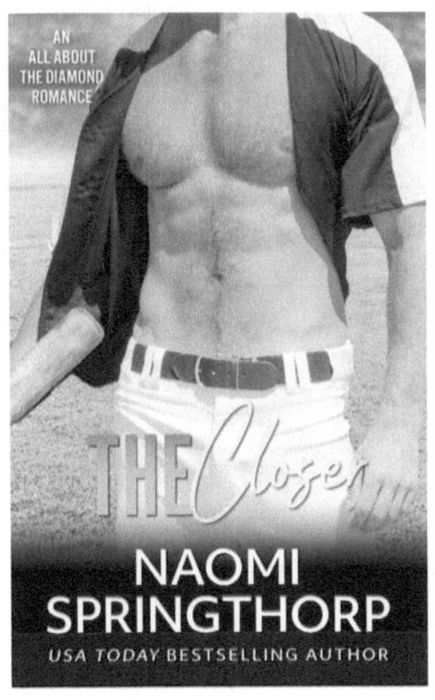

CHAPTER ONE

Houck

It's been a shitty week and it's only Thursday. I've blown two saves and my girlfriend dumped me. She said I use her for sex and don't care about her. Neither are true, but I compare everyone to Angie and nobody comes close. I never should've let her walk away from me. I didn't know any better and she didn't want to traipse around the country following a minor league player. Why would she? We were friends and nothing more. We were college kids. She had her own goals and she achieved them without me. She never needed me, not the way I need her. They say the last person you think about when you go to bed and the first person you think about when you wake up is the one who's most important to you, it's always been Angie. Nights like this when I've blown the save, I wish I had her with me. The girlfriends come and go. I keep hoping there's one out there for me, I just haven't met her yet.

I swear Angie has a sixth sense. Most times I have her on

my mind, she calls or something within a few days. Tonight a text comes in and it's not her typical fun message.

Text from Angie - I need to see you
Text from Angie - Already checked your schedule
Text to Angie - You want to get together over the All-Star Break?
Text from Angie - Just landed in San Diego

What the hell? I haven't been in the same room with her in thirteen years.

Text to Angie - I'll be there to pick you up in twenty minutes or less
Text from Angie - Thank you

I can't believe she's here. I don't have time to clean up, but I check the mirror to make sure I don't look like a fool. I shouldn't bother, she's a friend and has never been interested in me for anything more. But, when I remember her my blood pressure rises and I envision her with her head full of long fluffy dark blonde hair, wearing her cheerleading uniform with the short pleated skirt. Her legs toned, her breasts round, her strength and intelligence obvious. An unsolicited smile graces my face.

I slide into my car, voice texting her on the way to the airport, "On my way. Black Porsche 911."

Siri reads her reply to me, "Red dress."

I reply, "I know exactly what you look like," sending the message before I can reconsider and imagining her in a fitted red dress.

It's late and the airport is empty. I pull up to arrivals and she's standing in the beams of my headlights, gorgeous as always. I want to jump out and wrap my arms around her, kiss her senseless. I pull up calmly, hop out of my car and hug her, lifting her off her feet and kissing her cheek as I set her down. I load her suitcase into my backseat and chivalrously make sure she's in my car before I close her door for her. Everything about her is the same except the effect she has on me, which has become more potent. I attempt to calm myself down as I walk around to get in the driver's seat, but I'm consumed with how incredible she smells and how the kiss I gave her on the cheek should've been a closed mouth peck.

"I'm sorry about the short notice. I hope I'm not interfering with anything."

"You're always welcome. Is everything okay?" Wondering why she's here on such short notice, when she's always been prepared and calculated.

"I needed to see you," Her voice is different than I've ever heard. Her words pierce my heart with what I want her to mean, and I consider what the chances are that's her intent.

"Are you staying with me or do you have a hotel booked?" Please stay with me. Please say you're staying with me.

"I'd like to stay with you, if that's okay."

"Of course, you can use my guest room for as long as you want," unless you'd prefer to sleep in my bed, I will her to understand what I want and what she means to me.

"I don't have a plan, other than staying through the weekend and spending your off day with you. I'd like to watch you play. It's been years since I've been to a game."

I want to find out why she's here, but I'm happy to have her and don't want to push. She'll tell me when she's ready. "I'm the closer for the Seals. I don't get to pitch every game. I'm happy to get you a seat for the games this weekend."

She laughs, "I know you're the closer. I follow your career and your stats. I watch the highlights every time you pitch."

She watched me blow the last two saves. Is that why she's here? She thinks I need help getting it together? "Look, I don't need a keeper. I'll bounce back from the blown saves. I'm perfectly fine by myself. The team's got my back. This isn't like back in college. I'm a confident grown man and I can take care of myself." I hear my words accompanied by my annoyed tone and wish I could suck them all back in before they reach her ears. I add quickly, "But, I'm happy to have you visit." I drive into the parking garage and park in my spot.

"I'm not here because you're off your game. You know how I feel about that, it's still just a game. No pitcher is perfect. Besides, when you need the baseball talk you always tell me you need it somehow and you haven't in years."

I shouldn't ask, "Then why are you here?" I offer her a hand out of my car and unload her suitcase.

"We're turning 35 this year. I'm not baby crazy, I'm not worried about my biological clock being a ticking time bomb. But, I do want things in my life and time is getting away from me. Every time a guy I'm dating starts to get serious, I dump him. Why are you still single?" Her big bright blue eyes search mine, waiting for an answer.

I've been waiting for you. Nobody compares to you. "I guess I haven't clicked with the right woman." Our conversation continues as we take the elevator up to my high-rise penthouse and I realize she's never been here. I hope she loves it, maybe she'll stay longer.

She nods her head, "What if we dumped the right one and we don't get another chance?"

"I didn't dump the right one. I found her. She never found me." Find me. Find me.

"You know who the one is?" She questions me and her voice gets higher pitched.

"Yes. I mean, I haven't tested the theory. I've never kissed her or held her all night." I've wanted to since college. It's you, Angie. Tell me you want me, too.

Her voice is angry, "If there's a woman out there for you, why haven't you gone after her?"

"She lives far away and she's never been interested in me." The elevator opens and I lead her into my living room.

She stops in her tracks, not paying any attention to her surroundings, "Does she know how you feel?"

"She always seems to know everything."

"D, have you told her?" She shakes her head, "You're a major league baseball player and your record this year is 21 for 23, for Pete's sake!"

"My game has nothing to do with it, it can't be why she wants me. I've had too many of those and I've been dumped by the last one."

"Have you told her or not?"

"No."

"Wouldn't it be better if you were with her?"

"Yes. She's not interested."

"You can't be sure. You haven't told her."

"What if I tell her and she's not interested? Then I don't have her at all? I don't want to lose her completely."

"What are you losing out on by not telling her?"

She makes a good point. She probably wouldn't if she knew it was her. "Let me show you to your room," I refuse to respond to her question but bring her into the moment and she finally glances around.

"This is nice. Awesome view. I bet you spend a lot of time out on your balcony."

I smile, "Your room is on this side of the condo and you have your own bathroom. My master suite is on the other side of the condo, if you need me for anything." Fuck I'd love it if she needed me. "Please make yourself at home." I lay her suitcase on the bed and flip the light on in the bathroom. I open the closet door, showing her she has room to hang up her clothes.

"Thank you."

"I'll leave you to get unpacked and get some rest." I turn to walk away, but before I leave the room I continue with my back to her, "I'm happy to have you here with me. Stay as long as you want. Don't hesitate, if you need me."

I walk to my room and sit on the edge of my bed. I pick up the framed photo of us together from my nightstand, remembering the night it was taken. Her arms were wrapped around me and she was proud of me for pitching the complete game. I was a starter back then and I threw the complete game in 101 pitches. The experience wouldn't have been the same if she wasn't there with me. It was a milestone in my college baseball career and the part I remember in most detail is her. The excitement in her hands as she touched me. The natural curve of her lips as she squealed in celebration with me. Her fresh gaze on me, deep into my eyes. It was all going to change that night. I was sure she wanted to kiss me. I wished she wanted more from me, but it didn't happen. I should've known the game wouldn't have an affect on her, it never has. It's just a game.

CHAPTER TWO

Houck

I wake up early Friday morning and get up, quietly going about my morning routine. I don't want to disturb my houseguest. I wander into my kitchen after something to eat, wearing only my pajama pants and notice Angie's already up and enjoying my balcony. I change my plan and join her.

"Good morning, I hope you slept well." She's breathtaking standing there in the morning light with her hair blowing in the breeze. "Can I get you some breakfast? I need to go for a run, do you want to join me?" It's one of the things we used to do together in college.

"I'm up for a run. I love your view. It's a nice place you have here."

"Thanks," I get warm all over, and I catch her checking out my abs. "I have a few hours until I need to be at the stadium. Should be plenty of time to run and eat. There's a set of extra keys hanging on the refrigerator for you." We part to get ready and meet back in the living room ready to run.

I catch her staring at me again. There must be something different about me. It has been thirteen years. I hope it's not a bad thing. "What distance do you want to run?"

"I can always go for another run after you go to the stadium if we don't go far enough."

I glare at her and shake my head while we stretch, "I have stairs in my run. Let's go." We start off slow and pick up speed as we go. I lead and take her running through the East Village to the Harbor Drive Pedestrian Bridge. We run up the stairs and across the bridge, then down the other side. I watch in case she wants to stop and take in the view, but she seems to be more focused on me. Probably her competitive spirit making sure she keeps up with me. We run along the marina, then up and over the stairs at the convention center a few times before we take the paths at the marina parks. I lead her out the Embarcadero to Survivor's Park and back to run the Harbor path. "Too much?"

"It's a start," she winks at me and laughs.

We get home and she watches me in my kitchen, "What are you doing? I'm easy. Where's the cereal?"

I open the cabinet, "Which one would you like?" She points, choosing the healthy granola. I hand it to her with the milk. We sit and eat cereal together comfortably without words. I'm happy having her here, but my head keeps running possibilities. Is she right? Should I tell her she's the one? I wish she'd tell me why she's here.

Angie

This was a crazy idea. Why did I fly to San Diego? I've never done anything this spontaneous. I shouldn't ask why. I'm fully aware and I blame my business partner, Lucy. She's getting married and taking a class with her fiancé through their church. She's such a good girl. I could never take a class at the church. Honestly, I'm not sure I'm marriage material. She shared the lessons they did in the class and one of them hit me hard. If it was a rock, my windshield would be shattered into a zillion pieces. As it is, it sent my heart and brain into a tizzy. It's a workbook page with questions and you have to fill in the answers. Then you take the answers, only the answers, and create a list.

1. Who's presence makes you feel calm?
2. When you have something to celebrate, who do you want to tell?
3. Who's the first person you think of when you wake up in the morning?
4. Who do you enjoy spending time with?
5. Who has the same fitness and eating habits as you?
6. Who do you see when you think of the future?
7. Who's the last person you think of when you go to sleep?
8. Who do you dream about?
9. Who can't you live without?
10. Who makes you feel protected?

1. If you answered the same name to all of these questions with the name of your fiancé, congrats! You've found the right one.
2. If you answered multiple names and not only your fiancé, you might want to explore your options and make sure you're doing what's right for you.
3. If you answered the same name to all or most of these questions and you're not engaged, consider the following and don't waste time you could be spending with the one:

Does this person make you feel special?

Is this person always available for you and ready to do whatever they can for you?

Do you have a solid foundation of friendship?

What has stopped a relationship with this person from progressing in the past?

Have you ever been in a romantic relationship with this person? If no, it might be worth exploring.
Go kiss them already!

Anyway, point is, hell I don't need to explain to you. I'm sure you already get it. The answer to the first ten questions were the same—Super D. And, yes, it did occur to me that this pre-marital exercise feels a lot like a quiz from a fashion magazine. Regardless, it left me reflecting on the time I've spent with him and how much time I spend working and how the years keep flying by. I don't know if I want kids or not, it might depend on who the guy is. But, at this rate I'll never find out because I'll never pick the guy. Truth is, he's only a friend, though I've compared other men to him. Why shouldn't I consider him as a potential mate? Seriously, he checks off all the insignificant boxes, too. He has money, he won't be mooching off me and if he did, he'd be let down because I can't support his lifestyle with the penthouse he lives in. He's handsome and has a hot bod. I don't remember him having all those abs the last time I saw him. He should really think twice before he exposes a woman to his shirtless body. And those pajama pants? They left nothing to the imagination. I'm pretty sure he was going commando. He's a professional athlete. What more could I want?

I was going to spend today getting comfortable with the surroundings and kiss him tomorrow. But, who's this woman he's meant to be with? How have I never heard of this person before? Maybe he's wrong? He's a guy, he's most likely wrong part of the time. He doesn't think she's interested, that's in my favor. How'd he say it? 'He's never tested the theory.' I'd like him to kiss me and hold me all night. It would answer all of my questions.

"Did you hear me?" He asks.

"What?"

"I was talking to you."

"Sorry, not sure where my brain was," Lies, you have a fine ass.

He shakes his head, "I have to go to the stadium. I'll text you in a bit with your ticket information. You're welcome to use the jacuzzi tub in my bathroom. Eat whatever you want. Text me if you need anything. I'm texting you additional contact info in case it's an emergency, I don't always have my phone on me. Game starts at 7:05pm tonight."

Text from Super D - shared contact Carter

Text from Super D - Carter is the Clubhouse Manager. He can find me if you can't get me for some reason.

"See you tonight. Hope you enjoy the game." He turns to walk out and stops, "Hey, do you want to go out for a late dinner after the game tonight or maybe dessert?"

I smile, "Dessert sounds delicious."

He nods and steps onto the elevator.

Dessert could be interesting. He means ice cream or something, but my mind is going now.

CHAPTER THREE

Houck

I walk into the clubhouse and find Carter, "Hey, can you put my friend, Angie, on the early entry list? I need tickets for this weekend's games for her, too."

Seno walking by hears me talking to Carter, "Angie? Isn't she the one you told me about?"

"Yep." He high-fives me. "Nope, she's visiting for a few days. Showed up last night and she hasn't told me why. I'm not complaining."

Carter interjects, "Where do you want her to sit?"

"Best seat you've got."

Seno adds, "Put her next to Sherry, so she's not by herself."

"Works for me," Houck agrees. "Can you get her a jersey and cap, too?"

"Sure, with Houck on them?"

"Yeah, I guess."

"You don't want her to wear your name?" Seno questions me.

I chuckle, aware how this is going to sound, "She calls me Super D." They both stare at me waiting for more. "She never thought Doug was a good enough name for me. Originally it was Super Doug, but you know how nicknames change."

"Super D it is. Any idea what size?"

"Misses jersey size medium. Can you charge anything she wants at the stadium to my account? I don't want her paying for anything. I want her to feel special. And, can you deliver everything to her at my place? She's not a fan of surprises."

Carter willingly goes along with it, "No problem. Easy enough since you live across the street."

"Thanks."

Text to Angie - Carter is going to deliver your tickets to you at my place. He has a key. He's a short bald man.

Text to Angie - Batting Practice is at 4pm. You're on the early entry list if you want to come watch.

Text from Angie - I'd love to!

Text from Angie - Going to try out your jacuzzi tub. I'll be at the stadium later.

And now I'm imagining her naked in my tub. I want to be naked in my tub with her.

Angie

When he said jacuzzi tub I pictured a tub with jets, not a jacuzzi fit for four grown adults. I could swim in this thing. I turn the water on, and let it start filling up while I get a change of clothes and grab a magazine from his coffee table. He's got music set up to pipe throughout his condo, I hit shuffle and go for luck. The sound of guitar strings and "Angela" by the Lumineers fills the room. I walk into his bathroom and strip naked, setting my phone and the magazine to the side while I climb into the tub. The jets blowing against me and the hot water are a perfect combination. Relaxing. I bet he uses the jacuzzi. We could both fit in the jacuzzi together with no problem. Maybe we can skinny dip in the jacuzzi together later. It would be better than dessert, or maybe it could be dessert. It would definitely melt the ice. Who am I kidding? That's not what I want. It is what I want, but not quick. For now, I'll soak here and daydream about the possibilities. Would he hold me in his lap and kiss me? Would he take control and splash water all over his bathroom while he takes me, claiming me as his? Maybe he's not a do it in the jacuzzi kind of guy. Maybe some warming up naked together, making out, hot heavy...

> He walks in and finds me in his tub, jets on and water up to my neck. I'm relaxing and my eyes are closed. My hair tied up in a loose bun on top of my head. He pulls his shirt off, showing me his bare chest and abs. He turns around and drops his pants going commando, showing me his magnificent ass. He climbs in with me, sitting across from me with his feet stretched out at my sides. His hands out of sight under the water, reaching for me and caressing my

leg. I go to him and his eyes search mine, finding what he wants his smile brightens and he pulls me down to him. Our lips meeting for the first time. Why didn't we kiss before? The heat between us is instantaneous, but we aren't ready for more. We pull back and smile at each other happily, both of us wanting each other for the first time. Holding each other is more than I ever dreamed would happen, but this is more. This is a need to be close to each other, explore each other, finally not worry if the other is interested and simply be together. His arm is holding me to him and his hand is at the back of my head. My arms are around his neck with one hand climbing up into his short brown hair and massaging his head. His other head is against my leg, but I'm not ready for him. I don't want to miss this new stage of us. We kiss sweetly, turning more heated with each passing second. He licks my lip and I open my mouth for him, kissing him deeply. Wanting more, but trying to hold back. He holds me close to him and keeps kissing me, not anything more. Simply holding my naked body against his and worshiping my lips. Why did I wait for this? Is he what I've been waiting for? He's been right here all along. He's all man and he's been waiting to be mine.

I hear a noise and I'm pulled from my daydream.

"Hello? It's Carter."

"Sorry, in the tub."

"No problem. I'm leaving tickets for all the games this weekend, a temporary access card so you can get in early, and a present from Houck on the kitchen island."

"Thank you."

"Enjoy your bath."

The elevator door closes and I listen to make sure he's gone. I get out of the tub and wrap a towel around my body, anxious to find what he left for me. I go to the kitchen and the first thing I see is a jersey with his number 18 and the name Super D. I get closer and find a matching cap. The jersey is even the right size. I open the envelope Carter left on the counter and find a note:

> Angie,
>
> Here are your tickets to this weekend's games. Use the card to get in early and to pay for anything you want while you're at the stadium. For early entry, use the VIP entrance near the home plate gate. Batting Practice is at 4pm. You can sit in your assigned seat for BP or anywhere you'd like on the field level, I suggest behind the Seals dugout.
>
> Go Seals!
> Carter

I'm standing in the kitchen, wearing only a towel when the door opens again. I've got to get used to this penthouse elevator. I consider running for it, but there's no time.

Houck

She's naked in my kitchen. She has a towel wrapped around her and it could fall off at any time. I've dreamt about having her in my kitchen in many different ways. She's always barefoot and naked, though I've never actually seen her naked. Her hair, piled on top of her head, leaves her neck and shoulders exposed. I'm staring at her and I can't take my eyes off her. I need to say something. Every second that passes makes me more of a creep. Then again, she's the one naked in my kitchen. "Hi, just want to check on you and make sure you have everything you need." How about me? Do you need me? I want you.

"I'm good." She steps from around the island and I can see the slit of the towel up to the top of her thigh. "Thanks for the jersey."

"You look good," I can't take my eyes off of her. She's better than good, she's stunning. "You're welcome." I fidget nervously. I want to reach for her and hold her, but I need to get back to the stadium. We're not that kind of friends. We've always been friends, nothing more. I've always wanted it to be more. Why didn't I kiss her thirteen years ago?

"Thanks," I swear she blushes.

I turn away quickly, "I have to get back. See you at the stadium." The elevator door couldn't close quick enough. I need to get out of here before I do something I shouldn't.

Angie

I get ready for the game, putting a low-cut snug-fitting tank on under my jersey. I button the lower buttons on the jersey and leave the top open. It's cute with my matching bikini panties and I consider taking a pic for future use, or maybe to send to D now. Too much for an ice-breaker? Probably. He was surprised and uncomfortable seeing me in a towel. I slide into my skinny jeans and put my sneakers on. I let my hair down and brush it out, trying the cap to figure out how I want to wear it. I leave my hair down and put the cap over it.

I'm anxious to see BP. He probably won't hit. Why would he? He's the closer. Still, it's nice for him to get me in early. I toss the envelope Carter left for me and the extra keys to D's place in my bag and walk over to the stadium. The stadium is easy. Everyone treats me like I'm a queen when I flash the card Carter gave me. The stadium is empty, except for workers prepping food and cleaning. There are only a few people in the stands and some men in team polos on the concourse. A couple players are on the field throwing the ball. There's one woman sitting behind the Seals dugout, and not another single butt in a seat. I follow her lead and sit a few seats away from her. She's focused on one player, I'm guessing it's her husband because she's noticeably pregnant.

"Hi, you must be Angie," a short bald man startles me. "I'm Carter."

"Nice to meet you. Thanks for setting this up for me."

"This is all Houck. I wanted to introduce you to Sherry, since your seat is near hers all weekend and she knows the drill on everything."

The pregnant woman turns briefly, "Hi, nice to meet you." Then back to watching BP, obviously taking it seriously. "Looking good, Seno!" She calls out. One of the players grins at her happily.

"I'll leave you two to get to know each other. Let me know if you need anything," Carter excuses himself.

It's refreshing to see two people who are meant for each other, have found each other. Their connection is clear, even with the distance between them. My heart warms at the thought and my mind wanders, are D and I meant to be together?

"There's your guy," Sherry points to Houck as he walks out onto the field.

"He's not my guy. We're friends," and I wonder why I point it out when I wish he was my guy. Or, maybe, want to find out if he's supposed to be my guy.

She turns and focuses on me, taking her eyes off the field. "Sorry, I shouldn't have assumed."

"It's okay. I've wondered what it would be like if he was."

"What's stopping you?"

"I don't want to mess up our friendship, but I'm here to find out if it's worth the friendship risk and if there are any signs he's interested."

"Does he know?"

"He doesn't know why I'm here. I hopped a flight to San Diego and called him when I landed."

Sherry yells at the field, "Seno!" and waves him over.

He comes up to the stands and puts his arms around her after his next turn at bat, "Is everything okay, my queen?"

She smiles like her world is complete, "I'm fine, wanted you to meet Houck's friend. This is Angie."

He shakes my hand, "Nice to finally meet you. I've heard a lot about you."

"Why would you hear about me?" I laugh.

His eyes widen, "It was all positive. I have to get back." He kisses Sherry on the cheek and runs back to the field quickly, not wanting to elaborate.

Sherry turns back to watch BP, "There's your sign. These guys don't talk about 'friends' enough for their teammates to know who they are."

Seno yells to the outfield, but I can't understand what he says. He points at me. D shakes him off. He yells again, loud and clear this time, "Never shake off your catcher. I call the game." D shakes his head, irritated and runs toward Seno. I watch their conversation, but can't make out the details. Seno hands D a bat and puts a helmet on his head with a big grin on his face. D complains and curses him out. "Shut up and trust me. Hit the fucking ball!" Carter's behind home plate chuckling and a couple of the other players are chiming in on the situation. D walks up to bat awkwardly and uncomfortable with a bat in his hands. Banter around the backstop continues, a combination of jibes and encouragement.

The first ball, he swings and hits the ball up the third base line. I call out, "Wooo wooo, go D!"

His stance changes, he's more comfortable. The second ball, and he swings like he means it, but misses the ball completely. I hear him cursing from my seat. The third ball, and he smacks it out of the park. I stand up and cheer, "Yeah! Go Super D!"

"Isn't it fun to cheer when your guy does something?" Sherry grins. "He may not be your guy yet, but he's your guy."

Fourth ball and he hits another home run. I cheer for him again and get more enthusiastic, remembering my cheerleading days. I know how to turn on the pep and root for my guy. My guy? We'll revisit that later. Fifth ball and he hits it to the outfield wall, disturbing the guys standing out there doing nothing. His turn is over and he goes back to Seno who points at me. D shakes his head and gazes up at me in the stands. His smile is brighter the longer he's focused on me. He runs up to my seat, "The team is picking on me because I have a hot blonde visitor and I hadn't come up to say hi yet."

"Maybe you should hook me up." I say laughing and his expression changes. I test the water further, "Which one said I'm a hot blonde?"

He leans in to my ear and whispers, "Me." He kisses my cheek the same way he did last night when he picked me up at the airport, more than a peck on the cheek and runs back to the field.

Me? He considers me a hot blonde? Did I hear him correctly? "Is there a player on the team with a name that sounds like 'me'?" I ask Sherry.

She rolls her eyes at me, "I told you he's your guy."

"What if he's not? What if I test the theory and it all goes to shit? What if it ends our friendship?"

"What do you mean? Test the theory? This is love, nothing scientific about it."

Love? I hadn't even considered love. I guess its part of being the one. You know, those stupid pre-marital classes should be more specific about things. "D said he knows who the one for him is, but she isn't interested. He said he hasn't kissed her or held her all night, he hasn't tested the theory." My brain is still stuck on 'love' while I rattle off the words. "You look happy with your man. You love him?"

Sherry giggles, "I am and very much. I didn't know this connection was possible until I met Rick. I wouldn't trade it for anything."

"I've never done the love thing."

"You don't choose love. It finds you. When it finds you, you don't have a choice."

BP is over and Seno runs up in time to hear Sherry say those words. "And, I'm glad it did." He lifts her off her feet and kisses her. He leans his forehead to hers without putting her down, "How's Baby Seno treating you today?"

"Baby cheers when I cheer and I approve of the behavior," her happiness is overflowing.

He hugs her and sets her on her feet. They both palm her belly and make eye contact. "I love you, my queen. Don't over do it. I'll meet you at the car after the game."

"Make it a win!" She tells him and he takes off for the dug out.

Their interaction gives me hope. "Are you for real? Your whole demeanor changes and you smile bigger in his presence."

"What do you think you did when Houck was here to say hi?"

I gasp internally. "There's no way."

"You did. He did, too."

"Are you telling me to test the theory?"

"Finally, you're catching on. Have you considered you might be the one who isn't interested in? Then again, what if you're not. Maybe he needs to know you're an option." She stops, "Now, I need to watch BP for the other team and report in. We're winning this season and it's one of the ways I contribute."

I sit quietly and watch the rest of BP. Honestly, I can't tell you a thing about BP. My head is reeling at the thought of being with D. Taking a chance. The possibility of love. What's the first step? Luckily I have the whole baseball game to figure it out. 48 outs and hopefully he'll come in to close. I'd love to watch him pitch and get the save.

Houck

Why did I tell her she's a hot blonde? Whispering in her ear and kissing her inappropriately on the cheek again? Having her here makes it hard to control myself. The text messages and phone calls at all hours are one thing. It doesn't matter if I had a girlfriend or not, I've always been able to be there for her whenever she wanted me. I always found a way to get away for Angie. A phone call from Angie was more important than anything with any other girl. That's bad, but it's true. I guess they've all been placeholders. Maybe the last one was right, maybe I didn't care. Maybe I didn't care about any of them. Having Angie here makes them all seem insignificant. Shit. I never got any of them in for early BP. I'd get them a ticket to the game if they asked, but never anywhere special. With Angie, everything needs to be the best and I want her to have everything she wants.

Seno and Carter walk up to me, Carter starts, "Anything else I can help you with for Angie?"

"Yeah, can you take her my hoodie? I don't want her to get cold tonight."

"I already made her one up with Super D and your number on it," he grins like a know-it-all. "I'll take it to her before the game starts. She has food service at her seat and the server has already been notified she's to charge your account."

"Thanks." I want to talk to her, but Seno is standing in front of me.

"I already talked to Skip and told him we need you to come in to close tonight. I'm not giving up any runs to get you a save, but most likely you'll be pitching the 9th. She needs to watch you pitch and win. Women like winners." He has it all planned out. "I know you've had a couple bad outings. Nobody's perfect. There's nobody I'd rather have closing for my team. It's probably the only two blown saves you'll have all season. I'm happy you got them out of the way early." He smiles deviously, "Now, tell me you want this woman and the texts I got from Sherry aren't crazy."

"What?"

"She's been talking to Sherry. Never mind. See you on the field," he high-fives me and walks away.

I wonder what they've been talking about.

Text to Angie - Did you enjoy BP?
Text to Angie - You have food service at your seat tonight. It's already set up. You don't need money.
Text to Angie - Carter's bringing you a hoodie for me.

She isn't answering. I start to get ready for the game and my phone lights up.

Text from Angie - BP was fun
Text from Angie - You didn't have to do all this for me
Text from Angie - Thank you (picture of Angie in her Seals jersey and cap)
Text from Angie - Ordered a hot dog and beer. Saving room for dessert.

Fuck, she's hot in my jersey.

CHAPTER FOUR

Angie

Text from D - I'll meet you at my place after the game.
Text to D - What's for dessert?
Text from D - Whatever you want.

I want you. Can I have you? Maybe I need to test his theory. We need to kiss and he needs to hold me all night. How do I make both of those things happen?

Text to D - Where's your favorite place to have dessert?
Text from D - My bed, with a big bowl of ice cream or gelato watching a movie.

Ding! Ding! Ding! We have a winner!

Text to D - Sounds like a plan.

Text from D - You're going to sit in my bed with me and eat ice cream?

Text to D - Yea, is that a problem?

Text from D - No. You pick the movie.

Text to D - How have I never heard about the girl who's the one for you?

Text from D - Time for the game. We'll talk later.

Text to D - Have a good game.

I'm going to sit in bed with him and watch a movie with a bowl of ice cream.

I sit with Sherry and watch the team warm up. The relief pitchers walk out to the bullpen in a group before the game starts. D is leading the bunch. It's fun to cheer with Sherry and get involved in the game. I haven't had the opportunity to enjoy a baseball game like this since college.

I remember the night D pitched the complete game. It's probably the only time I ever considered kissing him, until recently. If my business partner wasn't getting married, I'd probably still be in control of my world and not wondering if I'm missing out. Have I been missing out on D all this time?

It's the bottom of the 8th inning and the Seals are ahead by 3. The score is 4-1 Seals. They flash the bullpen up on the big screen and D is warming up. D is warming up! He's damn fine in his uniform. I don't remember him being so much of a man. I guess it was college. He probably hadn't filled out yet and he definitely hadn't had the opportunity to work out with a professional baseball team. There's no denying it, he's hot. He's tall with larger than average shoulders. His hair is cut short and clean. His pants are snug around his ass and he's wearing them long, down to his cleats. No stirrups or fun socks, he's all business.

End of the 8th inning and no score change. The stadium goes dark and the speakers start blaring "Sex Type Thing" by Stone Temple Pilots. The light bars are blue with a neon green line showing the beat of the music, then flashing to Houck. The big screen changes back and forth from the ball in his hand to his eyes staring you down. His gorgeous grey eyes staring straight into my heart. It's hot, or maybe it's me. He can stare at me like that any time he wants. I find myself standing up and cheering for him as he runs to the mound. "Let's do this, Super D! Wooooo!" Did he smile at me? It's probably in my head. Seno's behind home plate and ready to go. D throws him a few pitches and the first hitter of the 9th inning steps into the batter's box. First pitch and he's challenging the hitter with a 100 mile per hour fastball right up the pipe. The bat connects and it's a come backer, straight at D and he catches it. "Woooooooooooo!" One out. Second hitter and he throws him a fastball low on the outside corner, he gets the strike call. Second pitch, exactly the same spot and the hitter reaches for it smacking it down the first base line. First baseman, Kris Martin, grabs it and tags the runner out. "Yes! Go D! Wooo!" I'm dancing around and all the Seals fans are on their feet for the last out of the game. First pitch, he throws a curve for a strike. Second pitch, 98 mile per hour fastball on the outside corner for a called strike. Count is 0-2. Third pitch, 102 mile per hour fastball but it's off the plate. Fourth pitch, heater straight down the middle, batter swings and misses. Strike out, the Seals win and D gets the save. I scream out at the top of my lungs, "Woooooo! Go Super D!" and I dance around happy.

He's staring at me and smiling. He meets Seno halfway between the mound and home plate for a bro hug. They high-five the rest of the team in celebration of the win and the on field reporter grabs him for an interview. They show it up on the big screen.

"Doug, your fastball tonight was on point. You were clocked at up to 102 miles per hour, your fastest pitch of the season so far. Have you been working on pitch speed?"

"I had a lot of adrenaline going into the game tonight. It felt good to get it out there. I've been throwing 100 miles per hour routinely in practices."

"How do you feel getting the save tonight after blowing the save on both of the last two outings?"

"I never want to let me team down, but nobody's perfect. I wanted to get it done in three tonight and show them I'm the closer. I think I achieved that."

"You most certainly did and brought some amazing heat. Great job."

"Thanks."

Houck

I search for Angie in her seat or around the dug out after my interview, but she's not there. It's okay, she'll be at my place waiting for me.

My mind switches gears. She's going to be in my bed with me eating ice cream? How's this going to work? I need to make sure I stay in control. Fuck, I've dreamt about having her in my bed and it's always amazing, but definitely not in control. In my dreams, I hold her close to me and kiss her until she gives herself to me. She gives up control to me completely. There's no words saying it, her actions are all it takes. She's mine before I do anything more than kiss her. Fuck, kissing her. Kissing her is a drug I can't get enough of, better than the adrenaline rush I get on the mound when I get the save. I have to kiss her. I need to taste her. It's a dream, not reality. I dream about her, aware it'll never happen and with no consideration for it even being a possibility. Is there a chance it could be real? No, she's not interested. Don't get your hopes up. Stay in control. Enjoy the time while you have her here. No more whispering things in her ear. No more kissing her on the cheek. She's going to be in my bed. My mind races because I know what happens when a woman is in my bed. This isn't some hook up. This is Angie. I take a deep breath to center myself. The bed is a big sofa. We'll prop the pillows up against my headboard to lean against and sit on top of the bedspread. Right. I can do this. What if we fall asleep? Doesn't matter, we'll be sleeping. I'm sure she'll get up and go to her room when she wakes up in the middle of the night. It's fine.

"Hey!" Seno calls out to me, pulling me out of my head, "You okay?"

"Yeah."

"You look confused. What's up?"

"Nothing." He motions for me to tell him and I spill, "Angie's going to watch a movie with me in my bed tonight."

"What's the problem?"

"She's not interested and I want more. It's always been this way."

"Why's she here? What if she's interested?"

"I'd love it, but..." he interrupts me.

"I'm just saying, maybe you shouldn't rule it out."

"I'm open to the possibility. She's more beautiful now than I remember her being before. The part that gets me though, is how she's still her. You know? She hasn't changed. I talk to her all the time, but it's different when she's actually here. The time apart doesn't matter. It's like we've spent everyday since college together." I stop and close my eyes, "That's the problem. I don't want to lose her. What if I do the wrong thing and she's gone forever?"

"What if you don't do anything and you never find out? What are you missing out on by not trying for more with her?" He turns to walk out of the clubhouse, "Good luck."

I'm going to enjoy spending the evening with her. Maybe tomorrow I can try something new.

Text to Angie - I have vanilla and chocolate chip ice cream in my freezer.

Text to Angie - Does that work or would you prefer to go get ice cream and take it back to my place?

Text from Angie - Works for me. I'll be here when you get home.

I'm warm all over, she's at my place waiting for me. I get out of the clubhouse in half the time I normally take and don't hang out with the team.

Angie

I change into my soft cotton PJ shorts and the faded Seals T-shirt I've had since D was signed by the Seals, comfy and ready to watch a movie. I skim through his movie collection and choose a romantic comedy. There's only a couple and they both feature baseball. I go with Bull Durham because I love the speeches and the passion in the sexy scenes.

I walk to his bedroom and lean in the doorway studying his bed. The leather upholstered headboard has aged-brass fasteners and beading. The king sized bed is covered with an oversized warm dark chocolate comforter, accented with a bordeaux throw and pillows. The materials and colors are masculine, yet soft and luxurious. It's inviting to me. His room is large with a full wall of windows covered in blackout draperies to match his comforter. The walls are all off-white and he has some enlarged photos from his college team on the wall, along with a framed print of a baseball diagram. A framed photo on his nightstand gets my attention and I go to it, imagining it's a picture of his family who I haven't seen in years. But, it's not. It's us in college and my arm's around him, gazing up at him as if he's the only one who matters. He's smiling back at me with heavy hooded eyes. He wanted me then.

What am I doing here?

The elevator opens, and he calls out, "I'm home. Angie?"

"I'm in here," I respond without thinking. Why am I in his room? "Checking if I should bring my pillow and blanket with me to watch the movie."

I turn to find him standing in the doorway, "You won't need them."

Text from Lucy - Do you want to learn about today's lesson?

Text to Lucy - I'm still stuck on the last lesson. Thank you very much.

Text from Lucy - Did you find out yet?

Text to Lucy - Working up to it.

Text from Lucy - Stop wasting time. I need you working, not distracted by a man.

"Are you okay?" D asks.

"Perfectly fine. Business partner getting me caught up on

today. It won't take long." I sit down on the edge of his bed while I text.

Text from Lucy - You're smart and gorgeous. Any man who doesn't want you is an idiot.
Text from Lucy - Your friends aren't idiots. Stop waiting. Do it.
Text from Lucy - Today's lesson was about being confident and comfortable in your relationship.
Text to Lucy - Stop! I'm not ready for the next lesson.
Text from Lucy - I think you're already comfortable, show your confidence.
Text to Lucy - How was business today?
Text from Lucy - Everything is under control. Handle your business.

There's a reason we're successful business partners. We support each other and push each other when we need to. I need to listen to her. Shit. Sherry said the same thing.

D walks back into his room with a huge bowl of ice cream, "I went with chocolate chip. Is it still your go-to flavor?"

"Yes, thank you," I say as he hands me the bowl with two spoons and disappears into his closet.

He comes back wearing sweatpants and a threadbare concert T-shirt. Damn he's sexy. I'm surprised the T-shirt is staying together as it's stretched across his chest and shoulders. Ugh, and he smells all fresh and manly. "Great game tonight. You were perfect on the mound. Form, speed, location, everything on point. I guess you don't need me to tell you, the on-field reporter already did."

"It means more from you. You're never here. I'm glad you got to see me pitch." He smiles at me and stretches out on his bed, leaning back against the headboard. He takes the bowl of ice cream from me and I pull my feet up onto his bed as I move to sit next to him, so we can share.

He starts the movie with a remote without getting up. It's nice he's still the same guy. Yes, he lives in a penthouse and has some high-end things, but he's still him. He's still happy to stay home and hang out in an old T-shirt and sweats with a bowl of ice cream. Nothing snooty like Kulfi or Lavender Honey, simply the old standard vanilla or chocolate chip. He's relaxed and comfortable with himself the way he is. It makes him even sexier.

I take a spoon and dig into the bowl for a bite of ice cream, moving in closer and leaning against him in the process. He's warm and I don't understand how the ice cream in his hands hasn't melted. I take another bite and rub against him, waiting for a reaction and not getting one.

"So, tell me about the woman who's the one and isn't interested. Why haven't you told me about her?"

He chuckles, "She's successful and doesn't need a man in her life. Men are complications for her."

"She may not need a man, but it doesn't mean she doesn't want one. I'm guessing it's a possibility."

"Maybe, but she's never shown any signs of interest in me and she's had boyfriends right in front of me."

"How long have you known her?"

"Since college."

"Have I met her?"

"We don't need to have this conversation. It's not going to make a difference. It's not going to suddenly make her interested in me," his frustration shows.

I back off on the conversation. I consider who it could be and how I could've missed it back then. We were together all the time. My boyfriends used to get irritated at how much time I spent with D. Wait. Could he be talking about me? I go for another bite of ice cream and make myself comfortable up against him. He doesn't move or change positions, he let's me do what I want and shifts to suit me. He sets the empty bowl on his nightstand and comes back to exactly where he was, trying not to disturb my position. I lean my head on his shoulder and he rests his arm around my shoulders. Not holding me to him, simply getting more comfortable. Either way, it's nice to have his arm around me. We watch the movie together and my head runs away imagining how D could be the one. I'm comfortable with him and he's sexy and we get along, we've always gotten along. Is the girl who's not interested me? I need to show him a sign. He needs to know maybe I'm interested. Damn it! I'm interested.

I reach for the throw to cover my legs and he puts his legs over mine to help warm me up. I snuggle into him and he holds me there, like it's where I belong.

CHAPTER FIVE

Houck

Is this Angie? In my bed, up against me with my arm around her?

"D?"

"Yeah?"

"You think I'm a hot blonde?"

"Always have, Ang." I glance at her face to catch her smiling, but she's sleeping. I pull her in closer to me with both arms around her. "Do you want to stay here with me tonight?" I ask softly.

She mumbles something I can't determine, but her reaction is positive.

I hold her with one arm and adjust the pillows, sliding us down to lie on the mattress. She cuddles into me, nuzzling into my chest and my heart beats harder. I hold her, content. The theory is getting tested voluntarily. I'm holding her all night tonight and it just happened, I didn't have to do anything to get here. I consider step two of the test. Will the kiss come to me on it's own, too?

I'm holding her and her body is next to mine. She's wrapped her arm around me. I can't believe I've never held her before.

Houck

I wake up in the middle of the night and it's my dream. I'm holding her in my arms and she's wrapped around me. I didn't believe this would ever happen. I've wanted her for so long. I kiss her forehead and glide my foot along her bare legs, she's cold. I pull the blankets back carefully, trying not to wake her. I whisper to her, "Angie, you're cold. I'm getting us under the blankets and making sure you get warm. Sleep, everything is fine. D is taking care of you." I pull the blankets down behind me. I move back on the bed and take her with me, then pull the blankets up over us.

"Thank you, D," she sighs sweetly without opening her eyes.

Her sweet tone tears at my heart and I hold her tight, "I'll always take care of you."

Houck

I wake up again and she's gone. I didn't get to hold her all night. She must not have wanted to be in my bed. What was I thinking? Of course she doesn't want to be with me. She's not interested in me. She fell asleep. I take my shirt off and shed my sweatpants. I'm ready to go back to sleep when the toilet flushes and Angie walks out of my master bathroom. I'm stripped to my boxer briefs. Is she coming back to my bed or what? Come back to bed, Angie. Please, come back to bed. She walks straight back to my bed and climbs under the blankets, reaching for me and snuggling against me. She didn't fully wake up, but she's aware something is different. Her hands roam my body from my waist across my abs to my chest. She buries her cold feet between my legs. She giggles happily and is back to sleep with her fingers splayed across my chest within seconds. Fuck! Her hand touching my bare chest lights me on fire. She makes me want more. I'd give her anything, everything, if she'd stay with me.

Angie

I wake up in bed with D. His arms are wrapped around me and holding me close to him. I'm nuzzled against him with my hand on his bare chest and my feet snuggled between his legs. What happened? How did I get here? When did he lose his shirt? And pants? Should I get out of bed and go to my own room? My lips are pressed to his chest and he kisses my forehead. He's awake. "I'm sorry. I didn't mean to invade your bed." I'm surprised at myself and unsure about the situation. I move to get out of bed, but he stops me.

His grip on me tightens. "Please stay here with me," he says in a heartfelt raspy tone.

"Okay." My whole body relaxes. He wants me here. "D?"

"Yeah?"

"What are we doing?"

"Sleeping."

"You know what I mean."

"Do you like my arms around you, holding you?" he asks me.

"Yes." It's what I want.

"Then enjoy it with me. We don't have to talk about it. I'll never do anything you don't want me to do."

"D, am I the one who's not interested?"

"Testing a theory."

That's not an answer. I kiss and explore his bare chest as I go back to sleep.

CHAPTER SIX

Angie

Waking up in his arms with my hands on his shirtless body may be the best thing I've ever experienced. He's a professional athlete and has the body to prove it. His thick, corded arms protect me while his hands are splayed across my back with need. His long muscular legs warm my always cold feet between his calves. His lips touch my forehead with his nose buried in my hair. More than any of the rest of it, it's D. My Super D I've talked to or text messaged almost everyday since college. He's always been there for me.

I lie quiet and still, wanting as much of him as I can get and appreciating his manly scent while I wait for him to wake up. I'm happy to stay right here all day, but he can't. I'll be going to the baseball game tonight to watch his team play and hopefully cheer for him pitching for the save again.

Houck

I don't want to move. I want everything to stay exactly the way it is right now. I've stayed in bed longer today than I ever do during the baseball season. This could be the only time I have Angie in my bed. Test the theory is a fine plan, but what did I learn? She appreciates my shirtless body. Does it mean she wants me? I need more. I need the kiss.

I kiss her forehead, "Ang? Are you awake?"

"Yeah. Good morning," she says softly and doesn't move.

"Were you comfortable last night?"

"It was perfect. D, were you testing the theory?"

Angie

He pulls me against him, "I think the theory tested us." He gazes into my eyes and I can't help but to search his, wondering what his test results are and if they match the possessiveness he has in his hands. "Spend the night with me tonight?" He says low and raspy.

I smile and kiss his cheek while I glide my hand across his abs.

"I'm taking that as a yes."

"It's most definitely a yes." I stop and worry about what happens next. What about our friendship? "Are we still friends?"

"We'll always be friends. Nothing can change that."

What about part two of testing the theory? Will it happen? I don't want him questioning my intent, "I don't know who the one is that's not interested." I stop and drag my teeth across his earlobe, then whisper, "If it's me, you're wrong. I'm interested."

He pulls back away from me, holding me at arms length while he reads my expression and body language. His eyes shine and he laughs, "The first time I kiss you can't be in my bed when I'm mostly naked."

"Why not?" I need to kiss him. I need answers. Everything's right and I don't want to wait anymore. I run my fingers through his hair and pull his lips to mine. Chaste, not pushing it further. I pull away and get out of his bed with him watching my every move.

"Ang?" He calls out to me as I'm about to leave his room. I turn to find him sitting up in bed with the blanket covering him up to his waist and his strong chest bare. His eyes catch mine and he grins, "Have dinner with me tonight after the game?"

"I'll be here. Good luck at the game today." I walk away, leaving him to get ready for work. I take a quick shower and throw on shorts and a tank top. I pour myself some juice and sit out on his balcony, enjoying the cool breeze and bright blue San Diego sky. I'm buzzing at the idea of being with D. Kissing him wasn't weird at all. In fact, I want more.

Houck

I lie back down and stretch out across my bed. She kissed me and walked away. She's spending the night with me tonight and we're having dinner together. I need to get ready and go to the stadium. Fuck! I need to kiss her. No time for distractions, I already stayed in bed too long. I clean up and get ready for work. I sit at my kitchen island and eat a bowl of cereal, noticing she's doing yoga in the sunlight on my balcony. Stretching and bending, slow and methodically. I can't help myself. She's sexy and I'm not leaving her wondering until after the game. I need more now.

I join her on my balcony. Her eyes are closed and her hands are reaching for the sky. She's beautiful, calm and centered. I hesitate, examining every inch of her and suddenly worry the kiss might go bad. What if it's not special for her? Not the connection I'm anticipating? I don't have time for a second chance. It doesn't matter. I reach for her, leaning down to her ear I whisper, "Angie." I kiss her in front of her ear and she gazes up at me. My arm is around her and my other hand in her hair, I press my lips to hers asking for more. Asking for everything she's willing to give me. She's the one, she's always been the one. Her soft lips receive me willingly and kiss me back. Our kiss turns open-mouthed, our lips meeting repeatedly. She wraps her arms around my neck and arches into me. My heart pounds. She wants me. I slide my tongue against her lips and she opens for me immediately, greeting my tongue with hers and I'm done. I tighten my grip on her and control the kiss, my body ready to explode. I taste every bit of her lips and our tongues dance together. Her hands pushing up into my hair like she's trying to hold on. I glide my hands down her body and lift her up against me. She clings to me, wrapping her legs around my waist and arms around my neck. She throws her head back and giggles, then gazes straight into my eyes. "What are you looking for?" I ask her.

"I'm not sure."

"You don't need to look anymore. You found me."

"I have competition. Who's the one?" Her voice is concerned but confident.

I lean my forehead to hers and kiss her nose, "There's no competition. I didn't think you were interested in me."

She claims my mouth with hers leaving no question in my mind. She's more confident and forward than any woman I've been with. Not one of the skanks who goes straight for my dick because it's all they want. Is it because it's us or is she always aggressive? I'm hot all over, simply holding her and kissing her. This can't be like other women. I can't screw this up. She's only here a few days and this has to be at her pace. I can't carry her off to my room and fuck her, she's more than all of them together. This heat, her hands on me make my blood sizzle with desire. I've never wanted a woman more. I want her everywhere, not just wrapped around my cock. I tug on her sweet lips and I'm out of breath. I break the kiss and hug her close, whispering in her ear, "I'm all in. We don't need to rush us. Everything at your pace, Ang." I take a deep breath, "I need to get to the stadium, so I can pitch tonight. I'll be watching for you."

"I'll be there," she says as she slides down my body rubbing against my hard-on. "That's pleasing," she giggles. "We'll figure it out," she continues as she bites her lower lip.

I roll my eyes and give her a quick kiss before I run to the stadium. I'm glad I'm only across the street, I'd be late for sure. I adjust myself in the elevator and regain control.

I run into the stadium and Carter yells for me when I pass his office, "Houck!"

I turn around and lean in his doorway, "Yeah?"

"Running late?" he smiles. "Need assistance with anything today? BP is at 2:00."

"Can you arrange a candlelight dinner for two? After tonight's game?"

"Absolutely, where at?"

"My place on the balcony."
"No problem."

Text to Angie - BP at 2:00, game at 5:00 today
Text to Angie - Not that I'll be hitting
Text from Angie - I'll be there :)

Angie

There's a smile on my face I can't control. A man has never affected me this way. He's a tropical storm. Hot and sending lightning from my fingertips to my toes, leaving the thunder to rumble nervously in my belly. He's known I'm the one and didn't think I'm interested. Honestly, I hadn't considered him until Lucy and her pre-marital course. He's always been my friend D. That's it. Lying next to him last night, sleeping in his bed and simply being live, in person with him is a whole other ball game. I had to kiss him. I couldn't resist caressing his bare skin. He's known I'm the one all this time, and I didn't? Aren't women supposed to be more intuitive of these things? I guess I've always been more of a guy in some ways. I don't want to be a guy with D. Huh, what I found sliding down his body, Super D might be a description of him.

Since the game is earlier today, I don't have much time to get ready. I put my jersey and cap on over my shorts and tank top. I get distracted as I wander through his place and find myself leaning in the doorway to his bedroom. What am I doing here? I don't live here. I'm leaving in a few days. Can this work? Did I destroy our friendship? No. I can figure this out. But, right now all I can do is focus on his bed and the memory of his protective arms around me. The room is filled with his clean masculine scent and when I close my eyes he's pressing his lips to mine. I'm consumed by his heat and possessive fingers in my hair. Simply imagining him my pulse races and I'm unsure how I'm going to handle being near him alone tonight.

CHAPTER SEVEN

Angie

I find Sherry behind the dug out for batting practice and sit next to her. How does she do this everyday in her condition? Business alone could make it a challenge for me, but I'm not allowing any extra complications right now. I'm focusing on now and not how life will want to get in the way. "Hi, did I miss anything?"

"You're right on time," she turns and examines me, getting a big grin on her face. "Looks like you tested the theory with positive results."

I nod, "We'll find out after the game." We only kissed once, but damn was it an amazing kiss.

The team emerges from the dugout a few at a time. A bunch of pitchers walk to the outfield in a cluster and Seno drags D with him to take a turn at bat. Sherry yells at Seno and I follow suit loudly, "Go Super D!" She pats my knee and gives me a thumbs up. He smiles as he runs up to visit me. He grabs my hand and pulls me up out of my seat, then gazing into my eyes he kisses me. Not a sweet peck, no this was more. His hands are on my face holding me where he wants me while he brushes his lips against mine, sucking and nibbling on them until my breath turns ragged.

He breaks the kiss to whisper, warm in my ear, "I want to kiss you all night long. I have fifteen years of imagining what it's like to kiss you to make up for. I'll be happy kissing you and holding you again tonight." His tone, sincere and raspy, hits me directly in the gut causing the thunder to rumble. He kisses me below my ear and lifts me up to kiss and nuzzle at my neck, driving me crazy. I whimper uncontrollably and wrap my legs around him right there in front of everyone. The team catcalls at us, woots, whistles, "Get it!" and "Houck's got a hottie."

I lean down to whisper in his ear, hard to speak because he has me worked up, "You make me hot. You make me want more than kissing. You make me lose control." I tug on his ear with my teeth and sigh, "I want you."

He whispers back to me, "I want you, too. We'll talk over dinner, this can't be a game. You're the only woman I want." He smiles at me and I nod at him in agreement. He gives me a quick peck on the lips as he sets me back on the ground and he's gone.

"Looks mind blowing to me," Sherry comments. "I remember those first kisses when he left me punch drunk. I thought I was crazy. It was the new guy excitement." She laughs, "It still happens."

I smile and focus on batting practice, or at least pretend to because I can't focus on anything except D and putting words together is a challenge. He's right, we can't be a game and we should do the adult thing and talk about it, but it's new and I want to enjoy it. It's wrong, but I'd take his D out for a ride and find out if it should be the Super D. Not in a bad way, it's just that everything has been more than I've experienced before. Better than anything before and I'm a curious girl who's always taken a male perspective on sex. I'm not the village bicycle. I'm pickier than most, but if I find a ride I want to take—why wait? It doesn't have to be more than sex. Huh, maybe that's the problem? We've been friends for so long it can't be a satisfying fuck? We have to be more than sex? Maybe I'm not ready for this. Damn that Lucy!

Text to Lucy - I'm mad at you

Text from Lucy - What did I do now?

Text to Lucy - You told me about your workbook lesson

Text from Lucy - What happened? You kissed?

Text to Lucy - Yes we kissed.

Text from Lucy - And it was good?

Text to Lucy - No, it wasn't good

Text to Lucy - It was better than good

Text from Lucy - He's the one?

Text to Lucy - I'm not talking about the one

Text from Lucy - What else happened?

Text to Lucy - I slept with him all night and I'm going to do it again

Text to Lucy - Since we were friends, does it mean we can't fuck?

Text from Lucy - Umm

Text from Lucy - Stop being such a guy

Text to Lucy - But…

Text from Lucy - Seriously. You're a girl at heart. Stop hiding.

Text from Lucy - He's the one. Let him be the one.

Text from Lucy - Let it be different this time.

I shove my phone in my pocket without answering again.

She's right, but I have no clue how to be a girl. Let him take the lead? I guess? I'll consider it.

Houck

"Looks like it's going well with your friend," Seno laughs.

"Man, when I kiss her she makes me stronger. She's not like anybody else."

He hands me a bat, "Show me how much stronger."

Fuck. Again? I'm not going to argue with him, but there's no way I get brought in to hit. I'm the closer. I stand in ready to hit and everything seems to be moving slower around me. The ball is in focus. The pitch is obvious from the release and the grip the pitcher is using. The spin of the ball out of the two-finger grip, and it starts to drop. It's a sinker ball, but it doesn't appear to have much drop on it. I swing my bat hard and connect. The sound is clean and rewarding off my bat, but not as rewarding as the sound coming from behind the dug out. "Woooooo! That's my Super D! Go D!" at the top of her lungs as the ball flies out of the park. The next pitch is a four-seamer straight fastball and I see it coming, straight down the middle of the plate. Smack! Again and I have the power to do anything as the ball lands in the visiting bullpen. "That's my man! Go Super D! Super D!" Everything is clear. I connect to every pitch, hitting six more out of the park during batting practice and being rewarded by Angie's cheering every time. My Super D. My Man. She makes me better, indestructible, tougher, stronger. I'm a superhero for her. I'm her Super D and I want to be hers.

CHAPTER EIGHT

Angie

The game is going great. The Seals are up 7-2 in the 7th inning and D probably won't get to pitch because the team is ahead by more than 3, it's not a save situation. It's still a win. In the 8th inning the wheels come off and the visiting team scores 5, tying the game at 7 with a bases loaded walk and a grand slam. It's ugly and he's warming up in the pen. The game is tied and they don't play all of the closer lights when he comes running in. "Sex Type Thing" rattles the stadium and he's into it. I'm standing on my feet yelling from behind home plate, "Let's do this Super D! You can hold them!" He's ready and the first batter steps into the box. Seno gives the sign and the pitch is straight down the middle at 99 miles per hour, strike one. Second pitch is low, but catches the strike zone for a called strike. Third pitch is challenging the hitter, right down the middle and he swings getting a piece of it and fouling it off. Fourth pitch, a changeup thrown in to throw off the hitter's timing and a called ball. Fifth pitch, 103 miles per hour. Fastball straight down the pipe and the hitter swings and misses. Strike three. One out. The second hitter steps into the box and Seno does his routine of swinging his head from side to side and turning to wave at Sherry. He's funny. He does things to throw off timing and make the hitter's wonder. I wouldn't be surprised if he says things to throw them off, too. Sherry does. Seno gives the sign and D delivers the pitch on the high inside corner for a strike, exactly where the catcher is set up. The second pitch is on fire. A strike clocked at 106 miles per hour and flame graphics run on all the light bars and the big screen. The hitter never saw it coming. Third pitch is a changeup again, the hitter swings and misses. Strike three. Two out. Third hitter digs his cleats in and the pitch is delivered low and inside to push him back away from the plate. Ball one. The second pitch is 102 miles per hour right down the pipe, the hitter swings and misses. The count is one ball and one strike. Third pitch is a fastball down the middle again, this time at 104 miles per hour and the hitter is caught looking. One and two. Fourth pitch and he let's it rip, challenging the hitter. Flames light up the stadium again as he strikes out the side, this time hitting 107 miles per hour. I'm out of my seat screaming for him, "That's my Super D! Way to bring the heat!" He smiles at me as he walks off the mound. He kisses two fingers and points them at me. It's crazy how happy it makes me, but it does. It makes me more than happy and I can't explain it.

The Seals are up to bat in the 9th and they need to score or this game is going into extra innings. The leadoff spot is up and Chase Cross steps into the batter's box hitting the first pitch and getting a base hit. Shortstop Jones Mason is up next and smacks a grounder to the third baseman. He's out at first base, but Cross advances to second. Kris Martin digs into the batter's box intent on knocking it out of the park. He swings at the first pitch and pops it up, caught in centerfield. 2 outs. It's Seno's turn to hit and he takes four straight balls for a walk. The pitcher is in the fifth spot due to a double switch earlier in the game and I watch to find out who they bring in to hit with one out left. Super D is standing there with a bat in the on deck circle waiting for direction. Waiting for the coach to pull him back and put in a hitter, but he doesn't. I'm out of my seat, "Super D! Super D! Super D! Go Super D! Woooooo!" He focuses on me and smiles, the stress of the situation melting away from his face. "Let's do this, D! Woooooo!" Seno is clapping at him from first and Cross has a huge lead off of second. All he needs is a single to bring in Cross and the Seals win with a walk-off. The intensity of the situation is getting the best of me. My whole body is buzzing and I'm anxious for him. I might as well be in the batter's box. The first pitch is delivered and it's a ball outside. The second pitch is high and inside, Sherry and I are both out of our seats yelling at the pitcher. I'm louder than her and that's saying something, "Watch it meat! Don't be throwing at my man!" I don't know what's come over me. Next pitch and it's in slow motion. His grip changes on the bat and his eyes track the ball. He swings and the same sound I heard at batting practice rings through the stadium. I'm screaming again, "OMG! Super D! Wooooo!" I watch the ball sail over the wall in left field. Home run. Seals walk it off with a final score of 10-7. I climb over the seats in front of me to watch him cross home plate at the net and witness his joy as he runs into the scrum of his teammates waiting for him. It's a celebration, and he made it happen. His teammates disperse and he turns to me, kissing two fingers and pointing at me right as they dump a vat of gatorade over his head. He's pumped up and he doesn't care.

He does a quick interview with the on-field reporter, but the whole time he's focused on me. He walks straight to me at the net and gazes at me without speaking.

"You were awesome tonight."

He blushes, "You were cheering for me. Nothing matters as much as you calling me your man. You make me stronger. I ordered dinner in, it might get there before me. I'll be home as soon as I can." He holds my hand on the net and the lightning is back shooting through my body.

"I'll be waiting for you." I smile and he takes off for the clubhouse.

"Nice job," Sherry high-fives me. "You'll see there's nothing better."

I don't doubt her one bit.

CHAPTER NINE

Angie

I get back to his place to find a table for two with candles set up on the balcony. Place settings set out perfectly and a long stemmed red rose sitting on one of the chairs. It's romantic. I run into my room to change into something more appropriate for a date night dinner and thumb through what I've brought with me. I brush out my hair, attempting to get rid of the hat hair I've developed and tie it up into a chignon, a little fancy, it accentuates my bare neck, and hides my hat hair. I throw on the black dress I brought with me along with my strappy black high heels. I add to the ambiance by turning on some music. I skim through his play lists and choose one titled "my heart." The first song is "Angela" by the Lumineers. The elevator opens and a personal chef walks out, going straight to the kitchen with a cart of plates and food. I think it's odd he doesn't say anything until D steps out of the elevator right after him. He's focused on me and walks directly to me in his dark blue jeans and black long-sleeved button up shirt. He's absolutely gorgeous and he slides his arms around me without saying a word. He pulls me against him and holds me there, simply gazing into my eyes. He kisses my cheek and takes my hand, leading me to his balcony. He pulls the chair out for me and pushes me in, handing me the rose from the seat. He pulls the cork on a bottle of champagne like a professional and pours us each a glass.

"You're beautiful and you're all I've ever wanted. I don't know what finally brought us together, but I'm glad it did. To us," he toasts and clinks his glass to mine.

All I can do is giggle. He's an adult who's learned how to do adult things. I missed seeing him grow into being this responsible and respectable adult man. He didn't think I was interested because I've always been able to take care of myself, but in reality he's the same way. Neither of us need someone else. It makes it more special when we choose each other.

We each take a sip of champagne and the bubbles tickle my nose. I play with the rose he gave me, brushing it across my cheek. I'm a teenager again. Everything is new.

Houck

"You never told me why you're visiting me."

"It's silly," She laughs it off.

"Whatever it is, it brought you to me. It brought us together and there's nothing I take more seriously." I have to be completely honest and straight with her. This is Angie.

She stares off into the night sky, "My business partner is getting married. She's taking a pre-marital class at her church with her fiancé and she shares what they learn with me. It's more her way of reviewing and making basic notes for her to have in the future. Last week, she brought me a copy of the workbook page and told me to answer the ten questions." She shifts her focus to me, "Based on my answers she asked me the follow up questions and, basically, it said I should be with you." She takes a breath and continues with her hands flying everywhere, "I didn't believe it. I could've done a quiz in a fashion magazine. It had nothing to substantiate it. I tried to blow it off, completely forget about it, but I couldn't. Lucy told me to visit you and kiss you. She actually kicked me out of the office until I did it. I decided I should at least visit you and spend some time with you, but that was it. Somehow it got us here. It's batshit crazy."

"I need to thank Lucy," he chuckles. "What do you want, Ang?"

"I want you. We're friends, but this is new and the beginning is always exhilarating while you're discovering each other. I don't know what the best way to do this is, but I don't want to lose the excitement. Lucy told me to stop being a guy and let the girl come out."

"I don't want to mess this up and lose you completely."

"What's being together worth to you? It's a risk we have to take. We'll always wonder if we don't."

"Do we take it slow or?" he shakes his head. "We can't start at the beginning and date. We're past that. You already spent the night in my bed. We know each other too well."

"Take the lead and follow your gut. You won't hurt me, and if you do? It'll be worth it. I'll regret it everyday and question if we would've been better together if we don't," her eyes fill with tears, though she's not crying. It's her heart coming out. The girl she hides away behind her facade.

I've wanted her for so long. I can't let myself in any

deeper if we won't work. I never want to hurt her. I stare down at my plate and talk, "I need to know if we want the same things. Not now, but in time. Do you want to be married? Have kids? Where do you want to live? What about me being a baseball player and everything that goes with it?"

"I want to have kids if it's with the right man and I don't care where we live or if we get married. All I care is that we're together. I love to watch you play, but I don't know how it'll mesh with my business. I need to figure out all the logistics. It might not be ideal, but I'm sure there's a way."

The chef sets a salad of mixed greens and arugula dressed in balsamic vinaigrette in front of each of us.

I stand up and take her hand, leading her away from the table. "Dance with me," I request softly, placing my other hand on the small of her back. She follows my lead and we sway to "Somebody" by Depeche Mode. Holding her close in my arms, she's all I've ever wanted. She leans her cheek against my chest and wraps her arm around my waist. If I didn't have this shirt on, she'd have her hands on my bare skin like she did this morning. I'd do anything for her to graze my bare skin. I lean down and kiss her. I want to be appropriate, but I can't control my kiss. I've wanted her for too long. It's a 15 year long date that never got to first base until now and fuck me if I'm not going to turn this into a grand slam. I shouldn't, but I find myself kissing her harder and sucking on her lips. Thrusting my tongue into her mouth over and over. She's sucking on my tongue and digging her fingers into my back. Fuck. We're not going to stop. She pulls my shirt out of my jeans and unbuttons it while she's kissing me. I kiss her neck, needing to catch my breath, "Dinner in might have been a bad idea."

"Everything seems about right to me, but I've lost my

appetite for food," she bites my neck and nibbles at my ear. "If I was some girl you met, what would you do?"

Fuck! "You're not some girl. I can't fuck you hard and put you away sore."

Angie

"What if I want to be fucked hard? What if I want you to take me and do all the things you want to do to me?" I can't help myself. Lucy said to be a girl, but some things don't change. Maybe someday if it's more than sex. Maybe if I sense something different, something more, like the flutters Lucy talks about in her belly. But, this is what I'm comfortable with. My guy-like perspective. I want to fuck. I bite my lower lip while I stare up into his eyes. No matter what, he's a guy. He can't turn me down.

He searches my eyes, "Is that what you want from me?" His body language changes and he steps away from me, "One hot fuck is not worth losing you. Don't you understand you're more to me? I've wanted you forever. Fuck! I've been in love with you since college. Damn it! I wasn't supposed to say that," he turns away and stares off into the night.

"Say what?" I ask without getting closer to him.

"That's not how you were supposed to find out I love you, okay?"

"You what?"

He turns to me from across his balcony, "I love you, Angie. You weren't supposed to find out because I blurted it out when I was mad. I've known exactly how I would tell you for years and it's too soon to say it. Shit."

"What else do you have planned out? I don't want plans.

I want to experience you," I walk toward him. "I want to experience us," I kiss his lips tenderly. "You bring out the girl in me, only you, D." I rest my hand on his chest and wait for a response. I'm not good at this. He doesn't speak. "D? Show me how it's supposed to be. Make me feel like a girl." Still nothing, "I swear I'm not using you. I don't want to be one of those girls. I don't want to wait. I want you, and I want to be with you—naked."

"You sound like a guy."

"It's a problem I have. Maybe you can change it."

"I didn't think you had any problems. I thought you were perfect. I still do."

"I'm not perfect. I'm a guy when it comes to sex. I don't get invested. Happy?"

"You need someone to treat you like the woman you are." He turns my head toward him, forcing me to focus on him, "That someone is me, and only me from now on. Do you understand? I promise you, I'll make everything right for you and you'll never want anyone else. But, I don't want even the thought of you ever being with anyone else again. I will always be your next and your last."

I shiver and the thunder in my belly expands throughout my body. "Yes, please."

He scoops me up over his shoulder and walks inside. He calls out to the chef, "Package the meal up for us. We'll be eating later. Thank you." He carries me into his bedroom and shuts the door behind us. He tosses me onto his bed and takes his shirt off, letting it fall to the floor.

I giggle, watching him stand there focused on me.

He smiles, "What are you giggling about?"

"You. You make me excited."

He crawls onto his bed wearing only his jeans and wraps his arms around me, "Hey, beautiful." He gazes into my eyes and presses his lips to mine, soft and tender. I love the sensation of his body, bare skin and hard muscles. I go for the button on his jeans, "Are you sure you want me?"

"Yes. I want all of you." He doesn't stop me. He tugs on my lower lip and groans. He moves his hands over my body and squeezes my ass. I unbutton his jeans and pull the zipper down. I reach in and find him hard in my hand.

"Oh, Angie. Please." His eyes close at my touch.

"D, you should take these jeans off."

His jeans disappear and he's throbbing in my hand, getting harder. I pull him out of his boxer briefs and take a peek. My earlier encounter with his hard-on told me he's above average, but he's better, bigger than I imagined. I'm possessed and have to kiss it. I give it a sweet peck on the tip and he shivers at my intimate contact. I run my hand up and down the length of his shaft, silky and ready to pound nails. I kiss his tip again and swipe my tongue around him, giving him a suck. I want him. I take him into my mouth and have to swallow to get halfway down his huge cock.

"Oh fuck, Angie. This isn't supposed to be first."

I suck on him and take him deeper, licking him and stroking him with my lips. He grabs me around my waist and lifts me up to sit on his chest.

"Tell me you're mine. I want to make you feel what I feel, I want to make you happy. I'll never do anything you don't want."

I pull my dress up over my ass, showing him my red lace panties and suck on him hard.

Suddenly he has both hands kneading my ass, and slides my panties off. "I've wanted you for so long." Gently caressing me along my seam, but not penetrating. He pulls me back toward him and kisses my inner thigh. He kisses my thigh again, open-mouthed and moves closer to my sex. I shiver and he gets closer again, pulling me toward him. I suck on his cock hard as I release him and D takes control. He lifts me at my waist and sits me on the bed beside him. He slowly removes my dress, pulling it over my head and sends it sailing across the room. His eyes settle on my breasts and his hands soon follow, cupping them appreciatively. He unhooks the clasp and bares me to him.

"Anything you want, D. I want to be a girl for you." He squeezes my breasts, playing with my nipples and kissing each of them. Licking and sucking at my nipples. The way his hands are on me is something I've never experienced before, more than need or want. It pushes the thunder through my body, shaking me to my core with want. He pushes his boxer briefs off and lies naked beside me. He's a gorgeous man, solid muscle everywhere. Classically handsome with his strong jawline, bright shining eyes, and perfect lips. He holds me naked and searches my eyes until he smiles. "What made you smile?"

"I found what I was waiting for," he presses his lips to mine, cherishing me. He pulls back and gazes at me, placing my hands on his chest, "Feel what you do to me?" His heart is pounding in his chest. I kiss his chest and pull his mouth to mine. I nibble on his lips and slide my tongue into his mouth to find his. Sliding my tongue against his until he takes control of the kiss with open-mouthed kisses and I'm suddenly out of breath. I take his hand in mine and hold it to my chest, his eyes light up and he immediately goes back to kissing me. He keeps his hand on my chest wanting to revel in my reaction to him. He's tugging and sucking on my lower lip when the whimper escapes my lips. "Let everything go. I'll take care of you. Let me be the one," he vows soft and sincere. He goes back to kissing me open-mouthed and sucking on my lips. He glides his hand down my body over my hip and stops with his hand on my upper thigh. The anticipation is killing me. He rolls us over. He's on top of me and keeps kissing me. Kissing me as if I'm all he wants and somehow a magic genie has given me to him. I'm drawn into his kiss and focus on his tongue playing with mine. The kiss is everything in my existence or he's found a way to take me to his. I'm not sure which and I don't care. I'm happy to be in the same place and I'm willing to do whatever it takes to get there. Right now, I'd do anything for him. He's the only man who matters. The only thing in my world and I'm revolving around him. How did this happen? Do I need him? He's the one. He stops and stares at my face as he slides his finger inside me. I moan in pleasure as he begins to stroke me. He's still kissing me and holds me tighter against him. He gets hard against my leg. He slides a second finger in and keeps stroking me.

"D, please."

"Sshhhhhh. I'm taking care of you. I want to make you happy. I promise I'll give myself to you, all of me, heart, soul and dick."

I writhe at his hand, "Oh, D. Fuck." I'm wound up and ready to go, but he won't let me. He keeps stroking his fingers in and out.

"You're so hot and wet, baby. Do you want more?"

"Yes. D, I want to come." I reach for my sex and clutch at his hand stroking me.

He takes my hand and shows me how wet I am, then sucks my fingers clean, "Mmmmm." I want to touch myself, but he takes my hand away while he draws a line of kisses down my body directly to my sex. He kisses my thigh and gives me a nibble up even higher on my thigh. He licks my seam where his fingers are sliding in and out of my heat.

I cry out a noise I've never heard before, uncontrolled and full of desire. I beg, "Please," and wonder who has taken control of me. Is this the effect he has on me? When did he become a baseball playing sex god?

He settles his mouth at my clit, kissing me there as if he's making out with me and it's all it takes. My body, ready to explode, spools up even tighter with his added tenderness and I'm lost.

I'm falling in the darkness and I can't catch myself. There's no ledge to grab onto. No safety net to catch me at the bottom. There's no bottom, it's an infinite fall. I'm screaming out to D, but I'm not sure if he can hear me or if I'm actually making any sound. He stops stroking me and now I'm being pulled somewhere.

He kisses my lips, "I need you. I'm going to have you now, baby. You want me?"

I answer him in a shaky tone, "Yes."

"That's what I want to hear." He rolls me over on my belly and spreads my legs, leaving them hanging off the end of his bed. "I want you doggie style on the bed now." His words are unexpected and I don't respond. "I said now." I giggle. "You must want to be spanked." He lays his hard cock on my ass, "Feel how big and heavy I am? I'm going in you and I'm going to slam you hard from behind until you can't walk, until you do everything I want. Until you beg me for more after you've already come more times than you have ever come in one night before." He rubs his hand across my ass, "Such a sweet ass to spank until it's red. Then fucking you and smacking into it over again and again. I can't wait. Okay, bad girl." Is he kidding with this? What game is he playing? He smacks my ass firmly, over and over. I'm squirming at the sting and move quickly in between spanks to get in position for him. "Have you had enough? All you've done is cry out my name asking for more." There's no way? Then again, I didn't get up and run away. "Are you ready, baby? I'm giving you my Super D." He holds his cock with both hands and lines it up, rubbing the tip against my entrance. He has to push to get in, he's huge.

I scream out at the intensity and how much he's stretching me. His pure size pushing into me relentlessly.

"You feel me, baby?"

"Uh-huh," I'm finally able to respond.

"Do you feel full? You should see how big your hole is stretched for me."

"Very full," still limited in my speech.

"Trust me. You're not full yet. That's only my tip."

He slams into me all at once and I scream out again as he slams into my wall. His girth penetrating all the way into me.

"Come on, baby, I need to fit all the way in. There's still a couple inches. You can do it. I want to mash my body against yours when I slam into you." He's in deep and pushes further, "Almost."

"Oh. Oh," I can't function. I can't put words together. All there is, is him.

"Ang, you need to be able to take me the whole way if you want me to fuck you hard. It's what you want, right? It's what you asked for and I'll always give you what you ask for. He slams me over and over, harder and harder until he's smashed up against me. "Yeah, you're my girl. Do you like it, baby?"

"Yes."

"I knew you would. Do you want more?"

"Anything for you, D."

He pulls out and rolls me over to my back, "Do you mean it? Anything for me?"

"Yes."

"Is it what you want? Fucked hard and fast?"

"Anything to make you happy, D."

"It's not what I want. I want to take care of you and love

you and be naked together. I did it because you wanted to be fucked and you should experience getting fucked. I'll do anything for you, even fuck you hard when you need it."

Breathless, "D? Fuck me hard and make me come. I'll be yours, anything you want for the rest of the night." I'm not sure what's come over me, but I have to see it through. This is an experience I can't pass up, I need him to fuck me. I want him to be in control.

He doesn't speak. He simply stares at me. I move back to the edge of the bed and get on all fours with my ass in the air. "Do you want me or not, D?"

He gets up and stands behind me at the foot of the bed, his hands on my hips, "It's what you want. I'll always give you what you want." He rubs his tip in my wetness and slams into me all at once. "If you want it, I should enjoy it. Fuck me." He slams into me over and over. I'm screaming out in pleasure on every stroke. "All me, Ang. Remember, nobody else can do this for you. Only Super D."

It's hard and fast and so fucking intense. I start to move with him, moving in time to meet his strokes and slamming us together. He's huge, my head hanging down and I watch him slamming me from behind. He's hard and his extra thick head... he's amazing massaging me inside, and anchoring him inside me. "Oh, D. Fuck. More. Don't stop, Super D!"

"Anything you want," his breath ragged. Did I send him over the edge? He pounds into me harder and faster. His fingers grip my hips tight and dig into the flesh. He holds on while we get lost together, "Angie, baby. I'm close. I need you. Hard and fast and I'm done. Tell me to come inside. I always wear a condom, but this is you and..."

"Anything you want for the rest of the night. I'm yours, D. Your call."

"Fuck me." He strokes into me harder and harder, his body tensing and cock rigid, "You're on birth control?"

"No. Your call."

He doesn't hesitate. "Come for me, Angie," he whispers. "I want you to come with me." He leans over me and cups my breasts, holding on while he fucks me. "You're mine," he possessively shoves himself into me as far as he can.

"Oh, D! Now."

He slams me harder than before and I come violently around his huge cock, "Oh, fuck." His pattern changes slightly, "Inside, baby. Coming inside you, Angie."

"Doug! Doug!" I cry out as I spiral out of control. The thunder turns to a hurricane of need and emotions and I already want him again.

He wraps his arms around me tight and kisses my back, "I've got you, Angie. I'll always take care of you." He shoves in hard a couple times, then moves slower, but doesn't stop. "Are you okay for more?"

"Anything for you, whatever you want all night, Super D," my voice is softer, more feminine.

He pulls out of me slowly and I roll over onto my back, giggling like a school girl. "That's a happy sound," he says and crawls up next to me. He kisses me tenderly and searches my eyes. Wrapping his arms around me, "I love you and I'll always give you what you want, the way you want it. But, sometimes I want to love you. You're not on birth control? You let me come inside, I want to come inside you all night. Fuck, I want to come inside every time from now on. You're where I belong."

"I love how you make me a girl. I don't want to be in charge when I'm with you, I want you to be in control. I want you in control of everything. I don't want to make decisions. I want you to take care of me. I want you to love me and sometimes fuck me, because I might be bad," I smile at him. "You want to keep coming inside me? Your call." There's no way I deny this man anything. Yes, he's truly Super D, but it's more. He's Doug. He's always been there for me. What took me so long to discover he's the one. Yes, it's true, he's the one. He'll do anything for me and always will, but he's taken my heart from me in trade. No, I'm giving him my heart and my body willingly. I'm his.

CHAPTER TEN

Houck

I want to love her. I always want to love her. I bow down at her sex and kiss it, licking her clit until she shakes. I move up to her body, rubbing my tip in her wetness and push in slow while I kiss her, "Isn't this better, baby?" I get completely buried inside her and wrap my arms around her, moving slowly. She doesn't answer me and I want her to come around me again. I sit up on my knees and take in our connection. I push into her until we're completely one, "Do you want to touch yourself?" She reaches toward her clit and I take her hand, making her grasp how big I am at our connection. Her hand on my cock is almost enough to set me off. I caress her swollen clit and she shivers. "It's okay. I've got you." I rub it and she implodes around me, squeezing my cock. I lean over her moving in and out slowly while she comes, "I love you, baby." I kiss her neck and wrap my arms around her, "I've got you." She's not with me. I hold her and wait. Her breathing is heavy and her heart is beating as strong as mine. She's amazing around me and our heat is crazy. I push and pull with her tight around me and I'm done at simply the idea of being in Angie. I'm throbbing hard and she's still contracting around me while I come. How is this better with her? Fuck! I can't keep coming inside her. Too late now, she's getting everything and I want her to have it.

I'm happier than I've ever been because I have her with me. Kissing her, holding her, getting inside her, all things I could only imagine and now she's here in my bed, willing to give me anything I want. She left it up to me to make the decisions and I didn't take care of her. She told me she's not on birth control and I came in her anyway. Here's the kicker, I'm going to come inside her every chance I get and I'm going to come hard. What the hell am I thinking? Shit! What did I do? We're not married. We're not engaged. We're not even dating. We don't live together. Shit, we don't even live on the same side of the country. My stupid ass makes a decision that has her living alone and finding herself pregnant. What decision does she make if I'm not there? There's no way for me to have a clue. She could keep it to herself and never say a word. She could hide from me and I'd never get to talk to her again. Fuck. I'm in love with her and she's going to leave.

I still have her in my arms when my mouth takes control, "Stay here with me."

"I'm staying right here with you all night, D. I told you I'm yours tonight."

I take a deep breath, "I meant don't go home. This should be your home. This should be your bed. You should be with me."

"D, I..."

I don't want her reasons for why she can't be here or how this is just a weekend or we need time to make sure this is what we want. It doesn't matter and I've had a long time to contemplate it. I'm not giving her up. "We can hire somebody to pack your belongings up and ship them here for you. We can set up a virtual office for you. I can go to your place at the All-Star Break and help you get packed and moved. I want you here with me. I want you to be mine. I want to take care of you." My internal voice is at full speed and ready to express my desires. *I want to get you pregnant. I want you to be my wife. I don't care what order it happens in.* Then in a soft voice, "I want you cheering for me at every game and screaming out my name in our bed. I only want to give Super D to you." Fuck she makes me crazy.

She places her hand on my chest and searches my eyes, "Douglas Houck, you need to get a grip. You know me. You know I consider everything and make calculated decisions. This whole weekend is outside my comfort zone." She stops talking and her expression softens. I open my mouth to speak and she places two fingers over my lips to keep me quiet. I kiss her fingers and wait for her to continue. "I'm not sure what to say. I guess, I don't let anyone else have control or make decisions for me. But you? I want you to be in control. I don't have to think when I'm with you because you'll take care of me. You always have. You make me feminine, more of a woman. Nobody does that. I think I need you."

She hasn't caught up to me yet. She doesn't know she loves me. I don't need her to say the words, her eyes have already shown me. I need to love her and prove it's real.

Houck

I wrap my arms around her, kissing her glorious lips. I spread her legs with mine and lie in between them while we kiss.

Our kiss grows hotter by the second, I push into her and pull a squeal from her lips. Slowly, I bury myself deep inside her and watch her face as she experiences me. Opening her mouth and dragging her teeth across her lower lip. Her hands grasp at the headboard. Whimpers and cries come from her sweet lips. I claim her mouth while I move slowly inside her, needing all of her to be mine, "I love you. Please be mine." My words are unstable in the pit of my stomach. It's what I hope for, more than asking her for anything. Expressing my love for her is something I never dreamed I'd be able to do and here I am, declaring the words to her with all my heart. She moves her hands across my back and digs her fingers in. I explore her neck with my lips, loving her tenderly.

"Oh, D," she releases on a sexy sigh. "There's only you."

"Good, I don't want to share you."

"No, you don't understand. Everything else in the world is gone. It's only you."

Fuck me, "Only me. All of me inside you?"

"Yes, D. Super D."

"My lips on yours kissing you, kissing your neck?"

"Uh-huh, and your words, oh... honest to my heart."

"Everything I do or say will always be true. I've been waiting for you." I keep moving slowly and she's amazing around me. "Feel me move for you? I want to stay right where I am forever." Her hands glide over my body, a lustful caress, and she palms my ass with both hands. She starts to move with me, responding to me as I stroke into her. It's pushing me, "I want to go slow, Ang. Let me love you. Can't you feel what we are together?" She must. This attraction and heat we have is undeniable. She must sense it, it can't just be me.

Angie

I want to move with him. My body has to move with him and meet his actions. I need to. I need him. Super D makes me lose my mind, huge and hard. Nothing from my past compares. If I'm being honest, it's more than the Super D. It's superior in every way, but mostly it's him. I can't close my eyes without visions of him, he speaks and I'm overcome by his devoted words. When he declares his love for me, I believe him with every cell of my being. This easy sex is making it undeniable and sending his love for me to every part of me. It's a slow burn and he's pushing me closer with every delectable stroke. How can I want him this bad when I already have him? "It's so much," escapes my lips.

He's at my ear, "Do you want me to stop?"

"No, don't stop. Never stop. Love me, D."

"Always." He starts to grind against me on every stroke and I'm lost to the darkness without warning, hit unexpectedly by my orgasm.

I scream out his name and thread my fingers into his hair, holding him at my collarbone where he's kissing me. He keeps moving at his steady, easy pace.

"I love it when you scream out my name. I'll have to have you a couple more times before I'm done tonight."

Fuck me. My emotions respond, "Yes, please. Anything for you." I'm still coming around his hard love, his strokes pushing me further.

"You're so tight around me. You make me want to come now."

It's getting hotter and he moves his hands to my head, holding me where he wants me and kissing me. His movements are consistent and deliberate, but his kiss pushes forward. I'm completely his, here for his every whim. He nibbles at my lips and licks me from the base of my neck to my mouth. It's hard to breathe. My senses are all overcome and I can't concentrate on anything, only D. The friction building between us with the kiss. Him tugging on my lips, sucking on my tongue, playing with my hair, completely in control. It's never been this way. I'm always in control.

"You don't need to be in control with me. You're my woman and I belong to you. The only thing I need to do in my life is make you happy and give you pleasure. Until now, all I've done is practice for you. I'm here to take care of you." He claims my mouth, kissing me hard and needy. I wrap my legs around him. "Oh, fuck. Hold on." I squeeze him with my legs around his waist. "Hands, too." I grab onto him around his neck. He sits up on his knees, taking me with him as I cling to him. His hands are splayed across my back, supporting me as he slides in and out of me. "Trust me," he requests and I let go of his neck. He leans me away from him, holding me in his strong arms and focuses on me as he smiles. It's a stretch with my legs snugly around him. He pushes into me completely, our bodies mashed together at our connection. He slides me back and forth on his hard cock, stroking himself with my body.

"Oh, D," I let my head hang back in pleasure.

He moves me faster and the friction grows quickly, "I want..."

The thunder inside me is rumbling and ready to release. I'm full and sated, yet want more of him when he moves me even faster and slams me on his huge cock over and over. His cock becomes more rigid and he's throbbing inside me as he pushes in as deep as he can get. "Please don't stop," I beg uncontrollably.

He growls, "I love how you want more. I'm ready for you." He lays me back down on the bed and goes back to his easy pace. He pats my thigh and he grabs my legs as I release them from around him. He's still hard and wanting more. He leans into me, spreading my legs and finding my deep place easily. I whimper. "Do you like me deep inside you, Angie?"

I nod, "I love it, D." He leans in to kiss me, getting even deeper, "More."

"Soon, baby." He sits back up, "You're beautiful." He strokes into me slow, "There's still more for you." He circles my clit, teasing as he closes in on it, and he has me tightly wound. He strokes into me harder and finally works my clit. The thunder wins and I'm coming hard around him in darkness. I'm lost again, each time seeming to be further gone and more his.

"D! Fuck. D!" He grabs my legs and bends me in half, pounding into me hard and I come again instantly. "D! Fuck, Super D! So deep." I scream out of my mind being pulled from my darkness and suddenly warm all over.

He's out of breath, "So deep, baby. You're my girl. I'm coming with you." Suddenly slamming into me even harder, "Fuck. Fuck! Angie, I need you." I reach for him blindly in my state of bliss and we move together. My hands are on his back, holding him while his warm cum fills me. Our hearts pound together, hot and out of control, "I love you, baby."

"I love you, too," the words escape my lips without even thinking. They've been hiding there, behind my lips and captured by my left-brain. Maybe I've loved him for years. He kisses me and I can feel the grin on his face broaden.

CHAPTER ELEVEN

Angie

I wake up in the middle of the night hungry with D on top of me and I've got to pee. His arms are wrapped around me. I love it. I start to slide out from under him and he grabs my hand, so I can't leave. He immediately locks his fingers with mine and that's all it takes to bring the thunder back. "I'm not leaving. I need to pee." He opens his eyes and gazes at me full of concern as he releases my hand. I stand up and start walking to the bathroom.

"I always use a condom, but I didn't with you. I'm not apologizing. I know what I did and I didn't pull out. You're perfect. I love you and it felt like the right thing to do. When I'm in you, I want to stay there."

My back to him, I close my eyes as his cum runs down my thigh. Last night is blurry. I remember he's truly the Super D and he showed me he can take control, but wants more. It's one night, I'm sure it won't be a problem. There have been a couple broken condoms in my past and they worked out okay.

I could get a Plan B pill, but I don't want to. What does that mean? I don't want to? I pee and find I'm cleaning up more from last night than I thought was possible.

Angie

His alarm goes off and he talks to me with his arms around me warm and protective, "The last thing I want to do this morning is leave you in my bed alone. I have to get ready and go to the stadium. No BP today and I understand if you don't want to get out of bed in time to go to the game. You don't have to." He kisses my forehead, "I love you, my beautiful girl."

I groan and don't open my eyes, grabbing his pillow to snuggle with. He goes about his morning getting ready and I go back to sleep. But as soon as the penthouse is empty, my brain won't stop replaying everything that happened last night. It's when I remember I told him he could do whatever he wanted, I was his and he chose to come inside me every time. I didn't care last night when it was happening and he was in control. Fuck, I love it when he's in control. He wants me to stay here with him and he wants to get me pregnant. He loves me.

Text to Lucy - How's business?

Text from Lucy - What happened?

Text to Lucy - Just checking in… Geez

Text from Lucy - You know I'm not working. It's Sunday.

Text to Lucy - You need me back at the office?

Text from Lucy - I'm Wonder Woman, I can do it all.

Text from Lucy - Run a business, generate new clients, and plan a wedding at the same time.

Text from Lucy - Piece of cake when you have a magic lasso.

Text to Lucy - I wasn't trying to extend my getaway

My phone rings and it's Lucy, "What?"

"Hello my missing partner. What's going on there? First, is he the one or not?"

"He's the one."

"Um, really? I mean, I knew he was, but you agreed too easily."

"I love him. He loves me. He kisses like sin. He's hung like a donkey. He wants me to stay."

"Hhhhmmmm, you had guy sex."

"Maybe, okay yes. I had guy sex, but it was only at first and I…"

"Finish your sentence. I hate it when you do this. Use your damn words."

"I like it when he's in control. I love his hands on me. He makes me feminine," I surprise myself with my words and feminine tone.

"You need to come home now. You sound like a girl. You're obviously ill. What did you do with Angie?"

"That's what I was afraid of. It's him, not me. I'm coming home."

"Wait. Is he what you want?"

"I'd like to stay in his bed and never leave."

"I'm sure he'd provide you room and board for your services."

"Not funny!"

"Sorry, it was too easy."

"Where's your manpiece?"

"I stayed home, didn't go to his place this weekend."

"You haven't spent a week without him in... ever."

"He may have pissed me off and turned into a stupid man."

"Passing or are we going to talk about it?"

"The pre-marital course is working out much better for you than it is for me."

"Sorry."

"Me, too. Could be a deal breaker."

"Pick me up at the airport tonight?"

"I'll be there."

She needs me. I need to get my head straight. I need to go home. Tears roll down my face. I'm not one of those women who cry at everything. I can come back in a few days. I'm not leaving him forever. Shit. I need to tell him I'm leaving. He's not going to like it.

Text to D - Do you have a few minutes before the game?

Text from D - I'll find you pregame behind home plate

Text to D - Somewhere more private maybe?

Text from D - What do you have in mind?

Text to D - I need to talk to you.

Text to D - I like your idea better

I get dressed and pack while I wait for him to respond. I hear the elevator close and turn around to find him standing in the doorway behind me.

"Where are you going? Tell me you're moving into my bedroom," D waits for an answer.

"That's what I need to talk to you about. Lucy needs me back at the office to help her with some drama." I walk toward him and reach my arms up around his neck, "I'm going home to take care of business and I'll be back. I'm not leaving you. I don't want you to get the wrong idea. I'm yours. No other guys for me. Only you, D."

"Wait until after the game and I'll go with you. I'm off tomorrow and don't have to report in until noon on Tuesday."

"This will take a few days to fix and part of the problem is her fiancé. Having you there probably won't help."

"Are you sure it's work? Not me?"

"Lucy needs me. She can't run the business by herself and deal with her personal drama at the same time." I take a deep breath, "I need to get my head straight and get the logistics figured out."

"Please don't leave."

"I promise I'll be back as soon as I can. Hopefully I'll be back in four or five days." I caress his cheek, "I love you, D."

He smiles at me, "I love you, too." He takes my hands in his, "Okay, we're together and you'll come back to me or I'll go to you, whatever we have to do. We'll call and text everyday."

"Yes we will. We have most days since we met."

He lifts me up and hugs me, "I have to get back before I'm missing."

Silent tears stream down my cheeks, I hug his neck and talk into his ear, "Play hard and win, I'll be watching every game. Tell Carter I need a permanent access card ready for me when I get back. I can't believe it took me so long to find you. You're the one. I'll be back to you soon."

He sets me down on my feet and walks into the other

room. He comes back to me, "I don't like not having enough time to do what I want to do. I want you to live here, take the key with you. This is your place, too." He kisses me goodbye and he's not happy about it. I'm not either. He turns and as he's running to the door, "I'm going to make you my wife someday. You know that, right?"

"You make me happy, D."

He's smiling when the elevator door closes, but it's as fake as mine. Why am I doing this? I need to get back to the office and help Lucy. Some space will be a good thing. I can do this.

Houck

I hate that she's leaving. She isn't supposed to be leaving yet. I should have at least another day. I have things I wanted to do. I wanted to put the key to my place on a nice key ring before I gave it to her. I wanted to buy a piece of jewelry for her, so she could wear it and remember me. I want her to have me with her. I stop in at Carter's office on my way back in and have a seat.

He looks up from his desk, "What can I help you with today?"

"Angie's gone for a few days, can you get a permanent access card ready for her?"

"No problem. Anything else?"

"Can you get a key ring engraved for her and delivered to her at her office tomorrow with some flowers? A nice sterling silver or something, engraved with D loves Ang. Long-stemmed red roses, not the cheap ones. At least a dozen of them."

"I'll get on it right now."

"Thanks," I get up and go work out, trying to get my mind off it. She said she's coming back, she's not leaving me. Last night was crazy. She loves me. Everything is fine. I'll talk to her tonight. I need to focus on the game.

I watch the game from the bullpen and get stretched out. I did more than I should've last night, I need to make up for it. It was more than worth it. It would be worth it everyday. The game is going slow, mostly because I have her on my mind and she's not here. I'm watching the score and I doubt I get called in to pitch. Seals win 9-4, no need for a closer.

Text to Angie - Thinking about you. Message me when you land.

Angie

Text to D - Landed. Thought about you the whole flight home

Text from D - Your flight to San Diego is your flight home

Text to D - I know. I'll be home to you soon, D.

Text to D - Lucy's picking me up, I'll call later

Lucy pulls up and I put my luggage in her hatchback. I hop in the passenger seat, "Hi, thanks for picking me up."

She simply stares at me, "Who are you and what did you do with Angie?"

"What are you talking about?" I laugh.

"You have a grin plastered on your face that I've never seen before and your voice is all light and breezy. Are you actually happy? It's a new look on you. I hope it doesn't affect the logical side of your brain. I need that part for business."

"I haven't changed. I was only gone a few days. I do have some things to talk to you about. But first, take me home and tell me about the potential deal breaker with your stupid man."

On the drive to my third floor apartment, Lucy tells me all about her fiancé and his inability to compromise. She finally gets to the things she won't compromise on, primarily other women. Apparently, the weekends together because they live two hours apart hasn't been enough. He's been spending the night with other women when they're not together. To quote Lucy, "He said it doesn't matter. It's in a whole different zip code." She's not a happy camper, but better to find out now. She's already made her decision and she's done with him. Which I figure is her being tough to get through it, until she giggles at an alert on her phone.

"What's that about?"

"Oh, this? Nothing," she giggles some more.

"It doesn't look like nothing."

"I figured the quickest way to get over it would be to move on. I joined this dating app. These guys are fun and some of them are cute."

I shake my head at her, but if it helps her get over the jerk then I'm fine with it. It's much better than helping her pick up the pieces and having her be a complete mess. We agree to sit down and discuss business tomorrow.

I get unpacked and start the laundry. If I'm doing this, I need to be ready. I've been considering the logistics and a plan I need to talk to D about. He's probably not going to be a fan, but it makes sense. I can't believe I'm doing this. Am I moving to the other side of the country for a man? For the Super D? It's all for Doug.

I call him, and he answers on the first ring, "Hey, beautiful. I miss you."

I giggle, "Don't be silly. I just left today." I pick on him, but it's the truth. I get warm all over simply hearing his voice over the phone, "I miss you, too."

"When are you coming home?"

"Discussing it with Lucy tomorrow, when we handle the business drama. What do you think about me keeping my apartment here and staying here when you're on road trips? Not permanently, but I'll need to be here sometimes for business and it'll help Lucy be okay with my move. Then we can figure out everything else in the offseason, maybe you can help me finish moving then? It's only five months."

"You'll be here with me when I'm home?"

"That's the idea. There may be minor schedule snafus, but in general we'd come and go on the same days. I might not need to go every time you do and I've been hoping I might get to go on a road trip with you," I smile at the idea of road tripping like a baseball groupie.

"It's better to wait until the offseason, as long as you'll be here. It'll be six months, Seno says we're going to the series this year. Plan on being booked for post-season and spending October with me."

I love the confidence and how the team believes it's their year. The way they play, it wouldn't surprise me. "I can't wait to spend post-season with you!" I have tears in my eyes again, softly, "D, are we crazy?"

"I'm crazy in love with you. Come home soon, baby."

CHAPTER TWELVE

Angie

Monday

Lucy agrees with my plan to move to San Diego half the time and hopes I will find us more clients there. I left out how I'll be moving there full-time in the off-season. Things change. I may need to be here some for business still.

The office drama isn't bad. Dealing with the sales end of things isn't Lucy's strong suit. She's going to have to get better at it. I spend most of the day on the phone with clients and schedule a couple meetings for later in the week. D's going to hate it, but business is business. I need to get better at using my virtual office and contacting clients through the internet and phone instead of walking into their office anyway. It would give me more time if I wasn't driving between clients.

Lucy carries in a crystal vase of long stemmed red roses while I'm on a call and sits there in front of my desk waiting for me to get off the phone. There's at least two dozen dark velvety red roses. I hang up the phone and the smile grows on my face. "They came with this fancy blue box. Open it!" I take the card from the flowers and open it.

> Angie—You mean more to me than you know. I'm going to show you how much you mean to me everyday. I can't wait to have you back in my arms. I love you.—D

"What the hell? You're doing it again! That happy smile," Lucy snatches the card from my fingers. She reads the card and shakes her head, "What'd he do to you?"

She tosses the box to me and I open it to find a key ring with a shiny silver heart shaped tag. It's engraved with D loves Ang. There's a note in the box and it reads "Key to my heart and my home. Love you, Ang."

I send D a picture of the flowers and the key ring with a thank you and heart emojis. I get a response of heart emojis back.

"Seriously?" Lucy walks around behind me to be nosey over my shoulder. "Fine, it's sweet."

"He gave me a house key before I left yesterday. You should see his place."

"You mean your new place?"

Huh, "Yes." I try to maintain my smile, but I can't. There's no way. I show Lucy photos of D and tell her about the photo I found on his nightstand. "Did I tell you I live in a penthouse now?" I laugh at the whole thing. This is my life.

Angie

My phone rings about 10pm, "Hello?"

"I wish you were with me today."

"I do, too. The roses are beautiful and I put my keys on the key ring you sent. Thank you."

"You deserve more," I can hear his smile through the phone.

"Lucy is on board with me moving. I have client meetings on Thursday. I'll be back on Friday."

"Can't you meet with your clients sooner and come home to me?"

"I need time to pack anyway. I'm moving in. I need to bring my stuff, right?"

"Alright, I get it. Clothes don't pack themselves. Pack up boxes of whatever you want to bring with you and I'll get them shipped for you. There's two walk-in closets in the master bedroom, one of them is empty and waiting for you. I'll be patient, I've waited fifteen years and it's only a few days." His voice changes, lower and raspy, "I love you, Ang. Now that I have you, I never want to be away from you."

Tuesday

I meet Lucy for lunch and go to a couple clients. I spend half the day packing and surveying my apartment, considering what should go and what should stay. Where did all this crap come from? I pack up most of my clothes and shoes I won't be wearing this week. I toss my favorite blanket in a box, along with my photos, and things I've collected following D over the years. Everything else can wait or go with me on the plane.

Text from Carter - Working on your access card. Please send me a current photo.

I send him a quick selfie and send it to D while I'm at it.

Then I get a link, with access to the game live or whenever I want.

Text from Carter - West Coast night games can be hard for East Coast fans ;)
Text to Carter - Thank you
Text from D - Hey, beautiful :)
Text to D - Hi, handsome ;)

He sends me a selfie in front of his locker in the clubhouse.

Text from D - How's packing?
Text to D - I'm done packing my initial boxes. I have eight boxes ready to go.
Text from D - I'll get them picked up and shipped, your stuff will be here waiting for you on Friday.
Text from D - I'll call after the game tonight.
Text to D - :)

I watch the game live and fall asleep before it's over. I'm woken up by my phone ringing, "Hello?"

"Hi, baby. I woke you up. I'm sorry."

"Don't be. I was waiting for you to call. I like to hear your voice. How was the game?" My voice is sweet and it's all because of him.

"We won. I slammed the door with three strikeouts in the ninth inning to hold the score to 4-3 Seals."

"Keep it up and stay focused. I can't wait for October baseball with you. I'll watch the end of the game in the morning."

"Go back to sleep, Ang. I'll see you Friday. I love you."

Wednesday

The boxes I packed get picked up while I'm watching D get the save in last night's game and trying to get motivated for the day. I'm spending the day in the office getting my desk cleaned up and organized, making sure I have everything prepared that I need to work with from San Diego. I might need a desk when I get there. Nah, I'll work from the table on the balcony. It's gorgeous out there and I love the warm sun.

Sitting in my office, I find myself daydreaming while I stare at my roses. He loves me and I doubt anyone else ever has. More importantly, I love him and it's not lust. Everyday I'm away I miss him more.

Lucy walks into my office and looks me up and down, "What are you doing now?"

"It's a day game today."

"You're sitting at your desk watching the game and wearing a baseball jersey. Have you looked at yourself? Where's your office attire?"

"Some things are more important," slips from my lips without a thought. Shit. Try to cover it up, "I have issues, Luc. You know what it's like. Especially at the beginning, in the honeymoon stage." I show her the selfie he sent me, hoping my hunk might buy me some understanding.

"I guess you can do what you want. You're one of the bosses."

I smile in victory, "Thank you."

I hear Sherry yelling when Seno comes up to bat. I want to be there to cheer for D. Seals won 9-2, no closer needed today.

I get home, counting down the hours until I leave for San Diego. I find a Thursday night flight and book it. I send the confirmation to him via text and my phone rings.

"Do you like flying on Thursday nights?"

"I guess. I wanted the flight that would get me to you soonest."

"I love it. I'll be there to pick you up."

"I'm counting on it. Going to bed early, I have a long day tomorrow. Love you, D.

Thursday

I wake up Thursday morning and I'm not rested. I get up and do what I have to do anyway. I meet with my clients and handle business, spending two hours on the road and a couple more in the office. Lucy is starting to freak out and I'm already anticipating the D thunder. It's an unstable situation. We hit happy hour and she follows me home, ready to give me a ride to the airport.

Text from flyaway - Your scheduled flight has been delayed

Fuck. I start to search for details and...

Text from flyaway - Your flight has been canceled

Text from flyaway - Please contact us to reschedule your flight. We're sorry for any inconvenience.

I check for available flights and the next one is tomorrow at 10am.

Text to D - Flight rescheduled to tomorrow.

Text to D - I hate this. Call me after the game.

CHAPTER THIRTEEN

Angie

I wake up Friday morning when Lucy is banging on my door, "Are we going to the airport today or not?"

Why is she yelling? I open my eyes. Why is the room spinning? I yell out, "Lucy, come in. Use your key."

My door opens, "Angie?"

"In my bedroom."

"Open your eyes and get up. You've got a flight and Super D waiting for you."

Tears stream down my face, "The room spins when I open my eyes. What do I do? Help me here!"

"You look warm and a bit green," she checks my forehead. "You definitely have a fever. Where's your phone?"

"Nightstand."

She picks up my phone and dials. The voice on the other end comes through clear, "Hey, I've been worried about you, beautiful."

"Why thank you, but this isn't beautiful. Well, I'm beautiful but I'm not your beautiful. This is Lucy and I'm putting you on speaker. First, it's nice to finally talk to you, I've heard a lot about you and I'm happy you have finally found each other. Only a little bit jealous."

"Where is she? She didn't answer my call last night. Is she okay?"

"I'm right here, D."

Lucy takes control, "She'll be fine, but she's not getting on a plane today. She may not be getting on a plane for a few days. She has an ear infection or something. She's dizzy and has a fever. I've got her taken care of on this end."

"Baby, are you okay?"

"The room spins when I open my eyes and my head hurts. Don't worry about me. I'll be fine. Play hard and I'll be there as soon as I can. I'm sorry, D."

"Don't worry, I'll take care of her."

"Lucy, please send me a text. I need your number. Thanks for taking care of my girl. I wish I could be there to take care of her myself."

"D, go play ball. I love you."

"Love you, too, babe."

Lucy chimes in, "You two make me sick, bye." She disconnects the call. "Fine, I like him. You can keep him. But, you heard me and I'm not kidding, you're stuck here for a few days. Go back to sleep. I'll check on you in a bit."

CHAPTER FOURTEEN

Angie

I wake up Monday afternoon, finally coherent and not spinning. I sit up and grab my phone. I lost three days.

Text from D - Been in contact with Lucy for updates, didn't want to wake you up.

Text from D - Hope you're better soon. Call me when you can. Love you, Ang. I always have and I always will.

I call him immediately, and he answers, "She lives!"

"Yes, I'm alive. I miss you."

"I miss you more. I think about you all the time. I always have, but now it's different. You're real and what I want isn't a fantasy anymore. I need more than one night with you. Please don't change your mind and stay there."

"I'm not changing my mind. I want to be with you, D."

"Your boxes are already here. The team is off on Thursday, but it's a travel day. I'm on a two week road trip starting on Thursday. Don't rush and fly out here. Relax and get better. Stay and work or pack or whatever you want. We'll be together soon. I wish I wasn't going on a long road trip. I love you, Ang."

Angie

I spend the next couple weeks watching every Seals baseball game and wearing my Super D jersey to the office for day games. Lucy laughs at me for yelling at D when he's playing, but I don't care. She took a video of me doing it and didn't tell me. I had no idea until D told me she sent it to him and he loved it. The office is tighter, cleaner, and running better than it ever has. Every room in my apartment has been gone through from top to bottom, sorted, cleaned, and reorganized. I miss D. I've done everything I can to keep my mind occupied and be productive. He's expecting me on Friday and he should be home late Thursday night. I can't wait anymore, I'm going a day early to get unpacked and be there waiting for him when he gets home.

CHAPTER FIFTEEN

Angie

I get off the plane in sunny San Diego and get an Uber home. Home. Interesting, it is home. I take my luggage up the elevator and I'm home when the doors open. I immediately go out on the balcony and take a selfie, texting it to D.

> Text to D - I'm home and waiting for you
>
> Text from D - I wish I was home with you. See you tonight.

I use every minute of time until he gets home, getting unpacked and organizing my closet. It's huge. There's a spot for every single pair of my shoes, hangers for skirts, pants, even a longer area for dresses. There's a built in dresser, even a velvet-covered ottoman to sit on. I lay my favorite blanket out over the ottoman and put my box of D memorabilia on top of the dresser. One of the nightstands is empty, I claim it setting my autographed books up neatly and plugging in my gaggle of electronic devices. I get rid of the empty boxes and hide my suitcases in the back of my closet. I'm home. It's perfect.

Houck

I'm almost home and I can't wait to see Angie. The last three weeks have been worse than the fifteen years I waited for her. It's not her fault or mine, it's the way it is. Neither of us have talked about the night we spent together. Maybe we don't need to. There was a connection, and now that it's been made we can't go back. It was special. It always will be special with us.

I get home and it's dark, "Angie?" The light's on in our bedroom. I walk in to find her sleeping in my bed. She's beautiful and I'm happy she's back home. I drop my bags where I stand and climb in bed with her needing to kiss her. I wrap my arms around her and roll over on the bed, holding her on top of me. "I missed you. I love you, Ang." I kiss her and squeeze her in my arms.

She giggles, "I missed you, too." She rubs against me and my cock gets hard instantly. "Super D missed me, too."

"We both did."

She unhooks my belt and unbuttons my pants, "Can you get rid of these? They're in the way. I'm going to need this dress shirt you're wearing to go, too."

"Yes, ma'am."

She climbs off the bed and turns her back to me as she slides out of her pants and pulls her shirt off over her head, revealing her matching black lace panties and bra. "See anything you like?" She asks as she shakes her hips and ass at me.

I'm lying on top of the bed naked and she walks to me, "Everything, except the pretty lace needs to go."

"Do you want me naked?"

"Yes, and I've got something waiting for you," he says as he wraps his hand around his huge cock and gives it a stroke.

"I was hoping you'd be ready for me. I need you, D," she climbs on top of me straddling my waist. Her tone changes, sweeter, maybe more feminine, "I want all of you, it's more than sex. I love you, Doug. I need to be close to you. Please let me love you."

My already open heart about melts as her hands caress my chest and her words reach my ears. She strokes my hard cock with her hand and she shakes with need. She moves, guiding me in and takes me completely. Her whole body shivers and she sighs in relief. She lies down on me, her cheek to my chest and her hands on my shoulders. I hesitate, "Angie, should we talk about the birth control thing before we do this?"

"Your call. Always your call."

Fuck. "Ang?"

"Yeah?"

"You can trust me with everything, but you might not want to trust me with that decision."

She gazes up at me in contemplation, "Why not?"

I wrap my arms around her, "I'm going to come deep inside you every time. I can't help myself." I take a deep breath and whisper, "I want to knock you up. I want you barefoot in my kitchen with a baby belly full of Baby D."

"I'm okay with that," she says plainly.

I sit up with her in my arms and she wraps her legs

around me. "I'm sorry, did you give me permission to get us pregnant?"

"Not exactly," she takes my hands and places them on her breasts. They're plump and round and obviously sensitive to my touch. "I haven't had my period since we were together. I'm late and I have symptoms. Your hands on me are driving me insane, I can hardly contain myself. Seriously D, I want to scream out your name."

"You're making me crazy. Are you pregnant with my baby?" She doesn't answer. "Angie? You need to answer me."

"It can't belong to anybody else, Mr. Fucked-me-bare-and-came-inside."

"Yeah, I did and it was better than I dreamt it'd be. I'm going to do it again." I grab her around the waist, holding her on my hard cock and she giggles.

Angie

I lean in to whisper in his ear, "I love you. I did a test this morning and it was positive. I'll schedule an appointment to get checked in a couple weeks. If not, keep doing what you do because I'm happy to give you what you want."

"I fucking love you," he takes my face in his hands and kisses me tenderly. He gazes into my eyes, "I promise to always take care of you and our Baby D's. Never leave me. Marry me and be my Mrs. D. Angie, seriously, please be my wife. There's nothing I want more in this world than to have you as my partner. Pregnant or not, Angie, I want you."

I laugh nervous, not often my defense mechanism kicks in, "I don't see a ring."

He reaches into the top drawer of his nightstand and

pulls out a ring box, “I’ve had this ready to give you for almost three weeks. I had this whole elaborate plan to propose when you got here two weeks ago, but none of it matters.” He opens the box and takes a simple diamond solitaire out of the box. He lifts me off of him, leaving me sitting naked on the bed and gets down on one knee at the bedside. He takes my hand in his and gazes up at me. His eyes teary and his whole body shaking, “Angie, I’ve loved you since the moment I met you and I want to spend my life with you. I know this is quick, but you’ve always been the one. We’re a match. I promise to love you and take care of you for the rest of my life. There’s no one else and there never will be. Please, make my dream come true and be my wife.” He places the ring on my finger and holds my hand up to show me.

I lean down to kiss him and he takes me in his arms, naked on the floor. “Yes. Always, D. You and me, and whoever may come from us,” I laugh happily. “Now, please love me all night, my Super D. Close this game.”

PLAYLIST

"Angela" by The Lumineers
"Somebody" by Depeche Mode
"Dangerous Night" by Thirty Seconds to Mars
"Something Human" by Muse
"Simplify" by Young the Giant
"Walk on Water" by Thirty Seconds to Mars
"Heaven" by Bryan Adams
"Wonderwall" by Oasis
"Sex Type Thing" by Stone Temple Pilots

UP TO BAT

AN ALL ABOUT THE DIAMOND ROMANCE BOOK 6

CHAPTER ONE

Michelle

"Jones Mason! You spent the last ten days away on a road trip. Will you kiss me and show me you missed me already?" I put him on the spot, going for luck.

He grimaces and leans in to kiss me. It's been weeks and the most I've gotten is a hug and a peck on the cheek or forehead. It makes no sense at all. The night we met he basically tackled me to the couch and held me there all night long. I remember the sweet words he whispered in my ear that night and the brush of his lips on my neck. *You're the prettiest girl I've ever seen. Your eyes call to me and your smile shines brighter than the sun. But your laugh, happiness, and girlish ways are what tug at my heart, making me wish you were mine.* He wraps his arm around me, "Not here. Too many people." He leads me off to a corner of the player's garage and pulls me in tight for a hug. He's finally going to kiss me. I've been waiting for this moment. He leans his head down to my level and gives me a peck on the lips so small that I'm not sure it happened.

I want to beat him on the chest and yell at him, "That doesn't even count!" But, before the words can form from my lips and be projected at him, he lifts me up with his hands on my ass. He grins at me with his boyish smile and his thoughtful brown eyes that remind me of mahogany-stained wood, strong with the details of his life ingrained in them. I reach my arms around his neck to hold on. His big hands on my ass have me distracted, though I'm sure his actions don't come with the intent that I'm hoping for.

He whispers in my ear "I missed you. I missed your face." He kisses my temple and holds his lips there, more than his typical peck. "I need us to take this slow." He presses his lips to my neck, warm and open-mouthed. It sends a shiver through my body. "I need you to be patient with me. There's more to us."

I want to dig my fingers into his short, thick, dark hair and kiss his full lips. Find out what us would be like. "It's just a kiss."

"With us, everything is more." His voice gets lower, "We have time for everything. Let's not rush this."

"Kiss me, Jones." It's the wrong thing to say, but I'm tired of waiting. It's just a kiss. I'm not asking him to get naked.

He puts me down and walks away, turning around, "You don't get it. I'm not good at this."

He can't be serious, "Are you a virgin?" I say quietly under my breath, but he hears me.

He laughs, "No. I started young. Probably, too young."

It's the first I've heard of anything like this. "I don't understand how you can be my boyfriend when we haven't even made it to first base. We're still standing in the batter's box!" I shake my head and turn away so I can somehow suck the threatening tears back in without him seeing. "You're a major league hitter. Probably the best on your team." I take a deep breath, "But with me, you're still up to bat. The longest at bat ever."

Jones

She's been learning baseball. I love her effort to understand the game I play. I chuckle, "You've been hanging out with Sherry."

"I've been watching your games from home, too. I haven't missed a single one." She shifts on her feet, "Are you going to take a swing or not?"

"I know you don't understand, but the last time I kissed a girl it didn't stop with a kiss." She looks at me waiting for more. I need to tell her anyway. "Let's go."

"Where are we going?"

"Someplace quiet. I'm taking you out for a nice dinner, we need time to talk." All we've done is pick up food and order in. Play video games and watch movies, mostly video games. It's time for something new. I hope it's not a deal breaker for her. I reach for her hand and tangle my fingers with hers, needing to touch her. It's more intimate than I expect. She's soft and receptive to my touch. Her fingers locking into mine like they've been waiting for me. I open the door to my truck for her and reach to give her a hand in, it's all I can do not to claim her right here.

She locks eyes with me, "You want to kiss me. I want you to kiss me. Do it." She places her hands on my waist, encouraging me closer to her. Her cornflower blue eyes shining at me through the sandy blonde hair hanging long in her face comfort me and remind me of the fields I grew up playing in. Her hands start to shake and she gazes up at me, "Mase?"

"I'm not good at control. You have to be able to stop me."

"We're in public and at the stadium. You won't go too far." She pulls me down to her and kisses my cheek, then below my ear, not getting close to my lips. She whispers, "I might not want to stop you."

She's perfect for me in every way. We need to work up to things. Take it slow. Get acquainted with each other. Spend time together without having sex. I know me. I'll kiss her for the first time and need to get in her as quick as possible. The only thing I'll want to do is have sex with her for days. I can't let this get away from me. I can have control. I can wait. I push her back against my truck. My right hand grabbing her hair and holding her to me while I claim her lips with mine. She whimpers and her whole body relaxes into me. Somehow I've managed to lift one of her legs up around me as I'm kissing her, and I'm pressing my body against her. Sucking on her lips, tasting her. I'm on fire. I separate her lips with my tongue and take what I want, finding her eager and willing for everything I have to give. Her hands move to my hair, pulling it as she plays with it. I want her, but I already knew that. This was a bad idea. I kiss her harder and stroke her tongue with mine. I pull away long enough to speak, "This isn't a game, GG. I'm not playing."

She moves her hands to explore my chest and pulls away from me. Gazing up at me, "If this was a game, I'd already have won."

I smile uncontrollably as I pull her back to me, kissing her, knowing I'm in charge of what's real and she can win every game. I can kiss her as long as it's in public. That'll work for now. I break our kiss before I get carried away. I lean my forehead against hers and we both try to catch our breath. "Do you count that as first base?"

"I think it qualifies. Feel free to do that again."

"I will later. One thing at a time." I help her into my truck and drive through downtown to Little Italy. I take her hand and walk to my favorite place to eat. They know me here and I know they'll seat us in the back, giving us some time to talk without interruption. I shouldn't have kissed her. She might not feel the same about me after our conversation and now I know I was right. She's perfect. I'll know what I'm missing.

I sit across the table from her and keep holding her hand, examining how our hands fit together perfectly and absorbing her warmth and femininity. Though I don't think she'd want to be thought of as feminine. She's obviously a girl, but she's not one to make sure she's all put together. I've never seen her in a dress. Since I met her, she's been living in my ball cap and a Seals T-shirt. I notice she's wearing a simple silver band with a small diamond on her left ring finger. I spin the ring around her finger, "I've never seen you wear this ring before."

"Oh, it's just a trinket," she tries to dismiss me.

"Where'd you get it?"

"I've had it a long time. I just wear it sometimes when I want guys to think I'm taken."

"Where'd you get it?" I ask again.

"A friend in high school."

"Do you have another guy?" I glare at her sideways. I haven't seen any other signs of another man.

"Mase, seriously? Of course not."

"It looks like a cheap engagement ring."

"It's just an old promise ring."

"What did you promise?"

"It was more him. He wanted it to be an engagement ring."

"And you accepted it knowing that?"

"He was my boyfriend. He'd been my boyfriend for two years. He was my first. It seemed logical at the time."

"You still wear it? You should wear a different ring."

"It's the only ring I have. I like it. It's simple."

I'm starting to feel like I have competition, "What happened to the guy that gave it to you?"

"I killed him. He asked too many questions and started to sound insecure," she glares at me deadpan.

"Hey honey," the waitress stops at our table. "You want your usual?"

"Yes, family style, with the starters."

"What about me?" Michelle asks.

"I ordered for both of us."

"What if I don't like what you ordered?"

"You will."

"What if I want something different?"

"What if I want you to take that ring off?" I stare into her eyes, unsure why an old ring has gotten under my skin.

"Does it really bother you?"

"Yeah, I don't want you wearing something that means you belong to another man," I want to go on and tell her she's mine, but I hold my tongue.

She slides the ring off and into the front right pocket of her jeans. "Better?"

"Thank you."

"But now men will think I'm available. You're taking a major risk here."

"I don't blame them for trying and I trust you to turn them away." I rub my thumb over her fingers.

All through dinner all I can think about is this woman. I need Michelle in my life. I want to kiss her and hold her and experience her kneeling in front of me with her lips around my cock. Her sweet, supple lips with me guiding her mouth by her hair snuggly twisted around my wrist. Sexy moans escaping her and sending vibrations through me. My dick is pressing against my zipper and fighting me, wanting to come out to play and get into her. Once she has me, she'll never want anyone else—or she'll hate me. I shouldn't have kissed her.

I completely lost track of what I was doing. Leaving the restaurant, she walks ahead of me and my cock is screaming as she sways her hips. I've kept control this long. It's just, I only know Dee's way. I've grown accustomed to it. She was my first and only for over five years, and after her it didn't go well. It's not what women want from me. I catch them off guard being from a small town in the Midwest and a country boy at heart. Why do I want to fuck their pretty little mouths? I don't know. It's what Dee wanted. It's what I know. She'd call me up and ask me over. I remember vividly the first time she invited me to her place. She made it clear that her parents would get home around 7pm and she'd be home from school by 3pm. We were fourteen. She said she wanted to talk and get to know me without our friends influencing us. I thought nothing of any of it. We all had access to as much freedom and private time as we wanted. And Dee hadn't bit when I asked her if she wanted to make out in the fields. That's all we had, fields of tall grains, Prairie Dropseed, and Black-eyed Susans for miles. I walked up to her house, Nirvana blaring and a note on the door inviting me to come in, directing me to the back of the house. I followed the instructions, closing the door behind me. Music getting louder as I got closer to my destination. There was Dee, kneeling on the floor silently and calm in a room full of chaos. Topless with her waist length brown hair tied back in a loose ponytail at the nape of her neck. Pert, rosy nipples mounted on breasts that were large for her frame. She was barefoot and still wearing the skirt from her school uniform, shorter than most and pleated red plaid. I didn't say a single word. She reached her hand toward me, waving me closer to her. She wasted no time unbuttoning my jeans and pulling them down to find me commando and hard as a rock pointing straight at her. It was the first time a girl had got anywhere near me other than rolling around in the hay fully clothed. I reached out to grope her boobs, she swatted my hands away. She wrapped her hand around my cock and guided it into her mouth, dragging her lips over me. I came immediately. She spit it out and told me if I did it the right way she'd swallow. I didn't know what the right way was. She stared into my eyes and brought her ponytail forward, placing it in my hand. "Tighter," she said. I stood there not understanding what was going on. "Pull my hair," she instructed sternly. She gasped and melted as I followed her instructions. Her lips parted once again and her tongue darted out to the tip of my penis. I wanted more. I waited for more direction. I didn't want to fuck up getting my dick wet. I wondered what would happen next and if she told me to bring a condom and I wasn't paying attention. I definitely gave her my complete attention from then on. She took my cock to the back of her throat and sucked on it as she pulled her mouth off of it. Her stare was penetrating. She asked, "Do you want more?" I nodded and she continued, "Then take it." I stood motionless. She maneuvered my hand into a tighter grasp of her hair at the root and licked my tip teasingly until I pushed into her mouth. I couldn't help myself. I didn't have a clue what I was doing or why, but I was getting a positive response. Fucking her mouth wasn't my plan when I woke up that morning. I'd never considered it. It felt awkward and changed my method. I used the grip she'd given me to move her head on my cock instead of having to do the work myself. She yelped and I stopped, pulling away from her. She scolded me, "Don't stop until you fill my mouth with cum." I did as I was told, using her like a toy to stroke myself to completion. That's what she always wanted, and at some point she started bending over in front of me wanting me to fuck her hard from behind, which was the only way she'd come. She was pissed when I got my full ride to college for baseball and didn't take her with me. What was I supposed to do? Hide her in my dorm room closet? Nothing I offered was acceptable to her. She never talked to me again. It's better this way. She wasn't good for me. She was only a good fuck. That's not what I want in my life. I'm pretty sure what I want is Michelle. All of her. Only her. Maybe I don't need to talk to her and it will be fine.

I reach for her hand and her smile makes me warm. I open my truck door for her and give her a hand in, stepping between her and the door. I turn her toward me standing between her legs as I gaze into her eyes. I lean in and kiss her lips, "You're beautiful. Never think otherwise." I run my fingers through her long hair, brushing it away from her face. Holding her head, I kiss her again and she moans into my mouth. I eat it up, craving more. I dig my fingers into her hair and pull. The worry that shot through me was immediately extinguished when she responds by thrusting her tongue into my mouth deeper. I slide in closer, rubbing my hard bulge against her. I draw a line of kisses from her mouth to her neck, enveloping myself in her intoxicating scent. Her hands on me, exploring my back and finding their way into my hair. She guides my lips back to hers wanting more and holds me there not wanting the kiss to end. She's sweet, soft, and as addictive as I knew she'd be. I love a woman who knows what she wants.

CHAPTER TWO

Michelle

"No Mason tonight?" my roommate Kristina inquires as I walk in the door of our two-bedroom apartment.

"He just dropped me off. Something about tomorrow's schedule."

"All players are reporting early tomorrow, and me too—1pm game."

"Thanks for the clarification. Are you announcing tomorrow?"

"Yes, they won't say it's permanent but..." she grinned at me. "Anyway, I thought you might need the details. Sounded like your brain got scrambled against the door before you came in."

"What are you talking about?"

"I could only see hair through the peep hole, but I know swollen red lips when I see them. So, spill. He finally kissed you and I want the details."

"Why? You have your own player and I know Chase eats you up like baked goods."

"What is so wrong with me making sure my bestie is treated right?"

I side-eye her wondering where this is really coming from.

"Was he worth waiting for or not?"

"I'm still waiting."

"Michelle, one thing at a time. You couldn't think he was going to drag you off to his bed when it took him weeks to kiss you on the lips." she stopped and continued, "He did kiss you on the lips right?" She rolled her eyes around as if she was reviewing files in the back of her brain. "Tell me he didn't spend the last ten minutes kissing your cheek into a frenzy."

"He kissed my lips with his lips and there was tongue. He has strong hands that I want on more parts of my body. Enough?"

"Did you go to his place tonight? You're always here or there."

"Nope. He took me out to dinner."

"And...?"

"Do you need the time schedule?"

Kristina shrugged and lifted her eyebrows in response.

"He hugged me, kissed me, took me to dinner, held my hand, ordered for me, made me take my ring off, held my hand some more, devoured me with his lips when we got back to his truck, brought me home, walked me to the door..."

"I know the rest. I heard it banging against the door." She examines me critically, "It's been a long time hasn't it? Since you've been with a man. Has there been anyone since Jared?"

"Look, just because I've only ever been with one man..." my roommate interrupts me.

"Does he actually count as a man? I'm not saying

anything about you, just that I've got experience with a player and those who came before him don't compare."

I'm torn between a snarky comment and defending myself. "One, if nobody compares to him why do you keep dumping him and make him win you back? Two, just because I'm not a slut..." okay, maybe two snarky comments, "doesn't mean I haven't kissed a real man before. Jared is a man, we were both younger then."

"It's been over four years since you left him. He still calls. Does he not understand that you have broken up?"

"He's a friend, my critique partner, and co-worker. You're aware of all of this."

"Is he? Does he include boyfriend in the list?"

"He's aware I'm not his girlfriend." Though he doesn't like it. "If I was, you would've seen him come traipsing through our apartment on more than one occasion."

"I'm not judging, but you've done way better for yourself bagging a baseball player. Jones is such a sweetheart and respectful. You couldn't have done better."

I leer at her, "Hands off my boyfriend."

"Oh, better for you not for me."

"What is that supposed to mean? What difference does it make if it's me or you?"

"I feel like I'm more experienced sexually and want a man who can rock my world, like Cross. I'm not sure you're up for that or that Jones has that in him. Nothing negative, I'm sure you two will be perfect together. Maybe slightly tamer than what I aim for." Kristina stops and redacts, "You get it right? I'm not saying you aren't as good as us."

"I get it. You're both hos and we're not. Nothing to be upset by." The biggest grin ever dons my face, "Mase wants to take it slow. There will be more to discover for a long time."

"You know that's not what I meant."

"Don't be upset. There's no reason to compare here."

"Whatever. Have a good night. I'm going to bed."

"Goodnight." I grab a pint of ice cream from the freezer as her bedroom door closes and flip on the television in search of a movie. Bull Durham is on the recently watched list, so I set it to play and snuggle into my blanket while I devour the remains of my chocolate chip cookie dough ice cream.

I'M hot and wet between my legs. His body on top of me is all consuming, with his hard cock rubbing against my leg and his lips controlling mine like I've never experienced before. It's sensual overload, but I don't want it to stop. I want more. I want to find out what happens next. Whatever it is—I want it. His lips are warm and demanding as he spreads my lips invading my mouth with his tongue. Driving our intensity and need with every fraction of a motion. Pushed to my boiling point I need release. I reach for his belt... and I'm woken up by my phone ringing.

I answer without opening my eyes, "Hello?"

"Hey GG, you didn't answer when I texted. Is everything okay?"

It was great until you cut me off in my dream. "Yea, I fell asleep."

"Okay, are you coming to my game tomorrow?"

"Planning on it."

Sounding relieved, "Can I take you out after the game tomorrow?"

"Why are you asking? We've been hanging out together every night for weeks."

"I don't know. I guess I want you to know I take us seriously. I want to take it slow for a reason."

"Well then, where are you taking me?"

"I'll let you know first thing in the morning. Goodnight GG."

"Goodnight, Mase."

My phone lights up with kissy face emojis as soon as he hangs up. Okay, that might've been worth missing the end of my dream.

As I'm falling asleep in my bed, my phone rings again and I answer without opening my eyes, "Hello?"

"Hey Chelle, I missed you today," says a male voice, and I consider if Kristina is right, Jared isn't as much of a man as Jones. Note to self: check who's calling before you answer, that's what caller ID is for.

"What do you mean? We didn't have a meeting or anything," I say and hope I didn't miss something.

"We haven't had any time together the last few months. All we do is work."

"We're critique partners. We already have the fantasy world and characters created, and the plot is outlined for each serial for the next six months. What's left other than trading with each other to read and critique?"

"We're doing great on work. We haven't spent any time on the phone for edits or to catch up. I miss your voice."

"We don't need to. We've got this working like a machine." I consider my words before I continue and yawn, "Anyway, I'm in bed and was almost asleep. Have a good night."

"Wait. Did you just dismiss me?"

My FaceTime rings, he's trying to switch over so he can see me. "What do you think you're doing," I ask.

"You're in bed, I thought you might be wearing something sexy."

"Bye." I hang up and I'm immediately bombarded by texts.

Text from Jared: I was kidding.

Text from Jared: You don't understand how much I miss you.

Text from Jared: Are you still wearing my ring?

Text from Jared: You know we belong together.

Text from Jared: We're a great team.

Text to Jared The only thing we're good together for is writing for our serial contracts.

Text from Jared: Ouch! Don't say that.

I begin to wonder what he did to get paired with me on our serials. We write two semiweekly serials, one in a magic-filled fantasy world with orks, ogres, wizards, and other mystical creatures, and the other is sci-fi set in another galaxy in a time parallel to current earth. I believe I could write both without him, but not at the rate of four per week. I'm not sure he could do it without me. He gets the world creation but sometimes his characters are lacking and I push him on plots. There is no arguing with the corporate office, the motto is two heads are better than one—which is why we created a character with two heads for our fantasy world and made it stupid.

Jones

I wake up thinking about Michelle. She's beautiful in her almost no make-up, natural way. I'm taking her out tonight and I told her I'd let her know where this morning. It's a perfect date night because it's an early game today followed by a night game tomorrow. I want to take her to do something fun and romantic. I don't have the contacts for what I want to do, but Carter can make anything happen. I call him up while I'm getting ready.

"Good morning, Jones. What can I help you with today?"

"Do you have me programmed on your caller ID?"

"Every single player who comes through my locker room is programmed in. I'm guessing you need something urgent since it couldn't wait for you to get here?"

"Not urgent, but I want to make sure you can make it happen before I tell her where I'm taking her."

"What do you have in mind?"

"I want to take Michelle out for a romantic dinner and a private paddle boat ride in one of those fancy swans."

"Great idea, but no paddle boats after dark and she'd get cold. How about renting a small yacht with a private chef to take you out on the bay? I can arrange the swan thing for you on an off day sometime."

"A yacht might be too fancy for us. Can you make sure she has a ticket for today's game? Maybe have one of those Seals wide brimmed beach hats delivered to her to protect her from the sun?"

"No problem. How about reservations for the fondue restaurant with a bay view and a carriage ride along the Embarcadero?"

"Let's do that. You always have the answer. Thank you."

I text Michelle immediately.

Text to Michelle: Good morning GG.

Text to Michelle: You'll have time go home and change or whatever you want after the game.

Text to Michelle: I'll pick you up for dinner. Wear layers and be prepared to be outside near the bay for part of the evening.

Text to Michelle: See you at the game.

I don't get any answer, but that's not unexpected. It's early for her. Some nights she works all night. She doesn't have a regular schedule. She'll be in the stands today cheering for me and that means the most to me.

CHAPTER THREE

Michelle

I'm startled awake by loud banging on my bedroom door that's followed by yelling, "I'm leaving for work. Don't forget it's an early game today. Starts at 1 pm."

I grumble incoherently in response and find I fell asleep with my laptop open again. If nothing else I can depend on it to be warm and in bed with me.

"Another all-nighter?" she inquires through my bedroom door.

"Half-nighter. Men kept calling and texting. They can't just leave me alone."

"You're going to make me late to work. Men, plural? Are you writing some crazy sci-fi reverse harem scene?"

I consider the idea and brush it off. "Mase and Jared. Nothing out of this world."

"Why were you talking to Jared that late?"

"I wasn't. I was hanging up on him."

"And he doesn't think he's your boyfriend?"

"I don't want to talk about it. He's not my boyfriend regardless of what self-serving, selective memory, fantastical ideas he has in his pea-sized male brain."

"That's a lot of words for not wanting to talk about it."

"Will you just go to work already?"

Kristina cackles as she walks to the door, "Are you considering the company motto? Two heads are better than one? Keeping both of the guys on the hook?"

She's not serious, "Just go."

The door slams and I reach for my laptop to find it cold and dead. I plug it in curious to read what I was working on last night and wishing I had a coffee maker on my nightstand, or maybe one of those mini refrigerators stocked with iced coffee and energy drinks. Either would be better than leaving my warm bed to dash across my apartment to the kitchen and wait for the coffee maker to do its magic. I leave my laptop in my spot and hope it will keep it warm as I peel the blankets away to go make coffee. I tie my hair up in a knot and wash my face while I wait for my caffeinated brew.

Typically, I know exactly what I've written. But when I find my laptop open in bed with me all bets are off. Especially since I've been kind of obsessed with this other project that's not for work. At first, it was short pieces similar to a journal or a diary except it wasn't completely what had happened that day. Pieces of the day would be there—let's just say it must've included daydreams. Remembering last night, all bets are off. I'm often surprised by the words I type when I go back and read them. It's different for this project than the serials. The serials are short and somewhat formulaic, besides its already plotted so I know what I'm going to write going in. This is different. Free-form, the exact opposite—pantser not plotter. It's a new experience for me. I'm used to specific assignments, topics, and organizing my thoughts ahead of time for creative writing projects.

The smell of coffee widens my eyes. I grab my mug and go back to bed for some morning reading.

...I WRAPPED my legs around his waist as he claimed me with his lips, pressing me against the door. His need hard and throbbing against me. His masculine hands working their way up my body, leaving a heated trail on my skin. He kisses his way to my neck and buries his face, driving me crazy with his actions. His warm mouth teasing me with kisses and suction in an erogenous zone that hasn't had much play. His fingers thread through my hair and pull tight. My body reacts like never before, pushing against him and wanting more. He maintains his grip in my hair and presses his lips to mine, demanding my lips separate and grant access to his tongue. He pushes forward and his tongue tangles with mine. His breathing ragged, he whispers in my ear, "You make me crazy. I have to have you. You're so fucking sexy." He shoves his hard cock against me, "Do you feel that? You did that to me. All for you." I want him, but I push him away. "I thought you wanted to dance," he questions confused. I'm perplexed by my own actions. He's all I've wanted for weeks...

WHY IS it that I never get to the good part? Is it me? Do I have some type of block? A phobia maybe? What-if-his-cock-is-too-big-phobia? I'm not afraid of his cock, but that doesn't mean there aren't at least a hundred other things that could go wrong. I'd never admit it to Kristina, but she's not wrong. I don't have much experience. Only Jared and I'm the only woman he's been with so not much to go by. What's good? What's big? I don't have anything to compare.

One thing I know for sure—I want Jones Mason. Yes, I've had his hard sex pressed against me and I've grazed it intentionally and accidentally. He's definitely more than Jared. Honestly, that's not the part that matters. It's not why I need to have him. He could have a peen the size of my pinky finger (thank goodness he doesn't) and it wouldn't matter to me. He's got me locked in just being him. He's got this captivating combination of things that own me, but I'm not telling him that. Beyond the fact that he's absolutely gorgeous and fills out his baseball pants like no other. Something in his eyes, a warm and content sincerity that shifts to something more when he focuses on me. His athletic hands are protective and possessive from the moment I met him. Mostly, his words. I've never been able to get over a man that uses his words. That's probably why I agreed to date Jared in the first place. Well, that and the fact that I was young and didn't know any better. I didn't have the necessary experience to decide what was most important to me and what might be a deal breaker for me. Mase whispers in my ear, and I swear, I don't think the actual words matter. The tone alone could hypnotize me. His soft-spoken low tone could make me wet telling me he was hungry. When he uses his words, I'm his. Stick a fork in me, I'm done. Plus, he has a bit of a drawl that comes out when he tells me how beautiful I am. It's only there when he whispers sweet to me.

My thoughts are interrupted by a text...

Text from Mase: Are you awake? Game starts in less than two hours.

I read his messages from earlier and respond.

Text to Mase: You don't need to plan special dates for me.

Text to Mase: A carriage ride sounds so romantic.

Text to Mase: I can't wait.

Text from Mase: Are you coming to the game?

Text from Mase: Sherry's supposed to be back today.

Text to Mase: Yes. I gotta go get ready!

Text from Mase: You're always beautiful <3

Sherry hasn't been to a game in the last couple months. She couldn't manage it with her pregnancy, but their baby girl is about a month old now. She's watched every game and complained when she thought she should be in the stadium. I've watched many games with her. She knows everything about baseball and the San Diego Seals. If she played baseball trivia with the team, she'd win.

I take a quick shower and throw on one of my Seals T-shirts with a pair of jeans. My room is starting to look like the team store. I tie my hair up in a wet knot and head toward the stadium.

Sam, Sherry's sister-in-law, has been at some of the home games that Sherry has missed, so it's refreshing to find Sherry back in the seat where she belongs. "Welcome back!" I reach to give Sherry a hug.

She smiles, "I've missed it. Sam is watching Elle for me today. I wish I'd brought her with me."

"I'm sure it will be time to bring her to the game soon."

"It will. I already have a hat and jersey for her."

"I bet she's the cutest Seals fan ever."

Sherry nods, "Yes, but I'm probably biased. I want her to

see her dad play and get comfortable with the stadium atmosphere as soon as possible."

"Michelle," Carter calls out as he walks up to my seat. "I have a delivery for you from Mason." He hands me a wide brimmed straw hat with fabric wrapped around it that's the Seals navy and lime.

"I miss the days of surprise deliveries to my seat," Sherry smiles.

"Those days are not over," Carter says as he hands her the new Hawaiian print Seals baseball cap with the number 6 embroidered on the back.

She beamed, "I suppose they're not."

"Please let me know if I can get you ladies anything. I already have orders to deliver chocolate ice cream in the 5th inning," he smiles and waits for a second before he heads back to the concourse.

Kristina's voice comes ringing through the PA system on queue with the announcements for the day and today's line-ups. We observe as the players make their way onto the field to stretch. Chase stretching his legs and running sprints while gazing up at the announcer's box. Lucine playing catch with Martin. Seno warming up our starting pitcher in the outfield. Mase and Brandt doing stretches on the first baseline. The ritual of the game starts on time as always. Mase runs to go back in the club house, but redirects to me.

Smiling from ear to ear, "Happy to see you made it to the game. I'll see you at your place tonight when I pick you up for our date."

"I'm looking forward to it," I giggle like a school girl. "Thanks for the hat." The effect he has on me is even worse when he's in uniform and on the field. Lord help me if he gets dirty.

"I don't want my girl getting sunburnt." He winks at me and blows me a kiss before he takes off for the locker room.

Sherry turns to me with a questioning glare, "What's going on with you two? Dates now?"

Seno strolls up to the net before I can answer, "Do you know how happy I am to see you here?"

Sherry reaches for him, tangling her fingers with his at the net, "Happy enough to make it a win for me today?"

"Yes my queen, and then some."

"Make it a win!" she yells out at the field. "Go Seno!"

"Music to my ears," he smiles and goes to work. "You heard my woman! Let's get this done!"

Sherry adds intensity to the stadium. Nobody cheers like her. Plus, I love sitting next to her because it gives me more insight into the game.

Sherry turns to me, "So, back to my question."

"He took me out to dinner last night. All I know for tonight is it's a date and to wear layers because we'll be outside near the bay for part of the evening."

"What are you going to wear? Is he still taking it slow? He's such a sweet guy."

"Haven't even thought about it."

Sherry rolls her eyes at me, and quietly, "Show him what he's missing."

"I'm sorry?"

She focuses on me, "I always see you in jeans and T-shirts. There is nothing wrong with that, but if you want to make an impact you should dress up all girly for your date. He'll notice."

"I have a sweater I can wear with my jeans."

"Okay, that's a start. How about you come over to my place after the game and I'll doll you up for the night? Curl your hair, make-up, shopping in my closet."

I don't know about this. I like the idea of showing him what he's missing. "I'll be there."

"Good. Do you have a nice purse and shoes that match? Dress shoes or sandals?"

"I have shoes and purses."

"Bring some options, whichever you like best and black."

"Okay."

The game has been moving along quickly. No score and we're in the 5th inning. Our guys are getting on base, but not making it home. The opposing team is either popping up to the outfield or getting out on grounders. Lots of action but no reward for either side. Mase has been sharp at shortstop the whole game. Bases are loaded with Seals in the 6th with two out and Mase comes up to bat. He smashes the first pitch out of the park. I jump out of my seat and scream, "Go Mason! Wooooooo!" Grand Slam! He's all smiles and points at me when he steps on home plate. Seals on top 4-0. We shut out the opposing team 5-0 with the addition of Seno's home run in the 8th.

I GET HOME and want to take a nap, but there's no time for that. I gather up my makeup bag, shoes, purses, and a couple nice things from my closet in my duffle bag and toss it over my shoulder. I'm not ready for this, but I'm doing it anyway.

I get to Sherry's and she's got a few options already pulled out of her closet. All gorgeous, none I can imagine myself wearing. "What do you think?" She asks.

"Those won't look right on me or fit me."

"Yes they will. I bet at least one of them fits you perfectly. Give it a chance. Try them on and show me." I stare at her like she's lost her marbles. "Go on. Trust me on this."

I take the three outfits she has pulled for me into her bathroom and hang them on her shower door. Staring at each of them trying to decide which might not be so bad.

Sherry through the door, "I want to see all of them. It doesn't matter which one is first. No rush, but we need time to do your hair."

Fine. I strip down to my panties and bra, suddenly wondering if I should've dug my nice stuff out of my underwear drawer. There's a black strappy sundress with a single button at the top center in the front and a thin elastic band at the waist; a sleeveless red A-line mini dress with a sash to tie around it; and a multi-colored knee length wrap dress that's printed like peacock feathers. "These are all dresses," I state through the door.

"Yes, they are. Put one of them on."

I'm not prepared for the black strappy dress, I didn't bring and don't own a strapless bra. I'm going to leave that one for last and see if I can get away with skipping it. I pull on the red dress, "I can't reach the zipper."

The door opens and Sherry zips up the dress. She grabs the sash from the hanger, wraps it around my waist twice, and spins me around. "How's it feel?"

"My legs are bare."

"It's a dress. Dresses show your legs. I think it looks great on you. Did you look in the mirror?"

I face the mirror and I'm surprised to find that I don't hate it. Also, I'm going to need to shave my legs.

"Okay, now take that off and try on the next one." She leaves the room and closes the door behind her.

Once I figure out the knot she made in the sash, "Sherry, this zipper is not my friend."

The door opens and she joins me, wrangling the zipper. She stands there waiting.

"How do women deal with these zippers? I can't reach behind my back. My arms don't bend like that." I stare at her while I stand there half naked with the dress falling off my shoulders.

"You either figure it out, have a friend help, or find a guy that wants to take your clothes off. In case you're wondering, I'm trying to help you with the last option." She stops and continues, "Do you want me to leave or stay to help? There's no way you'll figure out the wrap dress if you can't handle the zipper."

I nod and step out of the red dress, carefully placing it back on its hanger. I remove the wrap dress from its hanger and put my arms through the holes of the cap sleeves. It's hanging on me like a backwards hospital gown that exposes all my good parts. I reach for the ties and start to wrap it around me like a robe when Sherry takes over.

"You've got the idea. We need to make sure the seams are in the right places and see where we want the tie to hit you at. I think this is probably the best option for your shape," she glances up to my face as she adjusts the tie. "Stop looking at me like I'm crazy. Trust me. Your breasts will look amazing in this dress and he won't be able to take his eyes off them. You've got them, so let's flaunt them."

"I'm trusting you. Only judging a little. I'm not big on showing my boobs."

"You want more from Mason. He obviously likes you. Seems like he needs a little push. Boys like boobs. Okay, I think that's it." She spins me around to face the mirror. "The print isn't my favorite on you, but the cut of the dress couldn't be better."

"The print is kind of sexy. I like peacocks."

"What do you think of your shape in the dress?"

"I guess I like it. It doesn't look like me. I'm not into dresses."

"I am aware. I'm going to make you change your mind about dresses. I'm not sure you need to try the black one on." Ha! "But, let's do it anyway." Damn it.

I untie the dress and hand it to Sherry so she can figure out how to hang it up and slide the black one off the hanger, "I don't have the right bra for this one."

"Just try it on."

It slips over my head easily. No unreachable zippers. No tie that requires a code book to arrange. It's soft, simple, and the thin elastic band hits me perfectly at my natural waist.

"You like it," Sherry says.

"Maybe."

"Hold on..." Sherry leaves me to check myself out in the mirror. I enjoy the way the dress sways around my legs. It makes me feel sexy. She returns, "Okay, try this bra on."

The dress comes off and I switch bras. "Why do you have my size bra?"

"I was pregnant. I tried everything. We got lucky. I can't use it, so you might as well."

"Thank you. It's perfect and I hate bra shopping." I slip the dress back on.

"You need a sweater and a pop of color..." she disappears for a minute or two. She hands me a cardigan sweater, "Hold this for a minute." She holds up a simple silver tie belt and a brightly colored scarf, "Which one?"

"Silver."

She wraps the silver strands around my waist and ties the ends together in a bow placed slightly to the side. "Try the sweater."

I put the black cardigan on and its silver-colored buttons are perfect with the belt.

"I forgot about those buttons. It looks like it was made to go with the belt and dresses up the plain black." She gazes at me in the mirror, "What do you think? Dressy black or peacock boobs?"

"I'm in on getting his attention with my breasts, but I need a night in a starter dress first. So, I'm choosing black for tonight."

"Good plan. Don't push. One step at time. Did you bring some cute black shoes and a matching purse?"

"I've got a pair of black strappy wedges and a small black crossbody with silver details."

"Perfect. Let's get your hair curled."

Text from Mase: I'll be at your place to pick you up in about an hour.

"How long will it take to finish getting me ready?"

"I want to take my time with your hair. Maybe 45 minutes?"

Text to Mase: I'm at Sherry's. Can you pick me up there?
Text from Mase: Okay.

"He's picking me up here in an hour."

She puts the toilet lid down and gestures for me to have a seat. She pulls my hair back and dumps out my makeup bag, "There's not much here."

"I don't wear much. Maybe mascara, a little eyeliner, and sometimes lip gloss."

"That's enough. Let's add a light eye shadow and blush tonight. Are you okay with that?"

I nod, "As long as I don't look like a clown. I like natural."

"You can wash it off if it's too much. Try my way?"

"Okay." Five minutes later I'm beginning to accept that Sherry is always right. I'm good with the makeup and she's spraying something on my hair that will make it curl easier.

"Flip your hair over and shake it out," she directs me. "It'll give you more volume. Do you want all of your hair down or would you like part of the top up?"

"Whatever you think. I'm trusting you tonight, so might as well go all the way."

Thirty minutes later I get a text...

Text from Mase: I'm here.

Sherry sees the text, "He should come up to get you. Besides, I need a few more minutes."

Text to Mase: Come on up.

Text from Mase: Why are we at Seno's?

Text to Mase: Sherry asked me to come over after the game.

Text from Mase: We have a date tonight.

Text to Mase: Yes we do.

Text from Mase: I'll be up in a minute.

Sherry finishes curling every hair on my head and runs her fingers through it, giving it a shake to arrange it how she wants. She gives it a mist of hair spray, "What do you think?"

I get up and check the mirror, surprised at what's staring back at me. Who's this blonde with all the crazy full and fluffy hair? The perfectly outlined eyes that pop and a dress that's both dressy and slimming.

Sherry smiles, "Mason's going to lose it when he sees you. You look great. Get your shoes and bag, he should be here any second."

"Thank you," I smile at her. There's a knock on her door and I move to leave the bathroom, but she holds me back.

"Stay here. Let me grab your bag and bring it to you, so you can be completely put together when he sees you." She chuckles, "Besides I want a good view when he sees you."

We both stop and listen when we hear the door open. Seno answers the door, "Hey man, come on in. Are you picking Michelle up?"

"Yea," Mason replies.

"She should be out in a few minutes. Where are you taking her?" There's some indiscernible mumbling from Mason, and Seno continues, "Sounds fun, I may have to take Sherry on a date like that. She'd love that. Let me know how the restaurant is."

"Sure thing. What are they doing?"

"Women stuff." Footsteps walk toward the bathroom.

Sherry slips out the door returning quickly to give me my bag. I slide into my wedges and put the sweater on. I find the matching purse and move my necessities into it. I love the dress with the wedges. The extra three inches lengthens my body. I step out of the bathroom and Sherry grins, "Leave your bag. You can get it tomorrow." I drop it in the bathroom and walk out to meet Mase. I see him before he sees me. "I love those wedges on you," Sherry comments and Mase turns to me. The expression on his face says it all. He's never seen me in anything other than jeans and a T-shirt, even if it is his shirt. I'm the girl he plays video games with. Maybe Sherry is right, he needs to see me in a new light. Honestly, I need to remember I'm a woman and can be feminine. I don't need to hide my body. I could get used to wearing dresses, especially if it makes him stare at me like he is right now.

"Hi Mase. I'm ready to go," I don't even sound like me. It's like a more feminine version has taken over. A sweet voice that would never sneak up behind him and blow him up when we're playing video games. The opposite counterpart to me being as loud as Sherry at the game when my guy hits a home run. There's a time and place for everything. I can be sweet and sexy on our date, and a tomboy at the game. It's all for him.

CHAPTER FOUR

Jones

I thought I was taking Michelle on a date tonight, but I don't recognize the curvaceous beautiful woman standing in front of me. Sexy legs and hips to die for, topped off with undeniably feminine fluffy curls that I want to run my fingers through. Who am I kidding? I want to get a tight handful of those curls and take control. She's not overly made up and her glossy lips are calling to me. She'll taste like my GamerGirl. I reach for her hand, skimming her hip through her flowing skirt, "Are you ready to go, beautiful?"

She takes my hand with both of hers and gives me a sweet peck on the cheek, "Let's go." Her smile lights the whole room. She's close enough that I'm overcome with her sweet, light scent. I place my arm around her waist and lead her out the door.

"Have fun," Sherry yells after us.

I've never imagined my girl like this. She is absolutely a woman and always has been, this is more than that. She's more than a girl I like and I'm comfortable with. I already knew there was more than that to us. She's an absolute knockout. This increases the stakes. The guys were interested the night we met. If they saw her like this, I could have some serious competition. I check her finger to make sure she's not wearing that ring again and notice her bare sexy neck. I wasn't thinking. This is a date. She took it like a real date. I didn't bring her flowers or anything. I'll make up for that this evening.

We've made it down the elevator and we're almost to my truck when Michelle asks, "Are you going to talk to me this evening or just hold my hand with that titanium grip silently? I'm good either way. Maybe cut back to a more mild-mannered Clark Kent grip instead of full-on Superman."

I stop in my tracks and stand in front of her, releasing her hand. "I wasn't expecting you. You're always beautiful, but it's like you turned beauty into an extreme sport that you're the untouchable champion of." Not to mention that it's all I can do to keep from dragging her back to my place like a caveman and having my way with her. Focus. This is your GG. You have reservations.

"You noticed," she smiles, happy with herself.

"That's kind of my point. Every male out there tonight is going to be looking at you and trying to figure out how to take you from me." I stop and shuffle my feet, "Or, maybe, wonder why the gorgeous blonde is with that loser."

"They can't take me from you. I choose who I want. I want you. If they don't know that you're the best hitter in the division, that's on them. I'm not dressed up to be a spectacle. Don't you get it?"

"Apparently not," I shake my head and wonder if I should stop at my apartment to change.

"Idiot! Boys are so stupid."

"Do you think you might elaborate on that please?"

On a huff, "Do you think I spent two hours of my day trying on dresses, getting my hair curled, and having my makeup done so I could be a spectacle? I only want attention from you. You called it a date, so I thought I should be date ready. You know I'm a woman, right?"

"Everyone within a city mile knows you're a woman."

"Does that include you?"

"Yes, I definitely know you're a woman and I'm proud to have you as mine."

"About that..."

"What now?"

"I'm not sure about this 'being yours' thing. We've spent a lot of time together. We have fun together and get along well. When you finally kissed me I enjoyed it. I don't understand why you waited so long and I don't like you making decisions for me, even if it's ordering food."

"You *enjoyed* me kissing you?"

"I'm trying to be diplomatic here, not boost your ego."

"So you more than enjoyed me kissing you?"

"I guess. It was a positive experience that I hope to repeat in the future."

Suddenly I'm pressing her body against my truck with the need to prove myself. My hands exploring the curve of her hips through the silky material. I separate her legs with one of mine and rub against her center with my thigh. My hard cock strangled by my fly. I trail my nose along her neck, her skin soft and smooth. I'm trying to have control. The evening has only just begun. I wrap my arms around her and whisper in her ear, "You're special to me. We belong together. I want to take it slow and enjoy every second with you. I'm sorry if I haven't made that clear to you. In my heart and my head, you're my girl. Are you okay with that?"

"I suppose."

"You suppose?" I say frustrated.

"Well, you've only kissed me a few times and we haven't spent the night together yet really and I don't know if your key works for my lock."

"Look, we can always get a locksmith or whatever. I don't understand how that matters."

"Ooh, are you into that kind of thing? I'm not sure I'm up for a threesome. Kristina might be. Maybe you've got the wrong roommate."

I cover my eyes and press my hand to my face, "No, I'm not into those things. I'm a one-woman man and I don't share. I promise my key will satisfy the requirements of your lock."

"What if it's too big?"

"It's not."

"Then maybe it's too small?"

I push it against her, "It's not."

"Oh, okay."

"Please let me take this slow. I want you to understand how special you are to me. I don't want you to think you're my fuck toy."

"What if I want to be your fuck toy?"

"You want to be a fuck toy?" She's killing me.

"No, but I'm interested in having sex with you. A lot of it. On a regular basis."

"Trust me, we'll both appreciate it more if we take it slow."

"I'll consider it."

I get her in my truck and want to bang my head against a wall. I hold her hand in a more mild-mannered way while I drive to the bayside. The short drive along the embarcadero is lined by lights strung on ships and reflecting off the water on one side, hotels and skyscrapers on the other. I park and help her out of my truck, I don't want her hurting herself in her tall shoes. Fuck, they give a sexy curve to her calves. I could throw her over my shoulder and keep her off her feet for days. We walk through restaurant row along the bay until we reach The Fondue House and I lead her inside. I give the hostess my name and she replies, "We have your table waiting for you Mr. Mason. Right this way." I place my hand on the small of Michelle's back guiding her to walk ahead of me. The hostess leads us to a secluded table in the back of the restaurant where there's a bouquet of a dozen long stemmed pink roses waiting. We sit down and she opens the draperies to an unobstructed view of the bay.

"This is beautiful, Mase," she squeezes my hand and reaches for the roses. "This is so sweet of you," she smells the roses and reads the card. "Thank you, Mase. I love the color."

"I'm glad you like them," I want to refer to her by name, but for some reason she's Michelle tonight and not GG. I check my phone to find out if I'm missing anything and that it's on silent. It should be. She gets all of my attention tonight. A text pops through:

Text from Carter: Seno called me and said you need help if you're going to keep that girl. He said you showed up empty handed and she should get some flowers. I called in a favor from the restaurant manager. Don't worry about what the card says, they have a generic thing they do "I melt for you" or something like that.
Text to Carter: Thank you
Text from Carter: Also, Sherry said a silver necklace would complete Michelle's outfit tonight. I can arrange to have one waiting for you at the carriage if you'd like. Let me know which one.

Three photos pop through when I'm ready to say no and one of them is perfect for her. A dainty silver chain with a floating shiny silver heart on it. Simple and I think she'll love it.

Text to Carter: The second one. Thank you.

Text to Carter: Can you make sure there's a blanket waiting at the carriage, too?

Text from Carter: No problem. I heard your date is more beautiful than normal and you weren't ready for it.

Text to Carter: Learning curve.

I put my phone away.

She asks, "Is everything okay?"

"Yes, just making sure we're set for the after-dinner part of our date." I lean over and kiss her cheek, "You didn't have to get made up for me. You're always beautiful." She giggles. "Have you been here before?"

"No, but I love cheese and chocolate."

"Then we should start with the cheese course. You pick the cheese."

She slides closer to me in the booth and we share a menu, "How about the gruyere combination?"

"Whatever you want. The specialty cocktails look good, too."

The waiter walks up to our table, "What can I get for you this evening?" His eyes flash when he sees Michelle and he turns to her, "Hello beautiful! I've got a cocktail that's perfect for you. It's pretty and pink, it'll match you and your roses."

She focuses on him and smiles, "Sounds good."

"And for the gentleman?" he asks.

"Whatever microbrew IPA you have on tap will be fine."

He nods at me and I continue, "We'd also like to order the deluxe cheese course with the gruyere combination."

"Can I get you any salads to start?"

I glance at Michelle and she wrinkles her nose, "No, thank you."

"Then I'll be right back with your drinks. The cheese course will take a few minutes to get prepped and heated," He winks at Michelle as he walks away. I knew she was going to get attention.

"He'll bring out a big tray of things to dip in the cheese, all cut up to be bite-sized." I wrap my arm around her and hold her close.

"How many times have you been here?"

"Only once, with a couple of the guys."

The waiter brings Michelle her cocktail, "I told the bartender to be a bit heavy-handed for you. I hope you like it."

"Thank you," she replies and he disappears without acknowledging my existence or leaving me a drink.

He returns with a huge platter of things that go well with cheese: cherry tomatoes, cubed French bread, broccoli, cubed sourdough bread, cauliflower, apple wedges, pear chunks, bell peppers, asparagus, mushrooms, carrots. "If you want more of anything just let me know," he directs to Michelle and takes off again.

"That's a lot of food," Michelle observes. "We can't eat that much."

"We can skip the broth course, but be sure to save room for dessert," I grin at her and her eyes turn to saucers at the thought. "What kind of chocolate do you want?"

She grabs the menu and her jaw drops, "Milk chocolate with peanut butter."

"Are you sure you don't want to try the white chocolate?"

"It's good, but not really chocolate. Peanut butter trumps everything else."

"I'll tell the waiter if he ever comes back with my beer," I chuckle.

As if on command the waiter arrives with the fondue and forks. Speaking only to my beautiful girl, "Can I get you anything else?"

"This all looks lovely. Thank you."

"I'm so happy you're pleased with it."

"I can't wait to try the milk chocolate with peanut butter for dessert."

"That's the best choice." He leans in quietly, "I'd skip the broth course and go straight for the chocolate."

"I like that idea. Let's do that."

"No problem. I'll take care of it." He steps back ready to leave.

"Do you think you could bring my date a beer?"

"Of course, and I'll bring you another cocktail on the house."

"Thank you so much," she smiles at him sweetly.

He leaves and I get to talk, "Did you enjoy that?"

"What do you mean?" she chuckles. "It's the only way you're going to get your beer and I'm saving you money on the bill."

"Why do you think that is?" I glare at her cockeyed.

"He likes my hair? He thinks it's my birthday or something because you got me flowers? I have a friendly face? He wants a big tip?"

"You have his full attention because you're the most gorgeous woman he's ever seen."

"Don't be silly," she bats at the air as if she's pushing the thought away.

I shake my head and move a few things to dip onto my

plate. Michelle scoots even closer and we enjoy dinner together, forking different food choices, dipping them and sharing with each other—only using the one plate. Her hand on my thigh the whole evening, even when the waiter brought her another cocktail and told me they're out of IPA without offering anything else.

The cheese is gone. We got in there with the bread and our fingers and fed the last bites to each other. This is turning into a better idea than I thought.

The empty tray is replaced with a new one filled with foods to dip in the chocolate, everything from cubes of different kinds of cake, marshmallows, and donut holes, to fruit, graham crackers, and rice crispy treats. We turned it into a s'mores fest. It was a mess that turned into licking chocolate off each other's fingers and lips. I suck and nibble on her lower lip under the pretense of chocolate until I gaze into her eyes to find the heat I'm experiencing staring right back at me. I palm the back of her head and press my lips to hers softly, slowly. Tasting her delectable lips. Opening my mouth slightly more with each kiss until her tongue reaches for mine. Her warm body against me, her fluffy hair teasing my senses. I want more.

"Ahem, excuse me. I'm going to leave the bill here for you. It doesn't look like you're going to be needing anything else that I can offer tonight," and he walks away.

I leave enough cash on the table to cover it and offer Michelle a hand out of the booth. She grabs her flowers and I put my arm around her as we walk out of the restaurant. I want to take her back to my place and forget about taking it slow. That's not an option.

"Are you ready for the next part of our date?"

She smiles, "I'm happy just to be with you."

She's perfect. "A date means we're going to do something

on purpose. Could be just dinner, but not tonight." I check the time, "Come with me." I lead her to the end of restaurant row to find our horse drawn carriage waiting for us. "My lady," I bow trying to be funny.

"Are you serious? We're going on a carriage ride?"

"Yes, we have the carriage for the evening." The coachman steps down from the carriage and hands me a large shopping bag.

"May I help the young lady into the carriage?" he asks politely.

"Yes, please," she replies anxiously and he pulls a step down for her, holding her hand for stability. "Thank you," she gets comfortable as I climb in. I find a small box in the bag and set it aside. I pull out a luxurious faux fur blanket and place it over our laps, tucking it around the other side of Michelle. "This is so soft. You've thought of everything."

"I've had a little help, but I'm trying." I hand her the little box, "I hope you like it."

She stares at me surprised and opens the box to find the silver necklace with the heart, "It's beautiful and perfect for my outfit tonight. Put it on me." I do as she requests. She wraps her arms around my neck and kisses me on the lips, "I love it, Mase. Thank you." She gets her phone out and takes a selfie. I take her phone from her and take a selfie of us together, then another as I kiss her. No better way to start our carriage ride. We snuggle together and enjoy the ride.

Michelle

I'm not sure what's got into Mase, but this night has been perfect since it started. Everything has been taken care of. It's a step in the right direction for our relationship. I get it, take it slow. But until now it's been pizzas, movies, and video games. Tonight shows thought and a chance for us to be out as a couple. Maybe he has a romantic side. It could be why we're taking it slow. I'm okay with that. The carriage ride was more than I could've imagined. The lights in the trees throughout the embarcadero park sparkling like stars, the bay crashing softly against the jetty, his attentiveness and being near him. After the carriage ride he wraps the blanket around me and buys us hot coffee from a stand.

"What else would you like to do tonight?"

"Anything as long as I'm with you."

"Let's go home. I want to stay with you tonight."

Before I get my hopes up and then destroyed and ruin an evening that I'll never forget, "Do you mean you want to come over and play video games? Sleep on my floor or the sofa? I need more information before I approve of your plan. I don't want anything to ruin this evening."

He stops and puts his arms around me, gazing into my eyes, "I want to hold you in my arms all night long and sleep with you in your bed. One thing at a time, okay?"

"I'm good with that." I can't wait. "Will you take your shirt off?"

Why does this seem like the beginning of negotiations? "I can do that. Do you want to rest your head on my bare chest?"

"Yes, and I want to feel your skin against me. I'm good with it. I won't push. I like the progress. I don't need more." I stare at the ground, "Mase, I don't want to go too fast either. I just need to know where we're going. I want to kiss you more."

He squeezes me, "Let's go home, beautiful."

On the ride home I text my roommate:

Text to Kristina: This is notice that I'm bringing a boy home to stay the night in my room.
Text to Kristina: Okay, mother?
Text from Kristina: Would you like me to pile up all the extra blankets on your bedroom floor so he has a place to sleep?
Text to Kristina: That won't be necessary, but thanks for offering.
Text from Kristina: Oh! Are you going to build a fort together to play video games in?
Text to Kristina: You might want to stay at Chase's tonight.

We may not plan on doing anything loud, but I'm not a child. She can wonder.

Text from Kristina: You get it girl! Woop!
Text from Kristina: I want the details tomorrow.
Text from Kristina: I'm already at Chase's bungalow for the night.
Text to Kristina: Does that mean we can wander our apartment naked?
Text from Kristina: I don't want to think about his peen hanging out bare in our living room.

I can imagine her scrunched up face at the thought.

Text from Kristina: Have fun. Don't do anything kinky in the kitchen. That's just disgusting.
Text to Kristina: Enjoy Chase.
Text from Kristina: I already am. Gotta go…

"Kristina's at the beach tonight. No roommate to deal with," I share with Mase.

"What will we do with the whole apartment to ourselves?"

"Whatever we want, but Kristina said no naked in the common area and no kinky in the kitchen," I chuckle.

"That's not a concern."

"No, but wouldn't it be fun to make her think there was some of that? It'd drive her crazy."

He grins deviously, "Butt print on the sofa?"

"I was thinking of leaving a pair of panties between the cushions," I suggest laughing.

"What about in the kitchen?" his wheels are turning.

"We might need props," I stare at him bright-eyed. "Can you make a quick stop at the adult store?"

"Yes, ma'am. What do you have in mind?"

"Don't worry. I'm not pushing us. I understand enjoying the journey, and our destination will be all us," I giggle. "I just want to torment my roommate. I'm tired of her thinking I'm a good girl." I stop and continue, "Are you okay with it appearing that we're having a sexual relationship?"

He nods and grins, "As long as we know the truth and are having fun, nothing else matters."

He pulls up to the door of the adult store and I hop out, "I'll only be a few minutes."

I want a variety of flavored lube, potions that heat up, and a pair of dirty dice. I find everything I'm looking for quickly and the older woman behind the counter says, "Would you like to add a vibrator to your order? We're having a sale to clear out last year's models. This little one's only five dollars." She continues in her smoker's voice, "It's ribbed for her pleasure. I also have a vibrating ring for him, it's a couple bucks more." She stops then adds, "I can't speak to the ring. The five dollar one works pretty well, but it tends to go through batteries. They both have batteries included that'll get you through the night."

Thirty bucks later I walk out of the store with a bag that has Mase's eyes lit up when he sees it. "What did you buy?"

I reply simply, "Props."

I have Mase park in my spot since my car is at Sherry's. We take the elevator up from the underground garage. The mirror in the elevator foyer says it all: A couple coming home from a date, roses, blanket, and a shopping bag with Adult Fun Shop ~ Lotions, Lace, and Vibrators printed on it in large purple letters. Luckily, we didn't run into anyone on the way to my apartment. He holds my hand as we walk to my apartment and I get it unlocked. It's not the first time we've been here alone, but something is different. Maybe the fact that I finally believe we're a couple. I don't know. Something about dinner changed things. We never share a plate like that or feed each other, but those are things that real couples do. The intimacy of his touch without being naked or in bed. The closeness and snuggling, protecting me in a way. Or maybe that was protecting what he sees as his. Was Jones threatened by the waiter? Did me getting dressed up for the date make that huge of a difference? I'm going to have to test that theory.

Hmmm, when is it time for me to change out of this dress? It's comfortable and I'm over the exposed legs things now. I'm not going to sleep in it. Shit, what am I going to sleep in? I asked him to take his shirt off. Is he going to expect me to take my shirt off or my bottoms? I usually sleep in a T-shirt and panties, lately his T-shirt. It's long, super big on me, so soft, and hangs down to about my mid-thigh. Should I dig out my cutesy girl jammies? That'd be kind of obvious. I should've thought of this at the adult store. I could've bought something sexy.

"GG? Why are you just standing there?" he asks slowly and questioning.

"Not sure."

"Why don't you show me what's in the bag? We can get that set up and then go about our evening," he says as he wraps his arms around me and kisses my forehead. "I'm not used to you being this tall," he crouches down and slides each of my wedges off. The warmth of his breath hits my good parts. His strong hands touching my feet and ankles send shivers up my legs. This hasn't happened before. The blood rushing through my body desiring our connection, I want him. I run my fingers through his hair and his hands are on my legs as they travel up my body, the skirt of my dress being pulled up slightly. His hands finding a resting place low on my hips when his mouth finds mine. It's a charge of lightning shooting up through me from my ankles to my good parts. As if he's my own personal electrically charged superhero or sex god. I kiss him back, pushing him forward and out of control. He places his hands firmly on my shoulders and steps back. His face is red and his breathing is ragged. His eyes focus on mine, hooded and needy. "Michelle?"

"Yea?" Trying to catch my breath.

"We..." I cut him off.

"I want you," I say quietly.

"I want you, too," we can't."

"We could," I suggest.

"It's too soon, GG. You're worth so much more. It's a bad idea."

"Why?"

"Didn't you feel it tonight? We got closer. Let's be in this space for a while."

There was definitely a shift in our relationship tonight, "Enjoy the journey?"

"Yea, the journey will make the destination better," his boyish smile takes over his lips.

I can't argue with him. There's nothing wrong with waiting. One step at a time. "I'm good either way."

"You win all the games. Let me have this one," he says with serious intent. He nods, "Now, what do you have in the sex shop bag?"

I dump the bag out to reveal the many individual pillow packs of flavored lube, flavored gels for blow jobs, and lotions that heat up, the five-dollar vibrator, the vibrating ring, a can of body cream, and a set of sex dice.

"Do you have a plan for this stuff?" he asks.

"Mostly I want to leave the open packages where she can find them, but not too obvious. Maybe leave the can of body cream open and a mess on the kitchen counter. Sex dice out on the coffee table in the living room. The vibrators were on sale and the older woman behind the counter thought I should get them. I couldn't tell her no. I suppose we could leave them lying in plain sight in my bedroom so she sees them if the door is open." I turn to him, "We could save them for a later time or, maybe, try them out."

"I'm not into that stuff. We are not trying them out. And if you mean save them for when we're fifty, then fine put them away in your dresser for a couple decades. We might want a little something extra then. I don't require help getting off and I don't require help to get you off," he says decidedly.

"Okay. It was only a suggestion," Maybe I can try it when he's not here. He probably wouldn't like that either. I put the vibrators in the bag and wrap it up tightly, then stash it away in my nightstand. I return to find he's already got the body cream open and has a mouthful of it. I stare at him, "Ummm... okay. Starting without me?"

"I was just going to make it a mess, but it smells good," he attempts speaking with his mouth full and walks towards me with the can in his hand.

"Oh, no. You keep away from me with that can. I already know it's a sticky mess," I warn as I walk backwards to keep my distance.

"Come on. Have some fun. You bought this stuff. It smells better than it tastes, but it's not bad," he goes on and finally gives up, taking it back to the kitchen.

"Leave the can kind of on the edge of the counter by the back wall. Like we set it there and just forgot. Or maybe we should put it in the refrigerator?"

He nods and places it in the refrigerator door next to the condiments. I full belly laugh until tears stream down my face. I get the scissors and open some of the pillow packs, squeezing most of the contents into the sink and rinsing it down the drain. I leave the opened packages in the top of the kitchen trash and in the bathroom waste basket. I place an unopened one on the kitchen counter next to the scissors and leave another opened pillow pack on the counter like an afterthought.

"What do you think about the dice?" I ask him.

"They look like fun for another time. Maybe open the package and leave them sitting on the breakfast bar," he suggests.

I take his suggestion and observe what I've left for Kristina to find. I'm happy with myself and focus on Mase. "So, my boyfriend... what's next on your plan for tonight?"

He grins from ear to ear, "I think it's bedtime." He takes my hand and leads me to my bedroom, closing the door behind us.

I'm suddenly nervous, "So, am I supposed to change into my sleep shirt with you right here? How does this work?"

He pulls me closer to him and places my hands directly on his skin under the hem of his shirt. His eyes focused on mine, he nods and somehow I know I'm supposed to take his shirt off him. I've never taken a man's shirt off. I start to explore his muscular physique with my fingers and realize I could be getting a visual at the same time. I push his shirt up and carefully pull it off over his head. He's standing there in only his dark jeans. His thick muscled torso with a defined eight pack staring at me, or maybe I'm staring at him. I reach my arms up to hug him and pull him against me, but my hands have a mind of their own. Planting on his strong broad shoulders and tracing a line down each sinewy arm along the outline of his deltoid to his bicep and around to his triceps. His arms and traps flex at my light contact "Are you comfortable with me sleeping in my boxer briefs or would you prefer I keep my jeans on. I can sleep on top of the blanket if you'd like, too. But that's not what I want to do." I internally question if he's asking me or considering his own will power. *What exactly does he want to do?*

Hot baseball player in his underwear. Probably not a good idea if he wants to wait, but I'm not turning it down, "However you're comfortable is fine. I don't see how you can hold me all night if you're on top of the blankets." Let the bricks fall where they may.

"True. We'll make it work."

"What about me?"

"Wear what you usually wear to sleep."

"Maybe I like to sleep naked," I can't help myself.

He glares at me.

"Then turn the other way so I can change into your shirt."

He turns away and unbuttons his fly, "Yes, ma'am."

I pull the dress off quickly and put his shirt on. Then hang up the dress. I turn back to the bed and he's already in it, lying there watching me. "That's quite the view you're giving me. Do you have panties on under there?"

"I'm not telling."

"Then I guess I don't get to find out."

I turn the light off and climb into bed with him. He fluffs the pillows and pulls me into him. My soft figure against his athletic build. I want more and he wraps his arms around me. Curled into him, I place my hand on his chest. He's warm, having his body next to me is both comforting and exciting. I drag my finger across his chest and his breath catches, his heart beating faster. He rolls towards me and sweetly kisses my forehead. His hands splayed across my back, his brow creases, "Do you always sleep in your bra?"

"No."

"Why do you still have it on?"

I truly have no idea. I'm new to this. I was worried about changing in the same room. But that makes no sense because I can take my bra off and keep my shirt on, especially since I'm wearing this huge shirt. Plus, it's strapless so there's no straps to deal with, it says so right in the name. What will he think if my boobs are free? Is that an invitation? Will he think they're saggy? What if they're not round enough? Or plump enough? I have to respond, "I didn't think about it. I was trying to change quick." I hear the nervousness in my voice so that means he does too.

His finger at my chin guides me to stare into his eyes, "I'll never hurt you. I'll never push you for sex. I want to be here with you. It doesn't matter if we're clothed or naked. All that matters is that we're together." He brushes his thumb across my cheek, "And, I would like you to be comfortable." His hands glide up my back and find my bra, unlatching each of the hooks and pulling it off of me. He tosses it across the room and snaps the elastic band on my panties. "You're wearing panties."

I chuckle, "Granny panties."

"As long as they're not my granny's panties, I'm good with that." He holds me snug against him, his hands back on the outside of my shirt. I reach around to his back and explore the details as if I'm reading braille. Not missing anything. He kisses my forehead, then the tip of my nose, then a sweet peck on my lips, then another, and another. His soft lips begging me to open for him with his open-mouthed kisses. I lick is lower lip from crease to crease and he tangles his bare legs with mine. He pulls back and gazes at me, searching for something with hooded eyes. His kiss more intense and possessive as our tongues tango. He finds his way back under my shirt, his fingers digging into my back as he holds me to him. His hard cock pushing against me. My breasts smashed to his chest. I want more. I want his hands all over me with their intense masculine strength and heat. His body against mine has me soaring. His hands move down to find their home at my hips and I'm struck by lightning again. He groans and kisses my neck, then whispers, "I'm not going further. This is what I want tonight. I hope I didn't go too far for you. I think you'd tell me. I'm going to hold you all night. Feel us together. It will only get better." His arms wrap around me intuitively, and we fall asleep forehead to forehead.

Jones

I wake up in the middle of the night with my arms around GG, one hand on her ass and the other spread across her back under her shirt. Her naked legs vined with mine and her freezing feet buried trying to absorb my heat. I remember the night. It was more than I wanted. We vibe like a romantic couple—I've never had that and I only want it with Michelle. I didn't plan on taking her bra off or getting under her shirt. This was supposed to be baby steps. I want to stay in this place for as long as I can. Holding her and not going further.

CHAPTER FIVE

Michelle

Waking up in his arms, let alone with a man in my bed is both wonderful and stressful. I want to stay in his arms for as long as possible, but I also want to go brush my teeth and hair. I'm sure I have something stuck in my teeth, killer morning breath, and knots in my hair. I bet my appearance is simply breathtaking. I can only imagine my hair is flat on one side and sticking out funny in the back. He's still sleeping. I study his handsome face while he's asleep. Square jaw, long dark eyelashes, and full kissable lips. I nuzzle my face under his chin and use his chest as my pillow, stretching my arm over his abs and holding onto him. I close my eyes and relax with his protective strength around me until we have to move.

Last night wasn't expected. We're a couple, and I hadn't realized how much so until we were out last night. We're more than gaming buddies. Him waiting and keeping his distance could be his silent attack. It's easy for us to be together. We're comfortable and get along well. There's been nothing threatening at all or pushing in the slightest. In fact, I've wanted more from him, I guess that's pretty obvious. But last night? Everything was simply how it's supposed to be. He's such a gentleman and always treats me like a woman, maybe more so since I was wearing a dress, or maybe that's part of the date experience. It doesn't matter, we're more of a couple than I had any clue about. I sat close to him with his arm around me or he was holding my hand, one or the other, the whole night. Then the way he kissed me and held me left me with no questions about us. It'll always be Mase.

His hand flexes against my back and he kisses the top of my head, "Good morning, gorgeous." His thick morning voice echoes through my head.

I squeeze him and press my cheek to his chest, "Good morning, Mase." A smile creeps across my face uncontrollably. I don't want to get out of bed. Fuck my morning bed head.

"It's a late game today. I have some time before I need to be at the stadium. What would you like to do this morning?"

I consider the contents of my kitchen and the potential for making breakfast. Not much more than a toaster waffle unless I want to break into my roommate's baking stuff and use her supplies—I know better. I don't want to hear it, but more than that I don't have those skills. A box of pancake mix with instructions I can handle. From scratch? Not so much. I do have coffee. "I can make some coffee, if you'd like?" I offer and go on, "But, I'm happy right where I am."

"I like that. I'm happy right where I am, too," his voice positive and wispy. "I do need to eat before I go to the stadium. How about we stay where we are for a bit and then let me take you to breakfast? I can drop you off at your car after."

"That works. I have some work to do before the game, too." I have to get some words down for the next serial. If I stay ahead, I don't have to talk to anyone. That's the way I like it. Worst thing is Jared's critique and that's usually an atta boy. "How'd you sleep last night?"

He rolls toward me and gazes into my eyes, "Perfect. I love having you next to me. You?"

I hadn't considered it. I probably should've before I asked him. I'm well-rested and that rarely happens. My feet aren't freezing for a change. His arms around me are like an impenetrable protective cocoon. There's this uncanny sense that I have the power to do anything. "You make me feel like I can do anything, yet protected at the same time."

He squeezes me and kisses my neck below my ear, "I'll always protect you. It might be my most important role in this world." He gazes into my eyes and I find more than I expected staring back at me. He takes everything slow, so I don't expect to hear the words—but I can read them in his eyes.

Eventually we both have to get up. I quickly thumb through my closet for something feminine to wear, not wanting to put on another Seals T-shirt. Last night may have changed me, I want to be a woman for him. I may need a shopping trip with Sherry. I find a simple pale pink chiffon blouse with ruffled edges and pair it with my capris and the wedges from last night. Quick and easy and I don't have to change my purse. I scrub my face to get the leftover makeup off and brush out my hair. I decide to keep my leftover curls, though they are softer now and less defined.

I find him leaning against the kitchen counter in his jeans with a cup of coffee in his hand, "It's black, would you like some?"

I take a sip from his cup and admire the view.

"You look beautiful today," he grins. "You always do."

He pulls his shirt on and grabs my hand to walk out to his truck and take me to breakfast. I'm enjoying the time with him and don't want it to end, but my head is just not in it. I had planned to go up and grab my duffle bag from Sherry's but I get in my car and drive home. I don't know if it's work on my mind or if I'm distracted by the relationship shift.

I get home and find myself on autopilot. I sit cross-legged on my bed, open my laptop and start working on the serial. I have the plot line document open, which I follow and elaborate on. Four hours later, I've got a studly horse shifting stable boy who the virgin princess is infatuated with and watching from afar. A princess can't associate with the help, but she must learn to ride a horse. It explodes off the page and I write them riding off into the forest where their eyes meet and everything around them disappears. This becomes a daily routine until the princess is skilled with horses and her father no longer thinks she needs training. She rides on her own and is followed by a dark mysterious stallion. She's originally frightened until she finds he's watching over her and speaks to her revealing he's the stable boy.

I read my work and I've covered the plot requirements, but written more than double the number of words necessary for the weekly serial. I send it to Jared for his critique anyway. He can cut the stable boy if he wants.

I close the document and the other project I started pops up, still open. Kristina is aware that I've got a rogue project going, but nobody else. Mase doesn't have a clue what I do, other than I freelance from home. I read the story I've started and pick up where I left off. It's turning into a romance with a daily diary entry at the beginning of each chapter and dream recollection from the night before that transitions into desires.

I look up and I've completely missed the game. I keep writing.

I get an email notification from Jared, I'll read it tomorrow. I keep writing.

Text notifications are coming through, I turn off my sound and keep writing.

Around midnight, Kristina gets home and storms to my room, "What's going on?"

"What do you mean?" I respond without looking at her.

"I sent you at least five texts and you didn't respond. Do you know it's after midnight?" in her higher pitched exasperated tone.

"No idea. How was your day?"

She said something but I have no clue what. "That's good. At least you got home before it's too late."

"It's after midnight."

"Right. Much better than other nights. Were you PA today?" I continue the conversation without taking the focus from my laptop.

"Are you going to look at me during this conversation?"

"That's good. I know you belong in that job."

"This is a useless conversation, goodnight," she storms away.

A few minutes later there's banging on the bedroom wall and Kristina yells, "Will you please look at your phone? Mason is calling you."

"Okay," but I keep writing.

I WAKE up the next morning with the laptop open and dead, still wearing the same clothes I went to breakfast in. And I'm hungry. I check my phone and find missed calls and texts.

Text from Mason: The game's about to start, are you coming?
Text from Kristina: Your man is trying to reach you.
Text from Kristina: How was last night? Bow chica wow wow.
Text from Mason: You missed the game.
Text from Mason: Why aren't you answering my call?
Text from Mason: I'm home for the night. Miss you. Hope you're okay.

I plug my laptop in to charge and respond.

Text to Mason: Sorry I was working and I fell asleep.
Text to Mason: Hope the game went well.

I check email on my phone while I wait on my laptop. I have email from Jared:

Re: Serial Critique Episode 129
Are we going to write a new version of Shrek next? Should I be expecting the princess to suddenly become a shifter and run off to play with the herd in the fields? That could be a great segue into a horse shifter orgy. Will she be taken away by an ogre and fall in love with him because she's under a spell that turns her into an ogre every night?
I have no problem with adding the horse shifting stable boy as a character, but we haven't included any romance in this plot. Besides the fact that you know there's not that much space allotted in the magazine for the weekly serial, this is not geared toward our primary audience. Who are you and what did you do with my Michelle?

> Re: Re: Serial Critique Episode 129
> Maybe there should be romance in the plot. A little bit of love never hurt anyone. Cut what you wish.

I get an immediate response. What is he doing? Sitting on his laptop anxiously awaiting my reply?

> Re: Re: Re: Serial Critique 129
> You may have heard of Romeo and Juliet. They died for love. Kind of the epitome of hurt.

Whatever. I'm not going to justify him with a response. I turn the coffee on to brew and shower quickly. I tie my wet hair up in a knot and pull on my favorite V-neck T-shirt. I dig around in my dresser and find my denim cutoffs. Refreshed, I open my bedroom window and take in everything around me. I woke up with Mason here yesterday morning. The strapless bra he took off of me lies where he flung it. It smells a bit like his masculine, clean, woodsy scent. I move my bed to the other side of the room. Headboard on the wall next to the door, so I'm facing the open window while I sit on my bed and work. I rearrange, pick up, and vacuum under everything. I consider going through my closet and getting rid of everything that doesn't make me feel like a woman, but don't. I need new panties that are not granny panties, soft and sexy jammies, easy things to make for breakfast, and to finish drinking my coffee. I sit down with the cup in my hand and open my laptop. There in front of me is the beginning of a romance novel. Why? I don't know. Will anyone ever get to read it? I don't think so. Why am I writing it then? I don't have a choice.

The hero is a lot like Mason.

CHAPTER SIX

Jones

I want to know why my girl didn't come to my game yesterday. I don't get it. After our night together I was anxious to have her here cheering for me. It's not the first time or anything like that. I just... something is different. More intense maybe. Everything was better than it has ever been with us. Maybe closer is the right word, not better. We've always been good together. When I crawled into my bed alone last night all I could do was imagine having her with me. Fuck! I swear her hair was tickling my nose and her soft curves were plastered against me. My dick was rock solid and ready for action at the thought of her. My hand was wrapped around my cock, I couldn't help but stroke him. He's pissed at me for not letting him have her. He's been pissed for a while and apparently he thought it was his opportunity to get some. If I've learned anything from my experience, it's to not let my dick lead my life. It may be a more pleasurable path, but it won't be the most fulfilling. It's a difficult choice to follow and I'm sticking to it. I believe it's the best direction for me and Michelle. She's not like the others. I love how smart and quick-witted she is. The fact that she's learning the game for me and didn't give a crap about baseball until she met me makes me want her more. From the get-go, she's not a player chaser and she wants to understand and be involved in what I do, it's important to me. Huh, I'm not as good as she is. I haven't taken any interest in what she does. Honestly, I've got no clue. She works from home and she works at all hours. She can usually control her schedule to be at my games. She has to do so much each week and she gets it done. She told me she's a freelance contractor and she never has said anything about being short on money. She could be a drug dealer or just about anything, not that I think she is. I need to find out more about her work and get to know her better overall.

Worse than not showing up at my game, she didn't answer my call or respond to my texts until this morning and I haven't replied. I'm a bit lost with her. She may be out of my league. Shit, maybe she's not interested anymore. Seno would tell me to send her flowers and fix it, even if it's not my fault. She got flowers on our date, and they aren't the answer to everything. I'm going to assume everything is fine, it'll be fine.

Text to GG: Good morning.
Text to GG: I missed you last night.

I hope for an instant reply. I wait a few minutes.

Text to GG: 7pm game tonight.
Text to GG: It's retro night.

Nothing.

Text from GG: Busy working on a project today. I should be at the game tonight.
Text to GG: I'll have a retro jersey made for you :)
Text from GG: See you tonight.

That's better. She has her own life, I have to remember that.

I've been handling business since I got to the stadium. Carter has the retro jersey for Michelle handled. Worked out with Cross in the club house and let him drag me out to run laps on the warning track. I'm following his lead today to help me stay focused. He challenges me to sprint the last lap and I accept, but there's no way to keep up with him. He's the fastest on the team, none of us can compare to his 3.76 seconds to first base. I give it my best shot and push to keep up with him, he just runs faster. I swear he has an extra gear he can kick into. We cool off in the locker room and I take the opportunity to check in with my girl. No messages. No calls. I text her...

Text to GG: Thinking about you.

I taunt Chase, "I bet you can't beat me at hitting."

I have his attention, "What's the game?"

"Long ball."

"I'm in. When and where?"

"Batting practice. Most homers wins."

"You know Skip doesn't want us popping up."

"Then they better all be homers," I glare at him with a

crooked smile. My girl will be here and I'll be full of adrenaline. He nods at me, in to compete.

Text to GG: Maybe late-night dinner tonight?
Text from GG: Might have to go straight home after the game.
Text to GG: ?

Don't tell me you're going to miss the game. I want you here for batting practice.

Text from GG: I'm running late, but I should make it for the game.
Text from GG: Busy with work.
Text to GG: Batting practice?
Text from GG: I'll try.

I need to find out more about what she does. Maybe there is another guy. Something is going on here.

Michelle

I've been writing for hours. I turned the sound on my phone off because it kept making noise and interrupting me. It's frustrating, my train of thought is on track and then—boom—all the boxcars and the caboose in shambles. Thoughts tossed about like loose meaningless freight. All lost, irreconcilable goods that will never get to their destination.

Jones texting me. Jared emailing me. Kristina, who still hasn't come home, wanting the details on my night with Mase. I don't want to tell her anything until she comes home. I refuse to screw up the fun with the props I've planted. Seriously, I'm using a bag I've got hidden in my room for trash so everything is as it's supposed to be for her to find. And, to top it off, my brother left me a message and he only calls if he wants something.

The most frustrating part? I can't get anywhere with the hero I'm writing. He's as bad as Mase. I can't even get any from my fictional character! I created him and everything about him. I'm writing his entire fictional existence and he has the gall to defy my wishes. I should write a new fictional boyfriend that wants to give it up and dump the original one. Or maybe kill him off in some horrible accident—train wreck comes to mind. As soon as he was dead, the new boyfriend would probably dump me or cheat on me or want a threesome or insist on anal.

This simply isn't fair. I can't get to the end of a wet dream without getting interrupted.

I'm writing down my thoughts as quickly as I can because I know I'm going to run out of time before I need to leave for the game. I can make batting practice if I leave in the next hour. If I can at least get an outline of my thoughts in writing, a basic timeline and plot—it'll be okay.

It doesn't matter anyway. It's not what I get paid for. It's not my serials that I don't even get credit for writing. No joke, Jared and I ghostwrite for corporate and they say the author is one of their well-known traditional authors to help boost popularity on the books they publish and get paid big bucks for. Personally, I think the serials are the only reason anyone buys the magazine in the first place. There are four serials in each magazine, the two we write as well as a Star Wars meets Robin Hood adventure set in the twelfth century and a futuristic world with flying cars, where people survive on flavored food pellets because the limited food supply is controlled by colonists on Mars who have it all sent directly to them, not knowing it's all there is.

The thing is, this story is mine. There's no writing partner or critique partner that can veto me on anything or make me change a single letter. I don't have to correct a typo unless it's my prerogative. Corporate has no say over it. I can put whatever name I want on it as author. It's my choice to try to get published traditionally or stick to indie or forever leave this story on my laptop in limbo and never let another living soul read it.

In a hurry, I close my laptop and pick up my phone, accidentally answering it because it was ringing. Suddenly Jared is staring at me, apparently I answered a video call. Yay me.

"Hello Jared."

"Grumpy. What's got you all flustered?"

"I'm not flustered. I'm busy. I have things to do. I have to get ready and leave."

"Splotchy red neck, flushed cheeks, not the best mood... looks like flustered to me."

"Why are you calling?"

"Oh yes, don't forget grumpy and irritable."

"Jared."

"I'm concerned about this princess and stable boy thing you wrote into our fantasy story. I'm not convinced that it falls within the corporate guidelines for the story. The fantasy writer we're supposed to be emulating has never included romance in his books, at least not to the extent that you've taken it. It's all very Princess Bride. I'm waiting for Inigo Montoya to appear and threaten my life at any moment."

"Then change it. Have the king kill the stable boy in front of his only daughter who is in love with him for all I care. Relive the whole Romeo and Juliet fiasco if that makes it work for you."

His tone changes and his eyes shift, "Wait, do you have another guy?"

"What are you talking about?"

"Flustered, splotchy, red, new necklace, not wearing my ring, in a hurry, not wanting to talk to me, and willing me to change your work. You never want me to touch your writing to correct a misspelled word. It all makes sense now... adding unplanned romance to our fantasy serial." He frowns, "I understand it was probably out of your control, unplanned in your real life. You'd never cheat on me intentionally."

"Cheat on you? It is impossible to cheat on someone that is a friend and co-worker. There is no bond to cheat on. What do you think I'm doing, working with another critique partner? And if I was, that wouldn't matter either! Maybe I'm writing a novel on my own. Or short stories with my neighbor down the hall who submits pieces to the New Yorker? Honestly, I'm creatively writing dirty letters and sending them in to Penthouse! You should see the responses I get from the horny men across our perverted countrysides," I spit sarcastically.

"Chelle, darling. Please, take a deep breath and calm down. We can talk this through and work it out. Relationships have bumps, I hoped ours wouldn't. I should've expected it being so far apart for so long. I never should've taken this teaching job at Wisconsin State without taking you with me. I should've insisted you join me being the male and dominant in our relationship," he says calm and sincere.

"I don't know about Wisconsin State, but you definitely need to have your mental state checked. You did get one thing right, you are male. You wouldn't understand dominant if a dominatrix bound and gagged you, pet. I think it best if you consider a local girl. You've always enjoyed cheese."

"My dear, don't say those..." I interrupt him.

"To be clear, we broke up. I'm not saying I dumped you or you dumped me, because that doesn't matter." Though I am the one who went the opposite direction when he got the job in Wisconsin and pushed him to take it. "The end result is the point I need you to understand. We haven't seen each other in person for over 2 years. You don't love me. I don't love you. We never have. We were young and acting out a part we watched as we grew up. We were doing what we thought was expected of us. Everyone thought it was cute. It wasn't. We don't match and we don't belong together."

"So, you really do have a new man?"

I take a deep breath and release it, "I have a boyfriend."

"I see. How long has this been going on?"

"Long enough."

"Have you had sex with him?"

"That's none of your business."

"You haven't then. Okay. I'm still interested since you haven't been defiled by another man. We can get past it."

"There's nothing to get past. I'm not interested in dating you or anything other than being your critique partner. And right now I'm not too happy about that."

"Did he buy you the necklace you're wearing?" He's looking past me at my room. "Did you rearrange your room? What's with the baseball stuff?" His eyes get big, "You're dating a man who's not an intellectual."

I don't have a clue why I have to defend Mase, "He did buy me the necklace and I'm never taking it off. No one has ever treated me as well as he does. He's sweet and good with his words. He's an athlete. He wants to spend all of his time with me." Here I am arguing with your ass when I should be there watching him hit batting practice. Shit! I'm going to be late for the game.

"An athlete? That's not who's meant for you. You shouldn't be with an athlete," he says shaking his head.

"You don't know me at all. He's where I belong and you're making me late to get to him," I huff. "Bye." I hang up and hurry to get changed for the game. My phone rings but I ignore it because I know it's Jared trying to continue our conversation. I already told him what to do with our story and that's the only thing he needs to be concerned with.

I check my phone in the elevator on the way to my car and find that Mase was trying to call me too. I text him back...

Me: Sorry, I thought you were somebody else calling.

Me: I'm on my way.

Me: I was stuck on a work call.

Me: I'll be there cheering for you <3

Jones

I called her and she didn't answer her phone. She wasn't here for batting practice. The game is about to start and she's not in her seat. I stand on the field just past first base leaning on my bat and watching the stands for my girl to show up while my teammates focus on stretching and warm ups. "Mase!" I turn to find Michelle at the first base wall and run to her. "Sorry. It was a crazy day. I missed you," she leans over the wall, places her hands on my cheeks and kisses me like there's nobody around except us. My cheeks warmed by her contact and my chest lighter. "Show these guys what you've got! Remember, best hitter in the league!" She yells as she runs up the stairs to get to her seat behind home plate before the game starts.

I turn back to the field and Cross is grinning at me, "That's new. I've never seen that before."

"What?" I question as I start to stretch.

"Two things, actually. One, you getting mauled on the sidelines and two, the grin on your face. You're in trouble, dude. In the best way."

I nod. I've known the truth since I met her. It will always be her.

Chase points his finger at me, "Remember not to tell her you love her too soon. Chicks can freak out about that and you don't want her to turn into a runner. Figure out what she likes to do and do it, it's all that matters and it'll keep her happy." He turns to run sprints, "Oh, and they put up with a lot since we're gone on the road so much. We should all be making it up to them constantly, they don't have to wait for us and deal with our shit. It's not their dream to be a baseball player, it's ours and they end up paying for part of it."

"Stop talking crazy."

"Do you think that woman who kissed you until you turned red just now, and didn't know squat about baseball until she met you, ever planned on spending any time at the baseball stadium? That time is coming from somewhere else."

I'd never considered the changes it might have on her life other than me being in it. "Where'd you come up with this insightful shit?"

Chase smiles, "Sherry."

Figures. No way he came up with it himself. Sherry has firsthand experience. No reason to question it. I search behind home plate for my gorgeous woman and find her in her seat ready to cheer in the retro jersey I had made for her. "One question since you seem to know everything, did they give us retro uniform pants too? They seem tighter than normal."

"Yep," he replies pointing to the retro stripe down the leg.

Michelle

I get to my seat. There's no Sherry in sight and they're playing the national anthem. The team is getting in position and Seno is taking advantage of the time to stretch his legs. I stand up and as loud as I can muster, "Let's make it a win boys!" Sherry would want that. Seno turns and gives me a thumbs up and I jump out of my skin when someone touches my shoulder.

Sam sits next to me, "Nice job. You're learning." She chuckles. "Sherry is wiped out, so I'm here to help cheer for the team. Seems like you might have it covered," she smiles approvingly.

"I'm still learning the game, but I've got the basics and I can be loud."

"What you lack in knowledge you make up for in enthusiasm. Don't take this personal, nobody know baseball like Sherry. She should be the coach."

I nod and she sounds off like she has a bullhorn when Martin tags the runner out at first. The top of the inning is over quickly and Chase is stepping into the batter's box. I clap, "Let's go Chase!" He digs his cleats in. He never stops moving when he's at bat. Amazing focus, but his body is doing a constant shimmy. Sam is fascinated with the on-deck circle. Kris Martin is swinging a weighted bat while he observes the pitcher. Chase connects on the first pitch and punches the ball up the third baseline. He legs the throw out and is safe on first. I've been told that's what his job is. He's not supposed to be swinging for the fences. Team sport, trust your teammates to bring you home. Martin smiles at Sam all sexy like as he walks toward the batter's box. She giggles and waves at him.

She yells with force, "Out of the park, Kris!"

I turn and glare at her "So, what's going on there?" She puts her hand in my face and changes it to her single pointer finger, telling me to wait without speaking. I'm new to this group, but I've seen enough to be curious and I'm not stupid.

She's glued to the at bat. First pitch low and outside. Second pitch is wild and Cross steals second easily. Third pitch high and inside, Martin pulls a Matrix-like move to avoid getting hit and Sam is out of her seat, "Don't throw at our guys. I will hunt you down in the parking lot and I can take you, you skinny bastard!" Kris shakes his head, communicating without turning to make eye contact. Next pitch is straight down the middle of the plate, but you never swing on a 3-0 pitch. Wait and take the walk. Next pitch is just off the plate and Martin takes his walk to first.

Sam turns to find me staring at her, "What?"

"What's with you and Martin?"

"Nothing. He doesn't have anybody special to cheer for him so I do. I've been around these guys a long time. Family, you know?"

I don't buy it. "I don't know your story," I stop and think about what I want to say and say it anyway, "I call bullshit."

She turns red, "What do you want me to tell you? I'm a married woman with kids. I shouldn't be all gaga over a player. If I was picking a baseball boyfriend, it would be him. I'm sure you were hoping for something juicier than that and I'm sorry to let you down."

"Whatever makes you happy. I'm just sayin', I can keep a secret."

"There are no secrets. Simply a boring old married

woman who helps her major league baby brother when he needs assistance."

"You're an amazing sister," I say sincerely and nod my head not believing a word she said about Kris. I try to let it go and write it off to me being overly creative. I completely miss Lucky's at bat, but he's walking to first and the bases are loaded. Mase is knocking the weight off his bat, it's his turn to hit. I stand up and do my best to be louder than Sam, "Best hitter in the league! Show'm Mase!" The first pitch is low. The second pitch low inside. The third pitch just catches the outside corner. He stands there, stoic. Not even a flinch. The count is 2-1. The next pitch is a heater on the outer third of the plate. The crack of the bat as it connects to the ball is clean and sharp. I'm out of my seat screaming, "Yes! Yes! Yes! Go Mase!" He shoots out of the batter's box toward first and it's out of the park! Fireworks explode as he runs the bases. Cross scores. Martin scores. Lucine scores. Mase jumps on home plate and celebrates with the others waiting for him. Nothing like starting the game with a grand slam—especially at the hand of your man. I yell again, "That's my guy! Go Mase!" He points at me and winks before he goes back to the dugout.

The problem with a grand slam in the first inning? The rest of the game can end up anticlimactic. Especially when the opposing coach pulls the starting pitcher and basically turns it into a bull pen game. That's a term that Sherry taught me. It's a game that uses the relief pitchers and no starting pitcher. Most are pitching only an inning or two. It's interesting to watch the different pitchers and it's good that they're getting used because that makes them less likely to be available to pitch tomorrow. But the score is still 4-0 in the 7th. Seno hit a homer in the 8th and a couple runs got strung together playing small ball. Final score 7-0 Seals. Mason was the player for the night and Hannah was waiting for him to do an on-field interview. I watch as they put him live on the jumbotron and replay his grand slam. I scream and he turns red smiling.

"Jones Mason, you've really come into your own this season. The cleanup spot is yours and I think you proved that you know what to do with it tonight in the first inning. How'd it feel to have the lead early on?"

"We should always be in the lead. This team is going to the world series this season. Nothing is going to stop us," he says decidedly.

"That's a bold prediction at this point in the season, but the team is in first place for the division."

"It's not a prediction. Captain Seno said we need to make it happen and as a team we will." Cheers erupt from the dugout, "Yes we will!" and the entire stadium joins in. Mase stands there watching the reaction to his words

"Sounds like everyone supports the plan. Go Seals!" Hannah ends the interview and Mase beelines for me.

I'm at the net waiting for him and Sam is at the net already talking to Martin about 10 feet away. I'm doing my best to eavesdrop, but not getting anything good. My fingers curled in the net, Mase reaches for them to hold my hands.

Jones

The game took too long. All I've wanted all evening is to have GG in my arms and make sure the other night wasn't a fluke. I lean my head towards her on the net, "I've missed you. Can I take you out tonight?" I stop remembering what Chase said, *whatever she likes* "Or, whatever you want? I want to stay with you tonight."

"You don't have to take me out. I'm happy hanging out with you."

He grins, "I'll be at your place in an hour and I'm ordering pizza delivery, okay?"

"Sounds perfect."

I'm not asking for permission to stay with her. I take a deep breath not wanting to let her hands go and run for the locker room. I order delivery with the app on my phone, shower and change, on a mission to get to my girl.

Michelle

I get home and wander my apartment picking up a bit, mostly making sure my laptop is closed and put away. I get Legends of Fantasy loading up, so we can play online while we eat. My nickname isn't GamerGirl for nothing and playing games helps him to relax. Playing video games is the first thing we did together. Everything isn't the same. I want to go back to what was comfortable. The shift in our relationship has me wanting to be cute when he gets here. I dig through my dresser and find a cute pj set, but all I want to wear is his shirt. I pull his big soft shirt on and exchange my jeans for leggings. The doorbell rings and I go to answer it. Food delivery is here. I open the door to a guy with a bunch of bags and boxes.

He peeps over the load he's carrying, "Order for Jones."

It takes me three trips to take everything from his hands into the living room. "Thank you. Let me get you a tip."

"Not necessary. Tip was paid upfront and very generous. Thank you," he nods and disappears down the corridor.

Text to Mase: Food has been delivered.

Text to Mase: Did you order the whole restaurant?

Text from Mase: I wasn't sure what you wanted.
Text from Mase: I'll be there in five minutes.
Text from Mase: You can start without me.
Text to Mase: Legends is loaded and waiting for us :)

I open the bags and boxes of food. I find sodas and energy drinks, and get them in the refrigerator. Two pizzas, a dozen wings, a big salad, tater tots, cheesy bread, warm brownies, vanilla ice cream, and both alfredo and marinara for dipping. Enough for six people as long as I'm not sharing the brownies. I get the ice cream in the freezer and sit down with the tots and dipping sauces. I stop myself before I open the tots and take a minute to brush out my hair and check myself in the mirror before he gets here. It's simply different and I'm not prepared. I'm not comfortable in this new relationship place, but I love it. I take a deep breath and think about Sherry and send her a text...

Text to Sherry: Mase is on his way over. Everything is different now.
Text from Sherry: He still likes you for you. That hasn't changed.
Text to Sherry: I wish I had appropriate jammies or something to wear for lounging around gaming.
Text from Sherry: Nothing better than his shirt. Stop worrying. Be you.

Mase knocks on the door and there's no more time to think about it. I open the door and my handsome guy is standing there in his jeans and T-shirt. I reach my arms up around his neck and hug him tight. His hands hold me close to him possessively and he whispers in my ear, "This is what I needed."

My uneasiness is gone. I grab his hand entangling my fingers with his and lead him to the living room where I've got the game ready to go and the food laid out for nibbling. He kicks his shoes off and sits on my couch with his arm around me. "Are you up for playing tonight?" I ask.

"Anything you want," he grins and we get into the game. We sit hip to hip working through the challenges that will eventually lead us to save a forgotten fantasy world from an evil warlord.

An hour or so in, another character pops into our space, Lord_Jared_III. He's there long enough to say, "sorry wrong group" and leave. "I'm sure it was an accident, not," I say out loud.

"Who's that?" Mase asks. I ignore him. "Michelle?"

How do I answer him? He's my ex? That's my co-worker? Just a friend?

"Do you know that person?"

The easy answer here is no, but that would be a lie. "Yes."

"Who is he?"

"My ex."

"You still talk to him?" Irritation shows in his tone, "Is that the guy that gave you that ring?"

"We have to be amicable. He's my co-worker."

He puts down his controller and turns the power off, "Did he give you that ring?"

"That was a long time ago. Old news and doesn't mean anything."

"And you work with him?"

"Yes, but never in the same location. He's on the other side of the country."

"When's the last time you saw him?"

Fuck. "We had a video meeting today."

"So you were late to get to the stadium for me because of this guy?" He's turning red and up pacing.

"Will you sit down please? After the meeting today I made it very clear that I have a boyfriend and reiterated to him that we broke up years ago."

"I thought you're a freelance contractor. How do you have a co-worker? What exactly do you do?"

"I don't like to tell people. He's a freelance contractor, too. The company we're contracted with pairs people up for long term projects," I stop trying to think of the best words to use, "we're paired together on both of my freelance projects."

"Are you kidding me? You're spending time with your ex on a regular basis?"

"Not really. The projects pretty much run on auto pilot at this point. I do my part and send it to him for review. He does his part and sends it to me for review. We agree or make changes. Almost all of it is via email."

"Change it."

"I can't. It pays my bills and I love what I do. It's a great stepping stone and has my foot in the door at a company that most never get access to."

"What do you do?"

"I ghostwrite fantasy and sci-fi serials for a major publication. He's my critique partner. I also have other side projects that I'm working on myself."

"So, you're a writer?"

"Yes. Unless you want me to start writing letters to Penthouse for the money, you have to understand that he means nothing to me."

"Okay. Why'd you have to see him today?"

"You ask a lot of questions. You know that?"

"My girlfriend hasn't been answering my calls or texts and still talks to her ex."

"I usually turn my sound off when I'm writing. It's quicker and smoother that way."

"Why didn't you tell me you're a writer?"

"I don't like explaining myself. How nerdy can I be? I play video games and write stories about those worlds. You don't want a nerdy girlfriend."

"I want you. I don't think you're nerdy at all. You're clever, quick, beautiful, and mine." He wraps his arms around me. "Did he see you wearing your new necklace?"

"Yes, and he didn't like it."

"Good."

"Are you threatened by him? Because that's not attractive."

"No. I want to make sure he knows you're taken."

"I've made that very clear on multiple occasions. I suggested that he seek mental assistance if he thought otherwise today."

"I don't want to play games any more tonight."

It feels like all we've been doing. This is all a big game.

He gazes at me, "I'm sorry. I need you to talk to me. I realized that you are the most special woman I've had in my life and I didn't even know what you do for a living. I started wondering what else I don't know." He softens, "May I stay with you tonight? I'll do better at this stuff. I promise."

"I want you here with me, Mase." I place my hand on his chest, "There's only you."

Jones

The last couple days and finding out her ex is still in the picture is driving me crazy. Our date was perfect. Waking up with her in my arms was an experience I'd never had before and want to repeat. I want to wrap her long hair around my wrist, bend her over the couch, pull her head back, and show her she's mine. That's not my plan for us. I don't want to mess up what we've got started. Well, it may be in my plans somewhere in the future.

I take her hand in mine and walk to her room, locking the door and turning off the lights. I step into her bedroom, "Did you move your bed?"

"Yep, I needed a change. I decided on the different perspective of the window."

"I like it."

"Kristina and I put those slider things under all of the furniture to make it easier when we moved in and left them there. It makes rearranging easy. I just slid it a few feet directly across the room. I didn't even turn it."

"I'm always happy to help, make it easier on you to move things."

"I appreciate that. Kristina and I made it a point to move on our own and not need any guys to help us. It's a girl power, self-sufficient thing."

"You don't have to do everything on your own. I get it, there's something about doing it yourself when it's your own place that's fulfilling."

She stares at the bed, then speaks, "I haven't decided which side of the bed I like with the bed in the new position."

"We can try both ways and see which one works. Though, I should be on the side closest to the door," it's the gentlemanly thing to do according to my mom. Basically, being her guard so anything bad has to get through me first. She slides a pant leg of her leggings off while I'm talking and I get a view of pink fabric. She lifts her other foot onto the bed and slides the other pant leg off. I wonder if she's teasing me on purpose or doesn't realize she's giving me a show. I pull my shirt off over my head and delay taking off my jeans in a sad attempt to hide my excitement. Internally telling my cock that he still doesn't get her. I just hope that he doesn't retaliate later and decide not to stay hard when I want him. He's selfish and not picky, so I don't think it will be a problem. That's the difference in my two heads, and like I said before—I've learned not to follow the one in my pants.

I wait and watch for her next move. She climbs into bed under the covers and snuggles in. I turn away to take my jeans off quickly and slide into bed with her. I roll onto my side facing her, "What do you think? Are you comfortable on that side?"

"I need to try the other side," she replies quickly and takes action.

She's getting to the other side of the bed by crawling over me. Not what I expected.

She makes a noise like she's out of breath when she's directly on top of me, "You're like climbing a mountain." She's silent instantly, "What's poking me?" She wriggles and pushes down against me.

"You shouldn't do that," I place my hands on her back trying to still her.

She reaches down between us and rubs my cock. Her eyes widen when she realizes what she's doing, but she continues anyway. "Um, I thought you were wearing a jockstrap or something."

"Nope. All me," I say and my cock twitches.

She tries to roll off of me, but I don't let her, "Stay right there. You started this."

"But, ..."

"No buts," I slide my hands to her hips and snap the string on the side of her bikinis.

"Mase!"

I drag my hands slowly up her sides and find her bra. I

unlatch it and pull the cups off of her, finding one breast with each hand.

"Oh, Mase," she says on a moan.

Round, plump, and more than a handful. Her whole body is silky to the touch and reacting to me in a way I'd love if I was allowing myself to have her. I shouldn't be doing this. I need to get in control.

She rolls her hips against me.

"I want you, too." I whisper in her ear.

"Show me," she says.

"We need to not rush this. Be patient for me, please."

"You're still squeezing my boobs."

"You're pressing against my cock."

We both stop instantly. I wrap my arms around her waist and scoot over to where she was lying. "Ready?" I ask.

"For what?" A scream escapes her lips as I roll on my side, dumping her off me.

I kiss her forehead, "We'll get there."

Her body stretches and complains without saying a word. She settles in with her hand on my abs and fingertips slid under my waistband. I can work with that.

Michelle

I wake up in the middle of the night with my hand in his underwear and his cock resting against it. I'm not sure how this happened. Is he aware of the situation, because if he's not I don't want him to be. The question is: How do I move my hand without waking him up? And, if he is aware, will he be offended that I moved? I'm sure it was a combination of us moving in the night. Nobody's fault. My other hand is under my pillow and both of his hands are on my bare back. Crap. My shirt is riding up exposing everything below my boobs.

Things are going to happen when you're in bed together. I pull my hand out of his underwear and rearrange my shirt. He rolls onto his back and holds me against him without opening his eyes. I'm comfortably back using his chest as my pillow.

I need to sleep but my brain won't let me. It's stuck at 100 miles per hour and nothing makes sense. It's scene after scene of me and Mase, hot sweaty bodies. Making out, hands everywhere. A new scene every few seconds, that never shows the deed. It's probably happening and I simply don't get to see that part. I consider writing, but I can't get my laptop out and work on that project while Jones is here. I roll away from him and grab my phone to make some quick notes. It doesn't matter what I do, when I close my eyes, it's always us naked together.

CHAPTER SEVEN

Michelle

I'd been awake for over an hour possessed with the need to write when Mase finally woke up to a phone call.

"Yea dude. What's up?"

"When?"

He covers the phone, "GG, Chase wants me to go meet him and work out this morning. Do you mind?"

"Of course not," yes! I can write.

He goes back to his call, "On my way now, man."

He rolls to me and squeezes me. He gets out of bed, "I owe you breakfast." Dressing and out the door in record time.

As soon as the door closes I'm up and my laptop is out. My fingers are typing and I don't even have to think. It's a different experience than writing the serials. We plot those with intricate detail, and create character sheets with appearance, personality, background, quirks, and everything important. When I sit down to write, there's no question as to what is going to be included in the week's story. Romance authors do the same thing, but then there are the pantsers. I've always thought they were an unorganized lot and didn't understand how they could write as it came to them with no idea what was going to happen next. I get it now. It's not something you do because you want to, it's because you have no choice. I have to get the words out of my head. I've had others tell me that the characters talk to them and demand attention. I haven't experienced that, but I never thought I would be a pantser either so I'm not ruling it out. If this is inspired by my own relationship, can the characters talk to me? Wouldn't that be talking to myself? I may need a therapist. My male character is absolutely Jones Mason, though he doesn't have any qualms about giving it up. He'd strip butt naked and chase me around my apartment when my roommate was home, as long as she was in her room. He'd sleep nude in my bed every night and be wanting it every night and every morning and wake me for a go in the middle of the night. He needs me and wants me and can't control himself. The desire he has for me fans my fire for him. Wait. Is this the problem? He's not giving it up because he won't want to stop? I'm not sure that's a problem. It doesn't matter because he wants to wait. I can respect that. I can enjoy the character I'm writing for now. What if I write something that we haven't done yet and totally screw it up? Or, write it so well that there's no way it can match up in real life? It doesn't matter. I can't help myself. Whatever writing demon has possessed me refuses to take no for an answer. Honestly, why would I turn him down?

... he lifts me to the kitchen counter and I wrap my legs tightly around his waist. He shoves his engorged cock up into me repeatedly as I scream out his name. I reach for any part of him I can get and hold onto him, digging my fingers into his back. He lifts me from the counter still mounted on his cock.

His arms around me, he bounces me on him delectably. My naked breasts pressed to his chest...

> Text from Mason: I want to wake up with you in my arms more often.
>
> Text from Mason: Will I see you at the game tonight?

I silence my phone not wanting to lose my thought process.

Jones

I need to keep reminding myself that she had a life before me and doesn't have a passion for baseball. She attends games and is learning the sport for me. Which should be more than enough to prove I've got nothing to worry about. She doesn't need to uproot her world and change her daily schedule for me. We'll figure out how to make our schedule work together. When we move in together it won't matter anymore because we will be together every night unless I'm on the road. I shouldn't be thinking about that. That's a long time off. We definitely need to have sex before we move in together.

I meet up with Cross at the beach. We stretch then run to the pier and back a couple of times. The sand is a workout. I'm dripping with sweat. I walk into the ocean to cool off and wonder why I've never walked the beach with GG. We could get our feet wet and admire a sunset. But, even when we're at Chase's with the team, we play video games or snuggle by the bonfire. There's nothing wrong with that, but I won't miss the opportunity next time. There's something romantic about the beach, but I don't want to talk about that while I'm at the beach with Chase.

We have early batting practice today and a team meeting

before the game. I leave Chase and go home to make a sandwich, shower, and change before I go to the stadium.

Text from Mason: Early batting practice today.

Text from Mason: 7pm game.

Text from Mason: Hope you can make it.

She told me she turns her sound off when she's working. I'm not going to worry about it. It'll be fine.

I CHECK my phone after batting practice and no response. I call her and it rings. Right when I'm about to hang up, she answers, "Hi Mase."

"Hi," I'm happy to hear her voice. "Is everything okay?"

"Yes."

"It's a gorgeous day out. Are you coming to the game?"

"I'm going to try."

"Are you busy?'

"I'm writing and I have rewrite I need to do."

"I'll see you later then?"

"Can't promise right now. Make it a win," she says with no enthusiasm at all and hangs up.

Alrighty, I turn my phone off and toss it into my locker.

"Hey!" Seno is standing behind me, "I'm not a fan of what I'm seeing. Keep your head in the game. I swear you rookies need to be banned from dating during the season."

I put my AirPods in and turn them up. Rather than hang out in locker room, I go to the gym and work out hard on the weight machines. It always gets me focused.

When she's here I'm pumped up and want to impress her. Games like today when she hasn't shown up yet and it's already the 3rd inning? I play. It's not the same when she isn't here to cheer for me and scream like crazy when I get a hit or make a play. I have to keep my head straight. I'm still doing my best. Seno has his eyes on me. It's a good thing. I'm aware of it and will stay focused. Otherwise he'll call me out. He's done it before. She keeps telling me I'm the best hitter in the league and I'm going to prove she's right. That's it, the goal I need to stay on track.

The game is going well. Chase got on base and stole second. Seno hit a double bringing him home. Kranston, our starting pitcher, is on point tonight. Every play is textbook. I haven't had to move more than 5 feet from my position. The grounders are coming straight to me. I'm watching from the on-deck circle when Martin walks on a wild pitch. Two out and I'm up. Best hitter in the league... her words are rolling on repeat in my head. It's her voice encouraging me, she'd say it's a fact. I don't think the statisticians would agree. Maybe based on one stat, but not overall. I need to look up the current stats and find out how other hitters are doing, maybe set some specific goals. Three pitches in and I'm not chasing the shit he's throwing outside the box. He's edging in on the bottom corner, so I watch for it and smack it with a launch angle that should take it out of the park. Three run homer and I'm running fast for home even though it's not necessary. I'm hoping GG is watching. I got on base two other times, but nobody brought me home. Martin is on a streak, getting on base every at bat. Final score 7-1 Seals.

Before I shower and change I walk into Carter's office, "Postgame request?"

I chuckle, "I was thinking. We're all aware of our individual stats and where the team is as far as ranking. What if we did a challenge in the club house, pushing each other to do better?"

Carter glares at me and calls out, "Seno!"

The best beard in the league pokes his head through the door, "Yea?"

"Talk to Mason. He wants to do a clubhouse challenge."

"I like ideas," he turns to focus on me. "Let's talk over breakfast tomorrow."

Seno yells out, "Cross, breakfast with me and Mason 8am at the Yolk. No whining."

From somewhere Cross responds, "Got it."

Seno moves on to the showers.

Carter smiles at me, "He loves everything that pushes the team to be better."

I nod and head off to the showers.

I CHECK my phone as I'm leaving the stadium.

> Text from GG: Sorry, I'm not going to make it to the game tonight.
>
> Text from GG: I'm going to be up all night.

I call her from my car.

"Hi Mase."

"Hi, should I stop by?"

"No, I need to get this done."

"Okay. Call me when you want."

"I will."

"Goodnight GG."

"Goodnight Mase."

CHAPTER EIGHT

Jones

The next morning I'm up early and ready to go to breakfast. The more I think about it, the more I like the idea. I'm going to set a goal for myself and challenge Cross no matter what.

I walk into the Yolk early and get a table. I order some coffee and check my hitting stats. I'm making notes on a napkin when Seno and Cross walk in.

"Sorry to be a few minutes late," he cocks his head as if pointing at Cross. "My ride was running behind."

"Dude! You called me to get picked up this morning," Cross tries to defend himself.

"So, tell us what you want to do," Seno has his full attention on me.

"I want to give myself a goal. Something to strive for that will make me better and be a positive for the team. I think it will help me stay focused and maybe it will help the other guys, too. Something we do as a team, not competing against each other."

"What are you thinking?"

"Well, Cross is one of the best base stealers I've seen. What would it take for him to be the actual best?" I wait for a reaction and go on, "For me, I'm thinking slugging percentage or on base percentage. I need to get on base every time and the more bases I get the better. It needs to be something each player can impact. More runs batted in would be great, but I can't control if there will be players on base when it's my turn to bat."

"I like it," Seno claps his hand down on the table. "I agree Cross could steal more."

"Hey, my job is to get on base," Chase complains, "I do my job."

"Yes, you do what you're supposed to, but you could steal more," Seno explains. "What's your deal with the hitting stats?" he stares at me.

"My girl keeps telling me I'm the best hitter in the league. I want to prove her right."

They both stare at me and nod their heads, "Let's do this!"

Seno continues, "I keep telling you this is the year."

"Lucky could work on his on base percentage, Martin could steal more. The guys that excel at something could get better at it. We could remind them they could be the best." I turn to Seno, "Like you tell us, our women want to see us win." I didn't realize how important that statement was until I said it. None of it means as much without her. Seno already learned that.

"You two start it and talk about it in the club house. I'll join in and you can bet the others will follow," Seno suggests.

"You might make it on this team yet," he smiles at me approvingly.

Later that afternoon Cross starts in on me, "You can increase your slugging percentage. You've got it in you."

"I plan on it. The real question is, when are you going to show everyone how good you are at stealing?"

"I'm a stealing machine," He replies.

"How about a challenge stealing machine?"

"Bring it."

"Steal 15 bases in the next 10 games."

"Okay slugger, how about you get a 1.500 slugging percentage over the next 10 games? That's only an average of six bases per game."

"Stretching it a little bit, don't you think?"

"Naw, you have the ability to do it. A home run and two singles or a double per game and you're in."

Getting cocky, I ask, "What's the league record for slugging percentage right now?"

Carter yells from his office, "1.387."

"I'm in," I high five Cross and glance around the room to find our teammates checking their stats. Success.

Michelle

I slept with my laptop again. I stayed up writing until 7am and fell asleep with my finger on the f key apparently, at least I'd guess that's how I ended up with three lines of f's. I plug in my laptop and check my phone. It's 1pm and no contact from Jones since last night. Unfortunately, I do have an email from Jared.

Re: Serial Critique 129 - Rewrite
After reading your updated version without the stable boy, I actually prefer the stable boy. Do you think you can add him back in somehow without the romantic relationship? Maybe a Bat Man crossed with Zorro type of character that uses his shifter ability to listen in on private conversations and save innocents from danger? No? Too Much? My point exactly. The new melancholy princess is a downer. I liked her better shagging the horse.

Asshole.

Re: Re: Serial Critique 129 - Rewrite
I took out the romance. I think it works as is. If you don't agree, write it yourself. Oh, and there's no need for your sarcasm. This is work, so keep your attitude in check.

Re: Re: Re: Serial Critique 129 - Rewrite
I'm sorry. You're right. It's fine. Maybe take the princess out altogether?

Re: Re: Re: Re: Serial Critique 129 - Rewrite
You are welcome to delete the princess and do whatever you'd like with her. I hope you enjoy yourself.

I get a text...

Text from Jared: What's gotten into you?
Text to Jared: We're co-workers. Act like it.
Text from Jared: My dear... we are so much more than that.
Text to Jared: No we're not.
Text from Jared: We're friends.

Text to Jared: You're acting like a jerk and friends don't do that.

Text from Jared: Something is wrong with you.

Text from Jared: Since when would you consider adding romance to our fantasy?

Text from Jared: It's specifically listed as not an option on our contracts.

Text to Jared: That's why we have critique partners.

Text to Jared: Verify that we stick to the contract.

Text to Jared: Thank you so much for doing so.

Text to Jared: Now, I'm busy on another project and I'd appreciate it if you left me alone.

Text from Jared: Did you get another contract?

Text to Jared: None of your business.

Text from Jared: What are you writing?

Didn't I just tell him it's none of his business?

Text to Jared: If you must know. I started a series on sex with professional athletes.

Text to Jared: I'm enjoying the research, but the lack of sleep is starting to get to me.

Text from Jared: There's no way you'd do that.

Text to Jared: You don't know me at all.

Text from Jared: Are you writing romance?

Text from Jared: I don't blame you if you are. It's a big seller.

Text to Jared: You're cutting into my writing time.

Text to Jared: Texting me doesn't make it not work.

Text from Jared: Who's the warrior you were playing with?

Text to Jared: If you wanted to know, you should've stuck around and found out.

I grab an energy drink and the leftover pizza from the other night and go back to campout in my room. I spend a lot of time in front of the laptop, but it hasn't been this much since graduation. I read over what I had written before I fell asleep and my fingers are anxious to hit the keys. Everything simply flows.

Jones

I didn't call or text Michelle today. I don't want to be a needy guy. I'm focused on proving her right. She's not going anywhere. She's not a runner like Kristina. Everything will be fine. It'll be fine.

Our challenge worked. Cross stole three bases, one of which was a double steal with Seno. I got three doubles and a walk. The team was encouraging from the dugout. Lucine got on base at each of his at bats. Martin stole two bases. Brandt hit two homers, and Seno had a homer, too. Final score 8-2 Seals.

Michelle

I notice my phone flashing and I've lost seven or eight hours again.

"Hi Mase. How was the game?"

"Good game. Better if you were there, but I understand that you're busy."

"Did you show them all that you're the best hitter in the league?"

"Yes, ma'am."

"They're going to start walking you rather than chance your bat."

"I guess I'll have to figure out how to stay under the radar."

"If anyone can, you can."

"I'm going home. It's been a long day."

"I'll be up for a bit."

"Michelle—I miss you."

"Goodnight Mase."

CHAPTER NINE

Michelle

One thing about my bed facing the window is that I can't miss the sun coming up. It's a common occurrence for me. I'm up writing or playing video games and lose track of time. I've got the flexibility in my schedule to work the hours I want, so I don't sleep until I can't hold my eyelids open. Sometimes I sleep all day. I need about 9 hours of sleep to be awake for 20 hours. It's a vicious cycle that leaves me sleeping at any hour of the day or night. I try to go to bed when the sun comes up, but when I sleep until the middle of the afternoon I'm simply not tired yet. Lately, I'm not sure I'm present when I'm writing. I just write.

When the sunlight hits my window I stop and save my progress. I check my phone to find texts from a few hours ago...

Text to Mase: I can't sleep.

Text to Mase: I'm lying in bed thinking about you… us.

Text to Mase: I wish I was with you.

I could call him, but it has been hours and he's probably sleeping now. I should go to bed, but I grab an energy drink and go back to writing.

Jones

It's an early day for me. Early batting practice. Early game. I hardly slept. Nothing from my GG. Not the way I like to start my day. I get my shit together and grab a double shot coffee on my way to the stadium. Smashing the ball at batting practice is what I needed to get my frustrations out. Seno was all over it, "That's it. Teach that ball a lesson!" He's right and it keeps me focused. Her sweet voice adamant in my head with every swing of my bat *"Best hitter in the league."* Not a waiver to the thought or tone, she believes in me whole-heartedly. It's as if the words themselves are a spell that keeps me in line, giving me confidence that's she's mine and the power to prove she's right.

Every time I catch myself searching the stadium for her I have to remind myself; I can't expect her to change her dreams and goals for me. She would never consider asking me to quit baseball. No, what does she do? She encourages me. I need to be doing the same for her.

By the time the game started today, more of the team had taken on challenges and Seno had vowed to do whatever was in his power to help set the table and make it happen. Lucine committed to increasing his on base percentage. Martin says he's going to steal at least a base per game. Rock said he wants to increase his home runs. Even a couple of the pitchers joined in saying they want to work on getting more strike outs.

Halfway through the game and we're hitting on all cylinders. The score is 4-1 Seals. Seno puts his hand on my shoulder, "You did good kid. On top of everything else, it brought the team closer together and I didn't think we could get any tighter." My teammates are fist pounding when they achieve what they want to get done. Every little thing makes a difference, you have to get on base to score. Isn't that the truth in more ways than one? I've hit two home runs tonight, but with Michelle I just got to second base. Everyone assumes that guys want to score as quick as they can. With Michelle, I want to take as long as possible rounding the bases.

Rock came up with a homer in the 7th and the stealing machine stole two bases in the 8th. Brandt surprised everyone with an awesome diving catch to end the game. Lucine got on base at each of his at bats. Seno was a home run short of hitting for the cycle and tagged a guy out at home. Final score 9-3. I hope we can keep it up.

Hannah grabs me for the on-field interview, "Seno said to talk to you about the new life in the team tonight. What's different for the team on the field?"

I smile, "We reminded each other what we want to do here as a team, but the parts have to be great in order for the whole to win. We want to support each other in our individual goals, it'll make us stronger."

"You're a close-knit team and have been winning all season, if you get any better you'll be unbeatable."

"Wouldn't that be something?" I grin from ear to ear.

"Thanks Jones and good luck on the road trip."

"Yes ma'am, thank you."

I head to the club house and get ready for the flight out with the team.

Michelle

I wake up about 7pm and my phone is lit up like a Christmas tree. Messages from Mase started early.

Text from Mase: Hope you're coming to the game today.
Text from Mase: It's an early game and a getaway night.
Text from Mase: Team flies out to start a road trip right after the game.
Text from Mase: I was hoping to see you before the flight out.
Text from Mase: I understand if you have work.
Text from Mase: I'll see you when I get back.
Text from Mase: Hope your project is going well.
Text from Kristina: Are you okay?
Text from Sherry: Why aren't you going to the games?
Text from Sherry: Did you decide you don't like baseball?
Text from Sherry: Did Mason do something wrong?

Text from Kristina: Seriously, I know you're special but there's no way you miss the last opportunity to see Mase before he's gone for a week. Give me a thumbs up if you're still breathing.

Text from Mase: Call me please.
Text from Mase: I was hoping to talk to you before the flight.
Text from Mase: Don't forget me, Michelle. You're the only woman I want.
Text from Mase: Going into airplane mode.

I like Kristina's message and my phone rings instantly.

"Hello?"

"Don't hello me. Where are you? Where have you been?" My roommate is irritated.

"I'm at home. I've been working."

"What's going on? It's been days. You never spend that many hours working."

I open my mouth to answer, but...

"Never mind. I'll be home tonight. The team already left for Florida," she hangs up mumbling incoherently to herself.

I respond to Sherry...

Text to Sherry: Busy with work. I'm good with Mase.

Text from Sherry: It happens. Gotta pay the bills.

I wonder if Mason is getting the wrong idea. This obsession I have with writing this book has nothing to do with him and everything to do with him. Of course, he doesn't have a clue what I'm writing. I respond to Mase...

Text to Mase: Sorry I missed your call.

Text to Mase: Have a safe flight.

Text to Mase: I'll be waiting for you when you get home.

CHAPTER TEN

Jones

We land in Tampa Bay at 3am Florida time. I needed the almost six-hour nap I took. The day had a lot of positive progress, but I started with almost no sleep. I'm happy my girl responded to me. It's late, but I call her anyway.

"Hi Mase," she says with smile. "Give me one second," she disappears before getting my response. Then returns, "How was your flight? I saw you were awesome at the game today. I keep telling you, best hitter in the league."

"That's all you," I'm still tired and maybe not thinking straight. "You make me better. You make me want to prove to you that I am the best hitter in the league."

"Jones, I'd be proud of you if you were a bat boy as long as you did your best at it."

"I'm going to be the best hitter in the league."

"I love that. I believe you will make it happen. You're already the best hitter as far as I'm concerned."

"Can you tell me that again when I'm standing next to you in a week? I want to show my appreciation for your support."

"Yes, sir," she giggles.

"I'm tired. Goodnight GG. I wish my arms were around you."

"Goodnight Mase."

Michelle

He's the prince to my sleeping beauty. The moment our lips met I was brought to life with the electric charge in our connection. The first time his arms were around me I was home. I've never needed or wanted a knight in shining armor, nor a warrior—that's not what he is to me. He's awoken a desire in me that I'd never experienced. My need for him to follow through increases with every passing second.

Jones

I wake up thinking about GG and realize we talked about how much I appreciate her support yet I still didn't manage to show her I'm interested in what she does. I can do better.

Text to GG: Good morning GG.
Text to GG: I hope your project is going well.
Text to GG: I'd love to hear about it.
Text to GG: I'm sure you're sleeping. I'll call after the game tonight.

The locker room is full of smack talk and in the best

possible way. Bravo, Brandt, and Simms have all joined in with a challenge. Morale is high and we're all ready to put everything we have into sweeping the Tampa Bay Toucans. The other thing the challenge is doing is keeping our mind off the other thing that none of us will say. It's been over a week since we lost a game. I'm not saying the word and just thinking it could blow it. Even those of us players who change our socks every day and don't have a lucky batting glove can be affected by the superstitions of baseball. It's the oddest thing. The game could be the most exciting of the season and the dugout is silent. Our starting pitcher could have a no hitter into the 7th inning and everyone will stay away and not say a word to him when he's in the dugout. We're all aware of the situation and act like it doesn't exist. Fans are the same way, the words "no hitter" isn't coming out of anyone's mouth until it's done one way or the other. My phone starts buzzing...

Text from GG: Good morning.

I check my watch and it's 4pm, but I'm on the other coast and she was up all night.

Text from GG: I woke up thinking about you.
Text from GG: Can't wait for you to get home.
Text from GG: Go Seals!
Text to GG: You were thinking about me?
Text from GG: Yup.
Text to GG: What were you thinking?
Text from GG: My bed is warmer when you're in it.
Text to GG: Is it now?
Text from GG: Yes.
Text to GG: Why is that?

Text from GG: Maybe all your bare skin.

Text to GG: I've been thinking about what might happen if you were completely bare.

Text to GG: Don't go there yet. It's not time.

Text from GG: You were hard in my bed the other night.

Text to GG: I'm aware.

Text from GG: And, you were rubbing against me.

I remember waking up with my arms wrapped around her and her shirt around her neck. Her voluptuous bare breasts against me. I wanted to kiss them and suck on them, but I couldn't. She'd have been horrified if she found herself almost naked against me like that. I tried to adjust her shirt without waking her and settled for getting her breasts covered. When I woke up the next morning her shirt was pulled all the way down.

Text from GG: Isn't that what I'm supposed to do?

Text to GG: Yes, but not yet.

Text from GG: You didn't like it?

I liked it. I liked it so much I almost said fuck it to the plan to go slow and made her mine on the spot.

Text to GG: I more than liked it. We need more time first.

Text from GG: Whatever you say.

Text from GG: I'll try to be patient.

Text to GG: Thank you. It's important to me. You're important to me.

Text to GG: Call you later. Time for batting practice.

The balls are flying out of the park with no effort at all. Skip had us work on bunting and doing rotations around the bases that included stealing a base. He's a fan of the camaraderie but is reminding us of basic safety tips—he doesn't want any one of us getting hurt and ending up on the injured list. None of us do. We all need the voice of reason to keep us in line sometimes. Where your protective gear. Play hard. Play smart. This is not the season to lose any player to injury. Remember, we're going to the World Series. Okay, that last part is only in my head, but I'm pretty sure that's because Seno put it there. Happy Captain, happy team. I know it's supposed to be happy wife, happy life. My way works too and both statements are 100% true.

After a great day, the beginning of the game sucked hard. We were down 6-1 in the third. Seno got ejected in the 5th for the way he spoke to the umpire. I think he asked him if he was blind and stated that he couldn't tell the difference between a ball and a strike if he was using an electronic pitch tracker. Personally, he should've gone straight for the insult and at least got some pleasure out of it. Skip dragged him into the dugout before he could do more damage. Skip got ejected for voicing his opinion from the dugout in the 7th. And when we had no chance left, Cross and I found a big piece of cardboard and a sharpie to make a sign that read "Can you see this?" and drew a crappy rendition of a cartoon hand flippin' him the bird. That's what happens when there are no adults left to manage the kids, I mean rookies. Needless to say, Skip wasn't happy with us. Seno tried to be disappointed in us and simply couldn't be. We earned early practice with Skip, or it's supposed to be our punishment. You simply don't win them all. It's just a pisser if it's because of an ump that's inferior at his job. Either that or he's betting on the game and that's illegal. But the Toucan's pitchers could do no wrong and ours could do no right—even if the pitch was placed the same. It's part of the game. The human aspect is what we love and hate about baseball.

I go to my hotel room and order room service before I check in with my girl and get Legends of Fantasy going. I like to play on my own, I'm trying to catch up with her and I'm not sure it's possible. GG's character is this crazy powerful omnipotent wizard. She walks through fires and nothing does any real damage to her. Don't piss her off though, she'll kill you in a flash or turn you into a toad and make you beg for forgiveness. I've seen her freeze other players and leave them there that way.

I call and there's no answer, so I text her...

Text to GG: I'm in my room for the night.

Text to GG: Call me when you can.

Text to GG: Don't worry about waking me up, I'll turn my sound off when I go to bed.

Text to GG: I miss you, GG.

An hour into playing, I've finally gotten to the Hidden Oasis of Zoran. It took me three tries, but I managed to defeat the guardian and I'm about to claim the treasure when this character PinkPinkyToe pops into my space and blows me up. Dead. Then messages me, "see you again soon" and disappears. What the fuck did I do to him? I wait for my character Jonesin2Kill to rejuvenate and have to start back over from the beginning and make the trek killing all the things I've already killed three times tonight again. I get halfway there and in front of the Black Marketplace the PinkPinkyToe character shows up says "hello again" and blows me up. I don't need this tonight. I turn the game off, strip naked, and crawl into bed.

Just as I'm about to turn my sound off, my phone rings.

"Hello, is this my beautiful girlfriend?"

"Ummm, girlfriend? Let me think," she giggles. "Yes it is."

"Silly girl. I missed you today. It doesn't help that the game sucked."

"I'm sorry, Mase. Anything I can help with?"

"You're helping by calling and talking to me," I whisper.

"There you go using your words. I love words." She chuckled, "By the way, I saw you on the sports wrap-up flippin' off the home plate umpire with Cross. Sherry called me and Kristina to have a three-way discussion about it. She's concerned about how many more games you will have this season with that umpire and if there will be fallout. She also thought it was funny."

"Tomorrow's another day. We will get back to winning."

"I believe in you."

I adjust the sheets and get comfortable.

"What are you doing?"

"I just got in bed and I'm pulling the sheet out so it's not tucked in all the way around the bed. Hotels always do that and I can't stand it."

"I guess I should let you get some rest then."

"We can talk for a bit. How was your day? What project are you working on?"

"I think it was productive. My fantasy serial for the week got approved and I sent my version of the sci-fi serial to my co-worker for critique. That didn't take very long. I've spent most of the day working on another project."

"Do you want to tell me about it?"

"No."

"Why not?"

"I'm not ready. I've only done shorter solo pieces to submit to publications and this is different."

"Different how?"

"It's longer."

"How long?"

"Novel length I think. I'll know when I get to the end."

"That's some serious dedication."

"Thank you."

"Are you ghostwriting for somebody?"

"That's the thing. This is my thing. Nobody asked for it."

"I'm proud of you. I can't wait to read it."

"That'll never happen."

"I can read. Contrary to popular belief athletes have to pass their other classes."

She laughs, "I know you can read. I also know you will not be reading this."

"What if I buy a copy?"

"No."

"No?"

"No."

"So, when your book is a worldwide bestseller your boyfriend is supposed to play dumb and not know anything about it? I'm a public figure. I might get asked about my beautiful girlfriend's amazing book and my answer will be 'She won't let me read it?'"

"That works. Or maybe, something cliche like 'I've read it a few times and love her creativity. I'm sure somebody will scoop up the movie rights sooner than we think.'"

"Using the sports figure boyfriend to further you writing career already, damn!" I belly laugh, "I'm kidding. You don't need me for that."

"Question, what do you sleep in when you're on the road? Like now."

"Nothing."

"What about when you're at home?"

"Nothing."

"So, it's not just a thing about packing light."

"It is not."

"You don't sleep naked with me."

"No and I don't sleep naked when I crash at Cross's or when I'm at my mom's."

"Did you just say staying with me is like staying at your mom's?

"In a way yes, but that's not what I meant. It's a respect thing."

"I wouldn't find it disrespectful if you slept naked with me."

"You wouldn't, huh?"

"Nope."

"Soon, GG." I want to keep talking to her, but my hand keeps traveling to my cock and she seems willing to take this conversation in a blue direction. I'm not ready for that. "I need to get to bed. Cross and I have early training with Skip due to the sign fun." I chuckle, "It was worth it."

"Okay, Mase. Sleep well."

"Goodnight GG. I miss you."

"I miss you, too," she hangs up.

I fall asleep with my hand wrapped around my cock and visions of her naked next to me.

CHAPTER ELEVEN

Michelle

Re: Serial Critique 257
This one works perfectly with the plot we have planned. Nice work.

Re: Re: Serial Critique 257
Thank you. I can't say the same for yours. I'm not a fan of the hydra type character. It seems out of place here.

Re: Re: Re: Serial Critique 257
I appreciate your honest opinion and will review it. Thank you.
PS: Are you ever going to talk to me about anything other than work again?

Re: Re: Re: Re: Serial Critique 257
I'm sure I will at some point. You're going to need help

keeping a girl if you ever find one.

I've got to get back to my other project. I'll watch for your serial update.

Text from Jared: When are you going to give me the details on the other project?

Text to Jared: Never.

Text from Jared: I'm happy to critique for you.

Text from Jared: We're a partnership.

Text to Jared: This is a solo project. No critique partner necessary.

Text to Jared: Thank you.

I turn the sound off on my phone and flip it over so I'm not disturbed by any of the activity.

Every time I start writing I go back and read what I wrote the writing session before. I surprise myself. I don't remember typing the words I'm reading and there's no doubt that I did type them.

My bedroom door flies open, "What the hell is wrong with you?" Kristina stops and takes in the view, "Okay, let me try again. Michelle are you okay?"

"I'm perfectly fine. Why?"

"Well, you rearranged your room and have you looked in the mirror recently?"

"It's my room. If I want to face the window, that's my choice."

"You didn't have to move your bed for that. You realize you could've simply turned yourself around?" She shifts her feet and shaking her head, "Okay, we're going to Sherry's to watch the game. You need to be ready when I stop by to pick you up."

"I haven't slept yet."

"That's obvious. I'm not sure you've slept in days. Your hair is a nest. There's a pile of empty snack wrappers. Your eyelids are almost closed. Your laptop is gasping for air and considering filing for laptop abuse because it hasn't been powered down in, well, ever."

"No."

"No, what?"

"I can't go to Sherry's."

"Why not?"

"I have to finish this project."

"So finish it."

"It's not like that."

"How many more words do you need to meet the contract?"

"It's my project, not a contract. I don't know how much more there is."

"What?" Kristina glares at me like I have three heads.

"It's not a 'plotted out, fill in the blanks' type of thing. It just flows."

"Yeah, you're definitely getting out of the apartment and going to Sherry's for the game."

I shake my head negatively.

"Be ready when I get here or I'll get you ready. Do you understand?"

"Yes."

"You will be ready?"

"I'll consider it," but most likely I'll lock my door.

"Okay. I'll take that for now. I'll be back about 3pm, game starts at 4pm."

I wave her on and throw a shoe at my bedroom door so it closes.

She yells at me through the door, "That was uncalled for."

"Don't you have somewhere to be?"

"Yeah, I'm off to work. Please get some sleep." The apartment door slams and the lock tumblers latch.

She's not wrong. I'm tired. I set an alarm for 2pm. Power down my laptop so it backs off on its litigation plans. Close my blackout drapes and rest my head on my pillow. When my eyes close, it's movie time, I'm instantly dropped into a dream...

I'm with Mase at a huge party. Music is playing. People are dancing. There are lanterns strung across the ceiling of a romantically lit patio, with a dark sky overhead on a clear starlit night. Everything changes to a silent spinning blur, and we're all that's there. Nothing else matters. His arms around me, leading slowly on the dance floor. I reach my hands up around his neck, my fingers pulling through the ends of his thick hair. I rest my cheek on his solid chest as we sway happily together. I'm wearing a tee length navy floral print dress with buttons up the front and a sweetheart neckline, and matching navy heels, yet I'm still only as tall as his chin. He fills his suit out, perfectly tailored to his physique. He holds me possessively, whispering in my ear, "It will always be us." My bones ache with need for him, though we share our heat as we dance together. "1950" by King Princess plays and my mind spins at how all of my heroes have looked like him since the night we met. I never wrote a romantic hero until him. Yet I've written numerous books around a hero with similar features, speech patterns, and his slow sexy ways. His hand rubbing the small of my back familiarly. I loosen his tie and go on my tiptoes to kiss him. He smiles at me, content, and takes a step back with my hands in his. He kneels in front of me and gazes up into my eyes, "Be mine? Only mine? I only want to be yours." I lean down and kiss his soft lips...

I hate alarms! They always ruin things at the worst

possible moment. The dream is vivid in my memory. It was me, but somehow more mature and comfortable in my own skin—and the dress. Mase was closer to my soul. His words have had an effect on me since day one, but as he said the words I was already his.

I hear keys at the door and pull myself from my daydream, running to the shower before Kristina catches me.

A couple minutes later there's a knock on the bathroom door, "I'm ahead of schedule. Are you almost ready?"

"Yep. I'll be ready in less than 15 minutes."

"That works. We're picking up take-out on the way."

Kristina's right. I need to go outside and be with people in the real world. I didn't understand exactly how much until it took two rounds of conditioner to get my hair detangled. I may have fallen asleep on the last bite of a candy bar, which makes sense because I was wondering where the chocolate on my laptop came from. Yea, I definitely need to get out.

Kristina already has food ordered and everything planned out. I'm shotgun and she pulls up right in front of the deli, "I'll wait here. The order is under my name and already paid for." This isn't a request. She might as well have used a broom to push me out of her car.

I glare at her, "Yes, ma'am!" And go in to get the order. Of course, she didn't get energy drinks or dessert. I fixed that. The deli makes scrumptious individual desserts that are big enough to share. I bought three, the caramel turtle brownie, the macadamia nut blondie, the tropical fruit tart, and a container of their fresh whipped cream to go with them.

I walk out to the parking lot to find Kristina still parked right in front of the door, as if we may need to make a getaway. Her eyes like saucers, "I didn't order that much." Immediately checking her account to confirm how much they charged her.

"I added dessert," and smiled at her like the Cheshire cat in anticipation of how happy she's going to be with me.

"Why did you do that?"

"There was no dessert on the order. We need dessert."

She shakes her head and drives toward Sherry's, but pulls into another parking lot and turns to glare at me, "Next pick up. Order is under my name and is already paid for. Please don't get extra this time."

We're in front of the bakery. Shit. I go in and pick up the dozen fresh baked cookies. They're still warm in the box. I get back in the car, "Are we making any more stops? There's no room left."

She laughs and drives us to Sherry's. We walk in with the bags and boxes. I take the whipped cream directly to the refrigerator.

"How many of us did you think there were going to be here?" Sherry asks.

"I added dessert to the deli order," I explain.

"I'd already ordered from the bakery," Kristina adds.

Sherry nods, "Even better, we get dessert first and last! It's a long game. Why not have two?"

I'm not arguing.

"We can save some for another day," Kristina suggests.

"Who are you kidding?" I ask as I dip a warm cookie into the fresh whipped cream.

We settle in front of the TV and watch as the game is about to start. "We needed a girl's night. Elle might join us later. She's napping now." Sherry turns to me, "Why haven't you been going to the games?"

"That's a great question," Kristina says, and adds, "and what's up with the open edible body cream in our refrigerator, and all the empty flavored lube packets?"

"You waited until now to bring that up?" I glare at Kristina.

She shrugs her shoulder, "As good a time as any."

"Sounds like fun to me," Sherry jests.

"I thought it was for my benefit. There was too much of it." Kristina covers her eyes, "But then I saw the ass print on the sofa. I'll never be able to sit there again." She gazes up wide-eyed, "And now I'm wondering if I need to disinfect the whole kitchen or maybe never cook or eat at home again." She glares at me, "We may need to move. Don't ever do that again." She shakes her finger at me like a school teacher.

"I'll pay a cleaning service to come through," I grin in pleasure. It was worth it.

Our guys run out onto the field and our eyes are glued to the screen.

"The team has been playing extremely well, except last night. You have to lose sometimes," Sherry says.

"Chase told me he challenged Jones and it started something," Kristina said.

Sherry added, "To be fair, Mason started it. The three of them got together for breakfast the other day and ran with it. My king was telling me about it last night. He's proud of them and happy the team is having fun."

"I chewed out Cross last night for the sign stunt. What were they thinking?" Kristina shakes her head.

"No idea, boys will be boys," Sherry lets it go. "Let's hope the umpire crew doesn't hold it against them for the rest of the Florida series."

Cross starts the game by hitting a grounder, legging it into a double, and stealing third. Martin pops up to right field and brings Cross in to score. They're all hitting and defending their positions well. The Seals are ahead 7-2 in the 7th and Skip pulls Seno to give Stray some playing time. Sherry isn't happy and mumbles something to herself justifying the decision.

She redirects to me, "So, why haven't you been going to the games?"

"Kristina's only at every game because she works there," not sure why I find it necessary to bring her down with me.

Mouth dropped open, Kristina defends herself, "That's not true! If I didn't have to work I'd be in the stands yelling for Cross as many games as possible."

"But not every game. My point is that I have work, too."

"Cut the bullshit! You make your own schedule and we all know it," Kristina clarifies.

"I can't always control when things have to get done. Rewrites, meetings, things, not all in my control. I need income to cover my half of the bills unless you have a magic lamp hiding somewhere, maybe a mythical money tree."

"Nice try. Tell Sherry," Kristina commands.

"Tell Sherry what?"

"Stop being an obtuse child!"

"I'm the only one who's read it and I'm not ready to share," I say through gritted teeth.

"Read what? I want to read it," Sherry interjects. "What are you two bickering about?"

"Michelle's a freelance writer who writes serials for a magazine, but she's been possessed by writing this solo project to the point that I don't think she's sleeping, showering, or eating anything other than junk snack food, and simply can't manage her schedule well enough to get to the games," Kristina vomits.

"Thanks for that," I say dripping with sarcasm. "And, I can control my schedule. I can't control the compulsive need I have to work on the solo project. It's the only thing I can focus on. I even wrote a princess and stable boy into my fantasy serial, and romance is specifically prohibited from that contract. I got in a fight with Jared over it and told him off. Happy now? Want to share anything else?"

"Woah!" Sherry's eyes flick back and forth between us, "Creatives can be unique. I want to read it. Who's Jared?"

"He's my critique partner for the serials."

"He's her ex-fiancé," Kristina adds.

"Was that a necessary piece of information?" I glare at Kristina.

"I think so," she says and Sherry nods in agreement.

Brows furled, Sherry asks, "Does Jones know about Jared?"

"Yes," I reply plainly.

"He does not," Kristina says.

"He does so! You're not always there," I correct her.

Kristina shakes her head, "I don't think he does."

I'm ready to pull my hair out, "Who's life is this that we're talking about again?"

"Then what did Mason say when he found out about Jared?" Sherry asks.

"He told me to change critique partners."

"I think she told him," Sherry declares as she disappears to the bedroom only to reappear two minutes later with Elle.

"I should be at the games. A good girlfriend would be at the games. I get it. I intend to go to the games and then I lose an inane amount of time writing or fall asleep mid-sentence to wake up five to ten hours later. I've never had this happen with my writing before," I give a nod of finality.

"I'm interested. Tell me about what you're writing," Sherry asks sincerely.

"Romance. Steamy Romance. And my hero has the appearance of Mason, the voice of Mason, acts like Mason, tastes like Mason, basically Mason in every way, and he's a baseball player. Every time I get to the climactic part of a sex scene something happens so I don't get to write it. It's killing me."

"You need a cookie and that bucket of whipped cream," I listen and do as Sherry suggests. I've learned she's pretty much always right and I'll never turn down a bucket of whipped cream. Who would?

By the end of the night, we ate dessert twice and didn't touch dinner. We got used to Elle being a mini-Sherry attached to her somewhere. The Seals won but the margin was closer than we liked at 7-6.

"This is why you leave Seno in to catch the whole game. He's the glue and the best friggin' catcher in the league," Sherry proclaims.

Nobody was arguing. Our guys should always be in the game until the end without exception. The only reason to get pulled is injury or ejection, and our guys aren't allowed to get hurt. So, honestly stupidity, maybe. The rookies showed us yesterday.

Three hours later Kristina woke me up and drove us home. I missed my call from Mase.

> Text from Mase: Miss you.
>
> Text from Mase: It's late and I heard it's a girl's night. Have fun. We can talk tomorrow.
>
> Text from Sherry: Don't worry about Kristina. Do your thing and write your book.
>
> Text from Sherry: Mason will understand or he's not the guy for you.
>
> Text from Sherry: I'm here if you need me.

CHAPTER TWELVE

Michelle

I wake up at a normal time, which never happens when I'm alone. I don't remember climbing into bed last night, nor the ride home. Kristina is up and singing, so not like her. She doesn't sing. Well, that's not accurate—she shouldn't sing. She's a phenomenal announcer. She has clear tone and speaks articulately, with absolutely no ability to be in key. She's either in a wonderful mood, thinks I'm sleeping, or doesn't think I can hear her. She must think I'm passed out the way she's belting it out. I listen quietly as I get my laptop and do my best not to be discovered. One after the other, "Thrills," by Donna Missal, "1950," by King Princess, "Champion," by Bishop Briggs, and she's getting louder.

I check my phone and it's almost noon. She shouldn't be home. Texts have been popping for over an hour...

Text from Mase: Call me after you get up and talk to your roommate.

Text from Mase: She needs to come first today. :)
Text from Chase: Will you get up please!
Text from Chase: I wish I was there.
Text from Chase: I hate that I can't be there today.
Text from Chase: Whatever she wants today. I'll get you the money. You two need to paint the town.

Okay, my curiosity is peaked. I get out of bed, still dressed from last night, so that saves me a step and some time. I crack my bedroom door and take a peek at my roommate dancing around with her AirPods in and singing as she picks up the living room.

Text from Chase: We'll be in Denver tonight. Maybe you ladies can fly out and meet us?
Text from Chase: Double date. Mason would love to see you, too.

What the hell is going on? Kristina doesn't get days off. I lean against the door frame at the entrance to my room. "Good morning," I say loudly and get no response. "How loud do you have those things turned up, dancing queen?" I yell and she turns to me startled.

"What the fuck! Don't sneak up on a person like that! Geez! I about jumped out of my skin," she shakes it off and pulls the pods out of her ears.

I stare at her confused, "Shouldn't you be at the stadium by now?"

Her grin broadens, "I have the day off. Actually I have a few days off."

"How'd you manage that? Intern gigs are hard and you've been doing awesome."

She stops and glares at me deadpan, "I'm not an intern anymore."

Unsure how to respond, "Is that a good thing?" Did she give up and decide to be a player wife? Did she get in trouble for dating a player?

"Yes. I have a permanent position with the San Diego Seals," she squeals. "I start when the team gets back."

That's when it hits me, "OMG! You got it! They made you the PA Announcer!"

"Yes! I'm the PA Announcer for the San Diego Seals. Can you believe it?"

"You deserve it. You worked for that and nobody is better than you," I hug her and remember Chase's texts. "What are we doing to celebrate?"

"The guys are gone. I thought maybe we could all go out when they get back," slightly deflated but being an adult. "I'm excited to have the few days off."

I gaze at her kind of sideways and mumble, "We could go to them."

She drops everything and focuses on me, "This is a big deal. You should be able to celebrate today. We can meet them in Denver tonight."

"Should we?" She asks excitedly.

"Chase texted me and said you get whatever you want today. I didn't know why, but I get it now," I stop and consider his text. "He gets points for it, too."

I send him a text...

Text to Chase: Checking airfare. Don't tell Mase yet.

Text from Chase: Use my credit card and book first class roundtrip for both of you.

Text from Chase: No skimping for my girl.

He sends me a photo of his credit card. I'm about to argue that we can pay for our own, but he's doing this for Kristina.

"Pack your bag. I'm getting the airfare. We won't have much time," Kristina squeals again.

Text from Chase: Call Mason quick... we're starting batting practice in five minutes.

Shit. I call him up while I search for airfare.

"Hello, is this my girl?" I hear his voice and swoon internally.

"It is. How are you today?"

"I'm good. Staying positive."

"Maybe I can make your day better?"

"Your voice already did that, beautiful," the smile in his tone evident.

"I'll see you tonight in Denver. Kristina and I are on our way to celebrate," I'm as happy about it as she is and anxious to get my hands on Mase.

"I can't wait to see you. Will you stay with me?" I hadn't even thought about it. I'm sure Kristina will stay with Chase.

"Where else would I be?"

"Perfect. I'll have your name added to my room, so you can check in if you get there before me. I'm out of time. Gotta run. See you tonight!"

"See you then... miss you Mase." and he's gone.

Searching for same day first class flights, there's not much left to choose from. I yell out, "Kristina, can you be ready to go by 2pm?" Can I be ready to go by then? Shit, do I have clean clothes? "Kristina?"

"Packing."

"Pack for me, too?" I laugh. "I'm booking the flight. We need to be out of here in under two hours." I find a shuttle and book the town car instead, only $20 difference and that's what Chase would want. "A car is picking us up at 3:15."

Text from Mase: Check your email.

Text from Mase: What flight will you be on?

Text to Mase: Landing about 6:30pm.

Text from Mase: You'll be there before us.

Text from Chase: Thank you.

I have an email from Carter with hotel details. Then another pops through with confirmation and info on the car that will be picking us up at the airport in Denver. Is this what Sherry's always talking about when she says you'll never want it any other way once you've been with a player? I realize Kristina never responded to me, "Kristina?"

"Still packing."

"Shit... help me when you get done!" I run for my room and pull my carry-on out, throwing it open on my bed. Then immediately do the same with my laptop tote—I go nowhere without my laptop. I yell across the apartment, "What are you packing?" I need to be prepared to go out and probably more than once. Jeans? Crap... I fumble through my closet... "Kristina! Do I need to pack more than jeans and a sweater? What about a dress? If I have to bring extra shoes, I may have to check a bag." I consider what I need. Basics, panties and bras, socks, sneakers, something to sleep in. My head explodes, and I'm yelling, "Should I be packing my fancy panties? The lace bra? The thong? I know, I know, no granny panties. What should I take to sleep in? Do I need anything to sleep in? Can I leave that out and save room in my bag?"

"Stop yelling," She's standing in my doorway. "You're acting like you've never packed before. We both know you have. You're the master and commander in charge when we pack and move every time. You're the one who makes sure I don't screw things up with my work and keep me in line." She takes a deep breath, "What the hell has gotten into you?"

Without thinking, "I'm in love with Mase and we're going to Denver and he's there and I'm going to see him and I'm staying in his room with him and I don't know how to do this and I don't want to screw it up."

Her eyes freeze, focused on me, and her mouth drops open, "Breathe. Did you hear what you just said and do you realize your statement was a run-on sentence?"

I don't have a clue what I said, but me and run-on sentences are always epic. "No?" I say questioningly hoping she won't yell at me for not paying attention to my own words, and accuse me of doing the same to her like she has in the past.

"Sit."

"I don't have time to sit. I have to pack."

She points at my bed and I sit.

"Um, you're in love with Mase?"

I stare at her blankly, "What? Why would you say that? We're not you and Chase."

"You said that."

"Are you sure?"

"It was part of the run-on sentence."

"Oh fuck!"

"Yep, that's what I thought too." She stares at me trying to hold her smile in, "I'm packed and ready to go, so let's get you packed. It may be my celebration, but you have something at stake too." She pulls out a list and I gawk, "What is that?"

"My packing list. I use it every time I pack and adjust it accordingly."

That's why she's done packing.

"What time are we getting there and what time will the guys get there?" Kristina asks.

"We will get there first. Don't know when they'll get there yet. Mase put me on his room so I can check in and have a room," I spill.

"Okay, so we can get you ready when we get there. Let's go through the packing list. I'll ask for things and you give them to me to pack."

"Okay," I stand at the ready.

"Makeup bag, brush, toiletry kit."

"Jeans, hoodie, nice sweater, tank top, 2 T-shirts."

"3 pair of socks, cute PJs, 2 pair of leggings."

"3 pair of sexy panties including the thong, lace bras, all the granny panties."

Getting everything for her as she asked was working efficiently. I stop and glare at her, "All the granny panties?"

"Yes."

"Why?"

"Don't question me. I'm helping you."

I hand her all the granny panties and she drops them in my waste basket. "But?"

"No buts. Simply say thank you and bring your credit card. We will go shopping for more."

I nod and move on. She's helping me. It doesn't matter that they're comfortable. I can dig them out of the trash when she's gone.

She moves to my closet, "Okay, we need to find you a dress or something dressy." She goes through my closet one hanger at a time, judging each piece as she goes. She pulls out a purple sweater dress and throws it on the bed. "Pack your boots." She grabs my chiffon floral tunic that's almost see-through and adds it to the pile. "Pack a white or nude camisole." She continues going through my stuff, "That turquoise dress always looks amazing on you. The wrap accentuates your boobs." It gets added to the pile. "Make sure you have your Seals cap, jersey, shirt, and hoodie. We'll be going to baseball games. In fact, we should probably be wearing our hoodies on the plane. It will save packing space and it's going to be cold in Denver when we get there."

I do as she suggests and wonder when she got so good at this. I change into leggings and a T-shirt, then wrap my Seals hoodie around my waist. I slide my sneakers on and toss my laptop, phone, purse, AirPods, splitter, Peanut M&Ms, and charging cables into my tote. What am I missing? I toss my sexy nighty in my bag, and stockings and heels to go with the dress. "What am I forgetting?"

"I don't know about forgetting, but I think you've lost your brain."

I glare at her, "I have not."

"Prove it."

"I just don't want to get there and not have what I need. It's not like I can run home and grab something."

"That's what your credit card is for. You run to the store and get whatever you need." She stops and continues, "We'll be doing some makeup shopping for you. That little envelope thing you handed me doesn't count as a makeup bag."

This is going to be an expensive trip, "We can do that when we get back. My bags are already full."

She glares at me again. Yep, it's going to be an expensive trip.

I get a text...

Car Service: Your car will be there to pick you up in less than 10 minutes.

"That's our 10-minute warning. Are we ready to go?"

"As ready as we're going to be for this trip." I nod in agreement.

"Make sure you have your ID handy," I suggest as I put mine in the outer pocket of my tote. I put the tote strap across my body and roll my carry-on to the door. I focus on Kristina, "Ready?" She's standing there with her rolling carry-on and a huge purse slung over her shoulder. Both of us in leggings and a T-shirt with a hoodie wrapped around our waists and appearing to be walking Seals ads. I lock up our apartment and we make our way down to the street to wait for our ride.

On the way down the elevator Kristina asks, "What kind of car is picking us up? Uber?"

"I ordered a car from the airport shuttle service."

"Oh. What kind of car is that?"

We step out of the elevator and walk to the sidewalk. There's a shiny black Lincoln Town Car sitting there. "I think that's it."

A gentleman steps out of the car, "Michelle and Kristina?"

I nod and he opens the door for us. He puts our rolling bags in the trunk. "Ladies, do you need to make any last-minute stops or directly to the airport?"

"The airport will be fine. Thank you," I reply.

Kristina glances at me and sends me a text...

Kristina: This is expensive.

Kristina: We need to tip this guy?

Me: Already done with the payment of the service.

She sends me a thumbs up emoji.

On our way to the airport, I check on the game. It's probably almost over and I hope the Seals are winning. I don't want anything to be a downer tonight. "Can we watch highlights on the plane?" I ask Kristina.

"We might have to pay for wifi, but yea."

I need details. There's been two grand slams and an injury. Seals are winning, 9-6 in the 6th.

I turn to Kristina, "Did you tell Sherry you got the job?"

"No, and she should probably know we're going to be gone." My thoughts exactly.

I dial Sherry up on speaker phone and hope she answers.

"Hello?"

"Hi!" We respond together. "This is Michelle and Kristina."

"Hello ladies. You sound like you're up to something."

"I suppose we are. We're on the way to the airport to go to Denver and celebrate with our guys. Kristina got the PA Announcer job!"

"That's huge! Congrats! I wish I was going, but I'm grounded for a while still. You ladies have fun!"

"We hope to. We've been busy getting packed since this is last minute. How's the game?"

"Two grand slams. Mason hit both. Cross was on base both times. Seno hit the other homer. Team is looking good. Lucine got pulled for an injured finger, he jammed it on second base when he was stealing. It's going to happen when you play hard. Our guys are fine. Martin just hit a double and brought Cross in again. Have fun and let me know when you get there please!" She hangs up on us while yelling at the TV. Everyone will be in the mood for a party.

The car comes to a stop and our driver opens the door, offering us each a hand out of the car. He gets our luggage from the trunk, "Is there anything else I can help you with?"

"No. Thank you so much."

"Safe travels. I'll be here to pick you up when you return," he nods, gets in the car and pulls away.

We stare at each other with anticipation and walk into the airport. We stop to check the flight board and our flight is on schedule. Kristina turns to me, "I don't have a boarding pass."

"I've got both of them on my phone," I forward a photo of hers to her.

We approach security and I take the line labeled for first class, but she stops, "That's the first-class line."

"Yep," I reply.

She checks her boarding pass to find what seat she's in and follows me with a strut in her step.

"Round trip first class per your boyfriend's instructions," I confirm. "They've got a car scheduled to pick us up at the airport in Denver as well."

I text Mason...

Text to Mason: We're at the airport.

Text to Mason: Text me when you see this.

We get through security with no issues and have plenty of time to get to our gate. We stop and take selfies in front of an ad for the Seals. I get Kristina to pose like she's kissing Cross and another like she's grabbing his butt. She has me act like my arms are around Mason and I'm making out with him, then another where it looks like I'm giving him a sweet kiss on the cheek. We notice we're wearing our shirts with their names on them when we review the photos—they couldn't be more perfect.

We get to our gate and our stomachs growl. We got packed and here on time, but didn't manage to eat today. "Should we get something real quick or wait 30 minutes and take advantage of first class?"

"I'll take free over airport prices," Kristina chooses quickly. I nod in agreement.

We're first on the plane when it starts boarding. The flight attendant puts our luggage in the overhead for us and we get comfortable with plenty of room for our totes. We pull our hoodies on and get settled for the flight. Kristina plays with her seat, adjusting the foot rest. I check the personal screen to find out if we can watch the end of the game, but nothing is available yet. We order mimosas and the first-class dinner.

Text from Mase: GG?

Text to Mase: We're on the plane.

Text to Mase: Call me real quick?

My phone rings instantly, "Hey! We should be in the air on our way to Denver in about an hour." "Did you get the info for the hotel room?"

"Yes. I have all the info on the room and the car that's picking us up." I stop and want to tell him things that I shouldn't, "Mase?"

"Yea?"

"I miss you. I can't wait to see you."

"I'm looking forward to sharing a room with you for a couple days," his grin evident in his voice.

"I like that, too." I say sweetly.

Kristina waves her hands frantically and whispers, "Don't you dare tell him on the phone. Make him tell you first!"

I wave her off. I'm not telling him anything. I'm not sure she isn't hearing things.

"See you in a few hours. Text me if you want. I need to switch to airplane mode."

"Okay beautiful. I'll have my arms around you in about five hours." He hangs up.

Kristina is doing the same thing and both of us are smiling like fools.

Jones

I turn to Cross, "What's our plan for tonight?"

"I've been thinking about that. It's going to be late when we get in. We need to go out and do something to celebrate."

I reach out to Carter...

Text to Carter: Cross and I need reservations for dinner for four in Denver tonight.

Text from Carter: Any other details?

Text to Carter: Celebration dinner. Not too far from the hotel.

Text to Carter: Some place our women will love.

Text from Carter: I'll have something set up for you before you land.

Text to Carter: Cross needs flowers for his girl. It's her celebration dinner.

Text from Carter: No problem.

"These chicks, man," Cross starts. "Do you think they're the ones?"

"I know Michelle is. Knew it as soon as I saw her."

"It's weird though, right? I mean Kristina is the only woman who has ever made me only want her. Is that how we know?"

"Maybe that's how you know. With Michelle, I was jealous as soon as one of the other guys talked to her. The way she moves and how she responds—nobody else could have her and I couldn't risk them getting the chance. She's special. I need her."

"You're serious."

"I am."

"You're going to marry her."

"If she'll have me. She's the only one who deserves to be on my pedestal. I love that she's creative and quick, she can take care of herself. She doesn't need me for anything, yet she wants to be with me. It kind of makes it better that she didn't follow baseball and is learning it because of me, choosing me."

"Does she know you love her?"

"I haven't told her. I'm trying to take my time with everything. I don't want anything to be rushed. We have time."

"What if you don't?"

I turn and glare at Cross, "Why would we not have time?"

"Outside forces. Things we don't have control over. People and things we aren't aware of. Fastballs at our head. Shit happens."

Michelle

I get my laptop out on the plane and work on my project while Kristina watches a movie. My conversation with Kristina from earlier on repeat in my head. There's not much more epic than being in love. Do I love Mason? According to Kristina I said I do.

… I MISS him when he's not near me. The mere sound of his voice warms my heart. His hands on my hips melt me. His lips on mine create an electrical charge all the way from my toes. It's his words that have affected me the most. From day one he has whispered in my ear and used his words in a way that I never want to lose. I crave the vibrations against my ear. His pure words directly from his heart with no thought about what anyone else would think. We are the only two who matter. As

he has said, it will always be us. I can't imagine being a couple with any other man. His strong and honest presence, his true heart, his unspoken love—irreplaceable...

He's everything to me. I wait each day for what more can come from this amazing man. In awe each time he surprises me with something more. Aware of my emotions for him, I protect my heart and wait for him to decide it's the right time before I divulge the many ways I love him.

We land in Denver and I immediately turn off airplane mode, inviting the rest of the world back into mine.

Text from Mase: Getting ready to take off.

Text from Mase: Should land in Denver around 9pm.

I call the number for the car service to inform them we've landed.

The plane gets to the gate and the door opens. We sashay off the plane with our luggage in tow and follow the signs to where our car should be waiting for us. We step into the cold night air, happy to have our hoodies on. The brisk air has us putting the hoods on and drawing the strings.

"What kind of car is picking us up?" Kristina asks.

"I was told to watch for a vehicle with a seven on the rear window." A Hummer pulls up in front of us and parks a few feet past where we're standing. There's a big 7 in sports block lettering style on the rear window.

A man comes around from the driver's side, "Ladies, Kristina and Michelle?"

"Yes," we reply in unison.

"I was pretty sure. When I get a request from Carter and find two beautiful ladies in team gear waiting on the curb..." his statement drifts off as he loads our luggage. He offers each of us a needed hand to climb into the back of the Hummer. He gets in the front seat and rolls the glass barrier down, "Can I get you ladies anything on the way to the hotel? Any stop requests?" He waits quietly, then suggests, "Some hot coffee maybe?"

Kristina bites, "Yes please. A large hot coffee I can wrap my fingers around sounds wonderful."

"Agreed!" I chime in. I'm always up for caffeine, but the hand warmer idea is a plus.

A few minutes later we're parked curbside at a local coffee shop and a waitress comes running out in her cap sleeved red dress with white apron and white stockings. She has to be freezing. Our driver rolls down his window, "Thanks doll." He takes the coffees from her and hands them back to us.

"Any time, babe!" She turns and runs back into the restaurant quickly.

The heat emanating from the cup warms my hands instantly. I hold it, enjoying the heat almost burning my fingers. Kristina sips at hers cautiously and her eyes light up. I give mine a try and I'm suddenly alive.

It doesn't take long and we're being dropped off at our hotel. Our driver hands our luggage off to the bellman, "Have a good night, ladies!"

We nod and wave him off as we walk into the hotel. Everything shines, from the glazed tile floors to the brass accents and the crystal chandeliers hanging from the high lobby ceiling. The lights shimmering and reflecting off each other. We walk up to the check-in counter.

"Welcome, are you checking in tonight?"

"Yes. Jones Mason."

The clerk eyes me, "And your name?"

"Michelle."

"May I see your ID?"

I grab my ID out of the pocket on my bag and hand it over.

"Thank you," she hands it back to me and steps away from the counter for a moment. She returns with a small envelope. "This should be everything you need. The elevators are to your right. The coffee shop is open until 10pm and the bar will be open until 2am. Enjoy your stay."

I take the envelope and step away from the counter, surveying the surroundings. Kristina is standing next to me with a similar envelope, we stare at each other and open the envelopes. We each have a room key. I'm in 910 and she's in 916. We get our luggage from the bellman and take the elevator up to the 9th floor. We check out both rooms, they're identical with two rooms separating them. The stadium is only a few blocks away, we have a view of it from our windows. We each unpack quickly, getting things that might wrinkle hung up in the closet.

Text to Mase: What's our plan for the night?

I ask, not wanting to take my hoodie off and lose the warmth I've acclimated to. A few minutes pass and then I get a response.

Text from Mase: It's late tonight. We have reservations at the hotel bar.

Text to Mase: The bar?

Text from Mase: It's not just a bar. You'll see.

Text to Mase: Jeans?

Text from Mase: Whatever you want. You're always beautiful.

I turn to Kristina with an unimpressed tone, "We're having dinner at the bar downstairs. I'm told it's more than a bar."

"That means we don't have to go back out in the cold," she's happy and I get on board. "We need to be ready when they get here." She glares at me, "You should go with the purple sweater dress and boots. Do your makeup, nothing crazy. Let's see how much time we have left for our hair. We can always put our hair up."

I nod and don't argue. I have no idea what I'm doing here and I don't have to think.

"Sexy panties and lace bra."

I take a deep breath and start with the panties, "What if I don't like the sweater dress without my spanx?"

"Please tell me you didn't pack the spanx. You don't need those. You never have."

"Are you sure you're talking to the right person? My muffin top isn't going to be cute in that dress."

"You don't have a muffin top. Just put the dress on." She's rolling her eyes at me. I can't see her face, but she is.

I strip my bottom half quickly and keep my hoodie as long as I can.

I pull on black satin string bikinis, black tights, and my knee-high boots. I force myself to lose the hoodie and put on my black lace bra. Then slide into the purple sweater dress. It's soft and warm. I turn to Kristina, "Why do you get to wear leggings?"

"I don't have your shape. I'm cold."

"I was cold too."

"You have that warm dress."

"Is there a double standard at play here?"

"I don't think that applies to this situation. I'm in charge of what we're wearing. I packed both of us."

I huff, then gaze at myself in the mirror, "Okay, what should I be doing with this hair?"

"Brush it out, flip it around, and see what you get."

I brush out my hair after having it tied up in knot. The ends have a curled effect to them and the length has a bit of a wave. I flip my hair forward to shake it out and run my fingers through it when I stand upright.

Kristina checks it out, "Looks great. Get your makeup on."

Oh yea, that. I do my basic mascara and lip gloss. I stand there ready to go.

She pokes each of my cheeks, "Rub that in. It wouldn't hurt to put on some eyeliner."

I rub the red dots away to a light rosy pink on my cheeks. "I don't have eyeliner."

She shakes her head at me again and slams an eyeliner pencil down on the counter in front of me.

I pick it up and examine it. I take the cap off. I gaze at my reflection, then the pencil. "This is why I don't do this stuff. How do I do this without poking myself in the eye?"

She takes the pencil from me, "Look up." Poof I have eyeliner.

I'm happy with my appearance. I could get used to wearing dresses.

The door opens, "Hello?"

It's a familiar voice that makes my heart pound. "One second," I say running to the door and trying to give Kristina an extra minute to finish getting ready.

I throw my arms around him and he lifts me, kissing my lips. "I've missed you," he says as he gazes into my eyes.

"I missed you, too," I say sincerely and appreciate his large warm hands on me.

Kristina comes out of the bathroom, "Okay. I'm out. Where's mine?"

"He went directly to his room," Mase offers. "Congratulations on the PA gig."

"Thank you," she yells as she runs out the door to go find Cross.

He focuses on me, "Why haven't we done this before? Is there any reason you can't travel with me?"

I giggle and try to think like an adult, "I have a life outside of baseball and the airfares are not in my budget. But, I like the idea. Maybe I can sometimes?"

"I'm sure we can make it happen whenever you want," he gazes at me with intent. "The purple looks good on you." He backs me up against the wall and pulls my hands up above my head, leaning his body on mine and slowly tracing down my side. He whispers in my ear, "You're all I think about."

Knocking on the door interrupts the mood, and Mase opens it to find Cross with his arm around Kristina, "Let's go. I'm hungry."

We nod, all in agreement, and go to dinner.

The bar is more than a bar. The menu is like the fine dining menu of bar food. Everything smells delicious and the food on the tables as we walk in all make me hungrier. The hostess sits us in a rounded alcove booth of dark green velvet. Everything is decorated with dogs playing poker and wearing monocles, and accented with brass nail heads. The server comes to the table and Cross orders a bottle of champagne to start, "This is a celebration for my girl. We have to start with bubbly."

My glass was always full. I don't remember ordering. I think the guys ordered for the table. Bottles of champagne kept coming. Baskets of finger food arrived one after the other, cheese fries, popcorn chicken, sweet potato tater tots, onion rings, house made potato chips, spicy meatballs, pork sliders, corn dog bites—it just kept coming. And the sauces, are probably what made it. Every sauce you can think of and combinations you'd never heard of, at least a dozen different dishes of dipping sauce. Mase was feeding me and things got kind of blurry. He was sucking on my fingers. I don't have a clue what happened to Cross and Kristina, and at the time I didn't care.

Jones

Fuck me. I want her. I don't want to wait anymore. The sexy and soft purple sweater dress that shows her perfect curves. The way she sucks and licks at my fingers as I feed her. Finding us back in that couples place like we were before. Everything is screaming in my head to take her, show her you belong together. The bubbles may have gone straight to my head. It can't be because of the champagne. I want her present with me. She's giggling and lighthearted as we walk to the elevator. She leans on me and draws a line on my fly with her finger. My cock jumps, at the ready. I press my lips to hers and we're in the same place. She wants me like I want her. I unlock the door to our room and she walks in, immediately pulling her dress off over her head and falling flat on her face into the bed. Out cold. I roll her over and take in the view, black lace bra, tiny panties, black stockings, and boots. Amazing the difference the dress made. If I knew what she looked like without it, I may not have stayed at the bar. I pull her boots off for her and consider taking the stocking off of her, too. It's not time yet, but I can't help but take the stockings off. I glide my hands down her silky skin and hook my thumbs in her stockings, pushing them down over her hips carefully. I don't want to disturb her panties. I slide them down to her thighs. I catch the scent of her heaven and want to dive in. One hand on each of her legs, I glide down her body gathering the stockings as I go until I get to her toes. I set her boots and stockings next to her dress. I kick my shoes off, pull my shirt off, and take my pants off, gazing at her heavenly figure. Reliving her soft skin and feminine curves. I crawl in bed with her and pull the blankets up over the both of us, holding her as I fall asleep.

CHAPTER THIRTEEN

Michelle

I wake up and everything is bright. There's simply too much light. Where am I? I attempt to move, but I'm being held tightly, possessively. "Mase?"

"I'm right here, GG," he replies softly and half asleep. "Are you feeling okay this morning? I think you drank two bottles by yourself."

"Everything is so bright," I stretch and roll toward him, reaching my arm over him.

"I can help with that," he reaches over to the nightstand and the drapes close.

"You're magic," I say thanking him.

"It's just the drapes," he laughs.

There's a knock at the door, "Room service."

"Did you order?" he asks me and I shake my head. He climbs out of bed and I watch as he walks to the door in his boxer briefs. He cracks the door, "We didn't order anything."

"Delivery from room 916."

I suddenly realize that I'm lying here in my bra and panties with nothing to cover up with. Thank you for making me wear the sexy panties! I pull the blankets up over me.

"Give me one second," Jones tells them and fumbles to find something to put on.

"Robe in the closet," I suggest.

He points his finger at me and grabs it, wrapping it around himself quickly and getting back to the door. He opens it and room service wheels in a cart that they pop the sides up on and turn into a table. Then they get table linens, covered plates of food, and a pot of coffee from underneath and set the table. "Can I get you anything else?" they ask.

Mase chuckles, "I don't even know what this is, so I think we're good. Thank you." Room service nods and leaves the room, pulling the door closed behind them. He turns to me, "Hungry?"

"Coffee."

He laughs and I question, "Where did my clothes go?"

"You stripped as you walked in the door last night. I took your boots off for you," he stops and then adds, "and your stockings. I didn't want them to get ruined."

"You didn't, huh?"

"Nope."

"Did you consider putting clothes on me?"

"Why would I do that?"

I thought about his meant-to-be-rhetorical question, "Maybe I was cold."

He gazes at me with a grin on his face, "The only thing you are in those panties is hot."

He takes the robe off and tosses it to me. I put it on and join him sitting at the foot of the bed to discover what Cross had delivered. He calls Cross.

"Hey! Did you get your breakfast?"

"Yeah, that's why I was calling. Thank you."

"That's how I make sure I get up in the morning when we're on the road. I figured you might need some help this morning too."

"I appreciate it. I think Michelle needs it more than me."

"Kristina's the same way. Enjoy. Meet me in a couple hours and we can run to the stadium."

"Sure thing. Thank you."

Run? I don't consider running in my life. Not my thing. I get a text but I don't know where my phone is. Mase reaches for the nightstand and tosses my phone at me.

Text from Kristina: Lunch and shopping before the game?

Text to Kristina: How about sleep?

Text from Kristina: Don't be a pooper.

Text from Kristina: You're the one who needs to go shopping.

Text to Kristina: Fine.

Mase starts uncovering plates. I poor a cup of coffee and choose a cinnamon roll. He goes for the eggs and hash browns. We make our way, grazing across the plates. I take the remaining fruit and muffins, and we push the cart back to the hallway. The robe is cozy. I'd be content to stay in it all day and write. Kristina won't allow it, but it's still a nice thought.

"Cross arranged tickets for you and Kristina for today and tomorrow. Are you going to the game or do you need to stay here and work?"

I smile at his thoughtfulness and the way he doesn't take my time for granted, "I'll be at both games."

He grins, "I love it when you're at my games. Nothing

compares to you cheering for me. What are your plans today?"

"Lunch and shopping with Kristina, then the game."

"Going out with me after?"

"With you after, whatever you want."

"I like that too," he grins. "I need to shower and stretch. It's hard to keep up with Cross and he wants to run."

"Go get'm, Mase."

It's odd. I'm not freaking out that I'm basically naked or overthinking that I'm staying with a man in his hotel room. Somehow, I'm calm and everything in the world is right.

THE BABY STEPS that move us forward to places I've never been, could be more than the big step he's holding out on. The tenderness and learning to be together, sharing and taking care of each other. The trust that he will do the right thing without question. Undoubtedly, we have merged in some indefinable way that only those that are truly coupled can grasp.

I stop and question if he's having the same thoughts about me. Does he experience the same emotions and deep connections? Do men not do that? Is this a game to torment the female soul as it cries out for its mate when there are only part-time lovers to be had?

Or is this a question that's answered differently by others? Possibly not a question of male or female, but what each individual creature craves? What they're willing to do in order to have not only the one person who fulfills them, not simply the coupled effect, more than time together—all three and more somehow only when magically aligned by kismet no matter what individual effort is put into it. The love I crave. The hungered desire I hope to have fulfilled.

• • •

As soon as Mase leaves...

Text from Kristina: How long until you're ready?

Text to Kristina: I need to shower.

Text from Kristina: Me, too.

Text to Kristina: 45 minutes?

Text from Kristina: I'll knock when I get there.

I take a long shower. The heat and power of the shower pounding on me relieves everything. I dry off, taking the time to blow dry my hair, and get ready for our day out ending with the game.

Kristina knocks on the door and I open it, "Did you have a good night?"

She stares at me unsure of how to answer, "I don't remember."

I laugh, "Me neither." I tie my hoodie around my waist, grab my purse and my Seals cap, ready for our outing. "Do we have a plan?"

"I figured we could find some place to have lunch on our walk and we need to fix your makeup situation. If we find some cute boutiques, maybe do some clothes shopping."

We take off walking toward the stadium, checking out the architecture and styles of the neighborhood. Window shopping the many charming stores, but none pulling us inside. We walk by a coffee shop with an aroma of cinnamon and apples wafting from its windows and decide it's our destination. Or at least I assume that's what happens when Kristina turns around and walks in. Charming appeal inside and out. We sit at a window table and order coffee while we peruse the menu. The waitress brings us crispy cinnamon apple biscuits with our coffee. After trying the biscuits and reading the half of the menu that's desserts, we decide on a sandwich to share so we can order two desserts to share. We order a chicken pesto grilled cheese with sun-dried tomatoes that comes with a side salad. Then focus on desserts. If the delightful little biscuits are any representation of the dessert, we may need to come back tomorrow to try more.

Kristina starts, "What do you think of the dessert options?"

"Too many choices. What are your top five?"

"Five? You want me to only pick five?"

"If I'm picking one, it's that white chocolate thing."

"That's not really chocolate."

"True, but that's not stopping me. It's some sort of Hawaiian thing with the macadamia nuts and caramel, and dusted in milk chocolate powder with cinnamon and powdered sugar. Is it a bowl of puffs with stuff on it or swimming in the white chocolate?" I imagine myself sitting and staring into a pool of glossy reflective white chocolate and wishing the pool was big enough to dive into.

"Fine, but I'm ordering the apple pie milkshake."

"Are you sure you don't want to try one of the tarts? The homemade ice cream? The snickers pie?"

"Stop! That's why I picked the pie milkshake. We can try the ice cream and the pie, it'll just be all blended together," she holds her head up with her hands and stares down at the table. "I couldn't decide. I went with fruit to balance out your chocolate fat desert."

The food arrives and we eat silently, content and satisfied with every tasty bite. We order our desserts and gaze at the bakery display case from across the room.

"We need to come back here," I demand more than suggest. "Maybe after the game?"

"Chase would love the bakery case. I may need to get a box of baked goods for him."

"You don't want to take that to the game."

"No, not really."

The desserts arrive. It was like dessert soup with dessert dumplings floating in it and washing it down with apple pie. As crazy as that sounds, it was delish. I might've preferred no apple with the other flavors but it was all simply yum.

We walk the rest of the way to the stadium enjoying our time away from home.

Our seats for the game are right behind the visiting dugout. Not our normal behind the home plate, but I imagine those can be hard to get last minute. We're the visiting team. We hadn't considered that when we got dressed this morning. Is that why people have been giving us side-eye all day? We walk through the stadium to our seats, it's like wearing red in a solid sea of black. We stand out.

Cross is leading off and smacks a leadoff double on the first pitch. We both yell, Kristina doesn't usually get to being in the PA booth. Martin is up next and smashes a homer bringing Cross home. Brandt is hitting in the third position with Lucine injured, he takes the pitcher to a full count and walks. Mase steps into the batter's box, "Go Mason!" I yell at the top of my lungs. He hits a triple, bringing in Brandt. There's lots of action and I have to pay attention to keep up.

Balls are flying out of the park for both teams. "This is going to be a high scoring game."

"It's the stadium elevation. Supposedly, that impacts how the balls fly," Kristina adds.

"So, it's a wild card? Anything can happen?"

"Pretty much. Around the league, they say you can't have a big enough lead when you play here."

Who would think the field itself has an impact on the game? Then again, I'm new to this. I watch as ball after ball is moonshot out of the park. The ball carries.

At the end of the 4th inning the score is 10 - 8 Seals and the sky opens suddenly pouring rain and putting the game into rain delay. We find cover to stay dry and wait for details on the delay.

Text from Mase: Nothing yet on the rain delay.

Text from Mase: You should probably get a ride back to the hotel before everybody does.

Text from Mase: Too wet to walk that far.

Text to Mase: We're fine waiting to see how long first.

Text to Mase: We didn't fly to Denver to miss the game.

An hour later there's been no word on the rain delay and it shows no signs of letting up. I turn to Kristina, "What do you think? Should we give up and go back to the hotel?"

"Rain delays can be hours and they still finish the game," she says, her face crooked.

"So, we're staying here and waiting?"

"No, let's go."

I'm not arguing. I can go back to the room and write.

"Uber says it will be here in 14 minutes," Kristina says and I follow her to wherever we're supposed to be meeting the Uber.

Thirty minutes later I'm back in my room ready to take a nap.

Text from Kristina: What are you doing?

Seriously? She just left me.

Text to Kristina: I was going to take a nap.
Text from Kristina: Isn't there something else you want to be doing in Denver?
Text to Kristina: I'm here to celebrate with you and see Mase.
Text from Kristina: Okay.
Text from Kristina: The rain delay is supposed to be over in twenty minutes. You want to go watch the game in the bar?

Bye-bye nap.

Text to Kristina: Sure
Text to Kristina: Can we nap first?
Text from Kristina: Will twenty minutes work?
Text to Kristina: Yes. Thank you.

It's better than nothing.

Exactly twenty minutes later she's banging on my door, "Let's go!"

"Okay! I'll be right there." I get up and wobble to the door with my eyes closed. I let her in, wash my face, and run a brush through my hair. "I'm ready."

"You were really napping?"

"Yea, why?"

"I thought you were doing something else and it was an excuse."

"Nope. Let's go."

The bar is pretty full with the wet weather, but we manage to snag a couple stools at the counter with a clear view of the big screen.

"What are we drinking?" I ask Kristina wondering if its more champagne tonight.

"I'm thinking whiskey shots and coke."

I tap on the bar to get attention.

"What can I get you ladies?"

"Six shots of Jack and two tall cokes should be good to start," I nod at the bartender.

"Coming right up."

Kristina glares at me, "We don't need to drink all the whiskey at once."

We clink our shots and do all of them, one, two, three. Then we happily sip our sodas while we watch the game.

Jones

Walking into the hotel after the game we find our girls sitting at the bar playing cards.

I turn to Cross, "You see our girls over there?"

"Yep."

"What's your bet? I'd say GG is winning."

"I bet buzzed."

As we get closer the buzzed part is obvious and the bartender gets our attention, motioning they are cut off and to get them out of here. Alone they're easy, together they are trouble. A lesson that Cross and I both need to remember.

"Hey GG, how are you doing?"

Her eyes light up, "Hi Mase!" She throws her arms around my neck.

"How about we go to our room?"

"Whatever you want," she gets down off her stool and I hold her to keep her steady. I lead her back to our room with my arm around her.

Three hours later, "Why are you playing video games?" She asks from the bed.

"I like playing video games. I'm trying to build my character to catch up with my girlfriend. And, my girlfriend was passed out."

"I was not."

I stare at her, "The bartender told us you were cut off and to get you two out of there."

She glares at me.

"Do you remember coming up to the room?"

She glances around the room, "Nope."

"Passed out. I carried you from the elevator."

"You didn't strip my clothes off this time."

"I didn't last night. You did. Mostly."

I check my game, "Shit!"

"What's the problem?"

"This guy finds me and blows me up. It's a pain..."

"Right because you have to go back to the beginning and go through everything to get where you are again."

"Exactly."

"Who's the guy?"

"No idea. He started doing it last week. He's sneaky, he just shows up and blows me up."

"Sneaky? What's his name?" she asks.

"PinkyToe or PinkPinkyToe, something like that."

"Do you have another controller with you?"

"Of course, you want to play?"

"Yes." She moves to the floor and sits next to me. Good timing for her to start since I have to regenerate anyway.

"Are you hungry? Would you like to order room service?"

"I have a plan to freeze a pig right now," she says with a determined glint in her eye.

"Maybe some dessert then," I suggest and laugh, unsure

what she's up to. I've seen this focus on her before, the GamerGirl in full force. I wouldn't fuck with her.

"Where does PinkyToe appear?"

"Always about the same place. The Hidden Oasis of Zoran after I defeat the guardian and before I can claim the treasure."

"Asshole probably takes the treasure for himself, too."

"No idea. By then I'm pissed and not paying attention."

"Does he blow you up more than once a night?"

"He's blown me up three times in a night."

"The guy's a pain in my ass. What a stupid name Pink-PinkyToe."

"Let's do this."

The game is easier with her. She's the highest level of wizard and has powers that other characters aren't aware exist. She can basically do anything and take me with her. Which means that she can kill me in a heartbeat, and she has. "Where are you?" I ask. She's not on the screen.

"I'm cloaked. I don't want the PinkPinkyToe character to see me. He won't even detect me if he searches the game for my character."

I stop, "Wait. This guy's your friend?"

"Not exactly. Let's get him to find you and see if I'm right."

We get to the Hidden Oasis of Zoran and she defeats the guardian like he's a mortal. "Are we going to keep going?"

"No. Let's chill for PinkPinkyToe a few minutes. He's not expecting you to get here as quick as we did."

Sure enough he pops in and before he can blow me up he's floating frozen and WizardGG is visible. She circles around him deviously and types a message that shows on the screen:

WizardGG: I'm deciding your fate. Are you attacking what's mine? You're always hiding in a world of make believe where you're safe.

WizardGG: I have cast a spell of amazing power on Jonesin2Kill.

WizardGG: So, Jared aka PinkPinkyToe, I leave the decision of your fate to you. Do you wish that I show pity on you and leave you forever frozen or set you free for Jonesin2Kill to have fun with?

PinkPinkyToe: I beg of you high wizard, I know not what you speak of. Free me now and I will forever be in your debt. I'm merely a beginner at this game of life and I bow to you, your highness.

WizardGG: Silence your lies and hear me. Jonesin2Kill is mine. Do not fuck with me. Do not fuck with what is mine. I will not be as gracious next time. I understand that this may pain you, but I have explained many times to your deaf ears.

The freeze on PinkPinkyToe ends.

```
WizardGG: Jonesin2Kill, please beat
this guy to a pulp with your mace.

Jonesin2Kill: WizardGG, I would rather
claim my treasure and move on from
this waste of my time.

WizardGG: Jonesin2Kill, as you wish.
```

We continue to play the game for another hour. I fall asleep with my wizard in my arms.

CHAPTER FOURTEEN

Michelle

I wake up in the middle of the night and grab my laptop.

I'M HERE in the place that I want to be the most, yet I can't sleep. I've lost touch with reality and made a fool of the one who matters most, yet he rescued me. My past has haunted him and he refuses to bow to the level of the ghost. The light and positivity he sheds is a balance and reminder to move forward and let the negative go. All things do not require punishment, many deserve mercy and understanding.

The place I want to be most is the location where he is. Wherever the one who matters most is, that is my home. I hope to deserve his desire and presence. For he is my love, my balance, and my home.

. . .

I CURL BACK UP NEXT to Mase and hope for dreams of our future to come.

Jones

I wake with GG wrapped around me. It's my favorite thing, the way she melts into me and holds on throughout the night. It's still early, so I kiss her forehead and go back to sleep with her in my arms.

"GG?" I nudge her hoping she'll wake up. No response. I splay my hand on her bare back and pull her closer to me. "GG, let's get out together this morning." She releases a soft whiney noise. "You can come back and nap before the game."

"No I can't. Kristina won't let me." Her eyes are still closed and the blanket's now covering her entire face.

"Tell her no."

"I can't. It's her celebration trip."

I suppose it is. "I want some time with you in Denver and we're losing opportunities."

She pulls the blanket down and gazes at me bright-eyed, "Whatever you want." She smiles and I squeeze her. Her hand creeps up on my chest. "We could do other things and stay right here."

"Like what?" I ask wondering where she's going with this.

"Well, we're down to only underwear. We could take those off."

"Then what?"

"We could rub on each other. No sex of course."

"But we could rub on each other?"

"Yes, and we could kiss."

"We could have breakfast."

"Is that an euphemism for something else?"

"It could be, but I want actual breakfast."

"Then I know just the place," she bounces out of bed directly to the bathroom and the shower turns on.

I open the bathroom door, "Am I allowed in here."

"I'm naked."

"I need to pee."

"That means you'd be naked."

"The shower has a curtain on it, right?"

"Yes."

"Then don't look." I go for it because I can't wait. I rattle the shower curtain on my way out of the bathroom.

"Stop that!"

"Closing the door and leaving you to shower," I vacate the bathroom.

Michelle

What is with him this morning? If he's a morning person it could be a problem. He won't get naked with me, but he'll come into the bathroom while I'm in the shower. Maybe I should've invited him into the shower. I didn't think this through. I didn't bring clothes into the bathroom with me. It's okay. I got this.

I finish my shower quickly, thinking of the coffee shop for breakfast. A towel wrapped like a turban around my hair and another around my body, I walk out of the bathroom with a confident swagger. With my back to Mase, I drop my towel and wrap myself in the soft luxurious robe. I dig through my suitcase for panties, and decide it's a leggings and hoodie morning. It's cold, wet, and possibly still drizzling.

"Is the game postponed?" I ask.

"No. The weather report form the team said it would clear up in time for the game. Limited batting practice and all inside today," he stops and takes me in. "You're going to need something warmer than that hoodie for the game. You'll freeze."

He takes his turn in the bathroom and comes out ready to go in less than ten minutes. I'm still trying to get my hair dry.

He takes my hand and leads me out of our room with his fingers entangled with mine. When we get to the hotel exit he asks, "You have an idea where we should go?"

"Yes, I know the perfect place," and I take the lead almost dragging him down the street. I didn't even read the breakfast menu, but I'm sure it's fabulous.

He's texting with one hand. Then grins, "Carter's getting you my extra players jacket." He pulls me into the corner store, "And we're getting you a few things in here." He grabs a beanie with a matching winter scarf in navy to match the team colors, sherpa-lined insulated gloves, and some knock-off Ugg boots. "Did you bring long underwear?" he asks.

"That wasn't allowed on Kristina's packing list. She also tossed all of my granny panties out."

He drags me through the store until he finds the thermal underwear, "The soft girly ones or the waffle knit ones that will actually keep you warm?" He grabs the waffle knit ones without waiting for my answer. "That should do. Warm from your fingers to your toes." He grabs a couple hand warmers at the register then turns to me, "Should we get stuff for Kristina, too?"

"She gets colder than me. What if Cross already handled it?"

"You're right. Cross will take care of it." He texts and I'm sure he's reminding Cross just in case. What's the worst thing that can happen? She gets cold and we have to go back to the hotel? It's miserable out in the cold anyway. I guess that's his point. Most importantly, he wants me at the game.

We continue up the street until we get to the coffee shop.

"Why are we stopping here?" he asks.

"Use your nose."

He drags me inside and has coffee ordered before I can tell him they will serve it with biscuits. The breakfast menu does not disappoint. I want something warm and hearty. I want too many things. "Do you want to share?"

"I'm kind of hungry for sharing."

"I mean we order two meals and split them, so we can try more stuff."

"Can we get the banana nut pancakes and bacon and hash browns, and an omelet?"

"That's two meals, and yes. Which omelet?"

"When in Denver..."

"Denver Omelet it is."

We share breakfast and walk back to the hotel with packages in tow and his arm around me.

WHEN WE GET BACK to our room he starts getting ready to go to the stadium. "I want to stay here with you all snuggly today. It's cold, dreary and wet out there." He wraps his arms around me, "We could find a movie to watch and crawl back into bed together." He pushes closer and has me backed up to the wall, gazing down at me. He leans in and presses his lips to mine sweetly, then searches my eyes and kisses me again. I could melt right into him. My tummy is all widgey. I've never had butterflies, but my guess is that this is it. I'm fine yet a bit dizzy at the same time. I can't focus and when I'm with him I'm oblivious to everything and everyone else on the planet. I'm heated in my special places and if I checked a mirror, my cheeks and chest are most likely red or splotchy. All the signs, right? I just want him to kiss me again. His hands travel down my body, "Do you know how gorgeous you are? Perfect curves and a beautiful heart." I lean into him. My head tucked under his chin, "There was something about you the night I met you. I've known since then that we belong together." He kisses my forehead, "Let's just be us tonight. They can go do their own thing. Okay?"

"Sounds like you're going to need somebody to warm you up," I gaze up at him happier than I've ever been.

"Definitely, but not somebody—You. Save my spot?"

"Of course." I pull my fingers across his cheeks and give him a peck on the lips, "Make it a win."

"Yes, ma'am!" he replies as he walks out the door.

I WRAP myself in the bed linens with my laptop and write...

MOMENTS like these are memories that I'll never forget. I wonder if he's been this way with anyone else, or if it's just me. I've never been willing to give up a slice of bacon for part of an omelet for anyone else. I'd never give away my last chocolate chip cookie, but the one? I'd save it for him. I want to share everything with him. Is he always protective and thoughtful? Is it me?

MY PHONE RINGS and wakes me up, "Yes, Kristina?"

"Does this sound like Kristina?" Jared says from the other end of the line.

I need to stop answering the phone without checking the caller id. No, I just need to stop answering the phone.

"Slightly deeper voice, but not far off," I poke. "I have to go, getting ready to go to the game. Kristina is waiting."

"She can wait. Or is it someone else who is waiting?"

"Jared, what do you want?"

"I just want to talk. I can't believe you pulled the freeze on me last night."

"I can't believe that you were playing blow up my boyfriend!"

"I'm sure he loved that his girl ran in to rescue him from the PinkyToe," he laughs.

"He's better than me. I wanted to smash you to smithereens. He wants everyone to play and get along. Maybe you should talk to him."

"Is he there?"

"No he's already gone to the stadium."

"Oh, is he one of those guys who goes and hangs out at the stadium, watches batting practice, collects baseball cards, all that?"

"Yes and no," I don't want to tell him who he is.

"Which is it? Yes or no?"

"It doesn't really apply to him. He works there."

"Does he sell tickets? A member of the grounds crew?"

"Usually his position at the stadium is short stop," that ought to do it. "Bye." I hang up.

My phone rings again and I answer, "What else do you want?"

"What did I do?" Kristina asks.

"Sorry. Nothing. Jared's an asshole."

"Understood. What did the asshole want?"

"He never said. He didn't like that I froze him out on Legends of Fantasy last night. He's been bullying Mase, so any time you see Jared playing blow him up."

"Done. I've always wanted to blow him up," Kristina laughs. "Are we going to the game?"

"Yes, should we make sure there's not a rain delay?"

"Already did, scheduled to start on time."

"Come over when you're ready. I need ten minutes."

"Okay."

I put the layers of warm on. The new boots are cozy. I tie my hoodie around my waist until I need it.

Kristina bangs on the door and I open it. "What's with the snow gear?" she asks.

"Mase doesn't want me to get cold."

"You're adorable in a Stay Puft Marshmallow Man sort of way," she giggles. "But, I'm sure you're warm and comfortable."

I roll my eyes as we walk out the door and head to the stadium.

Jones

I hear her voice as soon as she gets to her seat. The happiness in her tone cuts straight through to my ears. I walk out on the field and find her chatting with Kristina. I wave and her beautiful smile shines. It's time for the game to start and the whole team is huddled in the dugout. I've got Michelle on my mind. I want to be with her, not in the dugout with a bunch of dudes.

The National Anthem plays and everything is off and running like clockwork.

Colorado's pitcher is on fire. Fourteen strikeouts in six innings. The players who have got on base can't get past first. 2-0 Colorado and it's starting to look like rain.

Michelle

The game is moving along, but nothing that keeps my interest. Mase has made a few good plays, but the Seals have hardly gotten any hits. At least I'm warm. Kristina has been sitting next to me shivering for an hour. You can only buy so many cups of hot coffee to warm your hands. I offered her one of my gloves but she declined.

"It's starting to sprinkle. Why don't we go back to the hotel? You're freezing."

"It's only the 8th inning."

"We're losing 3-0.We can't hit this guy!"

"I refuse to give up. Anything can happen here. 3 runs are nothing."

Maybe it was Kristina's hope or repayment for sitting in the cold or mother nature apologizing for the rain, but the unhittable pitcher slid on the wet mound and turned his ankle. He had help hopping to the dugout. There was a delay in the action while a pitcher got warm, but then? Home run city! By the end of the 8th inning the score was 8-5 Seals—every Seal had come up to bat. The 9th was a battle of the closers. A one inning pitcher's duel, and Super D prevailed with the save.

I turn to Kristina, "Can we go where it's warm now?"

"Yes, please," she shivers.

We walk quickly back to the hotel and when we get in the elevator, "You should take a hot shower to help warm up."

"That's a great idea and then I'm crawling into bed to wait for my personal heater to get home," her smile so bright it was starting to defrost her.

"Have a good night," I leave her for the evening and wonder how mine will go.

Text from Mase: Would you like to go out tonight or order in?
Text to Mase: Whatever you want.
Text from Mase: I want you.
Text to Mase: I'm here waiting for you.
Text from Mase: On my way.

Twenty minutes later, there's a knock on the door, "Special Delivery." I recognize the voice and open the door to find Mase with his hands full. He's got two big bags full of food and a dozen red roses. "I brought Italian," he says. He hands me the roses and give me a quick kiss.

I smell the roses, "Thank you, Mase."

CHAPTER FIFTEEN

Jones

I'm not looking forward to today. I've loved having GG here with me and she's going home. I get to go home late tonight. At least the home stand is a long one. More nights with my girl.

It's an early game today, but Michelle and Kristina have to be at the airport about the same time that we report to the stadium. Cross and I walk them down to their ride and see them off before we walk to the stadium. We pick up coffee to-go from the coffee shop and Cross goes nuts over the baked goods. He bought enough for the whole team and sent a package to Sherry.

You can always tell it's a getaway game by the way the team plays, especially if the team is going home. We like to be home. We prefer our home club house and usually play better at home, but we also like being with our women and sleeping in our own beds. Sleep can get scarce on the road. If it's the nights alone or a funky mattress or the room temperature just ain't right, home is always better. Lately, I've been thinking about Michelle's place. I like it there. I understand she has a roommate. I'm not planning to move in. I just want to be there with her. Then again her roommate is gone a lot, at least when the team is home. Anyway, my point is that the games tend to be quick because we have our minds on other things. I guess I made that point without saying so.

SEALS WON 10-2. Seno was keeping the pitcher on task and kept the pace up. He misses home more than any of the rest of us. Seno and Tommy Grace are always a great battery. Grace pitched the whole game in 92 pitches. The Colorado runs were both homers. The stadium has a life of its own, you can't control everything. Holding them to two is outstanding. Seno ruled today, all ten of our runs were off his bat—homers and runs batted in. I told you, he wants to go home.

***

I WALK into the players garage and wonder why I was in a hurry to get home. There's nobody waiting for me.

> Text to GG: Where are you?
> Text to GG: Should I go to your place?

I get in my truck and drive home. I get unloaded and shower, trying to give her time to respond. No reply.

MY PHONE RINGS as I'm crawling into bed, "Hello?"

"Hi," she yawns. "Sorry, Colorado wore me out. I've been asleep since I got home."

I smile, "Road trips can definitely wear you down."

"I'm glad you're home."

"Me, too."

"Get some rest, it's back to the grind tomorrow."

"I miss you, GG. I wanted to stay with you tonight."

"I want to be with you, too. But, I think it makes it harder."

"How does it make it harder?"

"Everything is more tempting when it is in reach."

She's not wrong. "Goodnight, GG."

"Goodnight Mase."

***

The next day...

Text from GG: Good luck at the game today.

Text from GG: I'm not going to make it.

Text from GG: I'm playing catch up on work stuff.

I call her on my drive home, but she doesn't answer. "Call me please. I miss you."

My phone rings after I get home, "Hello?"

"I miss you, too. How was the game?"

"We won by the skin of our teeth. I hit a homer and a double."

"I'm proud of you. Best hitter in the league."

I chuckle, "That's the goal. Should I come over?"

"Not tonight, I'm going to be up working all night. In fact, I better get back to it."

"Okay. Goodnight GG."

"Goodnight Mase."

***

And the next day...

Text from GG: I'm trying to make it to the game today.

Text from GG: I might be late.

Text from GG: Make it a win!

She showed up in her seat during the 3rd inning and cheered her heart out every time I did anything. I love that. She was gone as soon as the game was over.

She must be busy. I didn't call her.

***

The day after that...

Text to GG: Good morning.

Text to GG: Would you go out to dinner with me tonight?

Hours later...

Text from GG: Just woke up.

Text from GG: Can't go out tonight.

Text from GG: Working on getting to the game.

Text to GG: Early game today. Starts in 40 minutes.

Text from GG: Okay. Well, make it a win!

***

And the day after that...

Text to GG: Typically boyfriends and girlfriends spend time together.
Text to GG: I don't understand.

***

The following day...

I call her before I get out of bed and leave her a message:

Good morning. I knew you wouldn't answer for two reasons. One, you're sleeping; and two you haven't answered a call from me in a week. I've been patient. I understand that you have a life that doesn't center around me or baseball. I would like to be part of your life and right now I'm not.

***

It's been a week...

I saw more of my girl on the road than at home. Maybe I don't exist. When I'm with her everything is right. There's no doubt that she's into me. When she's near me I'm confident that she loves me the same way I love her. We haven't said the words, but they're just words. Our interactions, our electricity, us alone and quiet together, no words mean as much.

***

I'm done. If this is a game, GamerGirl just lost.

This woman completes me and frustrates me at the same time. I've never allowed a fury like this to take me over. She's mine yet she doesn't respond. She's mine yet she can't manage to get to my games. She's mine yet I can't reach her for hours at a time. I've been patient for weeks. I'm done with this. She's probably sitting at home with her laptop and if she won't acknowledge me, then I'm done giving her the option. I'm going to find her and force her to face me. If she's done with me, then she can tell me to my face. If she's not then she needs to explain herself.

I leave the stadium in the 7th inning, unable to focus on the game. I text Kristina...

Text to Kristina: Your roommate isn't responding to me.

Text to Kristina: I'm going to find her

Text from Kristina: I think she's home.

Text from Kristina: There's an extra key taped to the back of the welcome sign that's hanging on the door.

Text from Kristina: Go get her!

If she's home why is she ignoring me? Why isn't she here?

I drive to her place and run up the stairs, too impatient to wait for the elevator. I knock and there's no answer. I check the door and it's locked. I get the extra key and use it, locking the door behind me. There's water running somewhere in the apartment. I check her room to find her laptop open, but she's not there. I shouldn't, but I sit down and read what's on the screen...

... HE FINALLY TAKES *me as his after waiting for so long. Shoving his huge hard cock up into me as he holds me up against the shower wall. The hot water falling over us. I slick his thick dark hair back out of his eyes and kiss his neck, needing as much of him as I can get and fearing that I'll never get the chance to have him again. The journey to us has been a long one. My unspoken love and desire for him boiling. We belong together. I believe him every time he says the words. His magic words. I may not be worthy of his patience. The heathen in me unable to wait for him and have daily contact, forced to write my words to express my desires. Have I pushed him away? Will it be our breaking point? I hope I haven't ruined us. Everything with us has always been more...*

This is what she's been writing? I'm over it. I storm to the bathroom searching for her to find her naked in the shower. I strip quickly and throw the shower curtain back exposing her wet naked body.

"Mase!" she squeals.

I step into the shower and press my body to hers as I claim her mouth with mine. Spreading her legs with mine and rubbing my thigh against her sex. I take her chin in my hand and make her focus on me, "Do you see me? You make me crazy. I need you. I've been trying to do what I thought is best for us and you're hiding from me, writing what you want in silence. There will be no more of that. Is that what you really want? You want me to fuck you against the shower wall? You can't be patient for me? Wait until I can control myself and not want to take you over and over for days?" Her eyes get big with uncertainty. I take in the vision of her completely nude for the first time. She's beautiful. Her soft and creamy skin, like porcelain. Her curves are those of a woman that many only ever dream of. Her luscious, full, pink lips inviting and full of sinful thoughts. Droplets of water dotting her eyelashes like diamonds to highlight her telling blue eyes. I kiss her hard. I'm out of control. This isn't how I want it to be the first time. It's what she wants. "Is this what you want? I need you to say the words. Tell me you're writing what you want or tell me what you want." I've waited this long. I want us to be special. I believe in my heart that we belong together. We're not just sex. I've been there before, it's nothing but a meaningless waste of time. "Damn it! Do you understand how much you mean to me?" My tone is heavy and vicious. I hope I never use it again. "You mean more to me than anyone else ever has. YOU, Michelle. You are everything to me. How many times have I told you everything is more with us? Maybe I should've explained. Maybe you didn't understand my intentions. Everything with you has been more than it has ever been before. I'm not talking about sex, but I'm sure that will be too. I'm talking about the simple things. Holding hands. Sharing a meal. Walking together. Holding you. Sleeping with you. Games with you... pretty much anything and everything with you. The most basic things you can think of—it all means a thousand times more because it's with you. It's us. If there is an us." I turn around and face the wall, lost when I thought my world had been found. All of this and she has said nothing. I turn back around to find her crying.

"I don't know how to do this!" She sobs, "It's never been real before. Not a game, but I didn't have any experience to compare what real is." She tries to breathe, "I don't give a fuck about baseball or athletes of any kind." She shakes, "I was only there to push my roommate... But you, you grabbed onto me and claimed me with a whisper in my ear. Fuck! I'm a sucker for words. I always have been, but your whisper called to me with sweet yet masculine sincerity and pulled at my heartstrings. I'm the girl in this relationship. I'm not supposed to be doing this. I can't believe you're here naked in my shower yelling at me and you must've broke into my apartment to do it. Asshole! I love you!" she yells at me with her whole heart.

I grab her wet body and hold it against mine, my arms wrapped around her. I bury my nose in her hair and absorb the shocks of her sobbing. "I love you more than I can explain. There's no love that compares to ours." I move us under the shower and let the warm water wash over us, rinse away our sadness and misunderstanding. "We have to communicate," I gaze into her eyes. "That has to start now. Someday I'm going to marry you. I will give you everything that you want. You make me want to be the best hitter in the league. You make me better." I search her eyes, "Tell me what you want."

"You."

I kiss her with my entire being. Our souls make contact and fuse together. I drag a finger across her seam and she kisses me harder. Her hand grasps my ready cock and I'm charged by her handling. I drop to my knees, kissing from her belly to her clit. I hold her to me with my arms around her waist. Her back arched and body reacting to my actions. I kiss my way up to her breasts, caressing one with each hand and licking her nipples. There's so much I want to do, but I need to be inside her. This time everything else can wait. I lift her against the wall, nibbling on her lips and neck. She wraps her legs around me instinctively. My hard cock grazing her bare sex. I whisper, "Are you ready for us?"

"Yes, Mase. Please," she whimpers.

Slowly I push into her, giving her only part of me and she cries out. I hold her tight, "Okay, GG?"

"Uh huh."

I slide further into her slick heat, and pull back out.

"Please Jones," she purrs.

I shove into her completely. Her heaven made for me, squeezing my rock-hard cock. I stroke into her faster. I've been waiting for her and she's so much more than I'd hoped. She reacts to my every move and holds onto me, digging her fingers into my back as she screams out my name and convulses wildly on me. "I love you, Michelle," I proclaim as she takes me with her.

Michelle

He holds me close, not ready to release me. Our lightning current still surging through my body. It's never been like this. I need more of him. My cheek resting on his shoulder, "Mase, stay with me."

"I'm not going anywhere. You better tell your roommate you have a permanent visitor."

I laugh, "She's never home when the team's home anyway."

He turns the water off and grabs a towel, wrapping it around me. He reaches for another towel, quickly drying his hair and wrapping it around his waist. I towel dry my hair and wrap it up like a turban. He gazes into my eyes and grins as he picks me up and carries me off to my bedroom. I squeal in pleasure. We lose the towels and crawl into bed together naked.

"I'm on the wrong side of the bed. I've decided I like the other side better." I climb on top of him and lie there as if I'm rolling to the other side. I press my sex against his thigh and tease his cock, while I kiss him open-mouthed.

His hands grasp my waist, "I think you should stay right there."

I slide back, pushing onto his hard cock and rocking. I sit upright and grind on him. His hands on my hips, fingers spread across my ass. He's guiding me, moving with me. I'm so full yet I can't help myself. I need more. I bounce on him, balancing with my hands on his chest. "Mase?"

"I'm with you, you're unbelievable. Why was I such a stupid man thinking we should wait?"

"You said it would make it better, did it?"

He grins, "I may have done something right."

He flips me over and takes control, stroking slowly. He

rubs my clit and I'm instantly on edge ready to explode. "Not yet GG." He pushes into me harder and faster. I lose control, tightening around his huge cock. He falls with me.

He rolls to his side and gathers me next to him. I'm content, for the first time in weeks I have direction and my scattered thoughts are gone.

"Tell me you're mine," he says.

"I've been yours since the night we met and I always will be."

THE END

PLAYLIST

"1950" by King Princess
"Different" by The Academics
"The Last of the Real Ones" by Fall Out Boy
"Hold Me Tight or Don't" by Fall Out Boy
"The One" by Kodaline
"Something So Strong" by Crowded House
"Chasing Cars" by Snow Patrol
"Thrills" by Donna Missal
"Body Like a Back Road" by Sam Hunt
"Simplify" by Young the Giant
"Champion" by Bishop Briggs
"Goodbye My Lover" by James Blunt

FALLING FOR PRINCE

AN ALL ABOUT THE DIAMOND ROMANCE SHORT STOP

FALLING FOR PRINCE

"Are you going to your reunion or not?" My best friend, Faye, is exasperated with me before our morning coffee has had time to brew.

"I've..." apparently it isn't my turn yet.

"Sindy, there really isn't a choice here. The way I see it, you are going. There. Decision made. And, you're wearing your new dress design that just came in. The peacock blue will make your eyes shine. Oh! And those T-strap platform heels. The nude color."

"I'm putting my foot down on that one. If I go, I'm not wearing those shoes."

"You'd probably fall anyway," she glares at my ballet shoe covered feet.

"I can wear heels," I feign conviction.

"Can you wear heels and make it home in one piece? There's going to be dancing, mingling, lots of time on your feet."

"Forget it. I'm not going. Make the pancakes already. I'm hungry and the coffee is waiting." I turn to tend to the coffee, adding everything to it and turning it into a sweet creamy delight.

Faye rambles on, under her breath, "Nobody is ever going to see your fabulous designs the way you intend them to be if you don't show them. Seriously, nobody can do them justice other than you. Nobody has your figure. What I'd do to be six inches taller and somehow appear waif-like yet eat everything I want..." She drifted off and came back with a vengeance, "But, I've seen your ass, so don't think you're hiding anything. I know the truth. I saw cellulite and at least an extra inch of fat on your hips."

I start to spit out my coffee at the observation, but change my mind and add more cream. Fuck it. "Are you done yet?"

"Are you going to your reunion?" she stares at me expectantly.

"If I say yes are you done?"

"Yes."

"I'm going to my reunion."

"Did you agree to get me to shut up?"

"Yes, and we have to be at the boutique in an hour and you haven't made a single pancake yet. Make the pancakes, woman!"

Walking into our boutique, the peacock colored dress is calling to me. It stands out on the rack. It needs to be worn. It hasn't been unwrapped or tried on yet to make sure the seamstress got the measurements right. It's the only one of it's design, but we will have more made in different sizes if this one is accurate and fits as I expect it will. It's tea length, hitting me slightly below my knee. A slim A-line skirt with a deep cut halter on top. Metallic silver cord laces through the top and ties around the neck for the halter top, as well as around my waist as an accent. What was Faye thinking with the nude shoes? Silver will be perfect. I grab my silver ballet slippers from behind the counter and disappear into the fitting room with the dress.

"Ahem, not the ballet slippers." I open the door and she hands me a glistening pair of silver T-strap stilettos.

"Those are gorgeous. Perfect for this dress."

"But?"

"But, I don't wear heels. There's not a definition in the dictionary next to the word klutz anymore, it's simply a photo of me."

"Fine. I don't want to spend another night in the emergency room anyway."

I laugh, "Those were some hot docs last time."

"Maybe you should wear the heels," she laughed at herself so hard she turned red.

The dress is perfect. I hang it back up and spend the afternoon working on new designs. The quiet time allowing memories of high school to frolic in my head. I start to wonder about old friends, old boyfriends, and guys I was into. Will the cheerleaders all hang out together at our reunion and do they still have the perfect 36-24-36 figure? I wonder if that bitch, Jane, is still a bitch. I bet Marissa took over her mother's bakery. Are the jocks still paired up with the pep squad? Will the nerds be skinny and have tape on their glasses? I remember this one guy from high school who talked to me everyday, Kenneth. He was tall and lanky. His hair was always cut way too short. Always nervous to talk to me, but he didn't give up. I never understood why he was nervous. I'm not anything special, he simply wasn't my type. I guess it will be nice to catch up with everybody, and it's a perfect occasion to wear my new design.

Reunion day is here. Faye is covering the boutique. I've had it on my mind for the last month and I'm anxious to catch up with everyone. It's a two-hour drive to my hometown and I'm making a day of it. I'm stopping at my mom's house to take her out to lunch and then I'll go back to get ready there. I don't want to walk into my ten-year reunion in a wrinkled dress.

Mom is always happy when I visit and, as usual, dad is out of town for work. Everything is fine at home. I've been distracted by the reunion all day. Mom is excited to see my new design and loves that I decided to wear it tonight. Well, Faye decided I'd wear it.

I start to get ready and dump my bag to find my silver ballet slippers with a note pinned to them:

Please don't wear us. We need a night off.
~~ballet slippers

Of course, it was in Faye's writing. I get a text message, speak of the devil...

Faye - Are you getting ready?
Faye - The dress is beautiful.
Sindy - Yes. Read the note from my ballet slippers.
Faye - Interesting. What shoes are you wearing tonight?
Sindy - Haven't decided.

A photo pops through of my favorite fuzzy slippers with a butcher knife on top of them.

Faye - The silver T-strap stilettos are in your bag. Wear them or your slippers die.

Crazy! She means it. Last time I played this game with her my favorite jeans became shorts.

Sindy - I'll send photos.

I shake my head as I finish getting ready and leave the heels in the box until the last possible moment.

I walk into my mom's living room with my metallic heels dangling off my fingers, my golden blonde hair loose down around my shoulders, and a light spattering of makeup on my face.

"Give me a twirl. Let's check out this design. It's pretty, but not as beautiful as the girl in it," she says proudly and kisses my cheek. "I've always loved that color on you, makes your eyes pop."

"Thanks, mom."

"Have fun tonight. Remember you can always come back here for the night, but I'm not expecting you. I do have the ingredients for your favorite biscuits and gravy to cook for breakfast, just in case." She always does. Biscuits from scratch and sawmill gravy are always available at mom's kitchen. Considering the extra inch of fat on my hips Faye pointed out, I should probably avoid it.

"I'm sure I will. Should be entertaining if nothing else." I give her a quick hug and head out the door.

A FEW WEEKS ago I wasn't sure I wanted to go to my reunion at all, now I'm excited about it. I keep thinking of more classmates who I'd like to see. There was this adorable basketball player I used to sit in the gym and watch out of the corner of my eye during his practices. What about Eddie who had the locker above mine senior year? Or Tina who had the locker right next to me for three years? What did Tony end up doing after high school without me there to do his math for him? The closer I got, the more popped into my head.

I arrive at the venue and cruised the parking lot in search of a close parking space. When I say I'm a klutz, I mean it. I need the least number of steps between me and the door. No obstacles or potholes of any kind would be best. The worst part? I'm aware of it and I'm going to wear the shoes anyway. As much as I say I don't wear heels, I refuse to sacrifice fashion. Faye swears it's because I'm meant to marry a doctor.

I slide into my heels and grasp my car door securely as I stand with doe-like grace. I grab my wristlet pouch and walk the short distance across the well-maintained parking lot with confidence. If nothing else, I'm fashionable, independent, and haven't put on fifty pounds since high school.

I get to the hotel entry and the whole valet area is cobblestone. Fuck. It's a constant obstacle I can't avoid. Shit. I should've valet parked. I don't have the money for it, but it's better than wasting the fifty bucks I spent on my ticket to the event because I never manage to make it the last 100 feet to get there.

I stop at the edge of the cobblestone and inspect it. It's not that bad. This is stupid. I've been walking almost my whole life, well from the age of one and not during the eight weeks it took my broken leg to heal when I fell putting skis on, or the three months it took my foot to heal when I fell stepping off of a curb, or the three weeks I was on crutches while my sprained knee healed after I fell climbing stairs, or... Okay, maybe take a year off for injuries.

I gaze down at the cobblestone and quietly tell myself, "I will give you all of my attention as I walk across you. You will be the center of my existence. All I ask is that you take care of me and don't let me fall. Please." I take a deep breath as I step onto the cobblestone and it's not bad. Not slippery. Not as uneven as I expected. I can do this. I lift my head confidently and stride across the valet area, gracefully moving through the cars. I'm almost there, I've got this. A gorgeous man is walking up to the door the same time I am. Wavy, thick brown hair, crisp white button up shirt taut across his muscular chest, beautiful tan, warm amber eyes, at least six foot two, and a tapered waist that I'm sure is highlighted by an Adonis belt.

Shit! I'm down. Directly on my ass. Foot underneath me. It hurts, it hurts, it hurts. No tears, can't have tears, I have makeup on. Fucking cobblestone. *"You said you'd give me all of your attention. I'm not good enough for you or what?"* Never make promises to anything or anyone unless you're going to keep it, karma will make sure you get yours, or maybe I'm just a klutz. Everything will be fine as long as I didn't damage the dress. I've got this. I can get up by myself on cobblestone in 4" heels. I plant my hands firmly on the ground and unfold my body from what I imagine is a mangled pile in a spotlight for everyone to stop and stare at. As I realize that I cannot put a single ounce of weight on my left ankle, a pair of Havane Louboutin Mortimers appear in front of me. We're in the outskirts of Cleveland. Nobody wears those shoes here. Who has $800 for shoes?

Strong hands reach around me, lifting me up off the dreaded cobblestone, "Please allow me to help you." His voice hits me right in my gut, something is familiar. "Hold on." I tamp my natural instinct to insist he put me down immediately. It's the gorgeous man and he smells delicious, hints of citrus yet warm and masculine.

I reach my arms around his neck, "Thank you."

Our eyes meet and his eyes brighten, "Sindy Dearinger! You don't recognize me, do you?"

"It's been at least ten years. I probably won't remember anyone." Trying to think quick because I want more of this hottie.

"Imagine this: skinny with glasses, less hair, wanted you all through high school," he blushes.

I examine this strong, confident man closely. Nothing. He carries me into the hotel and through the lobby. There are signs providing direction to our reunion, but he sits down on a bench with me in his lap and pulls something out of his pocket. "Maybe this will help," he hands me his high school ID.

Oh my god. It's Kenneth! He's the size of two Kenneths, in a hot muscular way "Kenneth, I can't believe it's you!"

"I go by KC now," he grins at my reaction. He runs his hand down each of my legs, unbuckles my shoes and slides them off of me gently. Paying careful attention to when I wince, and trying not to cause me pain. He buckles my shoes together and places his warm hand on the spot that hurts, somehow soothing me. "Are you ready for the reunion?"

"I was, but I'm not really up for it now."

"Oh no, you're here—you are going." He picks me back up and carries me through the hotel convention area toward our reunion.

"You could just take me to my car. I'm parked in the lot. It's probably closer than the conference room we're supposed to be meeting at."

"We are going to the reunion. Sindy Dearinger, you're

my date for the evening and I'm not giving you a choice like I did in high school."

I giggle. I'm not arguing. I love his confidence, and, well… it's not like I can run away. Besides, only a dumb girl would turn this hottie down. I'm not a dumb girl.

Or, maybe I am. The more I talk to him. The more I have his hard body against mine. The more I want him. I hobble around the room catching up with old friends and enjoying the cheerleaders 40-42-44 figures. The jocks who are already losing their hair and the still good-looking pep squad who are stuck married to them. I was happy to learn Tony married an accountant, and didn't find my locker mates, but there were others I was happy to chat with. The whole time my eyes are on Kenneth as he works the room and everyone knows him. Everyone knows KC Prince, the All-Star third baseman who was recently traded to the San Diego Seals. Fuck he's hot. I'm out of here. I beat myself up mentally as I limp my way to my car. Such a dumb girl.

THE DRIVE HOME reminds me how happy I am with my decision to buy an automatic car. I couldn't have driven myself home if I had to deal with a clutch. My ankle is killing me and letting it hang there while I drive the two hours home doesn't help. It's swollen and feels tight. I can't walk on it. I dial Faye.

"Hello?" Oozing with irritation.

"Hey, would you please help me into the building?"

"What did you do now? Are you okay?"

"Well, I don't think I need a doctor. Sorry. I'll do better next time."

"Stay in your car, I'll be there in two minutes." I don't

have to see her to know she's shaking her head and judging me.

I open my door and turn in my seat, letting my feet hang out the door while I watch for Faye to rescue me. She appears like my fairy godmother with a pair of crutches in hand, always prepared and ready to take care of me. My wristlet hanging around my wrist, I pull myself up on the crutches as Faye assures I'm steady and holds my car door for me.

"I've got your duffle bag. Anything else I should grab from your car? Where are your shoes?" She asks helpfully.

Crap. "I forgot my shoes."

"If you didn't want to wear them, you could've sacrificed your slippers," she crosses her arms and glares at me.

"Hold on. First, are my slippers still intact?" It could go either way.

"For now," She adds a toe tap to her stance.

"I think my current condition proves that I wore the silver stilettos," I glare back at her wide-eyed. "Hands off my slippers."

She reconsiders her plans to decimate my favorite creature comfort, "Fine, let's get you inside gimpy."

It's been almost a week since the reunion and a day hasn't past without thinking about KC. I haven't said a word about it to Faye because I don't need her opinion. I've been watching the baseball highlights for San Diego, trying to catch a glimpse of him and damn he looks good in those pants. The way they hug his thighs and show the curve of his ass, I could watch him all day. I should never have left without getting his number. Maybe I should email the reunion organizer and ask for his contact info. I don't want to be needy. Forget it. If he was interested, he would've found me.

Faye finds me pouting in my office. "Who is he?" She says as she sets the crystal vase of long stem red roses on my desk. "I knew there was a guy. You've been pouty all week."

I glare at her and ignore her as I grab the card, it reads:

Sindy—I never thought going to my reunion would have an impact on me, but it did. I can't stop thinking about you. I'll be in town next weekend with the team, we're playing the Cleveland Cowboys Friday, Saturday, and Sunday. I hope you can come, I sent an envelope with a ticket for you. I'd love to see you again. Here's my number, please call me.—KC (*Kenneth*)

"Alright already! You're beaming! Who is he and why haven't you told me about him?" Faye spouts impatiently.

"KC Prince."

Her jaw drops, "The baseball player?"

Of course she'd recognize his name, "Yep."

"How did that happen?"

"Remember when I told you about that nerdy guy, Kenneth, who found me and talked to me everyday in high school?"

"Yea."

"Kenneth is KC Prince."

"What the utter fu...?"

I shake my head, still not believing it myself, "He doesn't look the same at all and he's gained confidence. Beyond hot."

With a smile crossing her lips, "And he still wants you."

"Maybe. I mean, I guess he could," trying not to show my excitement.

"Roses in an expensive vase like that? He's interested."

"I suppose." She smacks her forehead at my self-esteem lacking response. I grin at her, "I'm going to the baseball game this weekend."

"At least you can wear your tennis shoes."

"Smart-ass."

I call him immediately. I thank him for the beautiful roses and apologize for running out without saying goodbye. I blame it on the pain and don't give up my desire.

I WALK into the stadium and a short bald man approaches me, "Sindy?"

"Yes," I answer hesitantly.

"Hi, I'm Carter. KC asked me to meet you and escort you to your seat. First, you need the proper attire," he grins and hands me a baseball cap with a Seal on the front and Prince embroidered on the back, then a jersey with the name Prince and the number 7 on it. He watches me as I put them on and smiles, "Much better. Let me show you to your seat."

I follow as he rattles on about baseball and how excited KC is that I'm at the game tonight. He leads me down behind home plate, "Here's your seat." He hands me an envelope, "This is from KC and my number is on the envelope if you need anything."

"Thank you," I say politely as I absorb everything that's happened and wave at him as he leaves me in the stands. My seat is in the front row, directly behind home plate—an amazing view of the field. I open the envelope and find a note:

Sindy—I hope you enjoy the game. I'd love it if you'd hang out for me after the game and go out to dinner with me.—Yours, Kenneth

I'm not disappearing on him this time. I smile to myself and settle in for the game. He waves at me when he runs out onto the field and I giggle like a schoolgirl. His uniform fits him perfectly and moves with him as he plays the game with a mix of ease and intensity. When it's finally his turn to bat, he turns to me and winks before he steps into the batter box. He stands with the bat in his hands, holding it up at his shoulder with a slight bend at his hips and knees. He's focused on the pitcher, waiting for the release of the ball. His body almost dances as he prepares for the delivery and he doesn't swing. The umpire calls a ball and the process repeats, but this time he smacks the ball to right field and runs for first base. I'm instantly on my feet, cheering for him and hoping the fielder doesn't catch the ball. It's over his head and rattles into the right field corner. I yell louder as he turns at second base and goes for third. "Run, KC! Wooooooo!" The ball gets thrown to third and he beats it sliding in, safe on third base and oh so dirty. I'm clapping loud, "KC! Wooooooo!" The smile on my face broad, I'm proud to be here cheering for him. I love the dirt from his knees up, outlining his protruding features. His hair is a mess and sweat is building at his brow. The epitome of sexy.

I watch his intensity as he steps off the base, slowly edging closer to home plate. His stance wide, with his hands resting on his bent knees. He's focused on every move the pitcher makes, while he communicates with his teammate, Seno, in the batter's box. Seno is making the Cowboys pitcher throw as many pitches as he can and making sly gestures to KC. The lady sitting next to me is in Seal's gear from head to toe and yelling, "Work it, baby! Show these guys how we play ball in San Diego!" He turns toward her and grins, blowing a kiss her direction. Fourteen pitches in to the at bat, the pitcher is frustrated and getting sloppy. Seno jumps back to avoid being hit by the pitch and the ball bounces off the backstop. I hear a loud whistle out of nowhere and Seno is waving his arm around, staying back from the plate as KC makes a run for it and steals home.

KC and Seno high-five as he crosses the plate and Seno asks him rhetorically, "Why do we do crazy shit when we've got new women here?"

"You always seem too happy to help, captain," he yells back as he smiles at me and walks into the dugout.

Me? Did he just show-off for me?

The rest of the game goes smooth. He plays third base with ease and he doesn't let the ball get by him. He dives for it, jumps for it, blocks it—whatever it takes to win the game. He was no slouch at bat either. He walked twice and hit a double, pushing two of his teammates around to score. That Seno guy hit a home run with two guys on base and the lady next to me went ballistic. His team won 7-2.

As soon as the game is over Carter appears next to me, "Did you enjoy the game?"

"Yes, it was fun and who'd complain about a win?" I hadn't realized I was smiling from ear to ear until now.

He grins back at me, "Good, KC asked me to get you. Will you come with me?" I get up and follow Carter who is moving quickly, but I can keep up with his short legs easily. He leads me through a corridor and into a suite with a view of the field as the stadium lights go off. He nods and leaves immediately.

KC is here waiting for me. The fireworks start to shoot off on the field in big beautiful bursts, as he walks toward me still covered in dirt, "I can't take a chance on you leaving again." He gazes into my eyes as he reaches for my hand and pulls me in to meet him halfway. His eyes are hooded and I'm mesmerized by his inviting lips. He holds me close with his warm hand on my back and my eyes flutter closed as his lips meet mine. His hand drops to the small of my back and his other hand finds the nape of my neck, threading his fingers into my hair as he controls the kiss. His soft lips claim me, I taste him for the first time and need more. He pulls on my lower lip seductively, placing his hand on my cheek and pressing his lips to mine again, this time open-mouthed. I've never had this reaction to a kiss or anything else. The fire burns through me from his mere presence. His hard, sweaty body against me, I'm light-headed from the interaction and he's what's keeping me on my feet. He pulls back, eyes shining at me as he waits for a response.

I need more of him. I smile uncontrollably and reach up, nibbling on his neck as I find my way to his lips. I kiss him sweetly and repeatedly. My hands explore his muscular back. I want this man. I exhale my warm breath at is ear and whisper, "I didn't know you were the one."

His body relaxes, "I've always known it was you."

ABOUT THE AUTHOR

USA Today Bestselling Author Naomi Springthorp is a born and raised Southern California girl. She's a baseball freak who supports her team all season long and blatantly admires the athletes in those pants. Music has always been part of her life and she believes everything has a soundtrack. She loves her feline fur babies, though they're not quite sure what to do with her.

She writes Baseball Romance, Romantic Comedies, 90s Throwbacks, and Contemporary Romance--all with heat and sometimes a little sweet.

Join her newsletter at
www.naomispringthorp.com/sign-up

facebook.com/naomithewriter
instagram.com/naomispringthorp
amazon.com/author/naomispringthorp
tiktok.com/@naomispringthorp
bookbub.com/profile/naomi-springthorp
goodreads.com/naomithewriter
twitter.com/naomithewriter

ALSO BY NAOMI SPRINGTHORP

An All About the Diamond Romance

The Sweet Spot

King of Diamonds

Diamonds in Paradise

Star-Crossed in the Outfield

The Closer

Falling for Prince

Up to Bat

Stalking Second

Betting on Love

Just a California Girl

Jacks

Strings Attached

Standalone Novels & Novellas

Muffin Man

Finally in Focus

Confessions of an Online Junkie

The Panty Thief

Cookbook

The Naughties Family Cookbook

Anthologies & Box Sets

Sacrifice for Love

Storybook Pub

Storybook Pub Christmas Wishes

Young Crush

Storybook Pub 2

Hate to Want You

Tricks, Treats, & Teasers

Caught Under the Mistletoe

Hopelessly Devoted

Ruff Love

Craveable CockTales

STALKING SECOND

What happens when you put together a numbers girl, a second baseman, and night vision goggles? **You're Stalking Second.**

The difference between surveillance and being classified as a stalker? Surveillance sounds a lot nicer.

Binoculars or night vision goggles? Either one could ruin her life.

The one thing post-graduate student Maggie didn't consider the stats on: How much risk would she take for a crush?

Second baseman Drew Brandt is a hometown boy who just moved into his family home. He's dedicated to the game, but rattling around the big house alone is making him question if it's time for something more.

He's drawn to a beauty. He's curious about an adorable girl in a hoodie that's big enough for two. He's intrigued by... *his stalker?*

Get Stalking Second: http://books2read.com/stalkingsecond

FINALLY IN FOCUS
A NOVELLA

I want Kade. I've wanted him since high school, but it made no sense to be interested in a guy who never went to class and always had extra cash. What teenager ever had extra cash? It had to be bad news or illegal. His overgrown light brown hair hanging down into his eyes. His T-shirts were worn, old, and faded, sometimes not long enough to meet the jeans at his waist, and always stretched perfectly across his shoulders. He wore old school button-fly jeans, none of those relaxed fit or skinny jeans or anything stylish, and in fact he still wears those, but now it's usually topped with a black polo shirt (varying degrees of black, since it appears he doesn't care if they fade). Yes, I saw him recently. Shit. I see him all the time. Fine. I know where to find him when I want a glimpse. He's predictable and I'm good with patterns. I haven't spoke to him since senior ditch day, which was the longest conversation I've ever had with him. He had surprised me with his passion and intelligence. He hated school and the drama of everything it encompassed. He was on the home study program, but spent most of his time in the photography lab on campus. I remember learning about his schedule and being hit with my misconception, he wasn't ditching at all. I admired his mouth when he talked to me, and his hands as he used them to describe his words. He had passion in his hands when he held his camera and creativity shining in his hazel eyes. Yeah, I've dreamt about Kade since ditch day. What would it feel like for those hands to touch me? Would his mouth kiss with the same passion?

Get Finally in Focus: http://books2read.com/finallyinfocus

JUST A CALIFORNIA GIRL

Who knew I'd meet the love of my life on a girls night in Las Vegas? Definitely not me.

"Remember the moment we're together when I'm your world and nothing else exists. I've never had that with anybody else and I'm willing to bet you haven't either."

Those heartfelt words that fell from his lips have taken residence in my head, crushing my soul since I haven't told him who I am. What if he doesn't want the real me?

Danny's a hunky metal head with soulful brown eyes. His sexy tiger tattoo makes me burn from the inside out. He's everything I want and need.

I want to keep him. But, I can't tell him I love him until I confess my innocuous lie. I wouldn't believe it myself.

Betting on Love... could be the riskiest gamble of all.

Get Just a California Girl: http://books2read.com/caligirl

ACKNOWLEDGMENTS

The longer I'm part of this romance world, the more I find it true that my readers are what matters the most. I know who my loyal readers are—let's be honest, I don't have that many of them. I haven't figured out the magic combination that enables readers to find me. But, I cherish those of you who have and appreciate the patience you have with me as I navigate this journey.

Thank you Samantha for keeping me in line and helping me with everything you possibly can.

Thank you Jann and Jaime for keeping our group of Naughties going with consistent posts and appropriate funnies.

Thank you Alisa and Mary for always being there.

Thank you Irene for putting up with my constant requests for graphics and being part of my original book support system.

Thank you Andie for listening to me ramble and answering silly questions when I'm losing my mind.

And of course the rest of my OGs... Thank you for reading.

www.ingramcontent.com/pod-product-compliance
Lightning Source LLC
Chambersburg PA
CBHW032251020726
47495CB00001B/55

* 9 7 8 1 9 4 9 2 4 3 8 1 9 *